DATE DUE		
OCT 0 6 2001	DEC 0 7 2001	
NOV 0 3 2001	DEC 1 4 2001	
SEP 3 0 2002	DEC 2 8 2001	
JUL 2 8 2004	SEP 1 0 2005	
AUG 2 1 2012		

LOVE'S LAST CHANCE

A NIGEL AND NICKY MYSTERY
BY KRANDALL KRAUS

alyson books
los angeles | new york

© 2000 KRANDALL KRAUS. ALL RIGHTS RESERVED

MANUFACTURED IN THE UNITED STATES OF AMERICA.

THIS TRADE PAPERBACK ORIGINAL IS PUBLISHED BY ALYSON PUBLICATIONS,
P.O. BOX 4371, LOS ANGELES, CA 90078-4371.
DISTRIBUTION IN THE UNITED KINGDOM BY
TURNAROUND PUBLISHER SERVICES LTD.,
UNIT 3, OLYMPIA TRADING ESTATE, COBURG ROAD, WOOD GREEN,
LONDON N22 6TZ ENGLAND.

FIRST EDITION: NOVEMBER 2000

00 01 02 03 04 **a**   10 9 8 7 6 5 4 3 2 1

ISBN 1-55583-505-8

COVER PHOTOGRAPHY BY PHILIP PIROLO.

For Paul,
Who out-Nickies Nicky, out-Nigels
Nigel, and out-Nonnas Nonna without
ever leaving the sanctity of his bonsai
garden;
and for Andy, who couldn't be here
for this one, but appears all through
it anyway.

ACKNOWLEDGMENTS

Great love and deep respect to my primary patrons: Thao Ngo, for his love, support, and the financial underwriting of the expense of writing this novel; Carol Yaggy and Mary Twomey, for the house in the Redwoods, where most of this was written. Gratitude and respect to: Ron Baumhover, whose faith in me sustains me sometimes in dark, dark moments; Marge Poscher, my soul sister and physician, who has kept me alive long enough to write this book; Kim Storch, who reminded me how to recognize love when I forgot; Sasha Alyson, the first to take a chance on my writing; Scott Brassart, who possesses what every publisher should possess—abiding integrity, phenomenal editorial and reading sensibilities, and a sense of what's really important in life; D.J. Schmall, for the land in Anchor Bay, where much of the thinking and some of the best writing took place; Marjorie Baer, for her help with "things Italian" and her love; Annarita Grinvalds, for the use of her name.

"LAZARUS, COME FORTH!"
GOSPEL ACCORDING TO JOHN (11:43)

PROLOGUE

Love is a funny thing. You find it when you aren't looking for it and you lose it just when you've become comfortable with it. It's as though it has a mind of its own. A will of its own. Or maybe the ancient Greeks were right and we're all being toyed with by a bunch of Gods on Olympus.

Death is like that too, come to think of it. People who want it aren't allowed to have it, but just when you have the most to live for you open the door and the bugger's standing there grinning at you. That's how I see it, anyway. Love and Death, Death and Love. What a dance we do with them.

I'm going to tell you a story of love and death. This story begins and ends with a dream. In fact, as I sit here sipping my brandy on this cold winter night, talking about it like this, it seems like the whole damned thing was a dream.

Two or three nights a week for over 30 months I had the same fucking dream: my late partner Lyle and I are in a cab, train, subway, bus, or taxi. We stop; he opens the door and makes me get out. Then he closes the door and says through the open window, "You can't come with me now, but I'll be back to get you." And I am left standing on a dark, rain-slicked street or a dimly lit platform watching the taxi or train disappear into the night, carrying away from me the only person that I ever felt loved me.

But it wasn't the dream that was my enemy; it was waking up that I feared most. I dreaded waking each morning to find myself alone in bed with no train, no bus, no taxicab coming back to get me. At least in the dream there was hope.

I thought I would lose my mind if the dream didn't stop. And then suddenly, after all those months, a new dream: Lyle and I are in a limousine driving around Washington, D.C. We are drinking champagne, laughing, and kissing. The monuments are lit and crowds are waving at us as if we were in a parade, heroes returned from battle. The limousine stops in front of the Lincoln Memorial, where Lyle and I went on our first date, had our first kiss in the wee hours of morning. I step out and find an old woman waiting to greet us.

She has snow-white hair and is elegantly dressed in a tailored black suit. The old lady holds a red poker chip made of glass or gemstone in one hand; her other hand is poised palm-up beneath the red chip as though it were a communion wafer. Suddenly I'm terrified and feel the need to get away. I turn to leave, but she grabs my arm with two more hands that I hadn't seen before and holds me with unimaginable strength. She stares into my eyes and proffers the gleaming red wafer.

I try to break her grip but now I find myself holding hands with a starving boy who is all skin and bones; his huge brown eyes implore me. He clutches me with one bony hand and holds the other out, palm up, in an alms-begging gesture.

I scream and turn to look for Lyle and the limousine, but find myself facing a naked man with long black hair and brown eyes. He is dark-skinned, has two white wings coming out of each side of his head, and wields a knife. I know he is going to cut me, and I know I cannot escape. It begins to rain. He walks toward me. I begin to cry. I know it is the end of my life. He raises the knife and plunges it into my chest. Oddly, it doesn't hurt. I wake up startled and panting. And sexually excited. The first time I had this dream I wondered if I didn't prefer the other dream. At least it wasn't obfuscated.

In retrospect I should have paid more attention to that second dream. But I was pretty much a mess in those days. Full of self-pity and bitterness for everything and everyone around me. How dare the world go on spinning when I was lonely and deep in despair? But still I should have realized those dreams were trying to tell me something.

Yet how could I have? That was before Nicky. Before Nonna. Before the corpse floating in the middle of a lake. Before anyone knew how that corpse got there—except the person who put it there. It was before I was more "baked," as Nicky puts it. Before I was willing to give life and love one last chance.

ONE

"TAKE CASA Rota," Helen said, using the name her farm had been given by its original owner. She stirred her cappuccino. "I'm going to be here for at least another two weeks with"—she closed her eyes for the next two words as though she were about to be stuck with a hypodermic needle—"...*my mother*. Then I have to be in Verona for at least ten days."

Helen had moved to Italy in 1978 when she married an old Washington, D.C. colleague of mine who was in the diplomatic corps. He was from Florence, her family from the hills of Tuscany, so they had a lot in common. Evidently not enough. The marriage didn't last, but my friendship with Helen did. It survived even after I lost touch with her husband, Mauritzio.

When Italy legalized divorce, Helen and Mauritzio went their separate ways and she walked out of their marriage with a two-story penthouse apartment in the Campo dei Fiori in Rome and an 18th-century farm in Tuscany.

Helen had come to the states to take care of some family business in Iowa, but after a week she escaped to San Francisco to visit me and Carmine, a mutual friend who owns a travel agency. Helen, even in the harsh light of Just Desserts, the patisserie at which we had just stuffed our faces with Chocolate Decadence torte, looked younger than her 48 years. She had lost her father and one close friend to the AIDS epidemic, but had weathered it well. I couldn't help but look at her and think how loss affects different people in different ways. Or maybe it's the amount that determines the effect.

I wonder: How much loss is enough loss? One mother and two life partners? Two partners and three best friends? Six friends and twelve acquaintances? Is it enough when your address book has more names

crossed out than names still listed? When you can't think of anyone to
telephone to ask to go to a movie—not because everyone you think of
is someone you don't want to spend the evening with, but because everyone who comes to mind is no longer alive—would you call that enough?
At what point does the numbness set in so that you can't even remember when you reached "enough," and all you feel is the heavy stone of
loss that you carry in your pocket day and night?

"You look tired," Helen said, breaking my reverie. She was smiling
and leaning forward, her elbows resting on the table. Although we were
close enough in age to be siblings, Helen was like a mother to me. A
good mother: Not always there when I wanted her, but always there
when I needed her. She knew instinctively how to nurture a person, help
him take care of himself, rather than just rescue him. She claims it comes
from being Italian. I say it comes from paying attention.

"Weary might more accurately describe my condition," I answered
with a sigh.

"Why don't you write another book?" Helen suggested. "The last one
did well and kept you busy."

"The last one? You mean the only one."

"That's not the point," she countered. "Research, writing, rewrit-
ing…it'll take your mind off your troubles, give you something positive
to focus on."

"Nice try, but I don't think I have enough passion left in me for anything that big," I said. "I don't know what would make a difference, but
nothing that takes any energy."

"You look lonely," she continued, her lips on the verge of a sympathetic smile. "Are you seeing anyone?"

I looked at her blankly. She understood.

She lit a cigarette and inhaled deeply, taking me in with her deep
brown eyes, then she leaned back and prescribed. "You need love, ducky.
Someone to watch over you. When's the last time you had a date?"

"You wouldn't be trying to trick me into talking about my feelings,
would you?"

"You're a man. I know better." Now we both smiled. "OK," she continued, "when's the last time you got laid?"

"I've been busy with work," I said.

"*Too* busy from what Carmine tells me. He says he only talks to your machine."

"It's cheaper than a secretary."

"But not as much fun," she said, playing with her salt-and-pepper hair.

"You look terrific," I said, admiring her healthy complexion, her full figure, the light in her eyes.

"Gray hair notwithstanding," she joked. "I could stand to lose a few pounds. My mother's cooking will see to that." Her mother was the only Italian woman in the western hemisphere who couldn't cook. "We're all lonely," she said. "You've got lots of company in your misery."

I forced a smile. She got the message. She gathered her cigarettes into her purse and fussed with her leather jacket.

"Take the farm. Stay as long as you like. Just don't let anyone know where I am. The people in the village are so nosy. I had to move my mailing address to Malva because the woman in the post office was reporting the return addresses on all my mail to the village gossip chain. You remember where I keep the keys," she said, standing. I helped her with her jacket while two young girls with shaved heads and pierced eyebrows hovered, waiting to claim our booth. "In the tool room under the side porch where Signor Salucci keeps his tools. Go," she said, waving her hand in the air for emphasis. "You need a break. We all need a break."

I walked her up 17th Street to Carmine's. All around us, half-naked revelers costumed as everything from exotic birds to half-naked warriors to gossamer angels to crimson devils danced and shrieked. I had all but forgotten it was Cinco de Mayo and the *fiesta* in the Mission District had been going on all evening. In front of Carmine's house a band of androgynous, masked angels swooped upon us. They swirled in a circle around us, laughing and waving their arms, as if casting a spell, then fluttered off as suddenly as they'd appeared. In the distance, firecrackers popped, and over the top of one of the Victorians at the end of the block we could see the sparkling red embers of fireworks near the Embarcadero.

We climbed the steps to Carmine's front porch and hugged our farewell, Helen's face softer, sweeter in the porch light, her eyes bright, but worried.

"Nigel, when you go, leave it all here. Don't take any of it with you. The farm can be a wonderful place for healing. Nothing but the goats on the hill and the cuckoos in the valley. *Ciao, bello.*" She kissed me on the cheek and slipped through the front door.

From Carmine's front porch I could see the city skyline, the bay, the rolling fog moving silently over the water, creeping along the Embarcadero, consuming the lights of downtown. Only the very tops of the towers on the Bay Bridge were visible. Tonight the fog seemed not so much beautiful as sinister, creeping silently down the wet streets, overtaking buildings without warning, shrouding them in a cloak of gray so the people inside might not signal for help from any window.

As I descended the steps, the angels flew by again, heading up the hill. Now they were passing around a bottle of tequila. They had been joined by a single red devil, its eyes made of tiny red lights. He carried a pitchfork and wore only a red satin bikini beneath his red satin cape, which fluttered in the night air as he ran. He was laughing hysterically—they all were—caught in the frenzy of the celebration on this night of revelry and high jinks, of things seen and unseen. A line from a childhood prayer we used to say to St. Michael the Archangel came into my head, a prayer I hadn't thought of in years. "O prince of the heavenly host, be our protection against the malice and snares of the devil, and thrust into hell, Satan and all evil spirits who roam through the world seeking the ruin of souls."

Devils or angels, I thought. Heaven or hell. Tomorrow I would call Carmine to make my plane reservations for Italy. Helen was right: I needed the solitude of the farm. Thank God for Helen.

TWO

I WENT to Italy to hide. Not from anyone. From everyone. Including myself. I hadn't been anywhere except the desert in the three years since Lyle had died and I had been diagnosed HIV-positive. Helen had pointed out how my weariness was beginning to show, but she needn't have bothered. At a cocktail party in Pacific Heights about a week before her arrival, a friend's wife guessed my age at 50. I knew it was time for a rest. I don't mind being 45 and looking 45. I mind being 45 and looking 50.

I went, even though I generally hate traveling, even though it meant renting a car in Florence and driving the narrow dirt road a mile and a half up the mountain to the farm. It was a long journey with a delayed layover in New York. I had to take a train from Milan to Florence, then make my way in a steady rain through the city's dirty, crowded, maze-like streets to the car rental office. I picked up my rental car and drove in a downpour on the autostrada to the farm. The whole trip from San Francisco to Castelfranco di Sopra took 27 hours and I arrived at the farm long after midnight. I was beat. I couldn't get the lights to work, but found the flashlight Helen keeps next to the door and made my way to one of the bedrooms in the back of the house. I stripped and threw myself under the covers without even taking a shower. The heavy shutters, I knew, would keep out the light as well as the sound of the sheep and goats on the hill in the morning, and with luck I would sleep until the afternoon.

But of course I didn't sleep until afternoon. I woke at 4:30 A.M.— 7:30 P.M. San Francisco time—just about the time I would normally sit down to work on the novel I knew I would never finish, partly because it had to do with Lyle's death. It was my way of staying with the experience of our relationship, but it was also some sort of masochistic sentence I had imposed upon myself, an anchor I had dropped to hold me steady in the ocean of my life. I guess I thought that if I stayed still I might avoid any more hurricanes.

I lay in the lightless room for another two hours, trying to convince my internal clock it was wrong. I lost the argument. When I saw the tiniest crack of dim light peeking through one of the slats in the shutters I got up and threw open the window. It was still raining and the diffused gray light coming through the clouds fell softly on the green hills behind the house. A perfect day to sleep in, I thought, and laughed at the irony. I left a sunny month in San Francisco to visit the wet spring of Tuscany.

I sat on the loggia at the front of the house, drinking coffee from an oversized blue mug, and watched the rain fall on the Arno Valley below. Tiny villages dotted the wooded hillsides, and here and there along the river the stone towers of ancient churches and town halls rose into the slate sky, indifferent to one more morning's rain.

It was just before Lyle got sick, four years earlier, that I was last in Tuscany, but miraculously nothing had changed, at least visually. Even Helen's farmhouse, which had been undergoing renovation for the past ten years, looked, from the outside, like it hadn't been touched for two centuries.

The villa had ten rooms on the main level that were either restored or in the process of being renovated. The house was laid out in a neat U shape. The rooms wrapped around a thick central supporting wall, so one made the trip through the whole house by walking through almost every room. The bathroom was at the end of the hallway, which had bedrooms on either side, then the kitchen, and, through that, the dining room. Turn right into the study, another right turn and down one step into the living room, then a left turn through the ancient door onto the porch, or loggia. On each side of the loggia was a bedroom, each in some stage of reconstruction. There were also two outbuildings which were being reconstructed. One was a simple barn, the other a lovely cottage which looked small from the outside but actually consisted of seven rooms.

Wrapped around all of this were gardens, olive groves, forests of bamboo and fruit trees, all perched Italian style among the Tuscan hills above the Arno. The temperature was in the 60s and, in spite of the rain, or perhaps because of it, this was the perfect place to come after all. One thing was for certain: I wasn't going to be bothered.

THREE

I SPENT the first day wandering through the house and, between cloudbursts, taking little jaunts up the dirt road. The road to the farm wound through or near four other properties. First, about a hundred meters from the main paved road, the dirt road cut directly through an old couple's yard, as though they had built their home right on the path and planted their garden on either side. Or perhaps the men who built the road simply bulldozed right through their yard. You could literally reach out of the car window and touch the side of their house as you drove by. Helen was quick to warn guests of the old man's chickens that clucked haplessly back and forth across the road. She had hit one once and had never heard the end of it.

After winding 200 or so meters, a second farm is barely visible in a gully, a vacation rental, usually filled with German or American tourists. Just before the top of the hill, the road divides. To the left it rises to Ernesto's, the shepherd who lives at the top of the hill. To the right it leads to Helen's via an easement through a fourth property, another ancient farmhouse with an outbuilding owned by a dentist in Rome. He was forever renovating it but never finishing the job. Like the old couple's farm the road passed directly through the property, the main house above, a cottage below, each close enough to touch when you passed. From this point the road wound down the hill, ending at Helen's, directly below.

I walked up the road and stood in front of the dentist's outbuilding, a stone cottage with a tattered, red tile roof and dirty windows. From the small yard I could look down at the house where I was staying and the olive trees and gardens surrounding it. This is about as pastoral as any place gets, I thought. If I can't get some perspective on my life here, I may as well give up.

I felt like I hardly knew myself anymore. Three years without Lyle had made me a different person. With Lyle I was funny, clever; I read insatiably. The two of us had an active intellectual life, reading to one another at least a couple evenings a week. We had a spiritual practice of sorts. I had even begun meditating.

Now, I had no spirit, no joie de vivre; I barely felt the will to live. I detested the idea of being one of those people who can't function without a spouse, who's too ineffectual or diffident to function alone in the world. Yet the bitter truth, if I could bring myself to admit it—and here on a hill far above the Arno, in a distant country, I finally could—was that I wanted to live in a meaningful relationship with another person. I said it out loud. "I want someone to love. Someone to love me. Lyle is gone. The taxi's not coming back. God or Goddess or whatever you are, please send me someone to love. Please don't let me die alone."

The clanking of sheeps' bells on the hillside behind me broke the spell and I was immediately embarrassed. Dark clouds had sneaked over the top of the hill and begun another sprinkling of rain. I pulled up the hood of my yellow slicker and headed down the road. As I passed the dentist's house, I looked up and saw a young woman's face pull back from a window. I didn't stop because it seemed none of my business, but I thought it queer since there was no sign of anyone staying there. No car, no workman's truck, nothing but roofing tiles in a large pile near the side of the house and the raw ends of lumber stacked under a tarp near the front porch. It looked like no work had taken place in several months. Perhaps, I thought, it's Ernesto's wife, poking around the neighbor's empty house and not wanting to be caught. Helen said these people were nosy. Anyway, it was none of my business, and it was beginning to rain heavily. The wind had picked up considerably. It looked like it was going to be a big blow by evening.

I watched the rain the remainder of morning and all afternoon. I watched it rain a second day and then a third, waiting for "enough" rain to fall so the clouds could part and allow the sun to appear. But the rain continued into the fourth day. Small rivulets behind the house turned into streams washing through the olive groves. Fruit trees surrendered their branches to the driving rain. I sat wrapped in a wool blanket listening to the raindrops clattering on the red tile roof of the loggia, watching the endless downpour, waiting for something to lift—if not in me, then at least in the clouds sweeping across the valley.

I ate the provisions I found in the pantry: pasta, cheese, and, from the freezer, loaves of Tuscan bread which I slathered with butter and Helen's homemade plum and apricot jams. I drank coffee all day, wine all evening, then shuffled down the long tile hall and crawled, like a wounded soldier forgotten in a veteran's hospital, into the big feather bed, sinking slowly, heavily, into a deep, restless sleep.

Everything in my family on my mother's side is big: the men, the property, the emotions. And while all three are conspicuously evident at all times—especially the emotions—after the initial couple of weeks of crying over Lyle I had turned stony, cold, removed. I knew I was doing it, but I thought it was temporary. I thought I could haul out those feelings whenever I wanted, warm them like a touchstone, and get in contact with some deeper part of myself.

Then three years went by. I lost dozens of friends and acquaintances to HIV, cancer, and car accidents. Some of them I hardly knew; some were lifelong pals. There never seemed to be enough tears, enough feeling, or, as my Uncle Ernie would sarcastically shout when my Aunt Lizzie would start one of her tantrums, "enough opera."

I would get teary-eyed, sometimes cry, even sob for a moment or two. But then it would stop, As though a plug had been pulled and the emotions drained out. No matter how much I might try I couldn't muster more tears. But the sorrow, like sediment at the bottom of a well, sat thick and heavy within.

It occurred to me the fourth rainy night, as I sat finishing the last bottle of Montepulciano d'Abruzzo, that for all meaningful purposes, my life was over. I was not, at my age, going to meet anyone who would be attracted to me, let alone attracted enough to stick around and fall in love. I had few friends—or so it felt—and I hated socializing. After a ten-year stint in Washington D.C., which required embassy and Capitol Hill parties on a nightly basis, I detested social functions. So there was little opportunity for me to meet someone new. I had experienced the one great love of my life; he died and now I waited for my turn.

Yes, I was definitely feeling sorry for myself. I realized this as I watched the last drop of Chianti plop into the glass. But I also realized how very real those simple facts were, and how very difficult it would be for me to change them.

With the rain beating harder than ever on the tiles above me, I closed the blackout shutters in the bedroom, slipped into my bed of sorrows, and let the wine do its work. Perhaps Casa Rota was not such a good idea after all. I really didn't want to confront so much sorrow.

I still had two and a half weeks before my economy fare ticket would carry me out of Tuscany, so I decided to turn over a new leaf. I would rise in the morning, take a day trip in spite of the weather, and crawl out of the black hole of my depression before it got any worse. Also, I would cut back on the alcohol. Tomorrow.

FOUR

I AWOKE with a headache and a dull droning in my ears like the sound of water running in the distance. I sat up in the big four-poster bed, steadying myself with my hands. Thank God that was the last bottle of wine in the house, I thought, remembering the new leaf I had vowed to turn over. I went to the window and opened the inside shutters. It was still bleak outside, rain falling steadily across the green hills.

Perched on the hill above was the dentist's house, looking even colder and bleaker than Helen's house felt on this gray, tinny morning. I noticed the door of the dentist's outbuilding was open. It had not been open previously. The wind? A tourist like me, come to rent a villa in Tuscany, looking for a room with a view? The shepherd's wife? I was too hungover to care and groggily made my way to the bathroom without bothering to find my robe. I wanted hot water pouring over my body and I wanted it now.

I grabbed a fresh towel from the linen closet in the hall and opened the bathroom door to find that the running water sound I had attributed to my hangover actually was running water. Not only was the shower flowing full force, but standing in the steaming tub was a naked, dark-skinned man with shoulder-length black hair. I don't know which of us was more startled, but I reacted by wrapping the towel I was holding around myself. He stood staring. It seemed like a long time passed before either of us spoke, and then it was both at once. "Who are you?" we both blurted.

"I beg your pardon, but how did you get in here?" I asked, indignantly.

"Through the door, naturally," he replied. "Where did you come from?"

"San Francisco."

He rolled his eyes and placed one hand on a naked hip. "I don't mean *originally*. I mean just now. Have you been hiding here waiting to attack me?"

"What are you talking about? I've been asleep in the bedroom. I'm staying here. Attack you? Are you nuts?"

"Well, you *are* naked," he said. "Usually when naked men sneak up on people who are taking showers, they have something debauched in mind."

"Listen here," I complained.

"Say, if you don't mind terribly, this hot water isn't going to last much longer," he said, and began lathering what I now noticed was a thin but not unattractive body. He had the sort of waist I had always dreamed of as a husky child, one that actually formed hips. This was another reason not to like him. "No offense," he said, " but I'd also like to do this alone."

I gripped the towel tighter around my waist and stormed out. Who the hell was he and what was he doing in my, or rather Helen's bath-room? I'd get to the bottom of this—and fast. I threw on my jeans and shoes and began searching the house. In the bedroom across the hall sat two bags, one large, one carry-on, both white leather and very expensive. Who in his right mind would buy white luggage? In the armoire were half a dozen shirts and as many slacks. Three pairs of expensive Italian shoes sat in a neat row on the floor beside the armoire. He had not only arrived sometime during the night, but settled in.

The bed had been slept in and strewn on top of it were a pair of black silk pajamas. A copy of *The Tibetan Book of the Dead* rested on the night-stand. All this did not bode well. It appeared he had made plans with Helen to be here. It also appeared he intended to stay.

FIVE

IT TURNED out that Helen had double-booked the farm. At least that's what the two of us surmised, once he was out of the shower and dressed. She was notoriously scatter-brained, but this was the most annoying faux pas I had ever been the unwitting victim of. I only came to Italy because she insisted it would be the perfect place to restore myself and now she had made that impossible.

My first thought was to return home at once, but that wasn't really what I wanted. I had gone to a great deal of trouble to make this trip and I didn't want to throw in the towel at the first big obstacle. I decided to wait him out. I figured he'd get frustrated and leave; besides, from the looks of his wardrobe and luggage, he could stay in any hotel he chose. So I hunkered down and tried to outlast him.

He went about his business as though I were a roommate he had been living with for years. He fixed us meals, chatted about what he read in the newspapers, and tried to engage me in all sorts of conversations. He was a voracious reader and spent most of his time either sitting in the rocker on the loggia with his feet propped up on the railing or, when the rain finally subsided, lying on a blanket in the olive grove with a bottle of red wine and a pile of books. It was annoying how comfortable he was with this arrangement. Really annoying.

His body annoyed me as well. He had this exotic look about him. His skin was brown, but with a kind of green undertone to it, like the darker Italians in Tuscany. Not *dark* dark, like the Siciliani; more like the color of olive oil. His eyes weren't exactly almond-shaped, but they definitely weren't round. They were the only thing about him I found attractive, but I am always softened by any pair of brown eyes. Brown eyes are simply more soulful than blue or green ones.

His hair was shiny and black as coal, with an obvious softness to it. It constantly flopped into his eyes while he was reading or doing dishes at the sink. When he skipped down the stone steps to the garden or the olive grove it flew up into the air on both sides of his head, like Mercury's winged helmet. So cocky, so self-assured was he, that I became certain his entire persona was a deliberately aggressive act.

He probably took great pleasure in being just this side of effeminate, making people vaguely uncomfortable in his presence, but unsure as to why. I could picture him posing in one of his expensive suits at some formal function, the room filled with dignitaries and socialites taking surreptitious glances at this haughty young man, at home with the aristocracy yet with "hippie" hair falling down past his collar. Yes, he would love doing that. He was that kind of troublemaker.

He dressed simply and casually, but everything he owned was expensive. They weren't "label" clothes, nothing from designer boutiques or anything like that; nevertheless, they were made of the finest Egyptian cottons and Chinese silks, the supplest Italian leathers, and fine worsted wool. His trousers were box pleated like trousers from the 1940s, breaking slightly over his shoes, and were cuffed in the traditional style. They were probably tailor-made. He mostly wore white cotton shirts, open at the neck, the sleeves rolled one or two turns at the cuffs. This allowed him to expose his neck and wrists, the crisp white shirt contrasting starkly with his smooth, brown skin. Such a blatantly seductive ploy should have embarrassed him, but didn't. It was soon quite evident that nothing embarrassed him.

In spite of his sartorial folderol, he never looked "put together"; neither did he discuss his wardrobe or mention where he shopped for clothes. He also had the good manners not to comment on my casual California mode of living in khakis or Levi's, T-shirts, and sneakers. He was not pretentious. Still, I didn't like him being there. I wanted to be alone.

One evening over dinner I finally just came out with it: "How long are you going to stay here?" It sounded a little harsher than I'd intended, but after I said it, there was no taking it back.

"I haven't decided," he said, refilling my wine glass.

"Well, how long did you intend to stay when you left...wherever it is

you live?" I looked at the roasted chicken and vegetables he had prepared
for our supper, longing for a second helping, but feeling it wasn't fair to
harangue him and eat an extra portion of his cooking at the same time.

He took a sip of wine, thought for a moment, and said, "I hadn't
thought of it that way before, but actually, I guess that would be
nowhere. So I'm not sure."

He had a way of not making sense when he talked.

"Excuse me?"

"I came to Italy to see my grandmother. And Rosario's family in
Lucca," he said.

"Who's Rosario?" I asked.

"My lover," he said, only half paying attention. "I guess I really don't
live in any one place any more. I just travel from city to city. I hadn't
realized that until you asked the question. Thank you. I need to consider that." He sipped his wine and changed the subject. "Delicious, isn't
it? I think Helen trades olive oil for wine with some man in San
Giovanni."

This is how he talked. Back and forth from subject to subject. I never
knew where we were in the conversation or if it was a conversation at all.
He was driving me nuts!

"You must have a home somewhere," I protested. "Are you registered
to vote?"

"No, actually. I don't vote. Are you registered to vote?"

"Of course I am. Every citizen should vote. It's our responsibility.
Besides, I care what happens to my country." Looking back on the
evening, I realize now how hostile I must have appeared, and what an
arrogant fool he must have taken me for.

"Oh," was all he said. He got up and took our plates to the sink, then
began to brew espresso. "I never think of myself as a citizen of one country. I tend not to make those distinctions. At least I don't function under
those distinctions."

"That's rather cavalier of you, isn't it?"

"Yes," he laughed, "I suppose it is. But I don't see the world that way.
I just don't."

This guy didn't get annoyed by anything, which was annoying me ter-

rifically. "You don't see the world what way, as a place where individuals
have responsibilities and people should have a say in their government?"
I poured myself some more wine and waved a reluctant goodbye to the
chicken as he whisked it off the table and put it in the refrigerator.

"I don't see everything as being divided, broken up. Have you ever
noticed that when you're in an airplane you can't tell where one country
ends and another begins? Have you ever thought about that?"

"No."

"I look out the window when I'm flying from New York to San
Francisco and there arc no natural borders around states. When I fly
from London to Milan, I can't tell when I'm over France and when I'm
over Switzerland or Italy. The world isn't naturally broken up into coun-
tries. That's all arbitrary. We do that, not nature. You do like lemon in
your espresso, right? I never asked you; I just assumed, so I've been putting a bit of lemon peel in yours. I forget how American you are. Shall
I not add it this evening?"

American? What was that supposed to mean? "No, lemon is fine. We
have lemon in the States."

He smiled to himself, poured the coffee, and brought it to the table.
He sat across from me, lifted his demitasse as in a toast and said, not
unkindly, "To American lemons, then."

It wasn't until I turned out the light and pulled the feather comforter
around my shoulders that it occurred to me his toast may not have been
about citrus at all.

SIX

WE WENT on like this for over a week. It was infuriating. I began making day trips to some of the hill towns in the area. One day I would drive to Montepulciano; the next day I would take in Assisi; then I'd stay home a day, thinking he would take the hint and make himself scarce so I could enjoy being alone on the farm. But no, not him. He stayed home every day in spite of the silver Lamborghini parked in the drive. He preferred to lie around reading books on the I Ching and impossibly obtuse treatises by Carl Jung while I wore myself out traipsing all over the Tuscan countryside looking for a bit of privacy.

Finally I asked him, "Don't you want to get out a bit? Wouldn't you like to enjoy this beautiful spring weather?"

He was lying on a blanket at the edge of the olive grove. I had just parked the car after another of my daily attempts to find solitude and was on my way into the house. I saw him lolling there with a book and something inside me snapped. I marched over to where he was lying and blurted it out. He rolled onto his back, took off his sunglasses, and shielded his eyes against the sun with a perfectly manicured hand. "How kind of you. I'd like that, I think. Tomorrow's the first Sunday of the month and there's always a huge flea market in Arezzo. Why don't we go? I'll get up and fix us an early breakfast, then we can go to 10 o'clock mass in the village and we'll be in Arezzo by noon."

I was so taken aback by his assumption that I was asking him to come along on an outing that I couldn't even answer. I just turned and walked into the house. Maybe he's crazy, I thought. Maybe he has these little psychotic breaks from reality. Maybe he hears voices in his head. How could he possibly have thought that was an invitation?

Nevertheless, the next morning he woke me at 8 o'clock sharp with breakfast on the table and off we went. I didn't say a word in protest; I just followed his lead.

He insisted we take his Lamborghini, and also insisted I drive it. It was fun but nerve-racking. The slightest touch of the pedal and it raced out from underneath me. Finally I managed to get it under control and it maneuvered like a true sports car, nothing like the Fiat Uno I had rented for less than $300.

I didn't talk much on the drive, but he did. He went on and on about *The Tibetan Book of the Dead,* acting like it was the holy Bible. And this just after we had sat through a Catholic mass in a tiny village church where they didn't even have padding on the kneelers.

"Everything is a projection of your own mind," he said as we glided through the vineyards on our way toward Arezzo. The sun was high in the blue sky and everything was reflecting the most vivid colors: green leaves, red tile roofs, black soil. We were cruising through the Chianti district with the top down. It was warm and the air was so clear we could see all the way to the horizon.

"So I suppose all this isn't really there," I said, making a sweeping gesture with my right hand. "We're just imagining it."

"No, no, no. Not like that. Not literally a projection. Although in a sense that's true. No, the value we place on it is a projection. We project onto things the meaning we want them to have." He gave a little laugh, almost to himself.

The sun was warm on my face and the air was crisp and clear. "I love Italy," I said aloud. "It feels like home."

"Where are you from?" he asked.

"Calistoga," I said. "A small town in the Napa Valley in Northern California."

"Yes, I know it," he said. "It's the light that you love."

"What?"

"The light. It's the same here as it is in the Napa Valley. The same as most of Northern California, but especially in the Napa Valley. Rosario and I went there once, for the baths. He said it felt just like home to him. He said it was the blue light. Just like Tuscany. They're exactly the same, actually. Same climate, same air, same soil and, most of all, the same blue light." Then he closed his eyes and raised his face to take in the sun.

I turned my attention back to steering the car, to find a fat brown chicken in the center of the road. She had her head cocked and was staring with one wide eye at the Lamborghini bearing down on her. I swerved to keep from hitting her and we rocked from side to side. It scared the hell out of me, but he just laughed loudly, took off his sunglasses, and thrust his face upward toward the sun. Then he shouted, "*Mamma, mamma mia! Ti amo, Italia, Ti amo.*" We drove in silence the last 20 kilometers to Arezzo.

SEVEN

AREZZO was packed with people coming to the flea market and we had to park way out of town. We walked through the city gate and he pointed out places of historical interest or houses he knew because of his family connections. People milled about everywhere, sorting through the goods stacked on tables or piled beside carts the weekend merchants used to haul their goods up the steep, old-city streets. Women in aprons dragged children behind them, looking for a bargain. Young girls leaned out from red-shuttered windows above the narrow street. Children pointed and giggled at reproductions of Renaissance sculptures of naked boys. Haggling over prices went on at every concession we passed, a sign of respectful engagement.

"My grandmother used to bring me to this flea market when I was just a child. She lost me once and had the police and the *carabinieri* looking everywhere for me. An old lover of hers was the mayor at the time and they turned the entire city upside down. They even mounted huge speakers in the piazza and called my name."

"Where were you?" I asked, thinking he'd probably say he had fallen asleep reading under a tree.

We were climbing some winding brick steps between buildings, a shortcut he knew to the piazza. Almost matter-of-factly he said, "I was having sex with the most beautiful man I have ever seen. Right up there." He stopped and pointed to the tower of the duomo. "He was a young priest, probably a novice at the house of studies here. God, he was beautiful."

I was put off a bit by how casually he was imparting this information to a complete stranger, but I didn't want to appear unsophisticated or shocked, which is what, I am sure, he intended. "How old were you?" I asked.

"Ten," he answered and began climbing the narrow steps again.

"That's outrageous," I protested. "Did they arrest the priest?"

He laughed. "I hope not. It wasn't my intention to get him into trouble. I just wanted to see him naked."

"*You* wanted to see *him* naked?" I exclaimed, out of breath, as we reached the street that would take us the remainder of the way up to the piazza. Now we were in the thick of the crowds. Makeshift stands solidly lined the street and people were hawking everything from handmade lace tablecloths to antique furniture.

"Yes," he said, pulling out a white handkerchief and wiping his forehead. "I told you: He was the most beautiful man I've ever seen. I had to have him, so I lured him into the tower. He was huge and, of course, uncircumcised. And he was so cute. He ejaculated in my hand before he knew what was happening. No pun intended. You are Catholic, right? You get the pun?" he added as an afterthought, but didn't wait for my answer. "I wonder if he's still in Arezzo? Oh, look at this," he exclaimed, and went rushing through the crowd toward one of the concession tables.

I followed in a bit of a daze, trying to figure out what was true and what was drama for my sake. By the time we reached the piazza *centrale,* it was clear to me that he was completely at home here and that none of this was for show. This was who he was, and I was fascinated—as fascinated as I could be with someone I wished would go away.

When I caught up with him, he was dickering in Italian over the price of a bronze crucifix about a foot tall. The merchant was determined not to let it go for less than 50,000 lire, but he ended up parting with it for 20. "Isn't it beautiful?" he said, holding it up as we made our way through the crowd.

"I guess. It looks like any other crucifix to me."

"No, no," he said, raising it up for me to examine. "Look at the corpus. Look at the legs, those quadriceps, how they form and cut in near the knees. And look at the expression on Christ's face. His eyes are down, not up. He's defeated. You rarely see that. I think it's actually original and the guy didn't know it." He was more excited about this crucifix than I had seen him during the week and a half since he had arrived.

"Well, I guess as long as you're happy with your purchase," I conceded.

He looked at me with an expression I can only describe as incredulous. "Purchase?" He shook his head. "I forget sometimes how American you are. Your face is so…Roman, actually. I forget."

I hated this condescending attitude he resorted to whenever we had a disagreement. "You just bought the damned thing from a street vendor at a flea market. What would you call it?"

He put his arm around my shoulder, squeezed close and guided us through a particularly dense press of street shoppers. I could feel his breath warm against my ear as we pushed our way through the swarm of people gathered to see some sort of Punch-and-Judy show at a makeshift stage near the end of the street. We came out of the crowd near a park at the top of the hill we had been climbing. He smiled and his teeth gleamed in the Tuscan sunlight, his black hair shone so that it gave off an almost blue glow. "I would call it a memento of our happy day in Arezzo." Then he held out the crucifix to me and said, "Take it. I bought it for you. It's very valuable, you'll see."

Of course I was completely humiliated, having been so testy. I took the crucifix haltingly in my hand. It was much heavier than it looked. "Thank you," I said. "*Grazie.*"

"*Prego, amico,*" he replied, calling me *friend* for the first time. "Now go sit over there on the lawn while I hunt down some food for us, and don't let any of these Italian men seduce you. Or any of the women, either. They're very crafty." He laughed and trotted off down the next street, which was lined with food vendors. I watched him work his way through the crowd, the light brighter on him than on anyone else. It wasn't his white long-sleeved shirt, his black, shiny hair, the tan gabardine slacks, or the 500,000-lire shoes that caused him to stand out. It was the way he carried himself, with a confidence and grace I had never seen in someone so young, but that I imagined the lords of ancient Italian principalities must have also possessed. He was, if nothing else, a genuine aristocrat.

We ate on the park lawn, lying on a blanket he bought from one of the vendors. He brought us back a bottle of Chianti, some *pecodoro Romano* cheese and a long flat loaf of *ciabatta*. We ate mostly in silence, watching the people milling around the streets next to the park.

The park, which consisted of an expanse of lawn, huge cypress, oak and linden trees, and various hedges marking the walkways, was at the top of the city's highest hill. It was also the hub of a wheel of streets that fanned out to other parts of the city. People dotted the lawn around us, but it wasn't crowded. We sat under a huge linden tree sipping wine and enjoying the warm breeze rustling the leaves in the branches above.

I watched him while he dozed on the lawn. His body was nothing to look at. He obviously never worked out at a gym; he was neither fat nor skinny, just kind of in-between. His eyes, as I have already mentioned, were not round, not almond-shaped, but just oddly shaped, like they couldn't make up their mind what shape to take. Clearly there was some Asian influence. Eurasian trash, I couldn't help but think. Lots of money from the East being conspicuously spent in the West.

He was short, of course, too short to command authority, which was, I concluded, why he was so authoritarian. He weighed only about 150 pounds, so he could never be construed as a physical threat. His skin was soft and smooth, like a woman's. That was definitely one of his characteristics I did not find attractive. There was little or no hair on his body, except for his legs. There was a kind of ghastly green tint to his skin, as though he were about to be sick.

He always dressed like he was going somewhere special: slacks, white shirts, expensive belts and shoes. I never knew anyone who dressed like this except men in movies from the 1940s and 50s. He was so overdone. And while we were having an OK day, I wanted to be by myself. I just wanted him gone. I suppose some people would find him, if not sexy, visually intriguing. I wasn't one of those people. I didn't wish him any ill; I just didn't want him around the farm. I wanted to be alone.

He opened his eyes and looked at me. "What are you thinking about so deeply?" he asked.

"Oh, nothing, really. The farm, how peaceful it is there."

He closed his eyes again. "I'll leave soon. You can have it to yourself in a few days' time."

I faltered badly at this comment. It was as though he had been reading my mind, then tested me to see if I would tell the truth. "Oh,

I...no, it's not that, really. I mean..."

He sat up and began gathering our picnic remnants. "I can always tell when someone is lying," he said. "It's a curse that runs in my family. I get it from my grandmother, and it's infallible." He had a thin smile on his lips, as though he had just figured something out. It was a smile of recognition, not a smile of happiness. "Let's not talk about it anymore. Come with me now. I want to show you something."

EIGHT

WE carried our picnic leftovers through the streets and out the city gates to where we had left the car. We walked in silence, me falling back a little in humiliation. He had been so kind to me that day, so gracious, and I had been rude, sullen, even hostile.

When we got to the car, he asked for the keys, saying it would be quicker if he drove. And it certainly was. He drove like an Italian, speeding through the city streets and racing down country roads like he was running the Monte Carlo 500. As we made our way along the Arno we sent chickens and goats scrambling for their lives on the back roads between Arezzo and our destination.

About an hour later we arrived at the tiny village of Piantravigne, which, it turned out, was less than two kilometers from Helen's farm. He drove through the medieval town, through the tiny piazza, which was little more than an empty lot with a tree and a statue to Garibaldi. Two women bent over the village's central well washing laundry. They turned and watched us zoom past, shaking their heads in disdain. We careened down another road, which turned to dirt. The Lamborghini skidded to a halt in a cloud of dust in front of an arched, iron gate that opened to a field of high grass and cypress trees. "*Andiamo,*" he said, more a command than an invitation. He was out of the car and marching into the field before I could even get the door open.

Birds sang in the trees in spite of the heat. I could barely keep up with him. As I looked to the ground to make sure I didn't trip over logs or rocks I suddenly realized where we were. He had led me to a cemetery. Abruptly we reached the crest of a little hill and below us sloped a field of wildflowers, predominantly red poppies, most of which were less than half open, giving the hillside a look of being splattered in blood. He marched halfway down the hill and stood at a tombstone. I joined him and we stood together. I read the marker:

GIOVANNI ROSARIO DI COLOMBO,

FILLO, FRATELLO, AMOROSO, ANGELO

21 OCTOBER 1950—17 JUNE 1996

"You see, my friend. You aren't the only person in the world with heartache. You are in the most beautiful place on earth: Tuscany, the Arno Valley. Breathe the clear air, hear the birds sing, look at the river, smell the trees. Do it for the dead, if not for yourself. Life is not long enough for us to die with the dead. Our responsibility is to live. Your self-pity is wearing on me. Whatever it is, and I suppose it is grieving for your dead lover, get it over with and honor him by living a rich life. Stop feeling sorry for yourself. You too will have one of these some day." And with that he kissed his fingertips, touched them gently to the top of the tombstone, turned, and started walking back up the hill.

"Wait just a minute," I shouted after him, high-stepping through the dry grass behind him. "I am not filled with self-pity. I don't feel sorry for myself."

He stopped abruptly and turned. "I've never met anyone who felt more sorry for himself than you do. My grandmother has survived three husbands and countless consorts and her joy for living puts you to shame. You have no idea what suffering really is. You're not mourning your loss; you're feeling sorry for yourself and it's embarrassing. You have all of the spotlights turned on you and you like it that way." Then he headed back toward the car before I could respond.

I stood there shouting after him. "How dare you. You know nothing about me!" I was livid and on the verge of tears.

At the top of the hill he turned around one more time and shouted, "At least I know your name—Nigel."

NINE

WHAT was wrong with me? What had I become in the past three years? I stood in the cemetery watching this man disappear over the crest of the hill, feeling as though the last person on earth who might actually consider being my friend, in spite of my hateful ways, had just given up on me. I felt exactly the way I felt the day Lyle sputtered and gasped and stopped breathing in my arms.

I walked back to the farm beneath the blazing sun. I couldn't have accepted a ride with him even if he had waited for me, which he didn't. I was too ashamed of myself, too bereft. I shuffled through the tall, green poppy-speckled grass, through the arched gate and up the dirt road toward Piantravigne. Dogs barked at me in the village. Children huddled near the statue of Garibaldi, watching me make my way around the piazza. I must have been a sight, stoop-shouldered, trudging along like a defeated soldier or an escapee from a nearby asylum. I don't recall if the women were still at the well or exactly how long it took me to get back to the farm, but I do remember it was dark when I climbed the stone steps and made my way through the kitchen to my room.

I stayed in my room with the shutters closed tightly against the blue light of Tuscany. I lay in total darkness for two days thinking of ways to kill myself, concocting schemes for sneaking out of the house and getting to the airport without having to face him again. I even once fantasized bursting into his room in the middle of the night and murdering him in his sleep. I conjured up every self-indulgent way out I could imagine. Then the truth descended on me like a collapsing roof. He was right: I was drowning in self-pity.

The wretchedness of it came to me like a great inspiration or the solution to a mathematics problem. It seemed to come to me through my late partner, as most of my self-awareness had for the past eight years. I could hear Lyle as though he were standing beside the bed in the dark, taunting me in his inimitable way for being so childish. "You're a spoiled only child. That's your problem. He's right. You're proud and don't want to admit it. I'm dead and you're alive and you're angry about it. Get over it, queen! Live your fucking life. You've been moping around for three years, and frankly it's way past getting a little tiresome."

I don't know how long I lay there after that, but when I finally got up I didn't dress or shave or brush my hair or even look in the mirror. I just opened the door and went looking for him. The sunlight poured down the hall, blinding me temporarily.

I found him on the loggia, reading a giant book filled with symbols and pentagrams and bizarre drawings. He looked up as I stepped through the doorway onto the stone porch.

I must have looked a fright standing there barefoot, bare-chested, with two days' growth on my face, my pajama bottoms twisted and wrinkled. I probably looked like a character from a Fellini film, the crazy grandfather who won't come down from the tree in *Amorcord*. We stared at one another for a long time. Finally, I asked, "What *is* your name?"

He chuckled slightly, but it wasn't warm, and, of course, he didn't answer.

"No, wait," I said, wanting to do this right. "I'm sorry. You've been nothing but kind and generous to me and I've treated you very badly. Please forgive me."

His features softened at that and his chuckle turned into a genuine smile.

"I've been completely self-indulgent," I continued. "I've been feeling sorry for myself for the past three years and you're the first person who has had the temerity...no, the decency...the respect, actually, to tell me."

"Apology accepted," he replied, and it was sincere.

TEN

HIS name, it turned out, was a reflection of the absurd amalgam of East and West that also gave him such an exotic and unusual look. Nicholas Rosario di Medici Borja. "Nicky to my friends," he said. "Lucretia to my adversaries."

Nicky's mother sometime in the early '60s ran off and married Nicky's father, whom she had met during one of his many business trips to Florence from Guam. They had carried on a mad love affair for over a year during his stays in Italy. Nicky's grandfather, however, forbade his daughter seeing the man again and went so far as to hire bodyguards to watch her. She managed to elude them, however, and the two lovers fled to Guam and married. Nicky suspected his grandmother—Nonna, as he refers to her—had a hand in helping the two escape.

"How else could they have managed it?" he asked rhetorically, peeling a blood orange and handing me a section. "Only Nonna could have pulled that one off," he concluded.

"Why would she do that?" I asked. "Why would she defy her husband and help your mother do such a foolish thing?"

Nicky arched his eyebrows. "Foolish? You think love is foolish?"

"Well, your grandfather did have a point," I said. "They barely knew one another and she was awfully young."

Nicky gave a derisive laugh. "My grandfather eloped with Nonna when she was even younger," Nicky said. "He had no room to talk. In fact, I'm sure that's why he was such a shit about it. Her family had tried to stop their marriage and so he scooped Nonna up in the middle of the night, with the help of her duenna, I might add, and the two eloped to a Franciscan monastery, where a renegade monk married them. Very *Romeo and Juliet*, my family," he said, handing me another section of orange.

"OK, so what happened?" I asked, taking the orange, which was dribbling juice all over my hand.

"Naturally, being *Toscano,* my grandfather disinherited my mother and refused ever to see her again," Nicky said, but with glee.

"You don't seem very distraught about it," I observed.

"Everything turned out all right in the end," Nicky continued. "My grandfather died when I was 9 and Nonna sent for us right away."

"So the family had a reunion here in Florence?"

"Oh, no," Nicky said loudly. "My father is even more proud and stubborn than my grandfather. Turns out he's a descendant from the Spanish Borjas, who were related to the Italian Borgias somewhere along the line. No, there would be no family reunion that included my father."

"Well, how did you end up reconciling?" I asked.

"My mother sent my older brother and sister and me to spend a few weeks with Nonna that summer," Nicky said. "I felt like I had come home to a place I didn't even know I belonged."

"And your brother and sister?"

"They hated it. They went home within a couple of weeks, but I stayed until two days before school started. Nonna and I adored each other from the moment we met, and I loved Tuscany," Nicky said, looking out over the valley and smiling broadly.

"So you came back often?"

"Every summer," he said. "My mother, of course, had to stay at home. She knew that if she left Guam, my father would be insulted. His honor was at stake, and she loves my father above everything except her children, so she has never returned."

"God!" I exclaimed. "So your grandmother has never seen her daughter again?"

"No, every once in awhile Nonna would come to Guam, and check into one of the fancy Japanese hotels. My mother would sneak off to see her every day when my father went to work," Nicky said with amusement at the thought. "But now Nonna's too old to travel like that. Flying to Guam is an excruciating trip. So she has to be content with only me, but my mother talks to her every week on the phone."

We sat in the morning sunlight and talked at length about a variety of things that escape me now. But I remember the Tuscan sunlight falling through the trees, across the loggia, and onto Nicky's arms and legs. He was wearing only a pair of baggy gray-and-white striped boxer shorts and his feet were propped up on the stone railing of the porch, the book of symbols resting in his lap.

I also remember how translucent and beautiful his skin appeared in that light, unlike the way I had seen it in Arezzo. It was a delicate brown, the color of coffee and cream, but with the most sensual patina, like that of the men in Italian Renaissance paintings. In fact, this very tableau could have easily been a Renaissance painting had it been a little more formally constructed.

The other memorable thing about that morning was the feeling. I felt...different. I remember feeling, if not hopeful, not desperate either; if not happy, not unhappy. I felt light for the first time since Lyle's death. The air over the Arno and all through the valley was clear and it seemed we could see all the way to Florence. Cuckoos called to one another in the trees and the bells on the goats meandering along the terraced hillside above the farmhouse clanged lazily in the silent morning air. I felt as though I might finally rest. I decided then and there to be more congenial.

ELEVEN

THE NEXT morning I awoke to find Nicky standing over me holding a tray.

"Breakfast," he said, "Scoot up." He placed the bed tray on my lap, then went to the shutters and threw them open. It was a crisp spring day and the blue Tuscan light poured into the room. Breakfast consisted of a baguette, prosciutto, romano cheese, and a huge mug of hot coffee with cream and sugar, just the way I like it. A thin vase with some blue and yellow wildflowers sat in one corner of the tray. "Eat up, *caro*," he said, opening the closet and inspecting my clothes. "We're going into town today."

"Castelfranco di Sopra or San Giovanni Valdarno?" I asked, trying not to gag at the sight of food first thing in the morning. I reached for the coffee.

"Firenze!" he answered. "Nonna called this morning. She wants to rendezvous at the Brancacci Chapel. Something about a surprise. She said to bring you along. Here, this will do," he said, selecting a pair of blue slacks and a white long-sleeve shirt. "Where are your ties?"

"I didn't bring any ties," I answered, a little annoyed that he would not only plan my day for me, but also assume to pick out my attire. "This was a vacation, not a...." I remembered my decision to try to change my attitude and held my tongue.

"Well today is the exception. *La Baronessa* has summoned us and we must obey. I have plenty of ties. We'll find one for you." He came back to the bed, leaned over and kissed my forehead, surprising me so that I nearly choked on my food. "This is Italy, *caro*, not America. People here care obsessively about their appearance. They care about how others dress too. It is an insult to present yourself in polite society, especially to the elderly, in too casual a manner. You will like my grandmother, I promise. She is the real Italy." And with that he left the room.

As I showered, I mulled over the events of the past 24 hours and how I was feeling about them. I was forced to admit that I wasn't as depressed as I had been. While I thought Nicky was a bit presumptuous and very aggressive, I had to acknowledge that he was, if not charming, at least entertaining. Still, I should have been asked if I wanted to meet his grandmother, not roped and tied and washed and groomed like some prize bull. I would let it slide this time, but if I was going to turn over a new leaf, he was going to have to back off a bit.

TWELVE

TO AN ORDINARY Italian, the ride into Florence to meet Nicky's grandmother might be described as uneventful. After all, traveling at 165 kilometers per hour on the autostrada is simply touring for most Italians. I, however, was terrified. From where we entered the main highway, it was almost 30 kilometers into Florence, but we made it in about ten minutes. I sat gripping the Lamborghini's soft leather seat and pictured Helen's face when she was handed a photograph of my decapitated body mangled in the wreckage of Nicky's car. She would look at the coat and tie Nicky had "dug up" for me and tell the *polizia*, "No, that's not him. He wouldn't own a tie like that."

It wasn't that the tie was ugly; quite the contrary. It was exquisite, but it must have cost him as much as I paid for my plane ticket. To say that Nicky appreciated fine clothes is a huge understatement. It's not that he's gauche or flamboyant. He just seeks quality—in everything.

The church we were going to, Santa Maria del Carmine, wasn't situated in Florence proper. It was just across the Arno, not far from the Palazzo Pitti, in the section of Florence referred to as the Oltrarno. Nicky screeched to a halt across the street from the church, parking directly in front of the entrance to the Piazza del Carmine. He cut the engine and opened the door. "Nicky, this is a no-parking zone," I warned.

"What?" he asked.

"Right there," I said, pointing to the sign he had practically run into when he swerved to the curb. "*Sosta vietata.* In ten-inch letters. Even I know what that means."

"Oh, that's not for us," he said, and got out, reaching behind the seat for his jacket.

I climbed out of the car and stood in the warm sun. A series of win-

dow boxes spilling over with bright red geraniums lined each floor of the
sand-colored apartment building next to the piazza. "And why is that?"
I asked, dying to hear his answer.

"I don't get tickets in Florence. It's a family thing."

"And how will they know this is the car of the fabulous Nicholas Borja?"

"Him," he answered, hiking his thumb over his shoulder in the direc-
tion of the church. Across the street, standing next to a huge black
Mercedes, was a little man in a black suit and chauffeur's cap. "C'mon,
I'll introduce you," Nicky said, moving to cross the street.

"*Cesare, amico, come va?*" Nicky said, shaking the man's hand, while
at the same time kissing him on both cheeks.

"*Bene, signore. Grazie. E tu?*"

"*Molto bene, mi amico, grazie. Cesare, te presento mi amico, il signor
Nigel,*" Nicky said, stifling a laugh. He was using my first name only,
which I knew was a way of telling Cesare something, but I didn't know
what. I was sure it was some sort of joke at my expense.

"*Buon giorno, signore,*" I said, giving Nicky the evil eye, or *malocchio*
as it is called in Italy. "*Piacere,*" I said, "pleased to meet you." Nicky just
snickered and told Cesare we were in a hurry and would see him later.

I followed Nicky through the nave of the church, which seemed to be
under construction, *in restauro,* like almost everything in Florence that
tourists might want to see. We walked up a side aisle to a chapel on the
right, more of a side altar than a chapel, really, but it was magnificent.
"This is the Brancacci Chapel," Nicky said, his voice bouncing off the
walls and marble mosaic floors. "These frescoes are by Masaccio and
Masolino. And two of them they now think were painted by Filippino
Lippi."

The paintings were breathtaking. I nearly lost my equilibrium turning round and round, left and right, to take them in as we climbed the
steps toward the altar, where an older couple was engaged in conversation with a priest in white vestments. When they heard Nicky's voice,
they turned toward us. The old woman, who struck me as oddly familiar, smiled broadly and raised her arms to him.

Nicky took the last three steps in a single leap, embraced the woman
and then took both of her hands and kissed them, one at a time.

"Nonna, this is my very good friend, Nigel Love. Nigel, may I present my grandmother, La Signora Cecilia Medici Riccardi Giannini Bruneschi."

"Signora," I said.

"*Sì, sì,*" Nicky's grandmother said pensively, as though she had just remembered something important. "*Naturalmente! Il sogno.*"

"What dream, Nonna?" Nicky asked.

"*Niente,*" she said to him, then smiled at me, then again at Nicky. She said, "I am honored you could join us, Signor Love. May I present my fiancé, Senator Benjamin Tedeschi, of California."

I recognized Ben Tedeschi from my days in Washington, but he had no way of knowing who I was.

"Former Senator," the distinguished and charming man with thick white hair corrected, smiling happily. "Ceecee likes to exaggerate a bit on my credentials." He wore a black suit, a navy-and-silver striped tie, and he leaned slightly on a silver-handled walking stick.

We shook hands as Nicky exclaimed, "Fiancé! Nonna, what are you saying?"

"I asked you here to be our witnesses. Monsignor Graziano is about to marry us." It was clear the old woman was enjoying this. It was also quite evident that she and her beau, who must have been at least 80, were very much in love. They were like teenagers, trying to contain their happiness.

"*Allóra,* shall we to start?" the monsignor said, attempting some English for my benefit.

The ceremony was brief but touching, the ancient couple's eyes sparkling as they repeated their vows, barely able to stifle their laughter. At one point Nicky's grandmother giggled and had to start over. Our only task was to stand and witness the ceremony. Then everybody hugged everybody, several times, and the monsignor said something privately to Nonna before excusing himself and leaving through a side door.

While Nicky visited with his grandmother and her new husband, I examined the frescoes. They were all from the life of St. Peter the Apostle. A relative of Nonna's had at one time been the patron of the chapel and was responsible for saving it from demolition.

Nicky had remarked on the drive into town that the frescoes had recently been restored to their original condition and in his estimation they were possibly the most beautiful physical objects he had ever laid eyes on. I thought that was a curious, if not exaggerated, way of putting it; but now, standing beneath them, it struck me that he was right. One of the most arresting elements was the sheer beauty of the faces, particularly the men, and most notably the young men. In the *Baptism of the Neophytes* there was a young man with long hair, disrobing, waiting his turn to be baptized by St. Peter. I couldn't take my eyes off him. If his hair had been darker, it would have been a portrait of Nicky. He had Nicky's skin color too. It was eerie.

Another panel depicted St. Peter being freed from prison. It was one of the most delicate and sensitive paintings I had seen in all of Europe. A young, beautiful angel stands in the doorway of St. Peter's prison cell, listening as St. Peter speaks to him, and gestures with his hand. The face on the angel was obviously the face of some hypnotically beautiful Florentine the painter was enamored of. Beside the jail cell another equally seductive youth, a prison guard, sits sleeping, while his prisoner makes his escape.

While some of the other frescoes were more sensual, none held a greater fascination for me. The idea that God would send this delicate boy to free Peter from imprisonment, just when it was certain his life was over, moved me in some mysterious way I couldn't articulate. Now I see only too clearly that it was the perfect allegory for what was happening to me at that very moment. Nicky, like some heaven-sent angel, was freeing me from the prison of my grief. Unlike St. Peter, however, I was refusing to leave my cell. I blush to think how obvious it was to everyone but me.

I became aware of someone standing behind me. It was Nicky. "Beautiful, no?" Nicky whispered in my ear. "Didn't I tell you?"

"Yes, you did, but this is more than I expected," was all I could say.

"You like that boy in the Baptism fresco?" Nicky asked. I thought perhaps he had seen me admiring it and was teasing me. Before I could respond, he said, "Nonna says it is me in a former life. She's so funny."

We stood there for a few moments longer, then he placed his hand on my shoulder, indicating we should go.

The four of us walked in silence through the dark church of Santa Maria del Carmine and into the bright May sunlight. Nonna put on dark glasses with big plastic frames. She looked like an aging Monica Vitti, one of Italy's most famous actresses. For the first time I noticed what she was wearing: a tailored suit of black raw silk, a single strand of fat, perfect pearls, and a little hat with a veil. Her earrings were also pearl. I noticed that on her right hand she wore a round-cut ruby ring the size of Milwaukee; on her left, the simple gold band Ben had placed there during the ceremony.

"Now, you two," Nonna said, taking Nicky's arm, then mine, as her new husband made his way down the steps one at a time. Cesare stood holding the Mercedes door open. "I see something very special in your future, for the both of you."

"Nonna is clairvoyant," Nicky said, leaning forward, around his grandmother and looking me in the eye. "It's kind of spooky, eh, Nonna?"

"Nothing spooky at all," she laughed. "What is so special is about to take place at my house. A *festa,* and you two must come. Is that your car over there? That fancy one?"

"*Sì,* Nonna," Nicky answered.

"Such a gigolo," she teased, pinching his cheek. "You watch out for this one," she said, looking at me. "He steals hearts. *Ladro di cuori,* this one," she said. "You come now. Follow us. You remember the way, in case we go too slow and you have to give it the gas?" She gave Nicky a little slap and then kissed me on the cheek. "I see good things here for you," she whispered, then got in the car, leaving the two of us watching as Cesare climbed in and drove the two lovebirds to their wedding reception.

It was a poignant moment for me, a moment I wanted to savor, and Nicky sensed it. He put his arm around me and smiled knowingly. "Aren't they sweet?" he said softly. "That could be you some day."

"I doubt it," I said. "Those days are over for me. But I'm not complaining. I've loved once. That's more than many people get."

"You shouldn't settle for so little. You can have much more. You are still young." He leaned closer and whispered in my ear, "*We* are still young." Then he hopped down the steps like a child, one step at a time, jingling the car keys and shouting in a singsong voice, "Party, party, party. Nonna's having a party. Let's go."

And so we went to Nonna's party, which would change my life forever and prove true the prediction Nonna had whispered in my ear.

THIRTEEN

TO SAY Nonna's villa was palatial would be a preposterous under-statement. The Palazzo Medici-Riccardi on the Via Cavour is primarily a museum now, but Nonna's living quarters, which are actually on the street behind the palazzo proper, are connected through several wings accessible via a maze of corridors not open to the public. The entrance the family uses is on the Via di Genori, which runs parallel to the busy Via Cavour.

As a valet took the keys to the Lamborghini from Nicky and we ascended the main steps, Nicky explained that the commission for the Palazzo Medici-Riccardi was supposed to go to Brunelleschi. However, Cosimo Medici, Nicky's great, great, great something-or-other feared that Brunelleschi's design would be too grand and would cause Cosimo political problems with the citizens of Florence. So Cosimo gave the job to Michelozzo, who designed a palace of solid classicism and installed a tiny chapel rather than the traditional large chapel most affluent fami-lies of the day preferred. Also, Nicky told me, there was an even smaller private chapel for the family that no one knew about.

By the time we entered the grand ballroom, Nonna and Ben were already mixing with the guests, Nonna waving away the suggestion of a formal receiving line with her gloved hand. She wanted to keep things informal, Nicky said, interpreting some of her comments to me. "Just her and 200 of her intimate friends," he said, smiling and handing me a glass of champagne. "It's an international crowd. Look." He pointed to a heavy-set couple near one of the massive doorways. "See the man in the military uniform? That's the Georgian ambassador with his wife. She weighs more than he does. And there's the Swiss attaché and his wife. And there is the British ambassador and his boyfriend. Wonder where his wife is?" Nicky giggled and poked me in the ribs, making me spill my champagne. "Could be a naughty gathering," he said. "Look at the Jean Claude van Damme wanna-be over there."

I followed the direction of Nicky's nod to a 40-ish bodybuilder bursting out of a tuxedo. He was waiting while one of Nonna's domestics poured Peroni into a tall beer glass. "See, Nonna knows how to find something for everyone," Nicky laughed. I didn't know if he meant the beer for the guest, or the guest for our delectation. Either way it was amusing.

"I didn't know they had gay gyms in Florence," I quipped.

"Obviously, they do," Nicky said. "Want to get acquainted?"

"No, thank you," I said sarcastically.

"Just checking. I want you to have a good time."

Nonna gestured to Nicky from where she was standing with a small group of guests, and he excused himself for a moment. I took the opportunity to catch my breath. Two weeks ago, I'd been relaxing alone on the loggia of Helen's farm in the middle of the Valdarno. Now I was drinking champagne in the palace of the family who financed the Crusades and boasted more popes in its lineage than most people have relatives.

The room we were standing in was immense, at least 60 by 50 feet. The walls were Florentine marble, with columns built into them. Paintings by Raphael, Lippi, Leonardo da Vinci, and Botticelli lined the walls. A statue of David by Donatello sat in one corner. According to a conversation I overheard, the small fountain next to the David was cast by Bernini, but it was too small for the courtyard. Nonna, rather than discarding it or giving it to the government, had it installed in the ballroom.

The guests glittered with fine jewelry. I squirmed and tugged at my collar. The jacket Nicky had provided me was too small, but I was in no position to complain. I wandered around the room for a few minutes, then sneaked through some tall, leaded-glass doors that led to a balcony. The evening air was cool and bracing.

I leaned on the marble balustrade and looked down to a beautiful garden in a central courtyard. It was tended with great care, but it was simple and invited meandering. There were stone benches here and there, and in one corner, surrounded by a low boxwood hedge, was what looked like another bronze by Bernini, this one a naked Mercury holding up a message as he ran toward his destination.

The garden was lit by a series of stone lanterns, strategically placed to illuminate just the gravel walkways. There were no spotlights anywhere, which told me that someone, Nonna, I assumed, liked to spend time in the garden at night and had it designed so no lights hung high, where they might shine in her eyes as she strolled the pathways or sat in contemplation on one of the benches. It was quiet down there, in stark contrast to the noise of the reception behind me.

What on earth was I doing? How did I let myself get roped into this? I came to Italy to relax, to be introspective, to pull myself together. Instead, this international jet-setting gigolo had me attending weddings and grand balls and…

I was doing it again, I realized. Complaining about being alive. Why? Most people would give anything to be at a function like this, to stand in the Palazzo Medici-Riccardi, meeting interesting, colorful people or to be isolated on an 18th-century villa in the middle of the Arno Valley with an exotic and attractive young man. Nicky was intelligent, insightful, considerate, worldly, and not exactly unattractive. He just wasn't my type. And his jet set lifestyle wasn't what I was looking for. At least that's what I told myself.

I was still grieving, but why? Why couldn't I let go and enjoy life? Why wasn't I reveling in Italy the way Nicky was? And then, looking onto the quiet garden below me and listening to the din of the party behind the balcony doors, it dawned upon me: When I looked at Nicky I saw life. I saw someone who had his whole life before him. When I looked in the mirror, I saw a man with a death sentence.

True, the drugs I was taking for my HIV infection were working, and working well. But I kept waiting for the other shoe to drop. I expected to wake up one day and find myself short of breath, or step in front of the bathroom mirror to find a purple splotch on my cheek. I couldn't get those thoughts out of my mind.

Nicky had none of that to contend with. He was 30, maybe 31, rich, educated, attractive, and he had the world on a string. He could do anything, go anywhere. He didn't have to wake up each day to confront his mortality the way I did.

That's why I was so remote. That's why I was always irritated with him. I envied him. I envied his freedom, his devil-may-care attitude, and his reckless approach to life. He could fly down the autostrada at 165 kilometers per hour because Death had no dominion over him. And that made him different from me. He was smack in the middle of life. I was out on the edge, looking into the abyss.

It wasn't the surroundings or the high-powered people that made me feel so out of place. I had moved in these circles before when I worked in Washington. No, it wasn't that at all; it was all this goddamned life force, this fucking look-everyone-I'm-alive-and-well-and-having-a-fabulous-time-man-the-torpedoes-full-speed-ahead attitude.

He's going to live and I'm going to die: That was my attitude. That was the dark pit I was drowning in. I had fled half way around the world to escape that realization only to end up on a balcony of the Palazzo Medici-Riccardi staring it in the face all over again. I resented it.

"Nigel, I'd like you to meet someone."

FOURTEEN

I SPUN around, startled by Nicky's voice. Standing next to him was a woman I had seen him and his grandmother engaged in conversation with earlier. At the time, from across the ballroom, she seemed like a version of Cinderella; up close, she came off more like Zsa Zsa Gabor.

Even I could tell she had been under the plastic surgeon's knife more than once. The skin at her neck was pulled so tightly that her mouth was stretched into a perpetual smile. Her makeup, though expertly applied, was as thick as stage makeup, and her hair was a beautiful shade of unnatural blond. Her floor-length dress of blue-and-white bugle beads was outshone only by the diamond necklace and tiara she was wearing; even an unaccomplished queen like me could tell the stones were genuine.

In spite of all that, the woman, introduced as Mrs. Evelyn VanDeventer Iversen, was as charming and down-to-earth as everyone else was self-important. "It's the most amazing coincidence, Nigel," Nicky gushed, "It turns out that Mrs. Iversen's daughter and I went to college together. Isn't that amazing? Isn't it keen?"

"Yes, it is," I said. "Quite."

"I understand you're also from California," Mrs. Iversen remarked in a low, unassuming voice. "I believe Nicky said San Francisco."

"That's right. A native, actually."

"How unusual," she went on. "I mean that the two of you should be neighbors and have to travel halfway around the world to meet." She held, but didn't drink, a crystal flute of champagne.

"Neighbors?" I said, giving Nicky a quizzical look.

"The house on Sanchez Hill," Nicky said. "I told you about it."

"What house on Sanchez Hill?"

"Oh, never mind, I'll remind you later," he said, half teasing, half condescending. Then, to Mrs. Iversen, "He has a terrible memory. It's because he's so bright. An intellectual type. You know, they have a difficult time in the practical world. Let me freshen that drink for you." He took the champagne glass from Mrs. Iversen's hand.

"Oh, that's not necessary," she protested. "I don't drink much, actually, I just hold it because it makes people more comfortable if everyone is drinking."

"Well, I'll freshen it anyway, just in case you change your mind. Mrs. Iversen is a newlywed too," Nicky said to me, and with that, he was through the doors and making his way across the room. I watched him raise himself up on his tiptoes now and again, in search of one of the butlers circulating through the room with silver trays of champagne.

"So, a newlywed," I said, wondering which lucky man had latched onto this aging Barbie doll with the diamond tiara.

"Not really," she said, blushing like a schoolgirl and lowering her head in what seemed like genuine embarrassment. "Travis and I were married over six months ago. It's nothing like Cecilia. We weren't married today or anything."

"Well, congratulations, anyway. I raised my glass in a mock toast, but didn't drink, aware that her glass was making its way through the crowd in the hands of the impish, if not deceptive, Nicky Borja. Sanchez Hill indeed.

"It's quite remarkable, meeting you two like this. I mean meeting Nicky and finding out we know one another," Mrs. Iversen said, touching my arm lightly with fingers littered with jeweled rings.

"I'm not following," I said.

"Nicky went to school with Annarita, my youngest daughter. We just found out, when we met. He recognized the name VanDeventer and asked me if I was by related to a VanDeventer who attended the University of Texas. It turns out he and Annarita were friends in school, and as he went on talking I remembered her speaking of him. Quite frequently, actually." She threw her head back now in an unabashed laugh. "She told me she knew someone related to the popes. Frankly, I thought she had a crush on him in her junior year. Now that I've met him, I think they would make a wonderful couple." She stared into the ballroom as though she were watching Nicky and Annarita waltzing around the floor on their wedding day. "Don't you?"

"I don't know, Mrs. Iversen. I've never met your daughter."

"Oh, of course not. How silly of me. You must forgive me, Nigel. I'm just a romantic at heart. I think everyone should be happily married, especially women. My daughter is currently coming out of a very bad marriage and I'm feeling a bit protective of her." She touched my arm again, but this time left her hand there, as though she needed to draw some sort of reassurance from me. "I'm old-fashioned. I think a woman's place is with her husband. I think Nicky and Annarita would be perfect together."

I stifled a laugh as I conjured a split-screen image of Annarita and her mother waiting at the altar of the duomo in Arezzo while Nicky was in the bell tower giving the priest a quickie before the ceremony. Nicky appeared in the doorway with three glasses of champagne, which I helped him with. We toasted the "newlywed" again, Mrs. Iversen, that is, and while Nicky and I were drinking, she announced, "Oh, here's my husband, now. You can meet him. Darling," she called, "come meet my new friends."

Quite embarrassingly, both Nicky and I choked and drooled champagne, as her husband, the bodybuilder we had been dishing earlier, strode through the door. She didn't notice our faux pas, however, as she was already reaching to take his arm and commandeer him into our little group. Nicky and I sneaked a glance at each other and knew we couldn't look at each other again until we were separated from the two of them, or else we might give ourselves away entirely with explosive guffaws. The princess and the bodybuilder. Who would have guessed?

FIFTEEN

IT TURNS OUT the bodybuilder wasn't just a bodybuilder, if he was ever a bodybuilder at all. He was a cowboy! A real, live, honest-to-goodness, rodeo kind of cowboy, except instead of working with cows, he worked with Brahman bulls; specifically one white bull with huge forked horns that did things like count with its hoof and stand on a stool while the cowboy twirled a lariat.

We spent about ten minutes on foolish pleasantries with Mr. Iversen, or Travis, as he preferred to be called, not contributing much. He spent most of the time tugging at his collar and looking into his pilsner glass, as though more beer might have magically appeared since the last time he looked 15 seconds ago. I couldn't help but notice that now, for the first time since we met her, Evelyn VanDeventer Iversen was sipping at her champagne.

Travis was nice enough, but as Nicky wryly commented later, "sometimes nice isn't enough." Travis was clearly uncomfortable in this milieu. He was literally stuffed into his tuxedo; he wore cowboy boots, albeit designer lizard cowboy boots, instead of patent leather pumps, and he wasn't having anything to do with champagne or any of Nonna's high-society guests. The only contribution he made to the conversation was to say something about horses or Brahman bulls and how he had a ranch in Texas, besides the ranch that Evelyn and he just bought, and that he'd be real glad to get back somewhere where people spoke English.

Evelyn, the whole time, held onto his arm and donned a smile that didn't come from within. It was the kind of smile you see on a beauty contestant, one practiced in front of a mirror and easy to affect because she's coated her teeth with petroleum jelly. When she wasn't smiling she was telling us their itinerary. Travis had never been to Europe and she had been wanting to return for ever so long, so they decided it would be a kind of belated honeymoon.

They started in Paris, then took a private barge through a series of canals and locks to Amsterdam. From Holland they took the train to Brussels, Vienna, Zurich, Milan, Venice, and now Florence. "Tomorrow," she said, squeezing her husband's 22-inch bicep, "we return to Milan and fly back to California the day after that. You absolutely must come to visit Annarita in Concord. Now you have my phone number and you mustn't lose it. It's my private number and you can't get it anywhere. If you try to reach me through my secretary, you probably won't have any luck. She's a very protective gal."

Just then we heard the string quartet begin to play in the dining room across the hall from the grand ballroom, signaling that dinner was about to be served. Nonna had planned a sit-down dinner for 200. What I found so amazing about this was that she actually had a dining room large enough to accommodate that many.

We left the balcony with promises to call and visit and generally stay in touch. Once inside Nicky tugged at my sleeve, intimating we should lag behind and let them go ahead. A butler approached and exchanged our empty champagne glasses for full ones. I think those were probably our fifth by that time. "So what do you think?" Nicky asked, sotto voce. "Is he or isn't he?"

"Is he or isn't he what?" I replied, pretending I didn't know what he was referring to.

"Don't be dense. Queer, of course."

"How can he be queer when he's married to that lovely woman?" I persisted.

"Oh, my God. I hope you're not serious." He leaned back as if to focus on me better. "You are serious."

I stifled a laugh.

"Little bugger," he said a bit loudly. "I thought you meant it for a minute."

"You're easy," I taunted. "Not even a challenge."

"Well what's the story, then? He's after her money?" Nicky gulped his champagne like lemonade.

"I doubt it. He said he had his own ranch in Texas before he met her.

He must have some money of his own."

"Oh, please. He ropes horses in the rodeo and makes cows dive off a platform into a bucket of water. How much money can that bring in?"

"I have no idea. Enough to buy his own ranch, anyway." I had to admit it all sounded foreign to me. "Maybe rodeos are big moneymakers."

"When's the last time you went to a rodeo?" Nicky asked with exaggerated disdain.

"Well, I'm hardly typical, now am I?"

"There's something fishy there if you ask me. And did you see her face? I haven't seen that much plastic since I drove my brother's corvette. Are you going to drink that?" He clinked my nearly full glass with his empty one, then, without waiting for an answer, he exchanged glasses with me. He was quite different with a few drinks in him. Much more animated, I thought, as if that were possible.

"You have beautiful feet," he said, taking my arm and walking us toward the dining room.

"What?!" I exclaimed.

"Your feet, I've been noticing them when you come out of the shower in the morning. Or late afternoons, after your nap, when you walk barefoot out onto the loggia with your cappuccino."

"My feet?" I looked down at them, forgetting for the moment I couldn't see them through my shoes. "My feet..." I mused.

"Mmm," he moaned in my ear. "Very masculine." He squeezed my arm and picked up our pace. "I'm famished. I hope she's serving Brahman bull Bourguignon," he said, practically skipping into the room. He was quite entertaining when he was drunk. Well, actually, he was entertaining all the time, but especially when he was drunk. Entertaining and extremely funny. And kind of cute, too.

SIXTEEN

DINNER was a total extravaganza. Seven courses served by gloved butlers, four assigned to each table of eight guests. The dining room was set up in a series of round tables so guests could see one another without having to lean. Our table of eight guests was made up of Nicky and me; Dr. Njoto Bkumbe, an African tribal doctor consulting with a pharmaceutical company in Milan; his wife, Mrs. Iman Bkumbe; Ambassador General Andrei Boronovich, Ambassador to Italy from the Republic of Georgia; his wife, Vera; Dr. Michael Levy of the American International School in Florence, visiting professor of psychology and internationally known therapist and author; and Dr. Charlene Cardarelli, vice president of Olivetti International, based in Turin.

Nicky was the perfect host, engaging each person in conversation. He made sure everyone got to speak at regular intervals and paid special attention to the women, seeing to it that they received plenty of wine, or perhaps I should say wines, since there were a total of seven served, one with each course. Nicky hardly touched his food, but he kept one butler occupied throughout the entire dinner, just pouring champagne into his glass, which rarely left his hand.

The first four courses came and went without much attention, other than the polite comment on the quality of the food, but the fifth course, the "fish" brought a hush to the entire room. This course consisted of *salmone d'oro,* or golden salmon, with wild rice and porcini mushrooms. By golden salmon I don't mean done to a golden brown; the chef had prepared a salmon mousse, then put it into small, fish-shaped molds to bake. At the last minute, before taking the salmon out of the oven, the chef laid the sheerest sheet of gold leaf over the mold so that it would melt, leaving the effect of eating a mythic, golden fish rather than mere salmon mousse.

"It's quite all right, really," Nicky assured us as we stared at the plates before us. "Gold in small quantities can't hurt you. In fact, it's actually good for you. Like iron, I'm told. Nonna does this all the time and we've all survived." Then, as an afterthought, "Thrived, actually."

The Georgian ambassador's wife broke the ensuing silence.

"Signor Borja," she began, pronouncing the "j," which made Nicky cringe, "how long has your grandmother been planning this wedding to Senator Tedeschi? I had no idea they were so serious." I sensed that it was a passive-aggressive way of inquiring as to how long the couple had known each other, with a hint of approbation at the thought that some-one of the aristocracy should be marrying a "commoner."

Nicky saw through her catty remark and replied without missing a beat. "I'm not exactly sure. Probably shortly after they began sleeping together, I would imagine. She's very old-fashioned that way. How long have you and Comrade Boronovich been married?" The use of the word "comrade" made the ambassador choke and reach for his water goblet.

"Now, now," he said jovially, taking his wife's sausage fingers and squeezing them until her eyebrows arched, "We are an independent nation. A republic. Just like Italy. Isn't that right, dear?"

Mrs. Boronovich groaned her agreement through a mouth filled with mousse.

Dr. Levy entered the conversation and Nicky gave my leg a slight tap under the table. "Speaking of your country, Ambassador Boronovich, has construction begun yet on the IBM plant in your home town?"

"Not yet, sir. Many details are left to work out. Capitalism is still, how you like to say in the United States, a young zipper-snapper in my coun-try. But it will happen. Eventually. All in good time."

Dr. Levy lifted his wineglass in a toast, which he made while looking at the two of us. "To all the young 'zipper-snappers' everywhere. May they get bigger and bigger, even as the evening progresses."

Nicky gave me another kick under the table, a bit sharper this time. I took it to mean Dr. Levy was a friend of Dorothy, and upon second glance it was more obvious. His tuxedo was Armani—black label, not Emporio—and he wore a wing collar. I also thought I detected just a hint of exaggerated bicep in the sleeve as he raised his glass.

"Yes." Nicky, joined in, unable to help himself, partly because he was already loaded and partly because he was being Nicky. "To zipper-snappers everywhere. God bless us, every one." The entire table toast-ed, Dr. Bkumbe drinking the entire contents of his glass in one series of gulps, then smiling as he belched at about sixty decibels. Mrs. Bkumbe, who obviously had to remain silent in keeping with her cul-tural station, lowered her eyes in embarrassment, which I took to mean she had a bit more experience in the world than her husband. The Georgian ambassador and his wife seemed oblivious to bodily noises and didn't miss a beat.

Conversation continued in a convivial manner as the meat course, "rack of venison," was served. This was the deer equivalent of a stand-ing prime rib roast. The game was "harvested" on the Medici estate near Lake Como and prepared that morning with a remarkable mari-nade of garlic, fennel, and kumquats. Again, Nicky paid more attention to the champagne than the meal, but held his liquor well. Had I not just spent the past two weeks with the man, I wouldn't have known he was snockered.

"Dottoressa Cardarelli," Nicky said, holding up his glass for more champagne. The butler was now permanently keeping his station direct-ly behind Nicky's chair with the champagne bottle at the ready. "Tell me, how do you know my grandmother?"

Doctor Cardarelli, a striking woman with short dark hair and pierc-ing brown eyes, had maintained a reserved demeanor throughout the dinner. She was a diminutive woman with finely chiseled features. Her nose, while a bit Roman, was sharply defined and gave character to her face, which boasted high-set cheekbones and an olive complexion that radiated in the candlelight. At this question she became quite animated, setting down her fork, sipping her Montepulciano d'Abruzzo, and explaining, "Your grandmother saved my life, signore."

Now the entire table turned their attention to the woman. "Please," Nicky exclaimed, "we're on the edge of our seats. You don't mean that literally, I assume."

"*Naturalmente!* If it weren't for your grandmother I would be lying in a crypt in my family cemetery in Lucca, or worse, food for the gulls off Sorrento."

"Please, tell us," Nicky implored.

"Yes, yes," the others chimed in.

"The story begins in Naples," she said, folding her napkin in her lap. "I had gone there with a small group of coworkers from Olivetti to discuss a possible joint venture with one of our major competitors. We were trying to come to an agreement on the financial allocations and the talks were going badly. After six days of getting nowhere, I suggested we take a short holiday to Capri to let people cool their tempers. Everyone thought that was a good idea, so we left for the island."

"Both sides of the negotiations or just the Olivetti people?" Dr. Levy asked.

"No, both sides. I thought if we could be with one another in a more pleasant setting, we might see each other more as human beings and less as corporate adversaries. I hoped we would relate to one another better when we sat back down at the negotiating table."

"I see why you are a vice president, Dottoressa Cardarelli," Dr. Levy complimented, raising his wineglass in a gesture of salutation.

"*Grazie,* signore," she acknowledged, bowing her head slightly.

"Please continue, signora," Nicky urged.

"We checked into the Hotel Luna on Capri, all six of us. Two women, four men. After we had been on Capri only two days someone suggested we hike to Tiberius' Leap at the top of the island. It is one of the most breathtaking spots in all of the Aegean. There is a temple and the ruins of an old castle. It is where Tiberius took his traitorous comrades and threw them into the sea, thousands of meters below. It is a long, exhausting walk, but we were all in good shape. I thought it an excellent idea, to do something highly physical to work out the tension."

"You would make an excellent therapist, Dottoressa Cardarelli," Dr. Levy said.

Dottoressa Cardarelli simply smiled and went on with her story. "Two of the men—the president of the other company and our vice president of operations—had been arguing all week. They bickered all the way from Napoli to Capri on the ferry, all through our lunches and dinners. They took walks in the garden in the evenings and we could hear them shouting from where we sat on the hotel veranda. It was most disturbing. I thought the hike would be excellent. I secretly hoped they would get so winded halfway up the mountain they wouldn't be able to argue."

She took a sip of wine and wiped her lips with her linen napkin, then continued. "Now I must back up for a moment. The day we arrived on Capri, everyone's luggage was sent up from the dock and I ended up with someone else's suitcases. The porter delivered the most exquisite white leather bags to my room, six of them in various sizes. They were lovely, but they weren't mine, so I called the front desk and they came and got them. It seems your grandmother had checked into the Hotel Luna that afternoon also," she said to Nicky, "and somehow they mixed up the room numbers on the luggage. That evening, , while I was having a glass of vermouth on the veranda, the most startling vision appeared before me. It was a woman wearing a floor-length white gossamer gown with a white hat and a white shawl. *Allóra,* it was no vision at all; it was Signora di Medici Riccardi Giannini Bruneschi…Tedeschi," she said, giggling as she added Nonna's new married name to the list. "She apologized for the mix-up of the luggage and insisted on my having an evening Campari with her."

Dottoressa Cardarelli's demeanor changed now, becoming wistful and mysterious at the same time. "She was quite charming and we must have talked for two hours. Finally, the maître d' summoned her for dinner and she insisted I join her, which I did, of course. One doesn't refuse such a lady as the Signora, and she was an excellent conversationalist. It was the first relaxing engagement I had had with anyone since we had begun these meetings. So La Signora and I went to dinner and after dinner took a stroll in the gardens. We walked beneath the pergola, which was heavy with fat purple grapes. Through the arbor we could see the full moon, *la luna piena.* It was enchanting. About 1 A.M. we bid one another *buona notte* and retired for the evening."

"Around 4 in the morning I was awakened by a tapping at the French doors leading to the balcony. I sat up and could see a figure outside. It appeared to be a woman. I opened the doors to find La Signora di Medici standing on the balcony in the moonlight in her dressing gown, quite distressed, quite beside herself. She took both my hands and implored me, 'Dottoressa Cardarelli, you must not go on your excursion tomorrow. You must not. There is grave danger in it for you. I must insist you do not go.' As you can imagine, I was bewildered. But she was so insistent I agreed. She said she would not leave my side until I acquiesced to her request. She told me she had had a dream, and in it a messenger appeared telling her that if I left the hotel tomorrow I would die. She said she was experienced in these matters, that it had happened to her before, and I simply must trust her."

"The next morning, I vacillated. But before I could even get dressed, La Signora di Medici was at my door, making certain I did not leave the hotel grounds. She sat in my room while I telephoned the others to say I was indisposed and would not be joining them that morning, but that I would meet them for dinner that evening. So La Signora and I spent the morning reading on the loggia." Dottoressa Cardarelli sipped at her water now and looked around the table with a thin but charming smile. She was as beautiful as a Milanese fashion model, and I could easily picture her on the cover of a magazine.

"Well, what happened next, Dottoressa Cardarelli? Please, don't keep us in suspense. How did the *Baronessa* save your life?" The ambassador's wife was leaning so far into the table her bosom was in her plate.

"That afternoon the *polizia* came to the hotel to announce that the party that had hiked to Tiberius' Leap were dead. All but one, that is. It seems that the two men continued arguing the entire way up the mountain. When they got there, the president of the rival company went berserk and pushed everyone to their deaths in the waters a thousand meters below. They found him sitting in one of the temple gardens babbling to himself. If it hadn't been for your grandmother, I would most certainly have perished along with my coworkers."

"Remarkable!" said the ambassador's wife, brushing at her considerable bosom with her napkin. "Extraordinary."

"I have heard of many such clairvoyant events," said Dr. Levy, "but never have I met anyone to whom this has happened. You are quite fortunate, Dottoressa Cardarelli."

"I believe my good fortune was that I became a friend of La Signora. She has been like a grandmother to me for the past three years. She advises me on everything and is never wrong. Never."

"Is this common with your grandmother, Signor Borja? These paranormal events?" Dr. Levy asked.

"She has had a gift for as long as I have been alive, doctor," Nicky said. "It is not uncommon in our family for someone to have this gift, but Nonna has many gifts. You should talk to her about it some time, Doctor Levy. She would be a fascinating study for you."

Just then we heard a loud crunch and all heads turned toward the source. Directly across the table from where I sat, Dr. Bkumbe was enjoying the rib bone from his venison steak, crunching, chewing, swallowing, and smiling with great satisfaction. "Delicious. Best ever tasted!" exclaimed Dr. Bkumbe. He then turned to Mrs. Boronovich, "Are you to eat that?" he asked, pointing to the bone on her plate.

"Wha...wha...well...no. No, I...." the ambassador's wife stammered.

"May I?" Dr. Bkumbe said, not waiting for an answer, but reaching over and relieving Mrs. Boronovich of her venison rib bone. With a huge smile and a loud crunch, Dr. Bkumbe chomped down, nodding his head with exuberance. "Most delicious," he said through shards of bone. "Best. Best ever tasted!"

Nicky, of course, was beside himself with glee. He immediately jumped up and went around the table collecting the bones and taking them to Dr. Bkumbe. "Please, Dr. Bkumbe, enjoy! I'm so glad someone here appreciates Ricardo's fine cooking. *Allóra, Giuseppe, porti ancora piu ossi per il dottore,*" Nicky shouted to the butler. More bones for the doctor. "*Presto!*"

And with that the butlers around our table began scurrying to find more bones. Nicky turned to the table next to us and began asking guests if they were going to eat their bones, then scooped them up into a napkin and deposited them on Dr. Bkumbe's plate. "Eat up, doctor. Angelo," Nicky called to one of the staff. "Find Doctor Bkumbe a doggie bag for the bones he doesn't finish. May I?" Nicky asked Dr. Bkumbe, holding up one of the rib ones?

"Please do," Dr. Bkumbe answered, hoisting half a rib in the air in encouragement.

Nicky stuck the rib between his teeth and bit down. A loud crunch issued forth, along with a yelp. I jumped up and helped him from the

room. "I shall return," Nicky called back to our table as we went in
search of first aid.

SEVENTEEN

IT WAS ONLY a minor cut on his gum and we quickly patched it up in the bathroom on the third floor. I found some anti-bacterial ointment that contained an anesthetic in a drawer and proceeded to play doctor. The bathroom was, of course, the size of my entire flat. Nicky sat on a chaise lounge while I tried to administer help.

I dabbed some ointment on my index finger and stooped down to mouth level. "OK, open wide," I said. He complied. I stuck my finger in and began daubing the medicine on his wound. He closed his mouth and began running his tongue along my finger.

"You're incorrigibly drunk," I said, smiling in spite of myself, trying to be serious.

"Quite. I hope you don't take advantage of it," he said, his eyes half-closed.

"I think you need to get some sleep," I said, standing upright and slipping my finger out of his mouth against the suction he was now applying.

"I'm not sleepy," he whined. "The evening's just begun."

"Tell me something, seriously," I said, screwing the cap back on the ointment and returning it to the drawer. "Is it true what you said downstairs about your grandmother? The clairvoyant stuff, I mean. Does that happen to her often? I remember you saying something earlier today about her thinking the both of you had lived other lives. Is all this stuff serious with her?"

"Quite serious," Nicky said, looking around the room. "Where's my champagne glass?"

"Never mind that for now. What about you? What about those esoteric books up at the farm, like *The Tibetan Book of the Dead*. Do you believe in reincarnation too?"

"You have beautiful eyes, you know," Nicky said. He was slumped on the chaise, his jacket off, his bow tie hanging limply around his neck. He had tugged open his shirt collar, pulled out the studs from the top three holes and stuffed them into his pocket. His smooth brown chest was a stark contrast to the starched white tuxedo shirt.

"My eyes are hazel. Hazel eyes can hardly be described as beautiful." I countered, again stifling a laugh at how silly he was acting, but there was also something endearing about his innocence at this moment. "Green eyes can be beautiful. Blue eyes can sometimes be haunting. And brown eyes are beautiful in a seductive kind of way. But hazel eyes are just hazel."

"Your hazel eyes are beautiful," he said. "Nonna had hazel eyes once. Come, I'll show you." He stood, albeit shakily, scooped up his jacket, and headed for the bathroom door.

"What are you doing now?" I asked, growing a little exasperated with the fragmented nature of our conversation.

"You wanted to know if I believed in reincarnation and I want to show you Nonna's hazel eyes." He slipped into his tuxedo jacket and grabbed a champagne glass that someone had left on a marble table near the door. "Her *beautiful* hazel eyes. Come on, come on," he chanted impatiently. I followed him back into the dining room, where he told me to wait by the door while he approached his grandmother at the main table. They whispered back and forth to one another a few times, then she looked toward me and smiled, as Nicky made his way back across the crowded room now filled with the after-dinner chatter of the guests. As he passed one of the tables, he begged a water goblet from a woman in a sari, dumped its contents into the flower arrangement in the center of the table, and went straight to one of the butlers, who filled it with champagne.

"You do like your cocktails, don't you?" I teased, as he reached me.

"Now and again, when there's reason to celebrate. Mostly I drink to make life more like a movie. The same reason I smoke once in a while," he said, taking a cigarette case from his tuxedo pocket and opening it. He retrieved a cigarette and immediately one of the butlers rushed over to light it. He blew smoke in the air, sighed and said, "It raises the levity quotient." He lifted his glass to my lips. "Join me?"

I shook my head no.

"It's a test," he said, singing the last word and cocking his head sideways. He smiled and his full lips parted just enough to show his startlingly white teeth, which looked all the more white against his brown skin. It was a smile impossible to refuse. I sipped some champagne.

"Just please don't ask me to smoke," I said.

"No, I wouldn't force you to smoke. I'll smoke for both of us. Good little daddy," Nicky said, and patted me on the head. "A-plus. Oh, look, Dr. Bkumbe is waving at us."

Across the room, Dr. Bkumbe was waving a bone in the air in our direction. We waved back and made our exit.

"Nonna recognizes you," Nicky said as we walked down the long hallway.

"Recognizes me? That's not possible."

"She saw you in a dream a few weeks ago. You were standing on a hillside in the rain. She told me just now. It's why she was so weird when she met you this afternoon. She asked me to apologize for her. OK, now stay close to me. There probably aren't any lights on in this part of the house."

I couldn't stop thinking about appearing in someone else's dream as we worked our way down several hallways, through foyers and rooms and what seemed like a tunnel at one point. Finally we stood in an interior courtyard. Nicky approached a portrait of what I presumed was one of the early Medicis, which hung on a wall near a set of huge carved wooden doors, and swung the portrait out, revealing a small shelf with a large key. He retrieved the key, returned the painting to its previous position, and opened one of the doors.

We entered a room so dark I couldn't see my hand before my face. I heard the door shut and then Nicky found a rheostat of some sort and lights began slowly to come up all around us. We were standing in a small but magnificent chapel. It was stunning in the richness of its architecture and design. The walls and floor were made of various marbles and inlaid with gold and precious stones.

"Where are we?" I asked.

"This is the private chapel," Nicky said. "The one the tourists don't get to see."

The room was octagonal, about three stories high, rising into a domed ceiling that was lapis and gold mosaic. At the center of the dome was a leaded glass capitol of translucent glass. The eight walls of the chapel alternated altar, fresco, altar, fresco all the way around. The frescoes were painted above a molding about eight feet up from the mosaic floor. Around the chapel walls, just below the molding, ornate family crests were inlaid. The altars honored various saints favored by the Medicis. Each altar featured a statue of the saint, either sitting or kneeling next to the tabernacle. All but one.

"That's Lorenzo," Nicky explained. "Big ego. He had the statue of St. Peter placed above the tabernacle, supposedly to guard the host, but Nonna says it was because he thought he was bigger than God."

"He thought St. Peter was bigger than God?" I asked.

"No, puppy toes. That statue of St. Peter is a statue of Lorenzo. See the face? There's no mistaking that puss. It's all over the city. Lorenzo thought that Lorenzo was bigger than God."

It was a face I had seen on many statues and several paintings since I'd been in Florence. I knew it was common practice for the patron's likeness to be incorporated into works of art, but this did seem excessive.

"Everyone here in all these statues and frescoes are ancestors of mine. They're Medicis and Riccardis going back to the 15th century," Nicky said as we walked the circumference of the room. "Here is the expulsion from the garden of Eden, the court of King David, the journey of the magi, and the crucifixion. Look here," he said, taking my arm and drawing me closer to the fresco of the crucifixion. "What do you see?"

"The crucifixion of Christ," I answered.

"Let me put it another way. *Whom* do you see?"

I examined the painting on the wall more closely. There was Christ hanging on the cross, the two thieves hanging next to him, Roman soldiers sitting and standing around, waiting for the end. At the foot of the cross was a crowd of people I tried to put names to. St. John, an aging Mary Magdalen, a bedraggled Mary, the mother of Jesus, a few onlookers….Then something struck me and I turned my attention back to the figure of Mary Magdalen. I stepped closer to examine the face. Except for the brown-green eyes—the *hazel* eyes—it was an exact portrait of Nonna. Younger than 80, for sure, but it was definitely Nonna.

"It's your grandmother, right?"

"Sort of," Nicky said, impishly.

"Well, I mean, it's a painting of your grandmother that she commissioned to have put into the fresco. Your grandmother's face on the body of Mary Magdalen. Right?"

"Sort of," Nicky repeated, sipping at his champagne.

He could be so annoying. "OK, so what's the big deal? Nonna had her face painted into the crucifixion scene. It's a common practice, isn't it?"

"It *was* a common practice, 300 years ago."

"300 years ago?" Maybe it was the champagne, but I wasn't following.

"It was a common practice 300 years ago, when this fresco was painted. This is the answer to your question," Nicky said smugly, a sexy grin spreading across his lips. I hated when he toyed with me.

"Question? What question?"

"Do I believe in reincarnation? You're looking at Nonna, as she appeared in the year 1667. She had hazel eyes then."

It was true. There could be no doubt that it was the same woman. A shiver ran up my back. I moved closer to the wall. Nicky stepped up and stood next to me, slipping his arm through mine. I turned to look at him. He was looking at the face of Mary, a sweet admiration in his eyes. He turned and looked at me and smiled, and for no reason I can fathom even to this day I did something totally spontaneously and without forethought. I took him in my arms and kissed him.

EIGHTEEN

WHEN I opened my eyes the next morning, the room I was in was almost totally dark. Somewhere behind the thick draperies the sun was rising, but it wasn't strong enough yet to illumine the room. The bed was soft, a feather bed, I presumed. I rolled over onto my back slowly. My entire body was hung over. My joints were stiff and my muscles throbbed dully. I tried to remember if I felt like this after a night on the town when I was in my 30s, but this morning I couldn't remember my 30s.

As I turned, the top of the bed came into view. It was a canopy that looked more like the baldachin of St. Peter's. It loomed about half a story above me and was crafted of ornately carved mahogany. At the top of the four posts that rose from the bed, four archangels thrust their swords toward the center of the canopy, their shields raised above their heads as though they might ward off evil spirits.

As I slowly spread out my arms and legs in an attempt to stretch, my left foot contacted naked flesh. I lurched up on my elbows and, lying on his stomach, next to me in the bed, the coverlet pulled down below his thighs, lay Nicky, deep in champagne dreams.

A blade of golden light sliced through tall damask draperies at the windows and fell across the bed, splaying directly up the crevice of his buttocks, the small of his back, and across his right shoulder blade. His long black hair fell disheveled over his left shoulder. The sunlight, as it struck the pillow where Nicky's head rested, splashed in all directions, giving the effect of a halo. Whether it was the hangover, a dream I might have had, or simply the intoxication of Italy and the palazzo, I will never know, but one thing was certain: He was, at that moment, in that setting, naked in the chiaroscuro of the Florentine morning sunlight, a vision as beatific as any of the Lippi angels on the walls of the Brancacci Chapel.

I turned onto my side, propped my head on my hand, and drank him in through my eyes. His olive skin was smooth and soft, like the subject of a Venetian painting. His buttocks jutted upward and dark hairs curled across both cheeks in contrast to his bare back. The thighs were thick in spite of his being more slender than muscular.

I lay for what seemed like hours just watching him sleep. He had consumed an enormous amount of alcohol the night before and he slept deeply, not moving except for an occasional twitch of nerves in a hand or leg. I couldn't take my eyes off him. I wanted him. A typical male response, I know, but there it was. I hungered for him. I leaned toward him, bringing my face closer and closer to his body. I slid downward slightly, toward the foot of the bed, and brought my lips next to his left buttock. I was so close I could feel the warmth of his skin, then I felt the tiny hairs brushing against my lips, and, finally, my lips pressing lightly upon his flesh.

I held my lips against his bare butt for the longest time before I gently began to brush them back and forth on his warm, soft flesh. I increased the pendulum-like motion of my head, my lips grazing his skin and then the soft, curly hairs up to the small of his back, and back down to the fold where buttocks met thigh. Back and forth, lightly, gently, feeling the warmth of him, each sweep moving my face closer and closer to the warm, dark crevice that was my ultimate destination.

I could feel my heart beating harder and harder in my chest, my erection growing stiffer. I nestled my nose into the warm place where crack, thighs and scrotum meet and breathed in deeply. I pressed my nose just slightly between his warm furry cheeks and at that moment he arched his back and my upper lip met that moist hot place that was now my obsession. I placed the tip of my tongue at the very base of his scrotum and began to run it up the divide. As my tongue moistened the soft, tender hairs that made a trail for me to follow, the tip of my nose found its mark and I drank in his musky scent. I was millimeters away from my mark, from heaven itself, when suddenly his cheeks clamped shut and he turned slowly over, stretching his arms and legs and moaning in a totally unconvincing way, as though he had just risen to the surface of consciousness.

Now we lay looking at one another, my face inches from his erect penis, pointing toward his smiling face, and, I might add, dripping profusely onto the brown trail of dark hair just below his navel. "Looking for trouble?" he asked in a gravelly, morning-after voice.

"Not exactly," I said hoarsely. "Just looking."

"Hmmm. If I didn't know what an honorable man you are and how uninterested you are in having another relationship, I'd think you were getting ready to invite me to do the horizontal rumba."

I said nothing, but smiled and glanced sideways at the fluid now oozing out of him. It formed a little pool that was running into the recess of his belly button.

"But you're not doing anything like that, right?" he asked, raising his eyebrows and brushing his hair out of his face with one hand.

"No, of course not," I said softly. "It's just that, well…." I directed my eyes toward his cock, bobbing in and out of the pool of seminal fluid.

"Oh," he said, taking his finger, dipping it into the puddle of pre-cum and rubbing it onto my nose. "You mean this."

As his middle finger painted my lips with the warm fluid I closed my eyes and my own fluids gushed forth beneath me, soaking into the sheets and oozing into the hair on my groin in gentle spasms.

He ran his wet finger down the tip of my nose to my lips and then back and forth across my lips. "I'd love to, Nigel. When you're fully baked." Then he jumped up, threw his legs over the side of the bed, and scampered across the room and through a door, shutting it on his way out.

I buried my head in the sheets and lay there wondering how get rid of the sticky mess on the sheets before the maid arrived.

NINETEEN

BY THE TIME I arrived downstairs for breakfast on the loggia over-looking the central courtyard, everyone else was already there. Nicky was grilling Nonna about the wedding reception guests. Nonna and Ben sat at a bronze and glass table covered with a white linen cloth; Nicky sat across from Nonna. Ben sipped coffee and enjoyed the commentary his new bride was providing her grandson. His walking stick leaned against a potted palm behind him. I wondered if he really needed it, or if it made him feel more continental among these cultured Europeans, something to "lean on," literally and figuratively.

The maid poured Nicky another cup of coffee. A plate of food sat in front of him practically untouched. There was a bite out of one slice of prosciutto; provolone had been nibbled at. The only thing it appeared he had really eaten was half a roll with some jam.

As I approached, Nonna held up her hand in greeting. "*Buon giorno, signore.* Please join us for breakfast. Here," she said, indicating I should sit next to her. A place was already set and I had barely seated myself after kissing Nonna's cheek when a butler brought a silver tray loaded with choices. I helped myself to prosciutto, cheese, bread, jam, and melon. Another domestic, a woman, poured coffee for me.

"I trust you slept well?" Nonna asked.

"*Come un bambino, signora,*" I assured her. "Like a baby."

"Sometimes my guests have trouble sleeping here. The rooms can be drafty and the beds a bit lumpy. I'm glad you two had no trouble," she said, patting my hand.

"Good morning," Nicky said, reaching over and softly grazing my cheek with two fingers. "You look...relaxed."

"Very," I said, trying to have absolutely no inflection in my voice one way or another. "Please, Signora, Nicky, don't let me interrupt." I set

about preparing my coffee and piling the ham and cheese on my bread
as the two of them returned to their conversation. Ben passed me a silver creamer and sugar bowl but kept his attention on Nonna.

"*Allóra*," Nonna said, continuing where she had left off, "I don't know
why she can't find a husband. She is very beautiful, as you have already
remarked, and she is not averse to marrying. It seems to be the men.
They are afraid of her."

"They're discussing Signorina Bertolli," Ben explained, in a low voice.

"Men are intimidated by her, Nonna, that's clear," Nicky said with
authority. "She's quite self-possessed."

"Surely there must be some man who can handle a strong woman.
Gli uomini! Mamma mia!" she exclaimed. "Men!"

"Not many men are as fully baked as Signor Tedeschi, Nonna," Nicky
said, looking at me, as he then sipped his coffee.

"Then there's poor Evelyn," Ben interjected. "Sometimes, *cara,* having no husband is better than having a bad one."

"Now there's a truly interesting pair," I added. "What's their story?"

"I don't know much about it, actually," Ben said, reaching for *Il
Giorno,* the national newspaper.

"Nonsense," Nonna said sharply, but teasingly. "She's an old *amante*
of Ben's. He knows everything about it." She turned to Ben. "Don't be
burying your nose in that communist propaganda rag now. Speak up.
Tell the boys what you know."

He put the newspaper down on the table and slowly edged his cup
around and around in the saucer before him, his forearm resting on the
table. He stared at the saucer as though he were finding his story inside
it. "I really don't know that much, but I'll tell you my impressions.
Evelyn came to me about a year ago and told me she was in love. She
had met this man at a dude ranch in the Sierra foothills just north of
Sacramento. She said she had finally met the cowboy she'd been dreaming of and if he asked her to marry him, she intended to say yes."

"Not dreaming of literally," Nonna felt compelled to explain. "She is
not clairvoyant or mystic. Not by any means." Nonna did not add the
last sentence with any meanness, just emphatically.

"No, I wish she did have better intuition. She's had a bad time with men since Cyril died," Ben said. "That was her second husband. They were married for about 20 years. You may have heard of him, Cyril VanDeventer?"

"Newspapers, wasn't it?" I asked.

"Yes," Ben said. "Lots of them."

"Wasn't it a chain throughout California?" I asked.

"Northern California," Ben qualified.

"And if I remember correctly they were sold off to some larger corporation a few years back for an astronomical amount of money. Is that the same one?"

"Quite correct. Evelyn sold them. She couldn't keep up with it all after Cyril died. Actually, she had some trouble with the Board of Directors; nothing acrimonious, just that she was trying to give everything away. She's a generous woman—generous to a fault. They forced her hand and she sold to a national firm for half a billion dollars."

I whistled in admiration.

"Is that a lot of money, *caro?*" Nonna asked Nicky in a half whisper.

Nicky repressed a smile. "Yes, Nonna, in the outside world that is considered to be a lot of money."

"Ohhh," she said, nodding, but clearly having no comprehension.

I couldn't help but wonder if she had ever held any money in her hand. It was my observation that everything she needed was provided by the army of domestics and family that surrounded her. She was like a queen whose loyal and devoted subjects were intent on divining her every possible requirement.

"What was this business about dreaming of a cowboy?" Nicky asked. "What do you think the attraction was?"

"Evelyn grew up in Texas," Ben explained. "I think maybe she's reaching back to something out of her past, something familiar. She's very childlike in many ways. She isn't a complex woman."

"She seemed very happy last night," Nonna added.

I smiled to myself.

"What's so funny?" Nicky inquired.

All eyes turned to me. "Nothing, really."

"Oh, no, no, no. Sorry," Nicky said, "that doesn't work around here."

"I'm just thinking about how she thought you would be such a perfect match for her daughter. She kept asking me, every time you trotted off for refills, if I didn't think you were a good catch."

"Well, at least she got something right," Nicky said boastfully.

"*Sì,*" Nonna said, "And she knew precisely whom to ask."

It took Nicky a moment to figure out what Nonna was implying.

"Nonna," Nicky whined, clearly not used to her teasing him. It was apparent how close the two of them were. It was also easy to imagine their summers together and how she so willingly spoiled him just short of destroying his sense of reality. Somewhere in the process she gave him his sense of style. "Nonna," he whined again, waiting for her to say he was a good boy. It was gratifying to see there was someone who could tame this wild mustang.

She patted his hand and said, "You stay close to this man, *ragazzo.* You two are like *prosciutto e melone.*"

"Nonna," Nicky pleaded, "say you love me."

"*Ti voglio bene, prosciutto mio,*" Nonna said, telling him she loved him best and making us all laugh by calling him a little ham. She patted his hand. "You know this already. Now you and Ben go make something to do for yourselves. I have business with Signor Love."

"Now you're going to get it," Nicky said, leaning toward me and sticking out his tongue.

"*Basta!*" Nonna scolded him. "Enough!" She looked at me and shook her head. "I have ruined him. There's a way to say it in English." She thought for a moment, all of us waiting. "He's broke. I have a broke grandson."

Nicky and Ben excused themselves, trying to hide their smiles at Nonna's English, and I put myself into the care of La Baronessa for the afternoon. And what an afternoon it would be.

TWENTY

NONNA led me into the library. She directed me to sit across from her at a round gaming table, instructing the maid to pour us each a glass of sherry and then see to it we weren't interrupted. Once the door was shut tight Nonna produced a pack of tarot cards, which she told me were a deck of alchemical tarot given to her great-great-great-grandmother by an alchemist kept on staff to advise her.

"We have always been faithful to Rome," Nonna explained, shuffling the faded deck of oversize cards, "but we have never relied on the church to give us advice. We've had too many relatives in the Vatican to think any of them know what they're talking about. Saints, fools, and magicians are the only people to trust, young man. Remember that." With that, she handed the deck to me.

"Now shuffle them until you feel the inclination to stop," she said. "I like you, Nigel. I sense strength and devotion in you. Loyalty, commitment, spiritual fervor. You have come to the right place in coming here. Nicholas was waiting for you."

"Waiting for me?"

"Yes. He doesn't know that yet. He will."

I stopped shuffling the cards and set them down between us.

"Now cut the cards three times with your left hand," she instructed.

"Why the left hand?" I asked, as I cut the deck once, twice, three times.

"It is closer to your heart."

I neatly bunched the cards together, then took the top one, as she instructed, and handed it to her. She laid it face down on the table between us and told me to shuffle again, then hand her the deck when I was ready. She retrieved a pair of bifocals from a pocket in her dress and put them on. When I gave the cards over to her, she slowly placed the next twelve cards, also face down, in a prescribed layout.

Card number two was placed to the right of and slightly above the first card, but overlapping it. Number three was placed horizontally so that it was overlapping the top of card number two. These three formed the center of the spread, and the next four cards were laid out in a cross around them, number four at the top, five at the bottom, six to the right and seven to the left. To the right of all these she placed cards eight, nine and ten vertically so they formed a straight vertical line. Above these three, she laid out the final three cards horizontally, left to right, numbers 11, 12, and 13.

"Thirteen cards are used because in some quarters the number 13 is considered quite lucky. One plus three equals four, the number of wholeness and solidity. Thirteen is an aspect of four; it isn't exactly four, but it is striving toward it. It is associated with the 13 cycles of the moon and therefore is close to the feminine aspect of God. It is the moon that governs the unconscious, intuition, and the emotions. Do you know why 13 is considered unlucky, Nigel?" Nonna asked, picking up her sherry.

"No. I've often wondered," I said.

"Because it is too much of a good thing. It is too, too good. It represents the 12 apostles, plus one, the Christ, and therefore is too much for us to hold. So we avoid it. Just the way we tend to avoid all goodness in ourselves." She sipped her sherry, placed the glass on the table beside the cards, and began turning them over, one by one.

The first card was a picture of a man hanging upside down from a scaffold. He was hanging by one foot, around which was coiled a Cobra, its tongue sticking out. The man's arms were flailing and coins fell from his pockets to the ground. Nonna considered the card and mused to herself, "Of course, of course. This is you, Nigel; this is the querent card. This is what is happening to you, where your psyche is at present."

"I'm dying?" I asked, not impressed with the rather pessimistic beginning of this reading.

"No, no, *caro mio,*" Nonna chuckled. "Don't be so literal. It means you are upside down in your life right now. You feel like you're dying, like everything is falling apart, almost as though your life is over. Perhaps you even wish it was over, but that is not happening. See?" she said, tapping a wrinkled index finger painted with pale pink polish on the card. "The material world is falling away from you. Everything you value in life is escaping. See the money falling out of the Hanged Man's pockets?" She smiled, as though she already knew this of me; but, of course, there was no way she could know anything about me. I had just met her a little more than 24 hours ago and we hadn't spoken more than a dozen words to one another.

Card number two, overlapping the Hanged Man, showed two naked lovers embracing in a garden, Eros hovering above them on a cloud aiming an arrow at the man's heart. "This change you are going through, this transformation that has you upside down, has to do with love. Are you in love?" Nonna asked, looking up at me.

"In love?" I said, my voice cracking. What a strange, if not absurd, question. "No. No, I'm not. Quite the opposite, actually. My partner of ten years died recently and I'm still mourning the loss. No, love is out of the question," I said, a bit too emphatically.

Nonna stared at me for a long moment before continuing. "I see," she said. "Hmmm." She turned over the next card, the one that was horizontally intersecting the card of The Lovers. When I saw what it was, a chill ran through me as though someone had just opened a door in the middle of winter.

The card was Death and it was a horrifying illustration. A skeleton stood with a crow on his shoulder, an arrow in his hand. He stood on what looked like an eclipsed sun, the sky behind him black with smoke. Nonna laughed out loud, which I rather took offense at. I mustered a civil voice to ask, "What's so amusing about this card?"

"It explains the others. You should know; you just explained it yourself. You are fighting love with death. You want to fall in love, but you are clinging to death. This card is the Opposing Situation Card. It tells us what is acting in opposition or as obstacle to the current situation, The Lovers. I should have guessed as much. We are always the last to know when we are falling in love. Human beings are so silly. But now, thanks to me, you know: You are in love."

Before I could protest, she turned over the next card, the one at the top of the layout, just above the three lying faceup. As she turned it over she said, "This card is the future. *Allóra,* the Two of Staffs. It is a very big love, at that."

The illustration was of a tree on fire. A hand holding a flaming limb was reaching out of the heavens and joining the fire of the limb to the flame at the top of the tree, making one huge flame. "What does it mean?" I asked.

"Whoever it is you are in love with has much energy and when the two of you put your energies together it will be very potent. Very strong. See here?" she said, pointing to one of the tree's lower limbs that was igniting with a short burst of flame. "Your two flames could set the whole world on fire if you are not careful. Quick. Let's see what was in the past."

She turned over card number five, at the bottom of the layout, to reveal the Five of Coins. A one-legged beggar leaning on a staff was limping across a barren landscape with his hand held out in supplication. His downcast head was covered with a brown shawl; his eyes were closed. Littered around him on the ground were two gold and two silver coins. A fifth silver coin floated in the air above him, as though it might be the sun. "Is that bad?" I asked, not liking the weak connotation of this desolate creature.

"Bad? No," Nonna answered. "Sad, *sì.* Pathetic, *sì.* But not bad."

"Tell me more," I demanded.

"You've been wandering about thinking you are poor when wealth has been around you the whole time. You just have to open your eyes and you will see it."

"I'm not poor," I protested a little too strenuously. "I have enough money to live quite comfortably."

Nonna smiled thinly and sipped her sherry. She set the glass down without saying anything and started to turn over the next card.

"Wait a minute. Aren't you going to say anything?" I said.

"What should I say?"

"Well, that card is wrong. It's a mistake."

"I think not," she said, and once again reached for card number six.

"Wait!" I shouted. "Sorry, I didn't mean to raise my voice.

Signora Tedeschi, please, say something."

"You are having poor health?" she asked.

I could feel my face flush.

"You are lonely?" she added.

I turned my eyes away.

"You think no one cares and you are just waiting for death to come take you?"

"Why are you saying these things?"

"I am not saying them. It is here," she said, waving her hand over the cards. "It is all right here. You are in a state of transition. Love is beckoning, but you cling to death. You are blind to the abundance around you that is yours for the taking if you but open your eyes. It is all right here, signore. You shuffled the cards yourself. Do you wish for me to stop?" she asked, raising her eyebrows.

"No," I said softly.

She turned over the next card, revealing a happier picture. Thank God, I thought. Maybe there's hope after all. Two naked youths were playing on a hillside. One was standing on top of a small pyramid made of five gold and silver coins. He held a gold coin in one hand, offering it to the other boy, whose arms were outstretched, ready to receive it.

"This is your immediate future," Nonna said, "the Six of Coins. As you can see, it is the answer to the dilemma of the past. If you will open yourself up to receive a gift from someone who loves you, the world will be an easier place in which to live. Chaos will not claim you. This card tells us it is just as important to be open to receiving the world's treasures as it is to share what you have. Notice how young these two are? This means you must be like a child; you must be completely open, completely vulnerable. You see, Nigel, everything works out if we pay attention." She smiled and her voice was reassuring, suggesting I shouldn't be frightened of this reading of the cards. She obviously had sensed my growing distress.

"Let's look at your immediate past," she said, turning over card number seven. A knight lay in a pool of blood with ten swords stuck in his chest. An open book lay on the ground next to him. "Your ego has been shattered," she said. "Perhaps your persona, only. The mask you put on for the world to see has been ripped off. Someone has stripped you of your protective shield and you have become vulnerable. But here, on the ground, in this book, in words, you may find the answer, the antidote to the spell that has laid you in this grave may be within your reach. Remember the card opposite, the Immediate Future Card. Remember the Six of Coins. It tells you to open your eyes to love and to what others want to give you. Perhaps it only feels like you are dead. Perhaps if you take the gift in this boy's outstretched hands you will come back to life."

She turned over cards eight, nine and ten, one after another. "This will tell us the rest of the picture," she said. "This card," she said, pointing to number eight, "is what is going on inside you. It is the Two of Swords, the stable and the volatile." Two swords, one red, one green, were crossed, an owl hovering above the blades at the top of the card. "You are having an inner battle, probably between reason and instinct. Athena's owl is watching the battle. If you find a way to compromise, you will be victorious and wisdom will be yours."

"This next card, The High Priestess, tells us what's influencing you. This woman, floating on the ocean on a half moon, a book in her hand, her fingers to her lips, urging silence—this can only be one person I know. But it could also be a person I have never met."

"Who do you think it is?" I asked.

"Nicky. He rides on the surface of the unconscious and is carried to and fro by the winds of emotion. This is your soul. He is your soul mate. Be still and watch. That is what he is saying, or rather what this card is saying. Shhh. Stop fighting. Let go of *this*," she said, tapping her pink nail on the Death card.

The card above the High Priestess was beautiful, but frightening. Ten logs comprised a bonfire and in the center a red phoenix, wings outstretched, rose out of the flames, but was at the same time being burned.

"The number ten, as here in the Ten of Staffs, is the number representing endings and new beginnings. Something must die before anything new can be born. The ten becoming one. This card reveals your hopes and your fears, and they are related to the future card here." She pointed back to the Two of Staffs, the burning tree and the burning limb coming together to create an inferno.

"What does all this mean?" I asked. I was feeling physically uncomfortable. My head was growing light and it seemed there was less and less oxygen in the room with each passing second. "What do I do?"

"That would be these three cards here," Nonna said, turning over the three cards that lay horizontally above the three she just read. From left to right they were a naked couple inside the bottom half of an hourglass, a red rose in the top half; a frightened youth raising a sword, as if to protect himself from nine other swords, which hung suspended by ropes just above him; and a rose in a heart surrounded by the four elements of earth, air, fire, and water.

That was the last I remember of the tarot reading. The next thing I knew, a foul-smelling vial was being shoved up my nose. I woke with a start, my head throbbing. Two of Nonna's male servants were attending me. Ben leaned on his cane above me, flanked by Nonna and Nicky, their faces wrinkled with concern. The man with the vial passed it in front of my nose again. I pushed it away. "That smells terrible," I said.

"That's the idea," Nicky said, leaning over me.

I tried to get up, but the men restrained me. "*Non troppo presto*," one of the men said.

"You should take your time," Ben suggested. "Rest a minute, until the blood is circulating again."

"Maybe I should call the doctor," Nonna said to Ben.

"No, no. I'm fine. Really," I protested. "I don't know what happened. Maybe it's something I..." I stopped before I insulted my hostess. "I can't imagine what it was."

The butlers helped me to my chair, where I mopped at my face and neck. I was saturated with a cold sweat. Nicky was shaking his head and chuckling now.

"What's so damned funny?" I demanded.

"Must have been *some* reading, is all I can say. I'm sure you'll tell me all about it on the way back to the farm."

TWENTY-ONE

NONNA sent us on our way about an hour before sunset, after loading us up with nine bottles of wine, a loaf of *pugliesi,* cold venison, enough *bel paese* to constipate a horse, and a thousand kisses each. Just before we pulled away, she leaned down to my window and wagged her finger for me to come closer. I stuck my head out of the car and she whispered something in Italian in my ear, something which sounded like "turn the key." I was just about to ask her to repeat it, when Mr. Quick-on-the-trigger gunned the engine and tore away from the portico and through the front gate.

"Hey!" I shouted, grabbing at the packages of cheese and meat and bread that were falling between me and the door. "Your grandmother was telling me something."

"Sorry," Nicky said. "I want to get to the farm before dark."

We drove across the Arno, through a long, boring part of the suburbs and then onto the autostrada, weaving through cars and trucks and dodging pedestrians, none of whom seemed fazed by the silver Lamborghini nipping at the heels of their shoes. We settled down to a casual 150 kilometers per hour for our trip back to Castelfranco di Sopra.

"And another thing," I said. "What about this house in San Francisco?"

"What about it?"

"I thought you didn't live anywhere, or was that just for effect?"

"I don't live anywhere. I live everywhere."

"Oh, brother," I moaned, watching the cars blur by out my side window.

"I have a place in San Francisco. That's where Rosario and I lived while he was sick. My friend Pete left me some money when he died and Rosario and I were struggling at the time. I was working in a hotel;

Rosario was too sick to work at all by then. I didn't want to take any chances of being evicted while he was sick, so I bought the house. I don't like taking money from people, even Nonna. With her I can always send the money back, but when Pete died I had no choice. So I put the money to good use by putting a roof over our heads and by investing the rest on the advice of a friend. But since Rosario's death I've been look-ing for something, or avoiding something—like you—so I travel a lot. Is this a crime?"

"I just think it's strange you didn't mention it."

"I think it's strange you stayed in bed for two days, but I didn't call an inquisition to browbeat you over it."

He was reprimanding me again. So bossy, I thought. This is what happens to rich kids. Even I, as an only child, wasn't this spoiled. He was probably just a huge prick tease and everyone hated him. He probably doesn't even know how to have sex, I thought to myself.

"Stop thinking those evil things. You know nothing about me," he said directly, but without acrimony.

"I'm not even thinking about you. What an egocentric egomaniac you are."

"That's redundant."

"You think everything is about you," I charged.

"*Al contrario, caro. You* think everything is about me."

He was infuriating me, not to mention outsparring me. "I'm not hav-ing fun," I blurted out, trying to appeal to some cultural gene to make him feel guilty and stop attacking me.

"That's not my responsibility," he countered.

"That's just it, you have no responsibility. Especially toward me. I'm just a toy for you to play with, like some cat torturing its dinner."

"That's an interesting analogy you've chosen."

"Well, it's true."

"I have many responsibilities."

"Name one."

"To love you."

Well, that shut me up. It was another one of his non sequiturs that always ended up shutting down a conversation. I waited a couple min-

utes, then sneaked a look in his direction. He was smiling. He was just
too damned happy.

"What are you so happy about?"

"What are you so angry about?"

"I'm not angry. I'm sad."

"You're probably both," he said after a moment. "But if you could
stop being so angry and stop turning it inward, you might not be so sad.
Then we could start having fun together."

"Who said I wanted to have fun with you?"

"It's obvious, handsome," he smirked. "You're crazy about me."

"How is it obvious? Where is it so obvious?"

"Well, all over Nonna's sheets, for one place."

I could feel my face turn crimson. I was beginning to hate this person. He loved to make fun of me. Evil, I thought. Just like all the other
Borgias in history.

TWENTY-TWO

FOR THE NEXT two days I was mired in an inexplicable depression. Nicky continued to prepare us meals, plying me with bites and sips of everything he ate and drank. He brought me the newspaper in the morning, along with coffee on a tray. He followed me around the villa reading aloud passages from his ridiculously obtuse books, asking me my impressions. He acted as though nothing at all was wrong. Meanwhile, I was utterly miserable

On the second evening after we left Nonna's, I sat in the old green rocking chair on the loggia watching the sun set. He came out and sat down on the flagstones next to my chair, his feet resting on the stone steps that descended to the weed-ridden garden. We sat in silence for a few minutes. Suddenly I found myself speaking without realizing what I was going to say.

"I'm sorry I'm so difficult. I don't know exactly what's wrong. I…seem to be agitated." I sat thinking about what I had just said, as though I were an observer.

"I think I understand," Nicky said, resting his cheek against my thigh, but continuing to watch the sunset. His voice was soft and tender.

"Really?" I asked, hoping he did, hoping he might be able to explain it to me and perhaps even break the uncomfortable tension that I had created between us. "Your lover has left you. You are alone in the world and you don't want to be. You're sick, and you think you're going to die before you ever fall in love again and it's not fair. You're angry that life was so short for him and so cruel to you. You act out your anger at the least provocation. Even on the people around you who care for you," Nicky said.

What he said resonated with me. He was definitely hitting home.

"Now it's worse," he continued. "Here you are in this wonderful old villa, where you've come to be alone and cry yourself to death and what happens? I come along. Someone who engages you, challenges you, intrigues and provokes you. Someone who holds out all sorts of possibilities and each of them is appealing."

Nicky turned to look directly at me.

"And so you find yourself wanting to love me. But you can't. Not only would it be a betrayal of your late partner, but it would upset the applecart of despair that you've been pushing toward your grave. So you push intimacy away. It would be so much easier to die. Death seems so much easier than life when all the ones you have loved are dead before you."

Nonna's tarot reading flashed before me. I saw the Death card, ominous, foreboding. The Hanged Man, arms flailing, gold coins falling from his pockets. I did feel like that.

Nicky continued to face me, his head on my thigh. "But this fellow who has been placed in your path won't be avoided. I won't allow you to retreat into your tomb. I'm going to keep following you around the house, through the garden, calling your name, calling you back to the world. Come back, Nigel. *Torna alla vita.*' "

There was that phrase, the one Nonna had whispered in my ear as we were pulling away. It wasn't "turn the key," after all. It was "*torna alla vita.*"

"I tried to have sex with you," I offered in weak defense.

"I don't want to have sex with you," Nicky said softly.

That crushed me. A thousand reasons why he wouldn't want me spun through my mind: age, ugliness, illness. That was it. He'd already lost one partner; he wasn't about to commit emotional suicide by hooking up with me. All I could manage in response was a weak, "Oh."

"I want to make love with you. I want intimacy. I want a run-of-the-play contract. I'm not interested in casual sex. I've had enough of that to last a lifetime. I want the real thing."

"What? I thought you didn't like me."

"Why wouldn't I like you?" Nicky asked, as though he were talking with a child.

"Lots of reasons," I said.

"Such as?"

"Well, I'm older than you are. Considerably older."

"I like older men. I come from an island heavily influenced by Asia, a place where age is venerated. Age equals wisdom where I come from. Try another one."

"I'm not very good-looking."

"Beauty is in the eye of the beholder."

"But I'm not. Very good-looking, I mean."

"I'm not going to carry that for you. You want me to reassure you about your looks and your age. You have to do that yourself. I can only reassure you about how I feel about you." There was no rancor in his voice; he was just stating how it was. It was disconcertingly like talking with Lyle.

"Well, if nothing else, there's the HIV."

"The HIV?" Nicky asked, perplexed.

"I'm HIV-positive. Surely you knew that."

Nicky reached into his madras shorts and withdrew a flat silver box. "That's why God invented these," he said, handing me the box.

I took the box, which had his initials engraved on it.

"Go on, open it."

I slowly opened the lid. Inside I found a panoply of pills, most of which I recognized. "I don't get it. You carry these around in case I need them?"

Nicky laughed out loud. "You're so goofy. They're mine, nitwit. You are so completely hysterical that you forget there are other human beings with their own lives all around you."

"Oh." I sat with that for a minute. "Why didn't you tell me you were positive?"

"Why didn't you ask?" he responded.

"But I've never seen you take any pills," I said.

"I tend to forget. You don't have a monopoly on denial, you know. Perhaps you'll help me remember now."

He took the case gently from my hand, rose, planted a kiss on my forehead, and went inside. Across the hills, the sun disappeared behind the tree line. Two cuckoos were calling back and forth to each other across the valley below. Mourning doves cooed from the tall grass in the olive grove. I rocked in the old green chair. Rocked and wept, late into the night.

TWENTY-THREE

IN THE early hours of the morning, when it was still dark out, I woke from a dream, shouting, trying to speak but unable to articulate anything more than loud grunting sounds. The dream was a variation of my old dream.

Lyle and I were in a Metro station in Washington, D.C., and I got out, turned, and the doors of the subway car were closing with Lyle standing just on the other side. But this time, instead of saying anything, he raised his eyebrows and pointed excitedly to something behind me, mouthing the words, "Look, look!"

I turned and there on the platform behind me was a child with dark hair and brown eyes. I knew he had been abandoned. He was dressed in tattered clothes and his face was dirty. He wore shoes too big for him and no socks. I approached him, fishing in my pocket for some money, but when I walked to where he was standing, he held out his hand to give me something instead. Whatever it was, was so bright I couldn't make out its form, so I reached into my jacket pocket for my sunglasses, but I was unable to grasp them. I pulled my hand out and looked at it only to find I had no hand. I raised my left arm and there was no hand there either. I was shocked and horrified. The child kept nudging me with his unseeable object. I looked at my wrists and they were bleeding stumps. That's when I woke up wailing.

I lay in the dark room trying to remember where I was, trying to remember if Lyle was alive or dead. Within a few seconds, I realized I was in bed at the farm and that Lyle was indeed dead. I couldn't rid myself of the image of the abandoned child; neither could I rid myself of the image of my bleeding, handless arms.

I stared into the blackness of the room, feeling as if I were in a tomb, and slowly the tears came. I began to cry, then to sob, then to wail. I

wanted Lyle back. But I also wanted Nicky. I hugged the pillow, trying
to bury my face in it so Nicky wouldn't hear me, but it was no use. The
cries of anguish issuing out of me had their source in the very bowels of
hell. I could scarcely catch my breath between sobs.

Then he was there, gently, quietly holding me, cradling me in his
arms and stroking my head and whispering to me in Italian, then
English. "*Va bene, caro; va bene, bello mio.* It's OK, sweetheart; it's OK,
my beautiful one. It's all right. It will be all right now."

After a long time I fell back to sleep.

When I woke, he was still holding me, snoring softly into my hair,
one arm draped over my chest. I hadn't felt this loved, this cared for since
Lyle was alive. Perhaps I had never felt so taken care of, so genuinely
loved, with absolutely no expectations or conditions. It was at that
moment on that morning in early May, lying in Nicky's arms in the
dark, that I knew Nonna was right. I was in love. Against all odds,
against my better judgment, against every defense I could put up, I was
hopelessly, dazzlingly in love with the obnoxious, witty, insulting, truth-
mongering, charming, sassy, outrageous, contradictory, and—yes, I had
come to see him this way—exotically beautiful Nicholas Alex Borja.

TWENTY-FOUR

FOR THE NEXT few days we loafed around the farm, took day trips to Assisi and Siena, and roamed the Chianti district, marveling at the burst of spring color splashed all over the Tuscan hills. Entire fields near San Gimignano were red with poppies. Lupines and marigolds and flowers I had never seen covered every fence and roadside. Bright red geraniums cascaded down the sides of every window box. The sky was blue all the time and the air was provocatively warm during the day, sensuous at night.

Imagine my frustration, then, when Nicky refused to make love. He simply wouldn't go all the way. For example, one night we were lying in front of the fire and I asked if he would like a massage. "Mmm, that sounds heavenly," he murmured. I got up and got some eucalyptus lotion from Helen's dresser and proceeded to massage him. We were both in our underwear; he in Italian bikini briefs, me in boxer shorts. First I massaged his shoulders, then his chest, legs, and back. But when I tried to slip his briefs off to massage his butt, he rolled over and said it was time to go to bed.

He did this three nights in a row. Finally, the fourth night, I blurted out, "What the hell is wrong? I thought you liked me."

"I do. But I want you to be sure. I don't want just sex. I want love. Intimacy. The real thing," he said. "I want you to be sure."

"I am sure," I protested.

He stood up, his hard-on peeking out over the waistband of his briefs. He kissed me on top of my head, and said, "We'll see." Then he trotted off to his room where I could hear him slide the bolt on the door. I wanted to thrash him.

Nicky changed his airline ticket to return with me to San Francisco. He also upgraded mine to first class so we could sit together. I protested, but he said it was free because he had about a billion frequent flyer miles. I took his word for it, but didn't like the idea of being indebted to him. What if this didn't work out after all?

The day before we left, the phone rang, and when I answered an American woman asked for Nicky. It was Annarita, Evelyn Iversen's daughter, calling from the States. They rekindled their friendship for a few minutes before he hung up with a promise to call her when he got back.

"Her mother got home a week ago and told her all about us. She's dying to see me and to meet you. She sounds kind of depressed. I guess it's the d-i-v-o-r-c-e," Nicky said, sitting back down at the rough wooden table in the kitchen. A crude but shiny metal shade hung over a light bulb suspended just above the center of the table. Holes had been punched in the shade in various shapes, none of which I could ever make out, and tiny beams of light splayed across the walls around us. "I'm actually looking forward to seeing her. You'll like her, I think. She's very smart and lots of fun. At least she used to be."

I resisted saying I doubted I would meet her, since she was really Nicky's friend, not mine, that I don't really enjoy moving in that social set, and if he wasn't going to put out, I wasn't going to be traipsing out to Brahman Bull Boulevard or wherever these people lived to munch on crudités while he hobnobbed. "Where is the happy couple? Doing the rodeo circuit?"

"No, she said they were at the ranch in Scottsdale. Annarita spoke to her mother this morning and she was distraught," Nicky said.

"She was distraught or her mother was?"

"Actually, I think both. I didn't ask about it, though. I didn't want to go into it long distance, but she did say something about the 'cowboy,' so I take it she's not very keen on him." He reached for the bottle of wine and filled my glass before refilling his own. "You will come out there with me, won't you?"

"I don't know," I said, shrugging.

He put down his fork and leaned into the table. "Nigel, I need you to go with me. I don't want to get trapped out there. What if her mother's back? What if they both decide Annarita and I were made for each other? Her mother's probably in Phoenix right now registering us for china and crystal at Goldwater's. You can't let me go alone. It would be barbaric of you."

"Hmm," I said. "Barbaric, eh? I wouldn't want to be barbaric, would I?"

"Well, not in this instance you wouldn't, but I can think of certain occasions that might call for it," he said seductively. "Anyway, I insist. I want you there."

"Well, if you're sure," I gave in.

"I am quite sure," he said.

"So am I," I said, pointedly.

"Good," he said.

"No, I mean I'm *sure*," I said, bulging my eyes. "As in 'I'm sure that if you don't have sex—I mean make love—with me, I'm going to explode.'"

"Oh, for heaven's sake," he said, picking up his plate and carrying it to the sink. "Men! You're all alike." Then he turned and went down the hall. "You'd better start packing and hit the hay. We have to leave here tomorrow morning by five if we're going to be in Milan by noon. Remember, we have two cars to return in Florence. Sweet dreams, Poppa Bear," he said as he closed his bedroom door.

TWENTY-FIVE

SOMEWHERE over Iceland, as our Alitalia flight chased the sun across the ocean, Nicky woke me from a restless sleep. Most of the First Class section was finishing dinner and the movie was about to start. He leaned over and whispered, "I need you to help me with something in the bathroom."

"OK," I mumbled. I unfastened my seat belt and stumbled up the aisle behind him toward the front of the plane, trying to wake up.

He opened one of the bathroom doors and we stepped inside. It was so cramped there was barely room to turn around once I had locked the door. As I turned to face him he wrapped his arms around my neck and planted a huge wet kiss on me. "What do you want help with?" I asked.

"This," he said with a low, throaty voice as he pulled my right hand behind him and placed it on his butt.

I tilted my head back a little to get a better look into his eyes. I wanted to see if I could tell what he was up to. He was smiling, his mouth open slightly, revealing his movie-star teeth. "And what's wrong with 'this'?" I asked, squeezing his ass just a little.

"It's running low on vitamin B," he said, slowly unbuttoning my shirt.

"Vitamin B?"

"Yeah. I need a Vitamin *beef* injection, and I need it quick," he said. By now he had unbuckled my trousers and let them fall to the floor with a rather loud clank as my belt buckle hit something metal below us. He slipped his own pants off as well.

"You're awfully adept at this," I observed.

"Hmm, so are you," he said, looking down to where I was sticking straight out of the opening in my boxer shorts.

He hoisted himself onto the sink, lifted his legs and wrapped them around my waist. Then he reached over and opened the paper towel dispenser, swinging the door back so it was flush with the wall. He reached inside and retrieved a tube of lubricant, put some on his hand, and then his hand disappeared between us.

"What a coincidence you should find that in there," I said, stifling a laugh.

"There are no accidents, Nigel," he said. "Everything is laid out before us. Our only job is to pay attention."

"Yes, and I think you're the master arranger." His lubricated hand wrapped around my cock, wetted it, and pulled it closer to its target.

He raised his legs higher, his ankles resting on my shoulders. The back of his head pressed against the aluminum mirror above the counter. He placed his hands on my hips and drew me forward and into him. I closed my eyes and waited either to melt with the warmth of him or to burst with the release of my pent-up anticipation for this moment. He began a rhythmic motion that drew me very slowly inside him as far as I could go, then out until the head of my dick was exposed.

"Look down," he said.

I did and saw myself moving back and forth inside him.

"What do you see?" he asked, watching my face as I looked at where we were joined.

"I see us."

"Describe it to me."

"I see me moving in and out of you," I said, panting.

"More details," he whispered. His hands were still guiding me back and forth.

"I can see my greasy cock sliding all the way into your ass," I said, pushing myself in as far as I could. "And now I see it slide almost all...the way...out." I had only plunged in and out a dozen times, but I could barely stave off my orgasm.

"Mmmm," Nicky moaned. "It feels so fat and so hot inside me."

I looked into his face. His long black hair was falling around his shoulders, his brown eyes were like liquid amber, his lips parted slightly. He bit his lower lip as I thrust deeper. "I like it slow like that," he said, "especially when you pull almost all the way out."

I pulled farther out, then pushed back in. His hands gripped my waist, stopping my forward motion, then pushed me backward again. He guided me back and forth in tiny movements, saying, "I want you to fuck me with just the head of your dick. Just like that. Slow, with just the head."

I wasn't going to be able to hold my orgasm back much longer. With the unusual setting, the unexpected nature of the sex, his completely casual and uninhibited way of talking during the sex, and the sensation of being inside him, it was all I could do not to come. I attempted to break the mood to make things last longer.

"I thought you didn't want sex," I protested. "I thought you wanted to make love."

"I do," he said.

"This is making love?"

"I want to make you happy," he said, pushing my shirt aside with both hands and looking at my chest.

"This makes me happy," I said, my voice barely audible.

"Say you love me." Nicky arched his back and contracted his muscles, tightening himself around my cock.

"I love you," I said.

"There. Now we're making love and having sex at the same time," he said in a low, halting voice that told me he, too, was close to orgasm. "How talented we are."

Then I leaned my head forward, placed my lips on his and said, as I kissed him, "I love you."

As I did this, he placed both hands on my nipples, brushed them lightly, and sent me gushing into him, until I thought it would run out of his nose and ears. He gave a high-pitched moan, almost a squeal, grabbed me by the shoulders and pushed me back so we could both look down between us where his cock was shooting ribbons of white onto my chest and his smooth brown belly. He squeezed his buttocks one last time and pulled me forward so that I was resting on top of him.

We stayed like that for several minutes, drinking in our first sex/love-making. "I do love you," you know," I said with my mouth pressed into his shoulder, feeling the slimy wet fluid spreading against our slippery skin.

"I know," he whispered, and stroked my hair. "I've known for a long time."

"You've been very patient with me," I said.

"You deserve patience," Nicky said. "And you were worth waiting for."

"I feel like I'm on drugs or something. I feel absolutely high," I said, half giggling.

"You are, honey. About 40,000 feet."

TWENTY-SIX

WE LOST our race with the sun, and by the time we set down in San Francisco it was dark. We shared a taxi to the Castro. I got out first, gave Nicky my phone number, and told him I'd wait for his call. He kissed me on the lips and I realized how good it was to be back home.

"Get some sleep," he said as the cab pulled away.

I threw the entire contents of my suitcase on top of the washing machine on the back porch and decided I would deal with it later. I was way too tired to sort laundry. My friend Marge had kept an eye on the place for me, stopping by a couple times a week on her way to and from her medical practice to pick up the mail and water the plants. The pile of mail on the desk was spilling onto the floor. I couldn't even see the computer keyboard. Most of it looked like junk mail, and I decided it could wait.

I stripped off my clothes, letting them lie where they fell, switched on the stereo, and headed for the bathroom. The melancholy strains of Bach's Kantate 51 filled the flat. It was what I had been listening to the day I packed for Italy. It was a bit heavy, but I decided to let it play. I was too tired to rout through the CD bin looking for something airy.

I took a long, hot shower, letting the water run over my head and down my body for a good ten minutes. I looked down at my dick, still slick with lubricant. I contracted my abdominal muscles and it bobbed a hello. "Lucky pecker," I said aloud, wishing Nicky was with me in the shower.

I fell into bed, wrapping myself in the duvet, and was asleep before my head hit the pillow.

Sometime in the middle of the night, or what seemed like the middle of the night, I dreamed that Nicky slipped into bed with me, naked, that he wrapped his arms around me and kissed me on the back of the neck and that we slept that way. I was surprised and a bit disoriented when the next morning I woke to find Nicky actually in my bed with his arms wrapped around me. I turned over sharply to make sure I wasn't dreaming, and in the process woke him. He opened his eyes, then closed them slowly and smiled. "Good morning," he said sleepily.

"How the hell did you get in here?"

He slid a hand down, cupped my genitals and snuggled closer. "Don't be dense. Everyone hides a key to the front door somewhere. You should find a less obvious place."

"You have some nerve," I said, slipping an arm beneath him and rolling him over on top of me. I kissed his neck and licked his ear.

He moaned and squirmed. "Mmmm, that'll get you into trouble, for sure."

I hoisted him by his waist so he was straddling my chest, then took him into my mouth. At just that moment, the doorbell rang.

"Shit," I tried to say with my mouth full. I rolled him off, threw on my bathrobe, and stepped into the hall, pressing the button that released the downstairs door lock. I shouted, "Who's there?"

"It's just me," an unfamiliar voice called.

"That's probably my friend Thao," Nicky shouted from the bedroom.

"Me who?" I shouted.

"Me, Thao."

I heard the downstairs door slam shut and footsteps on the stairs.

"Let him in," Nicky called out. "He's bringing us breakfast."

By now, Thao was standing in front of me, holding a large pink pastry box and a cardboard tray with two lidded paper cups from Spike's, our neighborhood's best coffee shop.

"I'm Thao," he said. "Pleased to meet you. I'd shake your hand, but…" He held up the things he was carrying.

"We're in here," Nicky called to his friend.

"After you, please," Thao said.

"No, no, that's quite all right," I said, stepping aside. "You're bearing gifts. That takes precedence." Actually, I wanted to get a better look at him. I followed him through the door and down the hall into the bedroom. He was a handsome young Vietnamese man dressed in a black suit that looked like it cost at least $1,000 and shoes like those I had admired through the windows of the shoe boutiques in Florence. Those probably cost him close to a thousand as well.

He and Nicky hugged and kissed, then tore at the doughnut box "Honey, this is my best friend in the whole world, Thao," Nicky said, yanking madly at the taped edge of the doughnut box. "Thao, this is Nigel." Finally Nicky held the box up toward me. "Honey, would you? I'm weak from you ravaging me all night," he added for Thao's amusement and to embarrass me.

I rolled my eyes, took the box, and retreated to the study, where there was a letter opener.

For the first time since we started having romantic feelings for each other, he'd called me "honey," and twice in practically the same sentence. And he did this right in front of this friend of his. He was comfortable with intimacy. I liked that.

"Here. Don't get crumbs in the bed," I said, handing them the box of doughnuts. They rummaged through the pastries like children, tossing aside the ones they didn't like, pushing each other's hands out of the way.

"Ooooooh. Maaaaple Bars," Nicky sang. "My favorite." He took one out, held it up, opened his mouth wide and shoved half of it in.

"Chocolate for me," Thao said, devouring a chocolate cruller.

"So tell me everything that's been going on for the past month," Nicky said.

"Can't," Thao, said. "Got to go. Big audit. I might have to go to Seattle."

"Thao is the Securities Exchange Commission's ball-busting wunderkind litigator for the entire West Coast," Nicky said. "Very important, very busy, very eligible." Then to Thao, "Seattle's divine. Can we come?"

"We'll see. It's either Seattle or Honolulu," Thao said. "I won't know for sure until tomorrow."

"Ugh! Honolulu," Nicky groaned, giving it a thumbs down.

"Most people would give their first child for business trips to Hawaii," I said.

"Give me a business trip to Norway any day. Preferably in winter,"

Nicky said, rifling again through the doughnuts. "You forget, *asaguahu,* I grew up on an island."

About halfway across the Atlantic, on our flight from Florence, Nicky had called me some other Chamorro name as well. He explained that, counting Italian and Chamorro, he was trilingual and tends to revert to Chamorro more than he's aware of, particularly when excited.

"What did you call me?" I asked.

"Oh, sorry. It means spouse in Chamorro. It's a nice thing." Nicky looked up from the pastry box, his chin a palette of maple frosting. Two strands of his long hair disappeared into his mouth and were being chewed along with the maple bar.

"Bye," Thao said, licking his fingers and heading for the door. "Call me later. Nice meeting you, Nigel."

We shook hands and Nicky jumped out of bed, stark naked, and followed him downstairs to see him out. I took off my robe and climbed back into bed. I took the lids off the coffee cups sitting on the headboard and found a cappuccino. It was still hot. There wasn't much left of the doughnuts, though. At least nothing in one piece. I picked through the remnants and found half of a plain cake doughnut. I wanted something I could dunk. I was trying to find the coffee through the foamed milk when Nicky closed the door to the stairway.

"I hope this is your paper," he called out.

"It is," I answered. I could hear him sliding the rubber band off as he walked down the hall toward the bedroom.

"Holy cannoli!" Nicky exclaimed as he walked through the bedroom door reading the front page.

"What is it, another sex scandal at the White House?"

"Oh, my God," Nicky said slowly.

"What? Tell me," I pleaded. "Nothing can be that shocking."

Nicky turned the newspaper around so I could read the banner headline: NEWSPAPER HEIRESS DEAD; FOUL PLAY SUSPECTED.

TWENTY-SEVEN

"READ it to me," I said, staring at the open box of doughnuts and wondering if it would be in bad taste to eat while he read to me of the death of the woman we had met at Nonna's just a week earlier.

Nicky paced back and forth at the foot of the bed. "Evelyn VanDeventer Iversen, widow of the late newspaper magnate Cyril VanDeventer, was found late Wednesday afternoon drowned in an Arizona lake. She disappeared in the middle of the night while on a camping trip, according to her new husband Travis Iversen.

"'How she got to the bottom of the lake and how the boat ended up several miles away are just a few of the questions we have to answer,' said Lt. Larry Cochran of the Maricopa County sheriff's office. Cochran also said there were no obvious signs of a struggle, foul play, or suicide, in spite of concerns expressed by friends of the victim."

"Victim," Nicky exclaimed, pausing in his pacing momentarily. "Sounds like they're going to convict the cowboy in the newspaper."

"Go on," I said, sipping at the cappuccino.

"'Detectives questioned VanDeventer's husband, Travis Iversen, at the scene, but Cochran would not discuss the inquiry. VanDeventer, 65, changed her name to Iversen when she wed for the third time on November 7th of last year. She had planned to continue using the VanDeventer name in the Bay Area. The couple divided their time between a ranch in Scottsdale and her Concord estate.' Wow!" Nicky said. "She was 65. Way to go, girl!"

"No editorializing, please," I urged, waving a doughnut fragment in the air. "Just the facts. Although if that's a San Francisco paper there probably aren't too many of those. They get in the way of the really good stuff."

"On Tuesday, the third anniversary of Cyril VanDeventer's death, the newlyweds went to Lake Barnett, a reservoir in a recreational desert area about 30 miles northeast of Phoenix. The couple arrived at the lake around 5 P.M. and set up camp at Mallard Point, Iversen told investigators. They had a few drinks before going to sleep under the night sky shortly after 11 P.M. He remembers the time precisely because he had to walk a good distance around the lake to ask two men who were also camping that night to please turn down their radio. He says he checked to see how late it was to be sure his request wasn't unreasonable.

"Police did not know if alcohol was a factor in VanDeventer's death, or if anyone else was camping near the remote site.

"About 3:30 A.M., Iversen said, he woke to find his wife and their new jet boat missing. He searched for her on foot until dawn, then drove to an emergency phone a mile away, from which he phoned the Sheriff's office.

"Deputies located the 15-foot jet boat about two miles from the campsite on the opposite side of the lake. A few pieces of clothing were on the boat, but there was no sign of VanDeventer.

Nicky slapped the paper down. "I love how they keep referring to her as VanDeventer when she was married to Iversen," he said.

"Yes, dear," I teased. "Please continue."

Nicky was silent and I looked up to find him staring at me. "What?" I asked. "What's wrong?"

"We sounded so 'married' when you said that," Nicky said quietly.

"Sorry," I apologized and swallowed the doughnut I had been chewing. "I didn't mean to."

"No, no, I liked it. I haven't felt married in a long time. I do better in a couple." Nicky said.

"It's just that, I don't know, I... Well, you called me 'honey' earlier and I guess it made me..."

Nicky came over and sat beside me, crumpling the paper in his lap. "Stop apologizing. I liked it. I'm not afraid of love. You have me confused with you." He placed his cheek next to mine in a tender hug and whispered, "But I'm going to fix that."

"Hmm...I guess that's fair warning," I teased.

He looked intently into my eyes, as though he were divining something in me, then said, "You're a Cancer, aren't you?"

"Have you been peeking at my driver's license?" I said, but then I remembered Nonna's psychic abilities and wondered if they might have been passed down to Nicky.

"Because you're a different person on your own turf. Here in your own home you're a lot more relaxed, more casual. Typical Cancer trait. Great husband material, Cancers are," he said matter-of-factly, then returned to his pacing. "Just leave me anything that smells like maple," he said, nodding toward the doughnut box.

"Now *you* sound married," I teased, and watched to see if he would have a reaction. He gave a little smile, more to himself than to me, and went back to reading aloud.

"About 3 P.M. the camera crew of a Phoenix television station, circling the lake in a helicopter, spotted an object just beneath the surface near the shore close to the campsite. 'I saw what appeared to be human limbs,' said news photographer Ira Leakey. 'The dive team boat pulled alongside and the diver jumped in and within seconds he confirmed that we'd found our victim.'

"The body, clad in bra and panties, was floating in about eight feet of water no more than 30 feet from the shore and about 175 feet from the campsite.

"Lake Barnett is a reservoir surrounded by rugged desert. Cactus, scrub, and rocky slopes line the lake, which is about five miles long. It is one of a string of man-made lakes in the area popular with sports enthusiasts. Lake Barnett is probably the least used lake in the chain, however, as it is the most remote. The only access is a dirt road and there is no running water or electricity outlets, which modern campers tend to prefer. A medical examiner is expected to perform an autopsy sometime today.

"Debra Haber, socialite and noted San Francisco philanthropist, said, 'I can't imagine Evelyn getting up and going out in a boat in the middle of the night. Her daughter told me that when they went camping together, Evelyn wouldn't even get up and go to the bathroom by herself. This is all very bizarre, if you ask me.'

"Mike and Sarah Baldonado, neighbors of VanDeventer for the past five years, said she was a good swimmer. They had attended various get-togethers at the neighboring estate and more than once saw the victim swimming in her Olympic-sized pool. 'When our daughter Frieda was born, she came over and offered to baby-sit any time we needed,' Mrs. Baldonado said. 'She was a really nice lady.'

"VanDeventer is estimated to be worth about $350 million. The sale of her late husband's newspaper empire netted the widow close to $500 million, but $150 million went to establish the Cyril and Evelyn VanDeventer Foundation in Contra Costa County, and to pay off outstanding debts at the newspaper in Concord.

"There was no prenuptial agreement for the VanDeventer-Iversen marriage, according to sources close to the victim. Iversen, who refused to reveal his age when the marriage was announced, comes from a ranching family somewhere in the Rockies.

"On Wednesday evening, VanDeventer's son, Vaughn VanDeventer, and eldest daughter, Virginia O'Brien Leavitt, left for Scottsdale in the family jet. 'We're completely distraught,' daughter Virginia said as she boarded the plane. 'We are such a close family. We can't even comprehend life without our mother. We're just in a state of shock.'

"Son Vaughn had no comment at first, but stopped before closing the door to the aircraft to say, 'I'm sure this is just a horrible accident. My mother loved Mr. Iversen very much. I have never seen her as happy as she was during the last year of her life.'"

Nicky folded the newspaper and laid it on the dresser. "Don't throw this away, OK? I may want to read it again."

"Are you all right?" I asked.

"I think so. I mean, I have lots of experience with death, but this is a bit strange. And with our plans to visit Annarita and all, I'm kind of freaked out." He crawled to the head of the bed and peered into the open doughnut box on my lap. "Is that all that's left?" he cried.

"Excuse me, but that's practically all there was when you handed it to me," I said.

"Thao is a sugar freak," Nicky said, licking the icing off another maple bar. "Shall I call her?"

"You have got to be the king of non sequiturs," I complained.

"Call whom?"

"Annarita, of course. *Diable.*"

When he said this last word, which, even without interpretation, I understood to mean *devil,* he placed the accent on the *ble,* making it sound like it was spelled "diabbluh." It was more of his Chamorro ethnicity popping out.

"Well, should I?" I asked. "I doubt she's receiving guests."

"I'm not so sure. She was really depressed when I talked to her. And the paper said only her brother and sister went to Arizona, so that means she's at the house. You're right; I should call," he said, crawling over me, reaching for the phone.

"You have her number memorized already?"

"Of course not. I'm calling Matthew to get it off my desk."

"Matthew?" I asked. "Who's Matthew?"

"The man I live with. I guess I forgot to tell you that part."

TWENTY-EIGHT

FOR A moment I thought I might throw up on the bed. "The man you live with?" I said weakly.

"He's sweet. You're going to love him as much as I do," Nicky said as he punched the buttons on the phone. "He virtually saved my life when Rosario was sick in bed. Matthew? Hi, it's me…Yes, everything here is fine…*very* fine," he said, and kissed me on the cheek. "I need a favor. On my desk in the study is a pink slip of paper with a phone number. Can you get it for me?"

Nicky rubbed my nose lightly with his free hand. "You have specks of sugar on your nose," he said. Then he raised himself up and licked the tip of my nose. "You're sweet. Literally. Oh, Matthew, wait a minute. Got a pencil?" he asked me, waving his hand in the air, as though I was supposed to make one magically materialize between his fingers.

I slid open the panel on the slanted headboard and retrieved the steno pad and pen I keep to record my dreams. I opened it to a blank page and handed it to him. He wrote down the number, then hung up. He immediately began to push buttons on the phone again. I put my finger on the flash-button and disconnected him.

"Just a minute, OK, Speedy?" I said.

"What?"

"Let's slow down for a second. Who's this Matthew and why are the two of you living together?"

"It's a long story," he said, slumping his shoulders and cocking his head, like a child who's been asked to tell about his day at school when all he really wants to do is go outside and play.

"That's OK. I have lots of time," I said.

"Well," he began, placing the receiver on the hook and reaching finally for the cappuccino Thao had brought him. He took a drink through the slit in the plastic lid. "Ughh! This is tepid."

"We can heat it up in the microwave. After your story."

"There's nothing to tell, really. Matthew was sent by Shanti to help Rosario and me. He was our practical support volunteer. He worked all day at his regular job at the hospital, then he would come to our house after work and work all evening, doing the laundry, vacuuming, cleaning, washing dishes. Most importantly he would sit with Rosario, chain-smoking and talking about everything from the politics of high fashion to religion. Those two smoked so much that by the time I got home from work the house smelled like a bar. I never could have kept things together without him."

"You were working?"

"Of course. Why not?"

"I…I don't know. Excuse me for being so presumptuous and for butting into private matters, but I thought…well, I thought you were financially independent."

Nicky gave a loud laugh. "Why would you think that?"

"Well, isn't it obvious? Ferraris, palazzos in Italy, houses all around the world? That's not exactly *Lifestyles of the Blue Collar Class.*"

"Silly," Nicky said, placing his hand flat against the side of my face and holding it there. "You're so funny."

"Mind letting me in on the joke?"

"I didn't always have this money. I guess I could have if I let Nonna support me but, as I told you, I keep her gifts to a minimum. What I have is mostly death money, honey. People remembered me in their wills to show me how much they loved me and hoping, I suppose, that the money would help make their deaths easier for me to cope with. And Rosario, like all middle-class Italian men, was insured nine ways to Sunday."

"Oh, I thought you always….I mean, you *are* rather sophisticated and urbane," I observed.

"You flatter me. I'm a brown-skinned boy from an island in the middle of the Pacific ocean. Anything I learned about the world, I learned first from Nonna and then from Rosario. I'm the roughest diamond in the rough you'll ever meet."

"So how did this Matthew come to live with you? What was that about?"

"After Rosario died I was drifting. I decided that for six months I would make no decisions that would change my life in any substantial way. I also realized that I needed to stay in San Francisco, where I could get the best HIV care. So about nine months after Rosario died, I asked Matthew if he wanted to move in. I really liked and respected him. It was silly for me to stay in that place by myself. It's huge. Wait till you see it. Besides, Matthew and I got along famously and he was living in an apartment the size of an oven, even with a decent salary at the hospital. You must know what rents are like in this city."

"I do. Why do you think I've been in this flat for twelve years?"

"So, since it was either move or get a roommate, and since Matthew was the only person on the face of the earth I thought I could stand to live with, I asked him to move in. That was two years ago. It was one of the wisest decisions I've ever made."

"There's never been anything between the two of you? I mean, romantically," I asked.

"No, nothing."

"Because usually, sooner or later between two friends, at least one friend develops a crush on the other or falls in love, or something," I pressed.

"Don't get me wrong, ducky, we love one another, but not like that. We're family. Real family, as in 'family values–family,' the way the religious right thinks it is. We actually support one another. Besides, when I met Matthew he was in serious recovery and had a history of really bad relationships. You know, the old-fashioned, fun kind: drugs, sex, booze, what's-your-name-and-how-did-I-get-here kinds of relationships. He's still gun-shy on that score. But you'll see all of this for yourself," Nicky said confidently.

I liked how self-assured he was, even if it sometimes grated on me that he assumed I would agree with everything he said, thought, or planned.

Mostly, though, I did agree. Which was even more frustrating.

"I guess we have a lot of filling in to do, haven't we?" I said.

"Yes, lemon drop, but we don't have to do it all this morning. Now, may I please call Annarita?"

TWENTY-NINE

ANNARITA, it turns out, was a complete doll. A total mess, but a complete doll. And was she ever glad to hear from Nicky. She gave us directions to the house and asked us to come over immediately, before the family returned from Arizona. Nicky went home to change and I picked him up an hour later, after I had showered and sorted the mail.

Nicky's house was surprisingly nearby. It was a newer home on top of Sanchez Hill. I remembered, as I pulled up in front, that neighbors had tried for months to block construction of this stretch of four homes. They argued that with the housing shortage in San Francisco, building such large single-family residences was unconscionable. All that really meant was that it was politically incorrect or they were jealous of any-one who could afford the $1.2-million asking price. But the houses were tastefully built, the architect having designed a quadruple set of con-vincing neo-Victorian structures. Also, each home boasted a back yard, a three-car garage, and an elevator from the garage to the upper floors.

Nicky's was painted the color of celery. The trim was white. It was four stories tall and the rooms appeared to be massive from what I could see through the windows. The front two uppermost levels boasted jut-ting bays that overlooked the entire city and probably the whole East Bay. His was a corner house, bordered by a small patch of city-owned lawn, giving him increased privacy and views on two sides. I couldn't help but think that Rosario must have been insured on five continents; either that or Nicky was lying about not taking money from Nonna.

Nicky loped down the front steps as I pulled to the curb. I was glad I had passed up my khakis for dress slacks and a white button-down shirt. He wore camel-colored slacks with a brown lizard belt, cordovan leather loafers, a white cotton voile shirt, and a black cashmere V-neck sweater. He stopped at the curb, placed his hands on his hips, and whistled at my white Celica convertible.

"Just get in," I said, embarrassed, but glad he approved. I liked realizing there were things about me he didn't yet know and that would surprise him in a positive way.

"You little vixen," he said, closing the door. He leaned over and
kissed me before fastening his seat belt. "Did you bring food and a
gun?" he asked.

I paused to study his expression, which was completely deadpan. "We
are going to cross the bridge, after all," he said wryly. "God knows what
lurks in the suburbs."

The Iversen estate was not what I was expecting. I thought it would
be grander. More style maybe, perhaps a hint at tradition. I thought at
least there would be acres and acres of grounds. But it seemed to me
more like a giant tract home plunked down on a three-acre parcel in a
high-end subdivision. The neighboring estates were all different from
one another, true, but there was something distinctly prefab about them.
Cheap-looking columns attached to halfhearted porticoes with gaudy,
gold swag chains supporting overly polished hanging porch lamps.

A middle-aged woman in a blue, tight-fitting suit let us in and
showed us into a sunroom that looked out over a garden, a large lawn,
and a swimming pool. She said she would fetch Ms. O'Brien, calling
Annarita by what Nicky reminded me was her maiden name, the name
of Evelyn's first husband.

The room was elliptically shaped and painted entirely white with
white wicker furniture. The cushions of the large double chairs were
white with green leaves and tiny tan stems, as were the cushions on the
two facing sofas. The windows swung out and up, giving the room an
outdoor effect. In the tropics this room would be called a veranda. In
Concord it was a "California Room."

"Nicky?"

We turned from the open French doors, where we were admiring the
back yard, to find a sturdy woman of about 30 coming toward us. She
wore slacks and a blouse, with a gold chain around her neck. She was big
without being fat, and wore her hair closely cropped. She reminded me
of a lesbian attorney friend with whom I wouldn't want to engage in

fisticuffs. Her feet scuffled along in an incongruous pair of rubber thongs, and as she walked to Nicky and gave him a hug, the noise her feet made on the terrazzo floor reminded me of the Chinese women who shuffle around the produce store down the street from my house.

Their hug lasted a long time, but eventually they separated and Nicky introduced me. Annarita sat on one of the sofas with Nicky; I sat on the facing one. She looked weary.

"I can't tell you how glad I am to see you. I was so thrilled when mother called from Europe and told me she had run into you there. How odd. I think it was meant to be, don't you?" she asked, grasping Nicky's hand with both of hers.

I could see his jaw tighten. This sounded like the matchmaking he had been afraid of, but now it was coming directly from Annarita. Nicky started to look toward me, but changed his mind, probably fearing Annarita would see the panic in his eyes.

"That's one way to look at it," Nicky said. "I suppose there was some fateful purpose in your mother being at my grandmother's house. Nigel and I were very glad to meet her. We had a pleasant time with her in Florence and we were both shocked when we read what had happened. Of course, we called immediately."

Any more "we's" in that answer and she would have thought he had a mouse in his pocket. "Yes," I threw in for good measure, "when Nicky brought up the morning paper and opened it, we were both speechless."

None of this seemed to faze her in the least. "I couldn't believe it myself when the police came to the house yesterday. I thought for sure there had been some horrible mistake. I still can't quite make myself believe it's true." She sat back against the plump cushions and sighed. "Vaughn called this morning and said he had identified the body. It was definitely mother. I kept hoping it would be someone else."

Nicky and I exchanged a look, which she picked up on. "Oh, it's no secret that no one in the family is thrilled with mother marrying Buffalo Bob." Annarita paused, realizing how she must sound to outsiders. "I suppose that's cruel. Travis isn't really a bad person. It's just that no one trusts him. I mean, would you?" she asked, looking directly at me.

"I don't know," I said. "I barely met the man."

"What do you think?" Nicky asked her.

"I don't know what to think. They met, had this whirlwind fling that no one—and I mean *no one*—could talk mother out of. Then they sneaked off to Hawaii and got married. We thought they were just going on some sort of romantic getaway to Maui, but they came back married! Can you imagine? Virginia was furious. She actually threw things at mother and told her she was going to have her committed to an asylum." Annarita held her hand to her mouth to stifle a giggle. "It was pretty funny, actually. My sister never loses her cool like that. I liked it a lot."

"All of this has to be terribly upsetting to you, though. Do you have any reason to suspect foul play?" Nicky asked.

"No. That's Virge's paranoia. And I suppose some of mother's friends who thought Travis was after her money would agree. I think he's just a slow-witted farm boy who found a woman he liked who had money to boot. They seemed awfully happy. At least she did." Annarita hesitated, then added, "Most of the time."

With this last sentence, Annarita seemed to drift off into a kind of daydream for a few seconds. "I'm just coming out of a bad marriage myself," she added.

"Your mother mentioned it to us when we spoke," Nicky said. "No details, just that you were living at home again while the divorce goes through."

"But I want to hear about you, Nicky. Please tell me what you've been doing since I last saw you."

The woman in the blue suit startled us by appearing out of nowhere, carrying a heavy silver tray with cups, saucers, and a teapot. "I thought you'd like some tea," she said, setting the tray on the glass-topped white wicker table between the two sofas. Then she left the room as quietly as she had entered.

"Thank you, Hudson," Annarita called after her. "She's been a life-saver in all this. She's such a mother hen. I don't know how she holds herself together though. She and mother were very close. Go on, Nicky," Annarita said, pouring tea for us, "tell me everything."

"I don't think there's a whole lot to tell," Nicky said. "I graduated,

went to Europe to visit Nonna for the summer, as usual, then came back
to the states and started working for a hotel. Then about a year later I
realized I wanted to be a priest, so I went into a Franciscan monastery
in upstate New York. Two years later they asked me to leave. I asked too
many questions for them. After I left I went back to Guam for a year to
recuperate, during which my family tortured me daily without mercy, all
except for my younger brother, Kenny, who you met once, I think."

"Isn't he the one who married his high school sweetheart?" she asked,
picking up her cup and saucer. She blew gently across the top of her
teacup, smiled at me, and turned her attention back to Nicky.

I pretended I had heard all this a million times. Monastery? Priest?
That explained the esoteric books he was reading in Italy, those theo-
logical and philosophical texts, the introductions to which, when I tried
reading them, put me to sleep.

"Yes, that's right," Nicky said. "So I put up with that for almost a year,
and then my father and I had a huge falling-out and I came to
California."

"Do you have family here?" she asked.

"Cousins, but I didn't stay with any of them. Well, actually, that's not
quite true. I stayed with my cousin Laurie for about four months, but
really I was just crashing at her place until I could save enough money
to get an apartment of my own. Then I moved into the city. I was working at a hotel when I met my late partner and moved in with him. We
were together for almost eight years before he died." Nicky and I
watched Annarita for a reaction.

"Oh, I had no idea," she said, touching his hand again. "I can't imagine what that's like. To lose a spouse, I mean. Divorce notwithstanding,
I've never gone through that. I guess losing mother is the closest I've
come. I never really knew my father. He might be dead for all I know."

Then came the inevitable, if not obligatory question: "How's your
health?" she inquired. Coming from her, it somehow wasn't so grating.
She seemed to genuinely want to know.

"I'm fine, thanks to modern medicine and ACT UP!" Nicky grinned.
"Nigel and I are on a cocktail of new drugs and we're coasting along
smoothly, at least for now."

Annarita turned her attention to me in a once-over assessment to gauge my health. The telephone rang somewhere inside the house. "Hudson will get that," Annarita called over her shoulder. "More tea, Nigel?" She poured tea for both of us and was replacing the porcelain teapot on the tray when Hudson appeared again in the doorway.

"Ms. O'Brien, it's your sister on the line. I'm afraid the extension in here isn't working, so you'll have to take it in the office," Hudson apologized. "One of the puppies must have chewed it."

"Thank you, Hudson. I'll be right in," Annarita said. "You two make yourselves comfortable for a minute. I'll be right back."

"Did you say puppies?" Nicky asked.

"Yes, Dreamer had a litter three weeks ago and they're a handful," she explained as she stood, smoothing her slacks front and back. "I breed Doberman pinschers. I'll show them to you when I come back if you like."

"Oh, yes, please," Nicky said, smiling broadly. Then he added, "We'd like that very much." He turned to face me, sporting a Cheshire cat grin, his eyes the size of silver dollars. "Puppies!"

THIRTY

I WAS HOPING that when Annarita returned and began talking about her sister's phone call, Nicky would forget about the puppies. The look in his eyes when he heard about them made me nervous. I was just getting to know him and thinking maybe we would be boyfriends. I wasn't ready to make an entire family. I might as well have hoped for a cat to forget about a mouse it had chased behind the refrigerator.

"Where are the puppies?" he asked as Annarita entered the room.

"Oh, follow me," she said.

We walked outside and across the lawn to the east wing of the house, through a pair of sliding glass doors and into a bedroom being used as a temporary kennel. Oddly it didn't smell and was fairly orderly, given the fact that seven puppies and a full-grown dog occupied it. In a far corner sat what Annarita called "the whelping box." It was a square-shaped box, about three feet deep by six feet long with slatted wooden sides. The bottom was constructed of two-by-twos spaced about six inches apart and covered with wire mesh to allow "puppy droppings" and urine to run through and into a metal tray which could be slid out and cleaned.

The puppies were sleeping in a huge pile, as though they had been dumped out of a wheelbarrow and slept where they fell, all in a heap. As we entered, the mother, a red and tan Doberman, raised her head, her cropped ears pointing straight up to detect strange or familiar voices, her amber eyes watching our every move.

"Walk slowly," Annarita instructed, "and speak in a high voice. If you have a deep voice, sometimes dogs think you're growling. Also, don't stare at her or she might think you're challenging her." Annarita began baby talking to Dreamer as we approached. "Hello, pretty girl. Can we see your babies?" She reached down and stroked the mother, who paid her no attention whatsoever, but was riveting us with her stare.

"Squat down so you're at her level," Annarita said in a calm, flat voice. Dogs don't like to be towered over.

"Awful lot of things to remember," Nicky joked.

"Well, how would you feel," I asked, "if Godzilla walked into your room and stood over your bed?"

"That's exactly correct," Annarita said. "If you always put yourself in the dog's position, like you just did, you will almost always do the right thing."

By now the puppies were squirming, waking up, yawning, tumbling to and fro around their mother. One of them made its way toward the side of the box where a small gate was attached. He climbed up with his front paws, fell over backward, then got up and tried again. Annarita leaned over and lifted him out. He was tiny, but wiggling like crazy.

"I think he's got his eye on you, Nicky," she said, handing him to Nicky. Nicky took him and cradled him against his chest. "Oh, Nigel, look. Isn't he sweet?"

"Yes, he's very sweet," I had to agree, but I tried to sound uninterested. "How long have you been breeding Dobermans?" I asked in an attempt to get the subject off the puppy and on to Annarita.

"For about seven years. Mother bought me a dog when my husband started traveling on business so I wouldn't be alone and would have a kind of built-in burglar alarm. Oh, look," Annarita said, "he's trying to crawl to you, Nigel."

Sure enough, the puppy wasn't content in Nicky's arms and had begun to paw its way free and climb across Nicky's folded arms to me. He managed to get halfway onto my shoulder before I had no choice but to take him. When I did, he licked my face wildly.

"He really likes you," Annarita said. "You know, owners never pick their dogs; dogs pick their owners."

"I'm sure that's true. However, I'm not an owner. I'm not even in the market."

"You could be," Nicky suggested.

I quickly gave him a "please shut up" look and turned back to Annarita. "So all it took was your mother buying you this dog and you started breeding them?"

"Not exactly. Three people told me the dog was good enough to show and one day in the park a handler came up and offered to show the dog for me if I was interested. I thought it might be fun and before I knew it, Rex was a champion. Then I fell in love with a bitch I saw at one of the shows and bought her and the rest is puppy history," she said, making a sweeping gesture with her arm over the top of the whelping box.

As she did this, Dreamer raised her head intently to make sure there was no imminent threat to her brood. Annarita was beaming, as though she herself had produced the litter.

"We might be interested," Nicky said. "Will you hold this one until we're certain?"

THIRTY-ONE

ONCE back in the house we visited a little longer in the California Room, then Annarita walked us to the door. We said our good-byes and promised to keep in touch, especially during this difficult period. Back on the road, Nicky said, "Well, what do you think?"

"About what?"

"Well, everything. Annarita first. Do you like her?"

"She's pleasant enough. I don't envy her, that's for sure. Money and social position can be a burden, I think. Especially when there are siblings around. This complication of her mother's death is just going to make all that even worse. The media, especially the media in the East Bay, will hound them. I do like her, though."

"I do, too. We were pretty close in college," Nicky said, putting a CD in the player, a concerto for recorder by Handel.

"Why didn't you tell her you were gay when you were in school, if you were so close?" I asked. It came out rather sternly, but I didn't mean anything by it.

"I thought I was bisexual in those days. Besides, in spite of what you think, I don't go about the countryside trumpeting my sexuality."

"Tell that to the priest in Arezzo. The one you raped in the belfry," I said.

"*Diable!* I see I can't tell you anything," Nicky said in mock exaggeration.

"Sure you can. Just be ready to hear it again. When the time is most propitious."

Nicky smiled and rested a hand on my thigh. We drove along for a few miles listening to the heavenly sound of the concerto. We passed through the Caldecott tunnel and the entire bay and both bridges appeared in the distance. The Transamerica Pyramid gave the city its signature skyline. Without it, the city would be indistinguishable, a horrible hodgepodge of rectangular boxes hiding the truly inspired architectural feats of the past.

The city was, architecturally speaking, a tribute to graft and kickbacks to city officials throughout the '60s and '70s. Thank God for the Transamerica building. Yet I hated to think it was owned by an insurance company, one which had canceled my life insurance through a bureaucratic mix-up and then wouldn't do anything about it, naturally, since they knew I had HIV.

"Do you think he killed her?" Nicky asked.

"I have no idea. I met the man once for about 30 seconds."

"Oh, come on, Nigel, you're a better judge of character than that. Think about it. We thought he was queer the minute we walked in the room that night," Nicky said, squeezing my thigh.

"You mean do I think he's queer and killed his wife because of it? That makes no sense, Sherlock."

"Well, there's something fishy there. Married six months to the wealthiest woman in the state and then he takes her camping to some remote lake in Arizona and, what do you know, she ends up sleeping with the fishes."

"Look, we have no idea what happened. It could be just the way he says. She got up in the night after a few drinks and wandered out to the dock and fell in," I said without much conviction.

"That's just it, Miss Marple. She didn't just wander to the dock and fall in. They're saying she got into the boat, took it out in the lake, and then fell in and drowned. If she was too tipsy to swim, how the hell did she manage to untie the boat from the dock, start the engine, and buzz around the lake? If she was functional enough to get the boat out into the lake, why wasn't she able to swim, or at least hang on to the boat? And why didn't Travis hear the motor when she started it? No, no, Miss Jane, this is way fishy. Way, way fishy," Nicky said with more passion than I was comfortable with. He was too interested in solving this mystery.

"Well, luckily it has nothing to do with us," I countered.

Nicky scooted over on top of the console and wrapped both arms around my neck. "You did it again," he said.

"Did what?" I asked, craning my neck to look him in the eye.

"You made us sound married. You said, 'This has nothing to do with us,' like 'us' was a married couple and you were speaking for both of us. That's so romantic," he cooed and began tonguing my ear.

"If you say so, babe, but if you don't remove your tongue from my ear, we'll never live long enough to see if marriage is even a possibility."

"All right," Nicky complained. "I'll just find another place for it." And with that, he put his head in my lap, unzipped my trousers, and found that other place. He accomplished his task and zipped me up just as we entered the toll plaza.

I handed the two dollars to the toll-taker, a 20-something redneck with tattoos all over his arms and neck, including one that said, "Sex is Cool." I was feeling quite cocky about narrowly escaping his detecting what had just transpired in the front seat of my car. I shifted into first gear and turned to smile and wink at Nicky, only to find him with his tongue sticking out at the toll taker. Covering Nicky's tongue, and now dribbling onto the top of the console, was a thick white liquid, which could be only one thing, given no one in the front seat was drinking hand lotion. As I hit the accelerator, I actually made the tires squeal.

THIRTY-TWO

THE PHONE was ringing when we walked into Nicky's living room. It was Annarita. I listened to his half of the short conversation, which ended with, "Let me talk with Nigel. I'll call you back this evening." I didn't like the sound of that.

He hung up and asked if I wanted a drink.

"Why? Am I going to need one?" I asked, only half teasing.

"She wants us to help her," Nicky said, going to the bar at the far end of the room. "She thinks there's going to be trouble."

"How could we possibly help her? She has more money than the pope," I quipped.

"Be serious. Money doesn't buy everything," he said, pouring himself something clear. "Do you want one?" he asked.

"What is it?"

"Tonic," he said.

"Sure," I answered.

He brought both glasses and we sat together on an overstuffed, pillow-laden navy blue sofa. "I think she's scared," Nicky said.

"Scared of what? What did she say?"

"After we left, she got an anonymous phone call," Nicky said.

"And?"

"The caller said that if the cops knew what he knew, they'd call it murder and that Iversen has a past no one knows about." Nicky waited for my reaction.

"So? It's not a crime to have a past. It doesn't make you a criminal in the present."

"Why don't you want to help?"

"I don't even know what 'help' you're talking about. What does she want us to do?" I could feel my face flushing, my blood pressure rising.

"She just wants to know if we'll look into it."

"Into what? There's nothing to look into as far as I can see."

"Why are you so defensive?"

"Look, I don't even know this woman, and I certainly don't know anything about her family or her cowboy stepfather, or whatever he is. I thought you and I were going to get to know each other." I tried to appeal to the part of him that liked the sound of "us."

"We *are* getting to know each other, but why can't we get to know each other and help Annarita at the same time? All she wants is for us to see if we can find out something about this guy. You know, to try to put her mind at ease. I don't think that's asking a lot."

"My God, she hasn't seen you in almost ten years, and the first time she lays eyes on you, she's asking you to go to work for her. Sounds like she's a chip off the old block, if you ask me. Did she offer a retainer?" Listening to myself, I could tell this was going badly. I wasn't even sure where all this was coming from, but my emotions were getting out of control.

"What are you talking about?"

"Isn't that what all you people with money do? Buy other people to do the work? Do I look like I'm for hire? Besides, I'm sure she wasn't asking for my help. It's you she interested in."

"Actually, she asked if, quote, 'the two of you' would help. What's this really about, anyway? Are you jealous?" Nicky smiled as he said this.

"That's it. I don't need this," I said, getting up and placing my drink on an end table. "You go play your Sherlock Holmes games with your socialite friends and maybe you can psychoanalyze her while you're at it, her with her 50 Doberman pinschers and her short hair and slacks and her country club life. Then when you're tired of that dead end, you can come see if I'm still around and…."

"Nigel!" Nicky shouted. "What's going on here? I just wanted…"

"I know what you want. And it isn't me," I said and stormed out.

THIRTY-THREE

I DIDN'T sleep that night. Or the next. By the third night, I was so miserable, I called him. I got his answering machine. "Nicky, it's Nigel. I'm sorry. If you want to talk about it…well, if you want to, I'd like to see if we can iron this out. I'm sorry. Please call me."

It was after midnight when the doorbell rang. I got up and buzzed the downstairs door open, figuring it could only be one person. It was.

Nicky came up the stairs with a backpack and a bunch of flowers. He walked up to me, kissed me on the mouth, complete with tongue, then said, "Men who apologize are so sexy." He put the flowers in a vase he found in the dining room sideboard, then we sat on the sofa. A long time passed without either of us saying anything.

"You did say you wanted to talk, right?" he asked.

"Yeah. I just don't know where to start exactly."

"I can wait. Let's have a fire. Do you mind?" he asked.

"Not at all," I said, starting to get up and get a fireplace log.

"That's all right, I'll do it. You keep looking for your words." He rose, took a log from the box on the hearth, and placed it on the grate in the fireplace. Then he stuffed newspaper under the grate and rolled a single sheet of newspaper up. He lit the paper he was holding and shoved it up the chimney. "This gets the draft going," he said. "Rosario showed me this trick in our old, drafty flat on Divisadero."

The fire caught and he came back and sat on the sofa, closer this time. "What's the matter? Don't you like me?" he asked. Immediately I began to cry.

He held my hand and brushed at my tears as I tried to articulate what was going on. "I'm worried you're going to go away."

"Why would I do that?" he asked gently.

"Because I'm not good enough for you," I said.

"Why aren't you good enough?"

"About a million reasons I can think of."

"Name one."

"I'm not smart enough or rich enough or sophisticated enough or—"

"Who told you all this?" he interrupted, placing his hand on my lips to get me to stop with the list of self-negating comments. "Where did you get this notion that you're not good enough?"

"I don't know. My father, I guess. All I ever heard when I was growing up was that I didn't think straight, that I was stupid and didn't use my brain."

"I don't think you're stupid. In fact, I think you're quite smart and even clever," Nicky assured me.

"You won't if we try to help Annarita and I don't find out what she wants to know. Or what if I don't know how to do what it is you want me to do?"

"Nigel, silly puss, I don't care about the outcome; I just want the adventure. And I want it with you. I want to do everything with you. It's not about succeeding or failing. It's about being together. It'll be an adventure. It has nothing to do with Annarita or anyone else. It only has to do with us. If you don't want to do that, fine. We won't. Just don't shut me out. If you want to do nothing, then OK; we'll do nothing. But let's do nothing together." He sounded so sane, so grounded, so centered. Mostly he sounded so honest.

"Maybe you'll think I'm boring," I offered as yet another possible obstacle.

"And maybe monkeys will fly out of my ass," he said.

I couldn't help but laugh, which started him laughing. Soon we were both laughing so hard we couldn't talk. When we finally caught our breath, I pushed him over onto the sofa and crawled on top of him, pinning his arms with my hands. "I love you," I whispered and kissed him.

"But will you love my monkeys?" he said, which made us laugh again.

"Only if they don't get in the way," I said.

"So you are the jealous type," he said.

"That's just it," I said, sitting up and pulling him up by his hands so that he, too, was sitting. "I've never been the jealous type before, but I was jealous, even threatened, by Annarita. I think I was afraid I couldn't measure up and that you'd rather be with her than me. I don't know. None of it makes any sense. It's not about sense, I guess. It's just a bunch of crazy feelings."

"Yes, feelings can be crazy," Nicky agreed.

"If you'll put up with me until we get to know each other better, I promise to try to do better," I said.

"I'll put up with you if you'll put up with me," he said. "It seems to me that I give you a lot more grief than you give me. At least you don't go around shoving venison bones into your gums and making them bleed in front of a host of international dignitaries."

"I guess we'll have to put up with different things," I said.

"Yes," Nicky said softly, nodding his head. "We are very different, you and I. Yin and Yang, but I haven't figured out yet which is which. Anyway, you…" He interrupted his thought, distracted by something behind me. He leaned forward as if to see it better, whatever it was.

"What is it?" I asked, turning around. There was nothing but the bookcase behind me. He reached past me, grabbed a book and brought it out.

"This is your book," he said, his voice sounding incredulous. "You wrote this book." He looked at me now in disbelief.

"Yeah. I always joke that that's the book that got me out of my government job." The book's title was *How to Get A Government Job*. "I wrote that just before Lyle and I left Washington. It did pretty well. With the advance I was able to quit my job and Lyle and I moved back here."

"I'm impressed," Nicky said, leafing through the book.

"It's pretty good, actually. It wasn't all that difficult to write," I said, denigrating my work as usual.

"Maybe not for you. I couldn't write a book if my life depended on it. I guess your father was wrong, then, wasn't he?" Nicky said.

"Wrong? About what?"

"About you being stupid. I don't know any stupid people who've published books." He looked at me with one of the most loving looks anyone has ever given me, a look I wished my father had given me when I presented him with his copy.

He went back to the beginning of the book and noticed the dedication. He read it aloud, "To my father, the perfect civil servant." Then he looked at me again. "I guess that made him eat his words, eh?"

"When I gave him his copy of the book, he pointed to the bookshelf in his living room and told me that when I had enough books with my name on them to fill a bookshelf that size, then I'd be a writer." Just telling the story hurt me, and I had averted my eyes.

Nicky put the book down, drew me close, took my face in his hands, kissed me and said, "A writer is someone who writes, not someone who publishes books. An author is someone who publishes books and not always very good ones. Neither a writer nor an author is necessarily a good person. And Nigel, if there is one thing I would stake my very life's breath on, it is that you, my lover, my passionate, beautiful, kind, and clever lover, are a good person. And that is all that really matters, now isn't it?"

With that he kissed me. And after that kiss came another one, and another and another, until finally we were naked on the floor before the fire. Afterward, I lifted him in my arms and carried him to what I was now thinking of as "our" bed, where I made love to him all over again.

THIRTY-FOUR

NEEDLESS to say, we decided to help Annarita.

By the following morning the newspaper was running further details of the drowning, as well as spinning the tale into several other fabrics. The lead story said Evelyn's blood levels made her legally drunk, and that her body was clad only in bra and panties. The story used the term "bra and panties" so many times that Nicky checked the byline to see if it was written by Danielle Steele.

The real interest, however, was turning out to be the marriage itself, not the drowning. The story was filled with innuendoes that Travis Iversen had ulterior motives in marrying Evelyn VanDeventer in the first place. The story that held Nicky's and my interest the most began:

"When he answered the phone, former Senator Ben Tedeschi instantly recognized the voice on the other end of the line. It was his former lover and longtime confidante Evelyn VanDeventer. Although she was usually animated and optimistic, the 65-year-old Contra Costa County publishing heiress sounded troubled to Tedeschi. She voiced concerns about the new man in her life, Travis Iversen, a 35-year-old, exhibitionistic, body-building cowboy who made his living performing rodeo tricks with trained bulls. He was a common sight at rodeos, speedways and tailgate parties throughout the West and Southwest, often performing at county and state fairs.

"According to Tedeschi, his former lover believed God had finally sent her the cowboy she had been praying for. But she soon started complaining that he was thoughtless, inconsiderate, and rude. He would show up for dinner parties two hours late bringing uninvited guests who weren't dressed for dinner; he charged outrageous amounts on her credit cards; he kept secrets from her; and he spent most of his available time with cowhands and rodeo performers, frequenting bars in all parts of town, including gay and lesbian bars, private dance clubs, and Asian opium dens, she told Tedeschi.

"Tedeschi's advice was simple: 'Get rid of him. Now.'

"'I can't,' she said. 'I married him.'

"This was how Evelyn VanDeventer Iversen informed her former lover of her recent elopement. It is also how her friends and family found out: through phone calls after the fact."

Nicky threw down the paper and made gagging noises. "Isn't this the newspaper that invented yellow journalism?" he asked.

"As a matter of fact it is, but that was before your time. Mine too, come to think of it." We were having coffee and bagels in my back yard, having slept until ten, made love, taken showers, and called Annarita to tell her to sit tight until she heard from us.

"I wonder if Ben is here or if they called him in Florence?" Nicky wondered aloud.

"Neither, would be my guess," I said, slathering cream cheese on half a garlic bagel.

Nicky gave me a look of confusion.

"I'll bet you they found someone who knows Ben or works for him and got him or her to talk about it. All they had to do was get the person to quote him once and they were off to the races, attributing every conjecture to Ben. Especially when they realized he was out of the country and couldn't challenge the quote."

"But that's not fair," Nicky exclaimed, slapping his hand on the table. "That's deceptive; it's lying; it's—"

"Modern journalism, dumpling," I said, pushing the bagel into his gaping mouth. "For someone so worldly, you certainly can be naïve."

He took a giant bite. "Mmm, delicious," he said with his mouth full. "Well, we have to do something."

"OK, what do you suggest? Shall I send a letter to the editor saying I met the man for five minutes at a wedding reception in Italy and it is my learned opinion that he doesn't show up late to dinner parties?"

"No," Nicky said, "I suggest we dig up the truth about him, at least for Annarita's sake."

"And how do you suggest we do that?"

"You tell me. You're the one who wrote the how-to book."

"Yes, but in case you haven't noticed, it was how to get a job, not how to dig up a suspected murderer's history. Here, have one with peanut butter," I said, shoving a half-eaten bagel with peanut butter and black-berry jam in his face. Unfortunately, he clenched his mouth shut just as I reached it and his mouth and nose ended up a gooey mess. "Gee, I'm sorry, honey. I thought that thing didn't close."

He wiped his face with his napkin, then grabbed mine off my lap. "You sure are developing a sassy mouth. Who you been hangin' with?"

"It's my new imaginary playmate. He's very clever and has an acid tongue. I'm in training," I said.

"You're coming along nicely." He picked up the bagel with the peanut butter and shoved the entire thing in his mouth.

"At any rate, I'm serious," I reiterated. "I don't even know where to begin finding out anything about this guy. I suppose we could try to get hold of his family or—."

Suddenly Nicky's eyes grew large and he tried to speak through his mouthful of food. "Wathoo, ubh hort."

I waited until he could swallow, which took a considerable length of time, during which I said, "If you weren't such a…how can I put this delicately? Pig!"

"Matthew, of course!" he shouted, and charged up the back steps into the house.

I stood and held my arms out, turned, and addressed all the back yards that abutted mine. "Ladies and gentlemen of Church Street, I give you Nicholas Alex Borja, the Queen of Non Sequiturs."

THIRTY-FIVE

WHAT HE MEANT was that his housemate Matthew could help. Matthew, it seemed, was a genealogist and a history buff, which made him an excellent scholar and all-around good snoop. So after calling him on the phone, Nicky threw the dishes in the sink and said we had to go to his house right away.

"What about the dishes?" I protested.

"The maid will do them."

"What maid, Lady Astor? Cinderella doesn't live here."

"Oh, that's right. We're at your house. Hmm. We'll have to figure that out later. Right now," he said, grabbing my arm and tugging me across the kitchen, "we have to go to my house. Matthew's waiting for us."

As usual, Nicky was right. I liked Matthew. Matthew Mahony was his full name and, while I usually don't seek out Irishmen, having had bad experiences with two Irish boyfriends, I had to admit he was charming and intelligent, not to mention entertaining.

"But I've never read any Zane Grey," Matthew said, as he put on a pot of coffee for us. "I don't know the first thing about Americana, let alone Wild West shows. In fact, I don't know much about anything that happened after the War of the Roses."

Matthew was in his mid 40s, with reddish-blond hair, and had what my mother would have referred to as Midwestern good looks. I recalled Nicky's stories of Matthew's wild, prerecovery days and it wasn't hard to imagine that he would have been able to seduce just about anyone. Matthew occupied the rooms on the first floor of the house, but there was a connecting stairway, so it wasn't as though he lived in a separate unit. The two of them were like brothers, or what I always imagined brothers would be like, never having had any of my own. They knew each other intimately but kept a respectable distance.

We sat at the table in the kitchen in front of a window that over-looked Nicky's backyard which, unlike mine, was carefully tended. My backyard was in full bloom, totally overrun with morning glories. Even the palm tree was covered. The railings on the deck and the stairs could-n't be seen through the vines and the tiny porch at the back of the upstairs pied-à-terre looked like the bow of a Rose Bowl parade float. Nicky's yard, by contrast, was carefully tended. Bonsai trees lined the sides of the yard, tiered up three levels on step-backed shelves. Some of the tiny trees were azaleas in full bloom. I didn't know azaleas could be made into bonsais.

"All I know is what I've been reading in the paper," Matthew said. Although he had put up a pot of coffee for us, he drank diet 7-Up. He was still in his bathrobe and the pajamas he was wearing were a jumble of porpoises jumping through hoops and holding multicolored flags in their mouths. I wondered where he found children's pajamas in his size. "It all sounds rather torrid, if you can believe the newspapers. Of course we always believe the newspapers," he said sarcastically as he lit a ciga-rette and opened the window closest to him. He exhaled a cloud of smoke through the screen into the fresh spring air outside.

"What we're trying to find out is what this guy is really like," Nicky said, tearing open a packet of artificial sweetener and pouring the con-tents into his mug. "Annarita thinks maybe he hasn't been on the up-and-up."

"Yeah, Annarita and the rest of northern California," Matthew brayed, leaning back in his chair to open a lower cabinet and retrieve an ashtray, which had the gold seal of the Hotel Cavour in Milan. "I mean, c'mon, the guy was a rodeo clown. What do you think his chances were of meeting, let alone marrying, the richest woman west of the Rockies? About one in a bazillion? Who would believe he wasn't in it for the money?"

"That's true," I said, "but it doesn't necessarily mean he's a bad guy. I mean, maybe he was a gold digger, but maybe he was also decent to her. Maybe he liked her."

"The way I liked my grandmother, maybe," Matthew said. "I'm sorry, but marrying someone twice your age means one of two things to me.

Either you're on a treasure hunt or you quit therapy too soon."

"Can you help us?" Nicky asked.

"I can try," Matthew said. "It'll be fun, actually. What if he really is a nice guy and everyone is jumping to conclusions like me and we're all wrong? I doubt it, but it'll be fun looking into it."

"How long does something like this take?" I asked, getting to my major concern, which was that we have something to go on before either the family tore the guy apart or he rode his Brahman bull into the sunset with a quarter billion dollars of someone else's money.

"Depends," Matthew said, swigging his soft drink. "Do you know where he's from? Originally I mean, before he moved to California."

"Utah, I think," I said.

"He has a ranch in Texas," Nicky added, "Besides the one he bought with his wife before…."

"You mean the one she bought *for* him," Matthew interjected.

"Now, there you go again," Nicky said, "judging before the evidence is in.

"Objection sustained," Matthew said, banging the salt shaker on the table like a gavel.

"Anyway, I think Utah is the place to start. That's where the paper said his family lives," I offered.

"That shouldn't be difficult then," Matthew said. "I only have trouble before the fifth century. Should be a walk in the park. When do you want it?"

Nicky and I looked at each other and winced. Then we turned to Matthew and said, in unison, "Yesterday."

THIRTY-SIX

MATTHEW said it would take him a couple days to get the lowdown on Iversen. He needed to spend time at the library, on the Internet, and on the phone talking to a network of people he used in his genealogy work.

While he was digging up information on Iversen, Nicky and I set out to see what we could learn about Evelyn. I figured the more we could find out about her and why she would marry someone like Iversen, the better prepared we would be to sort out their relationship after Matthew dug up a profile on Travis.

Nicky thought we should start at the boutique where she worked when she met Ben, which I was sure had nothing to do with anything other than him feeling at home around haute couture. I thought we should start where she might actually have some enemies, or at least where there would be people who had strong opinions and a history with her: the newspaper. This time I won. We made an appointment to meet with Ron Baumhover, publisher of the *Contra Costa Chronicle*.

The newspaper offices were located in the tallest building in Concord, a 22-floor high-rise in the heart of downtown. Another monument to Cyril VanDeventer. A receptionist showed us to a plush lounge area on the 20th floor, where a secretary brought us coffee and croissants while we waited for Baumhover. The room was tasteful and imposing, littered with dark mahogany dining tables, one long one at the front, and several smaller, round ones scattered throughout the room. The chairs were mahogany, high-backed with plush velvet cushions. Three walls were paneled in wood; the fourth was a bank of floor-to-ceiling windows that looked out over Contra Costa County to the east. "Cyril VanDeventer's kingdom," Nicky whispered as we stood at the window, hands clasped behind our backs, taking in the view. "What an ego he must have had to build such an empire."

"Your family built an empire," I reminded.

"I rest my case," Nicky said, smiling, never one to shy from the truth.

I don't know what I was expecting in Ron Baumhover, but he certainly wasn't it. I guess I thought an entourage of lackeys would sweep through the mahogany double doors with Baumhover in the center in a Versace suit, dictating a letter to a blond wanna-be. Instead, a service elevator we hadn't noticed in the back of the room opened suddenly and out stepped a middle-aged, blond man, shirtsleeves rolled up, necktie askew with a half-smoked cigarette dangling from his mouth. He carried five or six sheets of paper stapled together.

He came right toward us and gestured for us to sit at the table where our croissants and coffee had been placed. "Gentlemen, please, sit," he said, smiling affably and looking around the room. "I'm sorry if I kept you waiting. Trying to get tomorrow's edition to bed," he said, looking all about the room, as if in search of something. "Jesus Christ, I wish these people would put some ashtrays up here." He went to the bar across the room and came back with a gimlet glass and crushed his cigarette out in it. "Californians," he said with exasperation. "All closet smokers. You should see them down in the alley. Standing room only, there are so many people out there puffing. But in here, oh no. Politically correct all the time."

He laid the papers on the table, reached into his pocket for a lighter, and lit another cigarette, which he retrieved by digging in his shirt pocket without taking out the pack. "I'm from the Midwest. And a journalist. How do you write without coffee and a cigarette, eh?" He extended his hand, then, to each of us in turn. "Ron Baumhover, publisher. Love and Borja, right?" he said, pronouncing Nicky's name correctly. I knew this was going to go well.

"That's right, Mr. Baumhover," I began.

"Please, please. Call me Ron. It's bad enough I have to wear a suit to work." He laughed jovially, flicking ashes into the glass and pushing the papers aside.

"We're friends of Annarita," I said. "I don't want to make this into something it isn't, but there's been a lot of speculation about what hap-

pened to Mrs….to Annarita's mother, and she's asked us to look into it
for her, see if we come up with anything unusual. You know, just to put
her mind at ease."

"Are you two private investigators?" Ron asked.

"No, not at all," Nicky said. "Annarita and I went to school together.
We're old college chums." Nicky smiled. I looked at him oddly. Chums?
I thought. Where does he come up with these terms?

"How can I help you?" Ron asked.

"We were wondering if you knew either Evelyn or Iversen and what
your thoughts on the matter might be, being a newspaperman and all,"
Nicky said, eyeing the croissants.

Baumhover dragged on his cigarette, giving us another once-over.
"Well, I'll be honest with you then, since this is unofficial and off the
record?" he said, raising his voice at the end of the sentence and pausing, as though he had asked a question.

"Absolutely off the record," I assured him. "In fact, there is no
record." Nicky and I chuckled. Baumhover didn't.

"A lot of people around here didn't like Evelyn very much," Ron said,
dropping his cigarette into the glass. Smoke drifted lazily upward, clinging to the side of the gimlet glass. "A lot of people thought she was a gold
digger, that all she wanted was Cyril's money."

"And you? What do you think?" I asked, taking my first sip of coffee,
trying to sound casual.

"At first I thought so too. I mean, come on, there's Cyril, building an
empire, no woman in his life. He was a sitting duck." Ron laughed and
lit another cigarette. "Every woman in the county was after him. He was
the perennial 'most eligible bachelor' around these parts. Then he met
Evelyn at her job at the Holiday Inn or wherever the hell she came from,
and the next thing we knew it was wedding bells. It's not like she was a
society dame or even a businesswoman. She was a secretary, for Christ's
sake. Of course we thought she was in it for the loot. We were wrong.
That's what makes this such a shame."

"This?" I said.

"This business with Iversen," Ron said, shaking his head and staring
at his cigarette. "She was unhappy in this marriage. Rushed into it before

she knew what she was getting into. Big mistake. She was depressed about it."

"How do you know this?" I asked.

"I sit on the board of directors for Ark of Hope, the battered women's shelter she established a few years ago. About a month ago she gave me a ride home after a Board meeting. My wife had to have the car for a pottery class she's taking at the college because her car was in the shop. Anyway, my wife dropped me off, but I had to bum a ride home with Evelyn."

"And she told you she'd had a change of mind about her marriage?" Nicky asked, finally reaching for a croissant.

"I don't know if I'd go quite that far," Ron said. "But she said this guy wasn't the man she thought he was."

"Did she get more specific than that?" I asked.

"No, she alluded to his temper and him staying out all night with his buddies. She was also having trouble keeping him in town. Ever since she bought that ranch in Scottsdale, evidently, he'd been spending more and more time down there. She wanted him here with her." Ron shook his head again mournfully. "Evelyn was a woman who needed a lot of attention. Cyril gave her that, but it sounded like this guy was straying from the roost. I've heard lots of men use the line about being out with their buddies."

"You mean you think he might have been seeing another woman?" I asked.

"I have no proof of that, but when you put all the pieces together it sure looks that way. Knowing this guy even the little bit that I do, I would say other 'women.' He definitely has a roving eye."

"So you and Evelyn were close, I take it," I observed.

Ron stretched in his chair, crossing his legs at the ankles, lacing his hands behind his head, but somehow keeping hold of the cigarette. A professional smoker, I thought. "Yeah, Evelyn and I got along fine. She was my best friend here, actually."

"How so?" Nicky asked, spreading jam on the croissant. I shot him a "we aren't here to eat" look, which elicited a mere smile of satisfaction from him. He loved annoying me, not to mention embarrassing me at every opportunity.

"She saved my ass here. Really saved it," Ron said, smiling as he remembered something out of his past.

"Can you tell us about it?" I asked.

"Sure. It's no big deal, really, but it meant a lot to me. I came here from New York, where I worked for *The Post*. I don't know if you know anything about New York newspapers, but *The Post* used to be a pretty decent rag. But it also goes for the market, so anything that sells papers makes it in. The more sensationalistic, the better. When I got here I was still that kind of editor and I kept having trouble with the staff and with Cyril. It wasn't anything I could put my hand on at the time. It was primarily stylistic. Reporters here would soft-pedal around issues, or they'd write stories in a vague way, not pursuing the in-depth angles. I thought it was shoddy reporting and kept after the staff about it. They got more and more fed up. One of them went to Cyril behind my back and said the staff was about to revolt.

"Cyril mentioned to Evelyn that he was about to have a talk with me and might have to fire me after only six months on the job and he hated doing that, since I'd moved my family all the way across country.

"Evelyn took me to lunch on the pretense of wanting to talk about some upcoming function the paper was sponsoring. In truth, she wanted to give me a heads-up that Cyril was upset. I confided in her that I just didn't get the 'West Coast' journalism and she explained very clearly that Cyril was an old-fashioned, rural editor. He wouldn't shy away from stories, but he didn't believe in gory pictures or lurid details. And he watched out for friends in the community. A very political animal. She gave me some advice about how to approach certain stories and how to handle Cyril.

"Well, the day he took me to lunch for 'the talk,' a lead hit my desk regarding some embezzlement charges that were about to be laid on the doorstep of one of Cyril's buddies at the chamber of commerce. There had been an ongoing investigation of a couple of businessmen who were conniving to get all the contracting jobs from the city and up to that point, it had been contractors from Sacramento taking the heat. Suddenly, there was evidence that Cyril's friend at the bank was part of the scheme, or at least part of the cover-up. When we went to lunch, I laid it on the table before he could start the conversation about me and the staff. I told him it was coming down and I wanted him to know about it first."

"Wasn't that illegal? I mean, in the ethical sense?" Nicky asked. "Aren't journalists supposed to be objective?"

"Yeah, supposed to be. I don't know any who are," I interjected.

"Well, I had no intention of ignoring the story entirely. That's not what I was suggesting," Ron said, lighting still another cigarette. By now there was a small fog bank hovering around us. "I told him I thought we ought to get his friend's side of the story first, before we went with the obvious scandal angle that all the other papers were going to play up. I knew the guy wasn't going to talk to any reporters on advice of counsel, but if Cyril called and told him we wanted to give him an opportunity to present his side to the public, I thought he'd probably be willing and we'd get an exclusive. If the guy got a 'heads-up' warning in the process, well, I couldn't help that." Ron smiled slyly.

"The politics of compromise," I said.

"The politics of negotiation," Ron said back. "It worked. He loved it and loved me for bringing it to him. From that day on, we were tight. When he bought the other papers and set up the corporation for himself, he promoted me to publisher here."

"And the talk about being too liberal, too sensational?" I asked.

"Somehow he never got around to it," Ron said.

"And you attribute that to Evelyn?" Nicky asked.

"Absolutely," Ron replied. "And it wasn't the last time she helped me out that way. She gave me lots of tips on how to handle her husband. She'd even call once in a while to say he was hopping mad about something and was on his way over. Evelyn was good to her friends. Actually, come to think of it, she was good to everyone. She was just a good person. A bit flamboyant. She might have been a bit gaudy when it came to aesthetics, but she knew how to be a friend. I'm going to miss her."

THIRTY-SEVEN

NICKY had planned the next stop. I figured since he gave in to me about the newspaper, I'd go with him to the boutique. He surprised me, though. He had made an appointment with Benito Capra, Evelyn's plastic surgeon. We parked at the Stockton-Sutter garage and walked to the doctor's office on Post Street. While we waited in the office, I read *Vanity Fair* and Nicky studied the office binder on face-lifts.

"Look what we could have done," he said, showing me a before and after page. "Isn't it fabulous?"

"She'd look OK in the first photo if she had the same hair and make-up she has in the second," I pointed out. "And in the first one she's wearing a surgical gown and in the second one she's wearing a turtleneck sweater that hides her flabby neck."

"You're no fun," Nicky pouted and snapped the binder closed.

The receptionist ushered us into the doctor's office where we were greeted by a man about Nicky's age. He was mildly handsome in a nondescript way with curly brown hair and a fleshy face. He was one of those men you know is gay, even though you could never point to any specifically revealing characteristic.

"Gentlemen, what can I do for you? My receptionist said you wanted a consultation."

"I'm a friend of Annarita's," Nicky said.

The doctor looked blank.

"Evelyn VanDeventer's daughter."

"Yes, of course," he said. "I only know her as Annie O'Brien. Sorry. As a matter of fact, she called and said you might be paying me a visit. She wanted me to know it was all on the up-and-up." He had a strained smile on his face that suggested Annarita had either threatened or cajoled him to get his cooperation. "Exactly what is it you want from me?"

"We're just talking with people close to Evelyn, trying to get the whole picture of what was going on at the time of her death," I said.

"You mean, domestically, I assume," he said, warming a bit at the semigossipy nature of our inquiry.

"Yes, that for one," I answered. "But anything at all that you can tell us would help in our research."

"That's what Annie said on the phone when she called. God, that was horrible, wasn't it?" the doctor said, picking up a thin bamboo letter opener that said "Pfizer" on it and twirling it around in his hand. "Are they going to lock him up?"

"Lock whom up?" I asked before Nicky could say anything.

"That cowboy. Who else?" the doctor shot back. "He's like an un-neutered dog. I can't believe she married him. Sleeping with a hunk is one thing, but marrying it is something else entirely," he said, rolling his eyes and arching his eyebrows. "Believe me, I know."

"What makes you think he did it?" I asked.

"Well, isn't it obvious? Money. What other reason does a gorgeous man have for marrying someone twice his age? They were hardly compatible. He couldn't even tie a Windsor knot. Except for those ridiculous string ties he wears with the big silver and turquoise slabs in the middle, she had to tie his ties for him. Hideous! Poor Evelyn," he pined. "I feel awful. And she was looking so good, too. We were just about to do her last implant, as soon as she came back from Italy."

"So I take it you didn't care for Mr. Iversen," Nicky said.

"No, I did not care for Mr. Iversen," the doctor replied slowly and with malice.

"Have you spent much time with him?" I asked.

"Not much," he said. He was bending the letter opener now and I thought it might break. "A party or two. Completely self-absorbed, and hormones out of control. He'd flirt right in front of her. Broke her heart."

"But he was never abusive to her," I said. "I mean physically."

The doctor looked back and forth at us, his eyes filled with hatred.

Nicky broke the silence. "Dr. Capra, I know that Evelyn was very fond of you and you of her. I also know she was rather obsessed with her looks and with growing old. It would seem only normal for a man like Travis to be attracted to young women, especially when his own wife is a bit...over the hill. Don't you think?"

The doctor glared at Nicky.

"Is there anything you can tell us to steer us in the right direction, Dr. Capra?" I asked, knowing how much doctors love being called "Dr." "Anything at all?"

He squirmed a bit and was obviously itching to talk.

"I can't say anything about it. Doctor-patient privilege," he said.

"Fine," I said, standing up. "So long as there's no evidence that he was abusive to her, I guess he's a free man."

Nicky remained seated and leaned toward the desk. "A free man with Evelyn's money and lots of pretty girls around," he said. "Come on Capra, you know something that could shed some new light on this, don't you?"

"I can't say anything as her doctor," he said.

"But she was your friend, as well," Nicky pleaded. Now she's dead and the murderer, if he is a murderer, may get away with it. Did he ever hit her that you know of? Did you ever see bruises?"

"No, never," the doctor said, derisively. "Nothing so kind."

I sat down again.

"There are many ways to be abusive without hitting someone," he said.

"But 'physically abusive' is the operative phrase here," I said. "It has to be physical or there's no evidence that he ever did anything on his part to harm her person."

"There are many ways to be physically abusive without hitting someone," he said.

Nicky and I looked at each other and sighed in exasperation. I reached over and took a pen and a notepad that were lying on his desk. I wrote my phone number down and said, "If you can be of any help, please call us." Then I stood again. The doctor stood, went to a filing cabinet, and retrieved a thick patient file. He put it on his desk, opened it, then placed two blank sheets of white paper over one side of it, laying them horizontally, so that only two lines of writing con-

tained inside the file were showing. Then he walked around his desk
and went to the door.

"I have another patient waiting for me. You'll have to excuse me.
Sorry I couldn't be of much help," he said. Then he left the office, closing the door behind him.

Nicky and I looked at each other for a split second, then tore around
the desk. The patient file was Evelyn's, of course. The name
VANDEVENTER appeared on the folder flap in bold green letters. Capra
had placed the sheets of paper so the only thing we could read was a
notation he had made two months prior to our visit. Nicky and I gasped
audibly as we read it. In barely legible handwriting the notation read,
"INTRA-MUSCULAR INJECTION. ROCETHIN/250 MG. GONORRHEA."

THIRTY-EIGHT

THE FUNERAL was to be held at The Cyril and Evelyn VanDeventer Center for the Arts in Concord that Sunday. Annarita asked us to attend.

It was a media madhouse. Television and radio news crews and newspaper photographers swarmed outside the pavilion where the service was being held. A large crowd of passersby gathered, attracted by the media vans and the dozens of limousines pulling up to the main entrance. There were even network and CNN people, because the governor was scheduled to attend.

Nicky and I had been picked up by a limousine Nicky ordered. We stopped for breakfast in Walnut Creek before proceeding to Concord. We arrived about 45 minutes early and sat in the limo waiting for the doors of the Center to open. Many others had also arrived early and were gathering on the front steps.

There weren't any people I knew, but Nicky seemed to recognize almost everyone who pulled up: restaurant owners, television personalities, CEOs of banks and corporations.

"How do you know these people?" I asked.

"I read the papers, I eat out once in a while, and I shop," he said. "It's not a feat."

"I'd never even heard of Evelyn VanDeventer before we met her in Florence," I said. "I can't believe all these people actually knew her."

"Well, Angel Burp, think about it for a minute," Nicky said, employing another of his dozens of impromptu endearments. "If you were opening a restaurant, who would you invite for a free meal, a sheet metal worker off the street or the wealthiest woman in northern California?"

"Well, I suppose—"

"If you were the head of a bank looking for depositors or a corporation development director trying to find investors, who would you be calling on, the woman who takes your shirts at the laundry, or—"

"OK, OK," I said. "I just didn't know this woman was so powerful. Until the story in the paper about her selling the newspaper chain for half a billion dollars, I don't think anyone beyond the East Bay knew her. I barely paid attention then if you want to know the truth."

"You'd be amazed at how much money is out there that you know nothing about," Nicky said, taking my hand and kissing it. "See that couple getting out of the Mercedes. The silver one?"

"Yes."

"Do you know who that is?"

"No," I said. "Do you?"

"Not the point, Muffin Crumbs. Do you recognize the name Porcelli?"

"No, not especially. Unless you mean that old porn actor," I teased.

"I don't think so," Nicky said sarcastically.

"Tires!" I shouted, causing Nicky to jump. "Porcelli tires. He owns the tire company."

"Good grief!" Nicky said, shaking his head as though I were hopeless. "That's Pirelli, not Porcelli." Nicky leaned forward and slid open the glass divider separating us from the driver. "Excuse me, but do you have a lighter on you? I noticed you smoking earlier and I was wondering if you have a lighter I could borrow for just a minute?"

"Certainly, sir," the driver said. He reached into the glove box and retrieved a blue disposable lighter, the kind you buy at the drug store for a dollar, and passed it to Nicky.

"Don't tell me you're going to smoke in here?"

"Just a cigar," Nicky said, reaching into his coat pocket, then bonking me on the head with the palm of his hand. "No, I'm not going to smoke. See this?" he asked, handing me the lighter.

"Yeah," I said.

"Turn it over and read what's on the bottom," he said.

I turned the lighter over and read, "AMP, Inc."

"You know what that stands for?" Nicky asked smugly.

"No, professor, I don't, but I'm sure you do."

"Of course I do. It stands for 'Angelo and Maria Porcelli, Incorporated.' He makes half of all the disposable lighters sold in this country. At 99 cents times about 500,000 per day divided by two to estimate the wholesale price, I'd say he was doing pretty well."

"Jeez," I said, looking at the couple walking up the steps. They had stopped to talk with an elderly man in a pin-striped suit.

"And you'd never heard of him," Nicky said. "Most of the wealthy people in this country are people whose names you wouldn't recognize. They like it that way."

"Never thought of it like that," I admitted.

Nicky smiled and kissed my hand again. "See? I can teach you something too."

"Paper bags," I said, watching the couple make their way into the pavilion.

"Excuse me?" Nicky said.

"Paper bags," I repeated, realizing I was catching Nicky's penchant for non sequiturs. I was thinking of all the things we take for granted that someone gets rich on: price tags for hardware, ballpoint pens, rubber bands, paper bags. I had said the last one out loud. Good, I thought. He needs to know how frustrating it is to try to follow his train of thought sometimes.

"Exactly," he said. "Paper bags."

I should have known better than to think he wouldn't track my thinking.

THIRTY-NINE

BY THE time the service started, about 500 people had crowded into the pavilion. The auditorium used for the service was the main theater of the center, located on the first floor, where concerts and theatrical productions were usually staged. At the center of the stage was Evelyn's open white casket, covered with a blanket of orchids that trailed to the floor on three sides. Behind the casket was a podium with a microphone.

It struck me as a theatrical setup where the speaker could look down upon the corpse of the deceased while the gathering of people looked up at the speaker for inspiration. Travis and Annarita sat in the front row with a middle-aged woman we assumed to be her older sister and the rest of her family. Vaughn sat next to Annarita. The service had been put together by Annarita's older sister, Virginia, and her younger brother, Vaughn, whom Annarita had introduced just as we were going in. She had not introduced Evelyn's pastor, Reverend Phil Simmley. He introduced himself. He probably smelled Nicky's money. Simmley, a little man of about 35, looked like he'd had Evelyn's plastic surgeon rebuild his mouth into a condescending smile. But try as he might to put on a happy face, he couldn't.

Nicky pointed it out when Simmley first started speaking about Evelyn. The minister was listing her charitable contributions and telling a story about how she came to build the battered women's shelter in Walnut Creek. Nicky leaned and whispered in my ear, "*Yes, yes* on his lips, but *no, no* in his eyes. There's a darkness in there that's much bigger than the smile."

"But I don't have to tell anyone here today about Evelyn's philanthropy, her generosity, her enormous goodness," Simmley said, outstretching his arms to figuratively embrace the entire gathering. "I'm sure each one of you could tell your own story about how Evelyn touched your life. And that's what we thought we would do here today. Evelyn's children and a handful of her most intimate friends will say a few words, then we will have a closing hymn, one of Evelyn's favorites. Afterwards the family invites everyone to attend a reception at the VanDeventer estate. Cards with directions will be handed out as you leave. Persons needing transportation will find vans out front to transport you to the house and then home afterward."

The first to speak were a few friends, none of whose names I recognized. They consisted of two women and a man, all of whom told stories of how they first met Evelyn and how she touched their lives. Nicky and I didn't pay much attention. We were distracted by the nearly constant whispering between Vaughn and Virginia, who kept leaning back and forth in front of Annarita to talk. Virginia was all in black, including a wide-brimmed black hat with a black silk sash that fluttered back and forth as she and Vaughn kept whispering to each other.

"They're fighting over who's going on first," I quipped to Nicky.

"I think you're close," he whispered. "My guess is they're arguing because one of them doesn't want the other to speak at all. Sibling stuff. Very familiar territory."

Next came the governor, a short, desperately blond politician hoping to run for president. He was a notoriously bad speaker. Not that he wasn't dramatic, but he almost always put his foot in his mouth. Friends from my days in Washington used to say he gave new meaning to the term "damage control."

He spoke of how he and Evelyn met at a political fund-raiser hosted by Evelyn and her late husband. "But my most memorable conversation with Evelyn was one day when she called me after reading something unflattering a columnist had written about how bad I looked during one of my speeches," he said jovially. "It was so like Evelyn to call me about something personal, rather than political. She said, 'Governor, don't pay that person any mind at all. Your backside is better looking than his face on a good day.' That lifted my spirits. I felt even better about a week later when I shared her remark with the columnist."

There was general chuckling as the governor stepped down, paid his respects to the children first, then to Travis, and then left down the center aisle under heavy security. As he passed where we were sitting on the aisle, he caught my eye, came near and gave me a small punch on the shoulder and a wink. Nicky gave me a bug-eyed look. When people had turned their attention back to the service, I leaned over to Nicky. "I know him from my days in Washington. Barely."

"Don't ever tease me about my social life again," Nicky stated flatly. "At least I have the good taste not to fraternize with politicians."

Reverend Simmley took the podium again.

"My, my. I guess that says it all, doesn't it? Imagine, having the governor take time out of his busy schedule to come say a few words at your funeral. What an honor. You really have arrived, Evelyn." Simmley said, beaming down into the casket in front of him. "Yes, ma'am, we're sending you home in style."

Nicky turned to me and crossed his eyes, as though he might start tearing his hair and running down the aisle at any second. "Can you imagine Nonna at this service?" he whispered.

"I can't imagine Nonna in Concord."

Annarita was next, forgoing words of her own, reading instead a letter her mother had sent her while she was in college. It ended in a very touching way:

"So, my darling daughter, study hard and do your best, so that someday you may be the master of your own destiny. And regardless of anything that may come between us, for mothers and daughters can sometimes quarrel, remember this when you think of me: I tried to give you what I never had. I tried to give you the ability to earn your own way, so that you will never be hungry and your children will never be hungry. So that you and yours may always have a roof over your heads, bread on the table and, God willing, a man who comes home to you each night. If I can give you this, I will die a happy woman." Annarita folded the letter, put it back in its envelope and took her seat.

Vaughn took her place at the podium. He too had a letter. He took it from his breast pocket and laid it in front of him. "It's funny how both my younger sister and I have chosen to let mother speak for herself today. As most of you know, she was a woman of strong opinions. She was powerful in her own right, but she needed, by her own admission, a man's love to feel complete. She had that twice in her life that I know of. Once with Cyril VanDeventer, and again, more recently, with Travis Iversen."

There was a rustling among the people gathered, as though everyone just at that moment realized he had sat on a pebble, and had to wiggle a bit to reach down and remove it. There were even a couple of coughs. Nicky gave me a glance, but it was expressionless.

"There has been a lot of innuendo in the media over the past few days about my mother's new husband. Innuendos that, quite frankly, the family finds disturbing. I want to take this opportunity to say that we are all 100% in support of Travis Iversen. He was good to our mother. He loved our mother and he has suffered a terrible loss. What's more, our mother loved him. I want to read you part of a letter she sent me shortly after they were married: 'Son, I truly believe that this man was sent to me by God. He is everything I have ever wanted in a man, and he is exactly what I have been praying for. He's even a cowboy, as silly as that may sound. Almost no one knows or remembers that I grew up in Texas. He's thoughtful and sweet, but a bit rough. I don't think people see him for who he really is, but I do. And I love him with all my heart. I hope you won't be angry with me. I hope you and the girls will be as happy for me as I am. He makes me feel like a real woman, like some-one who still has something to offer a man. I never thought I would fall in love again, but now it has happened. It is more than I ever believed possible: two great loves in one lifetime. I will die a happy woman.'

"And so my mother did die a happy woman," Vaughn concluded. "She was as happy as any of us can remember ever seeing her. We are all in a state of shock and grief, and no one is more shocked or more grieved than Travis Iversen. My sisters and I want to take this opportunity, as we say good-bye to our beloved mother, to say to Travis, we grieve for you as well. You have lost your life's companion. But as we say good-bye to mother, we say hello to you. To you, Travis, we say, welcome. Welcome to our family."

Nicky pursed his lips and arched his eyebrows. There was general dis-comfort throughout the assembly, a palpable tension. As the Reverend Simmley told us to rise for the hymn, Nicky said, a bit loudly, "So, he came to bury Caesar *and* praise Brutus. That ought to shut everyone up. For a while."

FORTY

PALLBEARERS carried the white casket down the center aisle while a choir in the balcony sang "Amazing Grace." The family followed the casket outside. By the time we got outdoors, the rear of the hearse was being closed, and as the family made their way to the limousines that would take them to the cemetery, the television camera crews had descended. There was a minor scuffle as county sheriff's deputies tried to maintain order among the media, but Vaughn raised his hand in the air and indicated he would make a statement or take a couple questions. Annarita stood next to him looking like a frightened rabbit. Travis quickly slipped into the back of the car and waited in the dark safety of the limousine. Virginia, holding on to her hat with one hand and looking like she just swallowed a cup of vinegar, climbed in with her husband and closed the door.

"Mr. VanDeventer," a woman with a microphone that had a big 2 attached to it shouted, "Why did you think it was necessary to make a statement at your mother's funeral regarding her husband's innocence?"

"I think you're reading into my remarks. Innocence? That implies guilt, which implies there was a crime committed. The media need to go cover some real news," Vaughn said, smirking a bit.

Another reporter, a man also holding a microphone, took the woman's lead. "But, Mr. VanDeventer, you're the one who brought it up. Why did you do that?"

"Look," Vaughn said, completely composed, "my point was simple. Even for those with an eighth-grade education. We are all in shock and mourning. The things the media have been doing to slander my mother's husband also slander the rest of us. We want it to stop so we can mourn our mother and get on with our lives. We want you to leave us alone." And with that he turned, took Annarita by the arm, and herded her quickly into the limousine, ignoring the rest of the questions being shouted all at once by the gathered reporters.

The hearse and the family cars, six black limousines, made their way to the cemetery for a private interment in the family mausoleum.

Nicky and I drove in an unexpected silence toward the estate, knowing we would be early for the reception if we went there straight away. Suddenly Nicky leaned forward and gave the driver directions to a nearby park, where he stopped the car beneath a huge liquidambar tree. Nicky opened the door and got out. I followed, curious, and content not to be in the crowd I knew would be gathering at Annarita's.

'Let's just walk for a while," Nicky said softly. "Do you mind?" Nicky took my arm, completely unself-consciously, but I was only too aware of being in a part of the Bay Area known for its antigay politicians.

"Not at all," I replied. "I think it's a perfect idea."

The park was lovely: a broad expanse of lawn and oak, cottonwood and maple trees with a few pepper trees and palms scattered about. A walkway meandered through the trees and past carefully tended flowerbeds, a pond, and eventually a small lake with paddleboats. We sat on a green wooden bench and watched a flock of mallards swimming about, trying to avoid a cranky swan.

"Tell me something about Lyle," Nicky said. He didn't look at me, but kept his gaze on the ducks. "Just a little something."

"Well, let's see. He was a lot like you in many ways," I said.

"How like me?"

I sighed, feeling the corpse of memory floating to the surface. "He was very, very bright, a genius perhaps. He was clever and witty and was quick on his feet, like you. And he loved to blow things up," I said with a chuckle.

"Blow things up?" Nicky repeated as a question.

"Just like you."

"Give me an example of how I like to blow things up." He continued to watch the ducks, which were now diving for whatever they ate that lived beneath the surface of the lake.

"Well, like this," I said, and lifted our still entwined arms.

Nicky laughed. "Oh. That's good. I like that, 'blow things up.' That's clever," he said softly. "How old was he, Nigel? When he died, I mean."

I felt a slight pressure in my throat, as though someone had begun to squeeze my neck. "Thirty-one," I said.

"About my age," Nicky said, now turning his head to look at me.

"Yes, he was very young."

"Was he brave?" Nicky asked. "About his dying?"

"Remarkably brave. Remarkably thoughtful, too. But there was sadness," I said. "I remember one day in particular, when we were working at our computers together. He swiveled around suddenly and blurted out, 'Is this all I get? Is this really it? Thirty years is all I get?' I looked at him and was speechless. We just stared at each other for a minute or so and then he swiveled back to his computer screen and said, 'Guess so. Doesn't seem like much, though. Thirty.' And once in a while, out of the blue, he would say, 'thirty' just like that. Just the one word. I think he was trying to comprehend it. It made me terribly sad, though."

"Nigel, I want to be brave, but I don't think I will be. I think I'll fall apart," Nicky said, watching the ducks, as the swan swam toward them.

"You, not brave?" I said, incredulous. "I doubt it. I'm sure you'll be remarkable."

"I'm not so sure. I think all my understanding of these spiritual matters is mostly understanding, not experience. You haven't seen me when I'm sick. You don't know how horrible I can be."

"No, I haven't seen you sick," I said. "But I do know how horrible you can be."

He turned his head toward me, but there was no expression on his face. "That's why I love you," he said, looking straight into my eyes.

"Why?"

"Because you see the horrible parts of me and you still love me. Nothing frightens you. You face the world and take what comes. Secretly I'm afraid of everything," he said.

"First off, I don't find anything about you horrible. Second, there are plenty of things that frighten me. Don't let my act fool you. And third, I'm more extroverted than you might think. I've been very different the past few years, since Lyle's death. I've turned inward more. I used to be very outgoing, but I'm changing. Part of it, I'm sure, has to do with growing older. My whole way of looking at life has altered since everyone close to me has died. I've slowed down a little and become more thoughtful. But it's painful."

"I know," Nicky said, leaning forward, his elbows on his knees. The swan glided through the dispersing mallards but didn't peck at any of them. Her mere presence was enough to send them in all directions. "I see how it hurts you. I have that same pain, but I've done the opposite. After being introverted most of my life, I got a bit wild after Rosario's death. I became more like him, I guess. I take more chances because I now know with certainty how uncertain life is. We're a good match that way. You know, opposites attract and all that. We complement each other." He turned to look at me again, but didn't sit back.

"I love you, Nicky Borja," I said matter-of-factly. "I tried not to, but it was bigger than both of us. I don't know what to do with it yet, but I love you big."

"We're going to be married, aren't we?" Nicky asked. He seemed almost shy, almost embarrassed.

"Yes," I replied.

"Soon, huh?" he said, his smile growing.

"Yeah, probably sooner than even we realize," I said, beginning to smile myself. I was glad we were talking about this.

"There's nothing like death to make a person want to live," Nicky said, leaning back and taking my arm again. "I want to live now. I want to live with you and for you."

"What brought all this on?" I asked. "Why today, why now? The funeral? Is that what it is?"

"Oh, I suppose that's the catalyst," Nicky said. "I looked at that ridiculous white casket and thought, someday I'll be as dead as she is. I don't want to die alone, Nigel."

"Neither do I," I responded. "It's my greatest fear."

"But more than that," Nicky said, squeezing my arm and looking at me with an expression more serious than I had seen him wear before. "More than that, though, I want to be with you when I die. I want to die in your arms. Or, if not in your arms, at least I want to be married to you when I die."

We were both silent for a moment.

"Do you understand what I'm saying? Do you know what I mean?" he asked.

"I think so," I said, choking back tears. "I mean yes. Of course I know what you mean."

Just then the swan went after a couple of mallards that were diving for food near the shore close to us. She chased them until they had to hop up onto the path near our feet. They scurried across the pathway and onto the lawn, where they shook themselves and cocked their heads to see if the swan was following.

"Like that," Nicky said. "Just like that. Together when the white swan comes. We'll be together no matter what."

"Do you have any idea how much I love you?" I asked, trying to comprehend it myself. "Do you?"

Nicky actually blushed and scrunched up against me. "I think I do," he said softly. "I actually think I do."

"How much?" I asked.

"A hundred and forty-four skyzillion tons?"

"Yeah, that sounds about right," I said. Then, quite unlike anything I had ever done before, I kissed him. Right there in the park in the middle of Concord, I simply leaned over and kissed him on the lips. "See what you do to me?" I said. "You make me want to blow things up."

Nicky laughed out loud. "Hey, dude," he said in an exaggerated valley girl accent. "Wanna like go blow up a big, like, party I know about?"

"Groovy," I said.

"Groovy?" Nicky said, mocking me. "Groovy?"

"I mean, I'm down with that," I said, adopting a scholarly tone. "Quite down with that."

"Beginnings and endings," Nicky said, sighing. "It seems always to come down to that. Beginnings and endings."

"This time it's a bit of both," I observed.

We stood and traced our path back to the waiting car and driver. "I'm going to concentrate on the beginning part, myself," Nicky said. "It feels good and right. When it's time for the ending, we'll be together for that, too. Together in the beginning, together at the end. You and me and the white swan."

"Could be worse," I said tenderly.

"Yes," Nicky said. "It could be a white casket."

FORTY-ONE

BY THE TIME we got to Annarita's everyone who had been at the funeral had arrived and the family was just getting back from the cemetery. In fact, we pulled up just as Annarita and her brother and sister were getting out of the limousine. A heated conversation was going on between Virginia and Vaughn as they walked up the front steps. The two of them paused on the landing, shaking their fingers at one another. Annarita, who was attempting to calm them down, spotted Nicky and me and came down the steps to join us on the front drive.

"Boy, am I glad to see you," she said. "Anyone got a cigarette?"

Nicky pulled a silver cigarette case and an engraved lighter from his jacket and lit Annarita's cigarette. I watched this tobacco ritual like an animal behaviorist observing the odd carryings-on of a lost tribe on some distant continent. I didn't get this "cigarette thing," although I had to admit there was something cinematic about the way Nicky would light one, then draw the smoke in deeply and blow it out. Very Bogart. Very Steve McQueen. And sometimes very Bette Davis.

"What are they fighting about?" Nicky asked.

"Pick a topic," Annarita said, rolling her eyes and shifting back and forth from foot to foot. "First the service, then the casket, then the governor being there. Now they're fighting about Vaughn's remarks to the media."

"Have they been going at it like this for long?" I asked, watching the two of them, still raging in each other's face beside the front door.

"Oh, only about 20 years," Annarita said. "I'm so tired of it. I thought mother's death would bring us closer together. I should have known better." Annarita turned to look at them, then turned back to us nearly in tears. "Can we take a walk?" she asked.

We wandered across the lawn toward the back of the house, but the grounds were littered with guests, so we strolled down the narrow, tree-lined lane on which the house was situated. It was a warm June afternoon and the sun dappled through the trees. Expensive cars lined both sides of the narrow street—reception guests, I imagined.

"I want you to know we are proceeding," Nicky said, putting his arm around Annarita's shoulder. "We should know something in just a few days. Think you can hold up that long?"

"Yes, of course. I really appreciate what you're doing to help," she said, looking at me, then at Nicky. "I have no one I can turn to right now. At least no one I can trust."

"Tell me something, Annarita," I began slowly. "What is your primary concern about Travis? Is there anything you're afraid of in his regard?"

"No, it's not fear so much as just not knowing," she said, tossing her cigarette onto the street and crushing it with one of her tasteful but sensible black shoes. She wore a black silk crepe pantsuit and a white blouse. A simple gold cross hung around her neck. "I'm not afraid of him. Just suspicious, I guess."

"Do you have any concrete evidence that he's done anything underhanded?" I asked. "I'm not talking about the speculation on the drowning, now. I mean in any other aspect of his life, say his relationship with your mother while they were dating, or even during their marriage, short as it was."

"I'm not sure I follow," Annarita said.

"Well, do you think he stole money from her?" I asked.

"No, he wouldn't do that. He didn't have to. She paid for everything and gave him huge amounts of cash. She always did that. With everyone." Annarita stopped walking, raised her arms in a hopeless shrug, and said, "Her last boyfriend she gave a quarter of a million dollars!"

Nicky and I looked at each other with amazement. "She what?" Nicky gasped.

"She gave the guy $250,000," Annarita said, very slowly. Then added, even more slowly for emphasis, "And he took it."

"Detes," Nicky said, taking her by the elbow.

I looked at him quizzically, scrunching my face. "Detes?"

"Details," he explained.

Annarita filled us in as we walked. "Mother was dating this guy from the fire department. Some deputy fire inspector or something. He was always extremely self-conscious about the discrepancy in their finances, so about three months into their dating she drove over to his house and presented him with a check. Actually, now that I think about it, it was more than that. It was $300,000" she said, raising her voice in exasperation. "I remember, because Vaughn found the check register and went through the roof. It's the only time in the last ten years that he and Virge have agreed on anything. They sat mother down and read her the riot act. Virge tried to stop payment on the check, but he had already cashed it. He broke up with mother a month later and a month after that was engaged to some young beauty contestant. Mother was crushed, Vaughn was furious and Virge blamed Vaughn for the whole thing." Annarita laughed. "That's our family in a nutshell. Mother does something foolish, Vaughn gets mad, and Virge blames Vaughn. I mean 'did' something foolish. I keep talking about her in the present tense, like she's still alive."

"Why would your sister blame your brother? Does he watch over your mother's finances?" I inquired.

Annarita let out a little squeal of laughter. "That's a good one. Just the opposite. It's Virge who watches the money. Like a hawk. It's really backwards that way in our family, come to think of it. It's as though mother was the wild daughter and Virge was the mother. Mother was always giving money away and Virge was always trying to get it back or trying to limit mother's access to the money, especially after Cyril died."

"And Vaughn?" I asked. "How does he fit into the picture?"

"He's the prodigal son," Annarita said. "Got another cigarette, Nicky? I hope I'm not starting to smoke again."

Nicky lit one and handed it to her. "I'll keep track," he said. "Number two. You can have two more today, then you have to switch to chewing tobacco."

Annarita slapped his arm in a playful gesture. "By the way," she said, "did you see Dr. Capra?"

"Yes," Nicky said. "It was helpful, but nothing we can run with."

"What did he tell you?" she asked.

I didn't want to go into that with her, for a variety of reasons. "I want to go back to something you said a minute ago. It might be important," I said, distracting her from the topic of Dr. Capra. "How is Vaughn the prodigal son? When did he leave home? When did he return?"

"Vaughn left early on. In some ways he was never even here. We girls got all the attention, I'm afraid, especially from Cyril. The only man who ever paid any attention to Vaughn was Ben." Annarita looked at both of us in turn. "You two know him, right? Isn't he your grandmother's friend?"

"Yes. In fact, he's her husband now," Nicky said, smiling.

"That's sweet," Annarita said. "Imagine finding love at that age. What must the odds be against that?"

Nicky and I exchanged a smile. I wondered if he was thinking about Nonna, about Annarita's chances at another marriage, or about the two of us finding one another.

"Anyway," Annarita continued, "Vaughn was the rebel. He never did anything anyone else did, and after he came out things just got worse."

Nicky and I each took one of Annarita's arms at the same time and halted where we were. Then, like Abbott and Costello in a bad comedy, we said in unison, "When he came out?"

"Yeah, don't tell me you didn't know," she half laughed. "Please! Look at those clothes. Get a load of that hair. He goes to the hairdresser more often than Mother does. Did, I mean. You should see his apartment; it looks like something out of *Architectural Digest.* I thought everyone knew just by looking at him."

"Not I," Nicky said.

"I didn't either," I added.

"Hmmm. Well, he is," Annarita said matter-of-factly as we began walking again, this time back in the direction we had come. "I don't think mother minded, really. At least she wouldn't have if Cyril hadn't made such a fuss. He was *such* a homophobe. Although even he calmed down as he got older. Of course by that time Vaughn was long gone. They weren't crazy about each other to begin with. All that father-son stuff, I guess. But when Vaughn came out, and the *way* he came out…"

"The way he came out?" Nicky asked.

"It was horrible," Annarita said, putting her hand to her forehead. "Everyone was *so* humiliated. Especially Vaughn. He's actually quite shy, at least he was when he was growing up. Kind of typical, I guess. Typical gay kid, I mean. He read a lot, didn't like sports, kept to himself. I was his closest friend and even I didn't know until it happened."

"Until what happened?" I asked.

Annarita lowered her head and looked at the ground.

"Come on," Nicky said, "stop teasing us. Spill it."

Annarita blushed. "It's embarrassing," she said. "I can't."

"You'd better, or else," Nicky threatened.

"Or else what?" Annarita shot back.

"Or else I'll tell the nightgown story." Nicky said with exaggerated menace in his voice.

"Oh, God, not the nightgown story." Annarita laughed. "I forgot all about it."

"Well, I haven't, so talk."

"We were all going to Puerto Rico for Memorial Day weekend. Everyone except Vaughn, that is, because he had a term paper he had put off and the teacher had given him an extension, but he had to hand it in over the vacation or he'd fail the class, and if that happened he wouldn't graduate from high school. I can't believe I didn't tell you this," Annarita said to Nicky.

"We didn't meet until our Junior year. I transferred in, remember? In fact, we met on my very first time at the school, because you were doing some intern thing in the registrar's office the day I arrived," Nicky said.

"Oh, that's right. This happened the summer before," Annarita said. "I guess I wouldn't have told you anyway. I didn't tell anyone."

"Go on, please. Now you've got me really curious," I said.

"OK, so we're going to San Juan and we're flying in the family plane. Well, the corporate plane, really, but same thing. We all go to the airport and Vaughn stays home. It's about two in the afternoon. When we get to the airport the mechanic is working on something and says it'll take at least another hour, so we go to the lounge and have coffee. Then they tell us it's going to take another hour, so we go have a sandwich. Then it's going to take until six o'clock, so Cyril decides we should try a commercial flight, but the commercial flights are booked, even in first class, which is the only way he'll fly. So he and mother decide that we'll wait and go the next day, when the mechanic assures us the plane will be ready.

"By this time it's around 7 o'clock. So we pile in a cab because the car and driver have gone away after letting us off. We arrive home and let ourselves in and mother says we should just put all our suitcases in the California Room so that the next morning we can head straight out the door after we get dressed. So we all go into the California Room to put down our suitcases. Now it's late May and daylight savings has started, so it's bright outside. As we set down our suitcases, I hear a gasp from Virginia, then a little cry from mother. I look at them and they're staring out the window toward the pool. Cyril is putting on his glasses to see what everyone's looking at."

At this point in the story Annarita put her face in her hands and said, "I can't, I can't."

"Annarita," Nicky said. "Nightgown."

"All right, all right. Well, I look out the window and there's Vaughn. Naked on the diving board. Sort of."

"Sort of?" I asked.

"Well, he was kind of lying sideways across the board on his back. His legs were up in the air and…" She paused a long time.

"And?" Nicky pressed.

"And he was, well, he was…"

"OK, I'll help," Nicky said. "He was getting fucked, right?"

Annarita nodded. "But there was a second guy on the other side."

"Let's see, he was sucking the other guy's dick while he was getting fucked. Right?" Nicky said.

"Yes," Annarita said, but she was in no way relieved.

"I hate to tell you this, canary lips, but that sort of thing happens all the time," Nicky said.

"Not with Cyril's two business partners, it doesn't," Annarita said.

Nicky and I gasped.

"Yes, Cyril's business partners. The only two he had at the time. They were the men he bought the newspaper with. They were lovers, almost

Cyril's age, and he didn't know it. He was mortified."

"Oh, God," Nicky said. "What did he do?"

"He ran out and turned the hose on them," Annarita said.

There was a moment of stunned silence as the three of us looked at one another, then we burst into uncontrollable laughter at the image. By the time we stopped laughing, we were back at the house. "How did they conduct business after that?" I asked.

"Cyril bought them out the next day and told them if they didn't leave town, he would call the police and have them arrested for statutory rape or something. It worked. They moved to Hawaii," Annarita said.

"And Vaughn?" I asked, thinking of how traumatic it must have been for him.

"He was devastated," she said. "He and Cyril had screaming matches for the next two weeks and then finally Vaughn disappeared in the middle of the night. We didn't hear from him again for over a year. Mother had a private investigator track him down and found out he was living in San Francisco with some guy."

"And this rift between Vaughn and Cyril never healed?" I asked.

"Not really. They could be in the same room for short periods, but only if there was some social function going on and they didn't have to speak to each other directly. After Cyril died, Vaughn started coming around a little more. Then about the time mother met Travis, Vaughn took over the Foundation for mother. That's when he and Virge really started going at it full tilt."

"Why was that?" I asked. "Was it about him being gay?"

"No, I don't think so," Annarita said as we headed across the front lawn toward the porch. "Although she threw that up to him all the time, how he was an embarrassment to the family and how he should tone it down. But it was really about money. Virge is obsessed with money."

"Why?" Nicky asked.

"I don't know exactly. I think because she's the oldest she remembers what it was like when we were poor. She was in high school when both Vaughn and I were born, so she remembers what it was like not to be able to go to the movies or even have the food she liked. It was pretty tough for my mother for a long time after she left our father," Annarita said. "They've been at each other's throats for three years now, and it's just getting worse."

"What's going to happen?" I asked.

"I don't know, but Virge wants control of the Foundation."

"And Vaughn isn't about to give it up, I suppose," Nicky interjected.

"Well, why should he? She's already president of the board of directors of the newspaper chain," Annarita said with exasperation. "How much more does she want?"

"Wait a minute," Nicky said. "I thought your mother sold the newspaper chain."

"She did," Annarita said.

"Then how can your sister be president of the board of directors?" I asked.

Annarita gave a sly, sarcastic grin. "By marrying the CEO of the corporation that bought it, fellas. Like my mother would say, 'Ain't no flies on that girl.' And Vaughn had better watch out. Virge has a temper. A *really bad* temper. She's capable of just about anything when she's angry."

"Anything?" I asked pointedly.

"Oh," Annarita exclaimed, "that reminds me. I meant to tell you this before." She looked at me with a deeply furrowed brow.

"What?" I said. "It can't be that bad."

"Mother's handgun is missing from her night stand."

"Her gun?" I said.

"Your mother had a gun?" Nicky blurted.

"Remember, guys, she grew up in Texas."

At just that moment a shot rang out from somewhere in the house. We all jumped, looked at one another, then tore up the steps and through the front door.

FORTY-TWO

WE RAN through the foyer, looking for everyone. The house was empty, but when we went into the California Room we could see that all the guests were assembled on the back lawn with their backs toward the house. We ran outside and pushed our way through the crowd. There in the center stood Travis, in chaps and what looked like a 50-gallon black cowboy hat, silver belt, silver and turquoise jewelry dripping from fingers, wrists and neck. He was holding a six-shooter in one hand, a target in the other with a bullet hole right through the center.

We all breathed a sigh of relief, but Annarita was angry. "Travis!" she shouted, walking up to him and tearing the target out of his hand. "You scared us to death."

Travis gave a hearty laugh, showing what looked like the teeth of a movie star who had had lots of cap work to make them perfectly straight. He put his arm around Annarita and hugged her close. "Simmer down, little lady," he said. "Just showing the folks how I won your momma's heart."

"OK, everybody," Annarita said to the guests. "That's all the rodeo for this afternoon. Please help yourselves to more food and drink." She gave Travis an exasperated look, which just made him laugh more, and walked through the crowd and into the house through the doors where the dogs were kept. She still had the target in her hand. In the room next to that one, Virginia stood in the open doorway, holding a drink. She was shaking her head in disgust. Her black tailored suit contrasted sharply with the Irish red hair wound neatly on top of her head. She wore a string of pearls around her neck and gave Travis a look that a witch might give someone she was casting a hex upon. I followed her gaze over to where Travis was standing, half expecting to find he had turned into a toad, but he was showing some hunky blond and his wife his rifle.

Virginia took a long drink from her cocktail and strode across the lawn, greeting people in a supercilious manner as she passed.

Nicky nudged me in the side and said, "Wonder if he's after the blond or his wife?"

"Nicky," I scolded. I put my hands on his shoulders, turned him in the direction of the house, and gave a gentle shove. As we walked toward the house, looking for the bar, I looked up to the second floor and saw a young woman standing in the window, partially hidden by the curtains. She was watching the crowd, particularly, it seemed, watching Nicky and me. Nicky had gotten a few paces ahead of me. I caught up and grabbed his sleeve. "Nicky, look up at that bedroom window on the second floor. Who is that?" We turned our attention to the window where the woman had been, but now she was gone.

"What woman?" he asked.

"Never mind. She's not there now," I said. "She looked familiar. I was hoping you would recognize her. I've seen her somewhere before but I can't place it. Oh, well."

Just then Virginia passed and I took the opportunity to ask, "Virginia, excuse me, but can you tell me what room that is up on the second floor? That third window from the right?"

She turned and looked up for a moment, then said, "That's my brother's old room. It's a storage room now. Why?"

"Just curious," I said. "I thought I saw someone I recognized at the window a moment ago, that's all."

"Quite impossible," Virginia pronounced, taking a drink from her highball. "That room has mother's business cabinets in it. We keep it locked at all times."

"Oh, I see," I said, but Virginia was already talking to someone else.

"Come on," Nicky said. "I need a martini and a cigarette."

"*Casablanca?*" I queried sarcastically.

"More like *Steel Magnolias,* I think," Nicky quipped.

"They didn't smoke in *Steel Magnolias,*" I pointed out.

"They should have."

FORTY-THREE

AROUND 4 o'clock we left Annarita's. Nicky had the driver let me off at my flat, and he went home. We had made arrangements to speak in about an hour to decide what to do for dinner. When I got inside, I stripped off my clothes and checked the answering machine. There was only one message.

"Nigel, this is Nonna. I have been trying to find your number for two days. I hope I am not too late. Today is Nicky's birthday. I know he won't tell you. He had bad birthdays as a child. Someone has put *il malocchio* on the child's birthdays. Make something nice for him. *Ciao, caro. Ti amo.*" Then, as an afterthought, she left me her phone number in Florence in case I needed her for anything.

I checked the calendar. June 11. A Gemini. I had dated a Gemini for two and a half years. It's true what they say about Geminis: they do have split personalities. At least the ones I've known. I picked up the phone and called the dining room at the Ritz Carlton. Luckily they had reservations available. Then I called the little tyke. I got his machine.

"Nicky, you sly puss," I said, using one of his favorite lines, "pick me up for dinner at 7:45. Oh, by the way, it's formal. Black tie. You do own a tuxedo, don't you?"

Promptly at 7:45, as instructed, the car pulled up in front. Nicky looked stunning in his tux and was completely perplexed. When I opened the door, he grabbed my arm and pulled me inside. "What are you up to?" he said.

"I just thought we'd have a quiet little dinner together. Just the two of us. It's our anniversary," I said, adjusting my cuff links.

"It is not."

"Is too."

"Is not."

"Is too."

"Which anniversary?"

"It's our 44-day anniversary," I said, having no idea if I was even remotely close to being accurate.

"That's absurd. People don't celebrate anniversaries on the 44th day."

"People don't, but I do."

"You're up to something," he said, squinting his eyes.

It was a perfect opportunity to use yet another of the *All About Eve* lines he was so fond of. "Eve, darling," I said, in my best Addison DeWitt voice, "sometimes I think you keep things from me."

"Smart-ass," he said, then sat back and sulked all the way to the Ritz.

We started with champagne. After the waiter had poured us each a glass and walked away, I lifted mine in a toast, leaned closer to Nicky, and said "Happy birthday."

His face blanched and for a moment he looked like he might bolt from the table. "How did you know it was my birthday?" he asked.

"A little bird told me," I said. "She also told me you don't like birthdays very much, so I didn't tell them when I made the reservation. I didn't want anyone coming out and singing to you in a crowded room."

"Thank you," he said. "Nonna, of course. I wonder how she found you?"

"I'm sure Nonna finds whomever she's looking for," I said. "Anyway, again, happy birthday." I clinked his glass and we sipped the champagne.

"I had lots of bad experiences as a child. Birthdays were at the top of the list along with Christmas and any other holiday. I prefer to let them go unnoticed," Nicky said.

"Well, that could be a problem," I said, grinning. "You see, in my family—at least the Italian side, my mother's side—birthdays are a huge event. A gigantic *festa*. My Aunt Anna used to close down her bar here in the city and drive to Benicia just to spend the day. Mine goes on for a weekend at least. Sometimes a couple weeks. Since it's on July 2, I get to celebrate until the Fourth, when it culminates in pyrotechnics. Just for me. At least that's what I imagine. When you're in Italy doesn't Nonna make a big fuss? It's so Italian to celebrate birthdays in a big way."

"She would acknowledge it, but she would do it subtly, with just a gift or a card. I'm afraid everyone in my family shies away from birthdays and Christmas," Nicky said.

There was a sadness in his eyes, so I let it drop. "Well, this dinner will be my only mention of it, if that will make you feel better," I offered.

"Thank you," he said, then picked up the menu. "What are you having for dinner?"

We ordered, then reviewed our situation with respect to Annarita's mother. "We have to talk to more people, I think," Nicky said.

"I think the people we need to talk with aren't around here," I said, rotating the champagne glass in my hand.

"Where are they?"

"Wherever Travis is from."

"I'm not following," Nicky said. He looked so handsome in his tuxedo. I wanted to leap across the table and make love to him right there.

"We need to talk to Matthew and see what he's come up with. We have to talk with people who knew Travis before he met Evelyn. I'll bet you anything we'll find people willing to tell us things we don't know about him." I leaned forward, my elbows on the table. "Don't you think it's weird that someone who wants to be a rodeo star would agree to marry a San Francisco socialite?"

"Yes and no," Nicky said. He held the champagne up, watching the candlelight refract through it. "For one thing she wasn't exactly a San Francisco girl. There's a tremendous difference between the City and the East Bay."

"I'll grant you that, but still, why not someone from Houston or Dallas or even Cheyenne?" I pressed.

"We both know the answer to that question," Nicky said.

"No, we don't. We're *guessing* he was after the money. But what if he was after respectability?"

Nicky paused to think that over. "That's an interesting theory, but we have nothing to base it on until we talk to people who knew him. You're right. We have to get Matthew to fill in the gaps. He said he'd have something by tomorrow. Hopefully it will be something concrete." Nicky smiled. "You look quite handsome this evening, signore."

"*Grazie*," I replied. "So do you." "In fact, I was thinking that afterward we might go to my place for a nightcap."

Nicky's face got serious. "Maybe not tonight," he said without looking at me.

"Why? What's wrong?"

He hesitated a long time, then said, "I dated two men after Rosario's death. It didn't work out either time. I'm old-fashioned."

"What are you talking about?" I said. "I thought we were practically walking down the aisle."

"Each time I was serious and they weren't. They said they were, but in the end, they couldn't commit. Or wouldn't," Nicky said.

"I'm not those men," I argued.

"They seemed as serious about marriage as you do," he said. "One of them talked about it all the time, about how we would travel, where we would live. In the end he faded away. Some men are incapable of committing to a lifelong relationship."

"I thought we were past that. I thought you understood that I'm serious," I said, feeling both angry and frustrated.

"It's one thing to say something," Nicky said. "It's quite another to follow through."

"Follow through? I'll follow through," I said. "You'll see. It's not like I've been seeing other men or not spending time with you."

"Well, you haven't actually proposed, either," Nicky said, looking away as if there was someone or something beckoning him from across the room.

I laughed at the absurdity of this, which angered him. Then his getting angry made me angry and before I knew it, he was leaving the table, taking the car, and leaving me to make my way home.

I thought everything was going so well. Now this. I needed advice and I needed it right away.

FORTY-FOUR

I DIDN'T sleep that night. I lay there, wondering why this sudden putting on the brakes on Nicky's part. I had to do something fast to get him back on track. I didn't want to lose him, but I didn't know him well enough to know how to appeal to him. There was only one person I could turn to. Thank goodness she had left her phone number when she called about Nicky's birthday.

"He's old-fashioned, *caro*," Nonna said, her voice sounding so clear she could have been talking from the house next door, rather than from halfway around the planet. "You have to win not only his heart, but his mind as well. He was badly hurt by this last man he was seeing, some horrible professor from Canada. He was a philosopher, so of course Nicky thought he was wonderful. But he was only wonderful in the abstract. I met him once and I don't think the man could even tie his own shoes."

"So what now, Nonna?" I asked, feeling like I was talking to my own grandmother.

"If Nicky is to trust you now, he must think you are serious forever. He wants to get married, not have an affair. Trust me, Nigel. Convince him you are willing to make a commitment and he will be yours."

"But how, Nonna? How do I do that?"

"Only you can decide that. Make him realize you are serious. You'll think of something," she said. "Come visit me, you two. When you take your honeymoon or whatever you call it in San Francisco, come here. We'll celebrate. *Ciao, caro. Buona fortuna.* Good luck," she said, then hung up.

Good grief. It was going to be like having to get his father's approval, except from him. How quaint!

Matthew was asking for two more days to assemble his information, and I let Nicky cool on his own. I thought it would do him good to see how it felt to not have me around for awhile. Unfortunately, it didn't feel so good from my end, either. I was really crazy about him and wanted him badly. The next two days were sheer torture. I shopped for groceries that I had no appetite to eat, worked in the garden, and went to a movie. I couldn't even remember the name of the film five minutes after I walked out. On the third sleepless night, 5:50 A.M. I told myself this had gone far enough.

I got up and went down into the storage room, where some of Lyle's old art supplies were still stored. I found a huge drawing tablet about two feet wide by four feet tall and took it upstairs along with some colored markers. In giant letters, I wrote:

June 14
6 A.M.
NICKY,
PLEASE MARRY ME.
I NEED THE SLEEP.
NIGEL

In the center of it I taped my mother's plain gold wedding band. I drove to his house and tacked it to his front door. Then I went home and put on a pot of coffee. Around 8:30 the phone rang.

"I accept," he said.

"You do?"

"Yes."

"You believe I'm serious now and you'll stop this game of reach and withdraw?" I asked sternly.

"Yes."

"Promise?"

"Promise."

"You won't change your mind?"

"Can't," he said.

"Why not? What's so different now?"

"I accepted a ring."

"You are so weird," I said. "I'm coming over for breakfast."

"I'll put on coffee," he said.

"See you in a few minutes."

"Wait a minute!" Nicky shouted into the receiver. "Aren't you forgetting something?"

I smiled. He was a handful. "I love you," I said.

"That's better," he said and hung up.

Matthew answered the door. He was in his bathrobe which, I realized, was the only thing I had ever seen him wear. It was an ancient, red flannel robe with Roy Rogers riding Trigger in a never-ending circle around Matthew's body. Once in a while Bullet, Roy's German Shepherd, trotted alongside. "Boy, has she been ferocious," he said as I stepped into the foyer. "What happened?"

"He hasn't told you?"

"He's been in his room for two days. Didn't even eat until Nonna called yesterday."

That made me feel good. Nonna appeared to be on my side.

Upstairs, the round table in the kitchen was littered with bacon, eggs, pancakes, coffee mugs, and orange juice. I waited in the doorway, unsure of exactly how to proceed. Matthew sat back down where he had apparently been going through a stack of papers when I rang the doorbell. He began shuffling through them. "Hey, you've got a real live wire here," he said.

"You ought to know; you've been living with him," I shot back.

"Not her," he said jerking his head in Nicky's direction. "Travis Iversen."

"Oh, tell me," I said, moving toward the table.

"Excuse me," Nicky said with exaggerated annoyance from where he stood at the stove with a spatula in his hand and a chef's apron around him. When I looked over, he was tapping his puckered lips with an index finger. I went over and gave him a kiss. "More like it. See that that doesn't happen again."

"I've missed you," I whispered.

"Ditto," he said.

My mother's ring was on his finger. I took his hand in mine and looked at it. "I can't believe this actually fits you," I said.

"Spooky, huh?" he answered. "I knew I had small fingers, but…"

"It's an omen," I said, smiling. I kissed him on the tip of his nose.

"A most auspicious omen," he said. "Now go sit down. I'm in the middle of my famous Florentine flapjacks." He pushed me toward the table.

"Here's what I've been able to dig up," Matthew said, his robe now falling open, revealing pale blue cotton pajamas with red fire engines and black-and-white police cars. "He grew up on his family's 3,000-acre ranch in Utah, where his family raised cattle and sheep and a few horses, and he raised Brahman bulls. He has no brothers or sisters, dropped out of high school in his senior year to help out full-time on the ranch. A year later he married his high school sweetheart, a girl named Tammi Truesdale."

Nicky slammed down a plate of pancakes on the table between Matthew and me. "Tammi Truesdale? Are these characters from *The Love Boat*? Who thinks up these names? Jeez." He shook his head and returned to the stove.

Matthew and I just smiled at one another. "As I was saying," Matthew continued, "they were high school sweethearts, so it was kind of expected they'd get married. They had a son right away, but I can't tell if she was pregnant before they got married. It probably doesn't matter; in those cases they get married anyway."

"I'm not sure I understand what you mean," I said.

"I'm from the Midwest," Matthew explained. "Iowa. High school sweethearts usually get married simply because it's expected of them. In small towns no one wants to leave their…"

"They're afraid to leave," Nicky shouted from the stove, flipping more pancakes.

"They're afraid to leave," Matthew corrected himself, raising his eyebrows and shaking his head. "So even if she was pregnant, the only effect that probably would have had is to hasten the date of the wedding. Their son, Travis Jr., was born exactly nine months after the wedding. Iversen's father died about two years after that. Looks like he had an accident on the ranch, a rather ugly accident. There was not only an obituary, there was an accompanying story in the St. George, Utah newspaper."

"What happened?" I asked.

"One of Travis's bulls gored the old man to death. According to the paper, it was his son's prize Brahman, the one he was training to ride in the state rodeo. Travis was out with his buddies on a Saturday and his father tried to pen the bull without getting anyone to back him up. Guess he thought he could handle it. According to the newspaper, it cornered him in the corral and gored him. He was DOA at the hospital. From what I gather from the list of surviving relatives, Travis and his wife were living with Travis's parents."

"Nasty way to die," Nicky said, setting plates in front of us with eggs and bacon on them. He retrieved the coffee pot and poured more for each of us, then sat next to me as Matthew continued.

"Now here's something that might be of interest," he said. "While I was going through the microfiches, looking up Iversen for genealogical data, I came across a notice of marriage in the Mount Carmel Junction paper. It lists the marriage of a " 'Thomas T. Iversen to a Ruth McGraw.' He was 28 and she was 34."

"Why's that so unusual? There must be hundreds of Iversens in Utah," I said.

"Wrong," Matthew said. "There are exactly 76 as of last year. The year of this particular marriage, there were only 43."

"Couldn't it be one of the other 40?" Nicky piped in.

"Not unless they lied about their residence," Matthew said. "Thirty-two of those lived in Salt Lake City, eight in Provo."

"I see," I said. "Leaving just the three others in the southern part of the state, which is where Mount Carmel Junction is located."

"What?" Nicky said, popping a slice of bacon into his mouth and crunching loudly.

"The other three were Travis, Tammi, and the kid," I explained.

"That means everyone is accounted for, so it has to be…" I began thinking out loud.

"…your cowboy," Matthew said. "There's only one way to find out for sure. You have to go there and snoop around."

"Cool," Nicky said, wiping his mouth and reaching for his coffee mug. "I'll make reservations after breakfast. I *love* the desert."

"You do?" I exclaimed. "That's great. So do I."

Nicky quickly qualified his remark. "Conceptually, I mean."

"What does that mean?" I asked.

"It means I love the idea of the desert," he said.

"But not the desert itself?" I was beginning to feel the deflation setting in.

"I don't know," Nicky quipped. "I've never been to the desert. I liked *Thelma and Louise* though," he said cheerfully.

My spirits brightened. "Oh. In that case, you have a real treat in store. You're going to see something unlike anything you've ever seen before."

"Like when I saw you," he teased.

"Yes, but this is much bigger and much more breathtaking, as difficult as that may be to believe."

"And it doesn't talk back," he said, winking.

"*Al contrario, caro,* I said. "It most definitely talks back."

FORTY-FIVE

NICKY BOOKED us on a 2 o'clock flight to Phoenix for the next afternoon. He called Annarita to tell her we were going sleuthing and to give her the phone numbers of the places where we would be staying. He also asked for directions to the ranch, as I wanted to see both the ranch and the site of the drowning. Annarita said the family was having a cookout that afternoon and invited us over for an early dinner. Nicky at first declined, saying we had to pack for the trip, but I jumped up and down and waved my arms in the background, trying to get him to accept. He said we'd be there around 4.

"Why do you want to schlep all the way over there?" Nicky asked, hanging up the phone.

"It's an opportunity to see the family dynamic at work. We don't know the first thing about either Vaughn or Virginia. I want to observe them in action," I said.

"You're so butch," Nicky teased. "My own Sam Spade. Now, what shall I wear? Afternoon in the suburbs. Hmmm. Something plaid, I think."

Of course Nicky didn't own anything plaid, so he dressed as usual: Armani slacks, white shirt, V-neck cashmere sweater. By the time we arrived in Concord the gas grill was on and Virginia's husband was wrapping potatoes in aluminum foil and placing them over the fire. He was a large man, about 55, with salt-and-pepper hair. He had a bit of a belly. "Executive paunch," Nicky called it. He was affable enough, and shouted hello, waving his drink at us as we stepped onto the lawn from the California Room, which seemed to be the center of activity for the household no matter what the occasion. I couldn't help thinking how "white" that was. In the Italian household where I grew up, it was always the kitchen. Nicky said that on Guam it was also the kitchen. Here, in squeaky-clean suburbia, the kitchen was foreign soil to the upper middle class. Better to lounge on wicker, sip cocktails and let the brown-skinned people do the cooking. I said as much to Nicky while we waited for Virginia to bring us a drink.

"Somebody needs to nurture these people, that's for sure. I suppose the kitchen help and the maid is as close as they get to smiles, hugs and warm milk," Nicky said sotto voce as Virginia came toward us with two vodka tonics.

"Here you go, boys," she said. "We were so glad you could join us for dinner. Annarita is so thoughtful that way." It was obvious she didn't mean a word of it. "How are those taters doin', Poppa?" she said, walking toward her husband.

Annarita came outside from the puppies' room. "Hi. I thought I heard the doorbell." She came forward and gave us both a big hug, rather stiff, but generous. "I see someone already got you a cocktail. Good. We probably won't eat for another half hour or so. Where did Vaughn go?"

Virginia turned from the barbecue and answered Annarita's question although she was far away from our conversation. I made a mental note always to notice if she was anywhere in the vicinity of my conversations unless I wanted her to hear what I was saying. "He and Travis are in the rose garden. They're talking business or something." She smiled and lifted her drink in a toast. We toasted back.

"She's in a good mood," Nicky observed.

"They just acquired another paper. It's a big one in Sacramento, so they're quite pleased with themselves. Especially my sister. Virge is the one who went after this one. I think *The New York Times* is next," Annarita said.

Nicky and I turned in unison to look at Annarita. "Just kidding. I think. Maybe it's because tomorrow is the formal reading of mother's will. It's the day Virginia plans to become a very wealthy woman. If you two weren't going away, you could come. I mean, I don't know if you could actually sit in on it, but you could be here. We're doing it in mother's study. It's just a formality. There aren't any big secrets. Travis gets something like 10 million, Virge and Vaughn and I get about 100 million each, and the rest goes to mother's charity. We all know how it's set up."

"No wonder she's celebrating," Nicky said. "That much money would put a smile on anyone's face."

"Except perhaps Nonna," I reminded Nicky.

"Well, it would if you explained to her what 100 million dollars was."

Nicky, Annarita, and I strolled around the lawn and the small garden toward the far end of the house talking about the yard and flowers. We talked briefly about our upcoming desert trip and she said she'd write out directions for us although she'd only been there once. We turned to head back toward the house when we heard raised voices coming from the rose garden on the other side of the little garden we'd been meandering through. We turned in time to see Travis shove Vaughn into a large rose bush, then storm across the lawn toward the house. We rushed to help Vaughn untangle himself.

"Those thorn pricks are nasty," Nicky said, "and they're bleeding. They need to be disinfected. Come on, I'll take care of it."

"That's not necessary, really," Vaughn protested. His Calvin Klein slacks were ripped at the pocket and his beige shirt was starting to show tiny spots of red, where blood from the thorn pricks had seeped through.

"Come on," Nicky insisted, taking him by the arm and herding him across the lawn. "I used to be a nurse."

Annarita and I stood speechless for a moment as the two of them trotted off in search of peroxide. "When was Nicky a nurse?" I asked Annarita.

"Must have been in another lifetime," she laughed. "The sight of a needle makes him faint. I had to hold his hand and talk him through more than one blood test in college."

Dinner was cordial. We ate at a large dining table in a room adjoining the California Room. By the time we sat down to eat, Virginia was soused, her husband was well on his way, and Nicky and Vaughn were just returning from the first aid intervention Nicky had initiated in an upstairs bathroom. It had taken nearly half an hour and Nicky looked distraught when they sat down at the dinner table.

We made small talk during the meal, took coffee and sherbet on the lawn as the sun set. Nicky and I were on our way home by a little after 7.

"What did you and Vaughn talk about?" I asked.

"He's weird. Very seductive, but distant," Nicky said, watching the hills east of the Caldecott tunnel disappear into darkness as night fell. He seemed distracted. "He told me he didn't understand why we were engaged in this witch hunt with Annarita."

"He said that?" I exclaimed. "He actually used the phrase 'witch-hunt'? What did you say?"

"What could I say? I asked why he thought we were on a witch-hunt," Nicky said in a halting manner. He seemed distracted, as he had all through dinner. "He said it was obvious that Annarita was concerned about her inheritance and was doing whatever she could to cut Travis out of her mother's will."

"You know," I mused, "I hadn't gotten to thinking about the will yet. I wonder just how complicated it is."

"Well, there's one way to find out. If you want to change our plane reservations, that is," Nicky said. "After all, we have been asked to come if we want."

"I don't know. What could we learn at the reading of the will that would change anything?"

"That depends," Nicky said.

"On what?"

"On whether there are any surprises," Nicky said.

"Like what?" I asked.

"I don't know," he snapped. "It's just my intuition. Ignore it if you want. I'm not so sure it's going to play out the way Annarita thinks, though. For one thing," Nicky said, lowering his voice a bit, as though he were embarrassed, "Vaughn was acting very odd upstairs."

"Odd?"

"Friendly," Nicky said, not looking at me.

"Friendly," I repeated, as though saying the word might tell me more about its meaning. And it did. "Oh, friendly. How friendly?" I could feel my stomach taking a roll, sinking, like I was on a roller coaster going downhill.

"Forward friendly," Nicky said. Now he was looking at me and he looked guilty.

"Do you want to tell me about it?" I asked, not sure I wanted to hear, but knowing I had to.

"Can it wait until we get home?" Nicky asked.

"Why?" I asked.

"I want to be holding you when I tell you what happened. I want to be closer to you than I can be in this car."

"OK," I said. We drove the rest of the way home in silence. As we approached the center span of the Bay Bridge, the fog bank enveloped us. It was like entering a strange world. A frightening, strange world.

FORTY-SIX

WE WENT to Nicky's place. I parked in the garage and we walked upstairs, went directly to the bedroom, and undressed. I got in bed and waited while Nicky took a shower. That made me more nervous. What was he trying to wash off?

By the time he got in bed, I had constructed an entire scenario of steamy sex between Vaughn and Nicky that would split the fabric of our new and still fragile relationship. Nicky dropped his towel on the floor and slipped under the comforter, wrapping his arms around me and laying his head on my chest. He lay there working his fingers through the hair on my chest, playing lightly with my left nipple. It was a surefire way to arouse me, but he wasn't trying to arouse me. He played with it absent-mindedly. I could tell that sex was not where this was going.

After a long while, he spoke. "You know I love you, don't you?" he began.

"I don't like the way this is starting out," I said before I could check myself. Nicky said nothing. I finally answered his question. "Yes, I know you love me."

"And you know that I only want to be with you for the rest of my life, don't you?"

"Yes, that's what you've told me," I said, twisting his words a bit. He caught it immediately.

"You believe me, don't you?"

I took longer to answer than either of us wanted, but eventually I said, "Yes, I do believe that."

"OK, then. Keep that in mind, please," Nicky said, moving his right hand from my chest and wrapping it around me, holding me tight, as though I might bolt from the bed. "When we got upstairs to the master bathroom, I went to the medicine cabinet and began looking for peroxide. I told him to sit on the side of the tub. There's a giant built-in tub up there with a wide lip big enough to sit on. I found the peroxide and some cotton swabs and turned to help him and he was standing there with just his boxer shorts on. I must have looked startled, because he said, 'Oh, I had to take my slacks off. They were ripped.' I thought that was clever, but I wasn't born yesterday. I was about to set the peroxide down and leave the room, when he said, 'I got jabbed below the belt, too. That's how the pants got ripped in the first place. It hurts like hell.'

"I looked at him and he seemed sincere enough, so I told him to sit on the side of the tub and I began dabbing peroxide on the little bloody pinpricks. Most of them were on his right side along the rib cage. He must have spun around when Travis pushed him, because there was hardly anything on his back. I couldn't think of anything to say and the silence was uncomfortable. It made it erotic. I won't lie; he has a really beautiful body. Years at the gym and all that. He's stunning underneath all those designer clothes he wears.

"So I just started talking about going to Arizona tomorrow. He said he knew we were going but he didn't know why. I said we were just going to look around, check things out for Annarita. He said he didn't understand why she thought that was necessary. By this time, I was working on his chest. He had this big hole in his right nipple where a thorn got him good. It was still bleeding a little. I got a fresh cotton swab and put some peroxide on it and rubbed it on the spot. He gasped a little and then said, 'That feels good.' I laughed kind of nervously, but it was still bleeding, so I swabbed it again. This time, took hold of my hand rubbed it back and forth on his nipple.

"I don't know why I didn't just get up and walk out. It was all so strange, so surreal, so out of nowhere. I guess he mistook my silence for compliance, because he stood up, reached into the slit of his boxer shorts, and pulled his dick out."

Nicky lifted his head and looked at me. The only light in the room was a candle he had lit before he went into the bathroom to take his shower, but I could see his eyes quite clearly. He was afraid. "Tell me if you want me to stop. I need to tell you this, but if you can't hear it, then you need to stop me."

"Don't stop," I said.

Nicky laid his head back on my chest and continued. "He started rubbing his dick on my face. I couldn't believe what he was doing. I thought I was having a psychotic break from reality, or hallucinating. It was like some porn movie, but it was Annarita's little brother instead. It was too weird. I couldn't think. All I could do was stare at him."

Nicky sighed, waited a moment, then went on. "Then he grabbed me by my hair and pulled my head back and with his other hand he forced himself into my mouth. All I could think was: *This isn't happening.* I kept seeing you and Annarita and everyone else at the dinner table, waiting for us to come back downstairs. It was like I left my body. Except I didn't. I have to be clear and honest about that. Some part of me wanted to do this. I don't understand it; I don't like it; I'm certainly not proud of it. In fact, I'm ashamed. But I would be lying to myself and to you if I said that on some level I didn't go along with him.

"I'll never forget his eyes, so narrow and intense. Mean. Even violent. Yet they looked vacant, like he wasn't really there either. He was just doing this because the opportunity had presented itself. It had nothing to do with me. All I could think of was you downstairs and how this could ruin everything between us and wondering why did this have to happen to me and if I screamed or hit him would that end up making things worse. So I just stayed there and let him have his way. I'm sorry. I feel rotten. *Diablé!*"

I lay there with him on my chest, his arms tight around me, almost hurting me. I asked, "Did he come in your mouth?"

Nicky didn't hesitate to answer. "Yes. He was so big that most of the time he was banging at the back of my throat and I was wondering if he was going to come in my mouth or pull out, and as I was wondering it, he shuddered and then said this horrible thing. He said, 'Eat this, you little nigger.' And then he finished. I pushed at him, but it was too late by then. I just went slack and tried to comprehend what had happened. I'm sorry, Nigel. I didn't go looking for that. I never wanted it to happen. I don't know why it did, but it did and I can't keep it from you. I won't have that kind of relationship. I won't keep secrets. I want you to be my best friend as well as my lover and partner. Please don't hate me," Nicky said and began to cry gently.

"I don't hate you, Nicky. I hate him. We'll get through this," I said, hugging him. Then he began to cry in earnest. We both cried. Just when I thought life was getting easier, the trickster Goddess threw a nice hard curve. Why wasn't I surprised?

FORTY-SEVEN

WE SAT UP most of the night talking. Not so much about what had happened, but about same-sex relationships in general and ours in particular. Around 4 in the morning, Nicky called the airline and canceled the reservations to Phoenix. We had to regroup. At 4:30, when it was abundantly clear we weren't going to get any sleep, Nicky went downstairs and made coffee. He came back upstairs carrying a tray with the coffee and some old anisette toasts he found in the cupboard. "These never go bad," he said, holding up an anisette toast. "Whether they were made yesterday or the day Vesuvius erupted, they taste exactly the same." He attempted a smile, but it was weak.

"I need to ask you some questions," I said. "Is it all right?"

"Of course," Nicky said. "I expect you to."

"Some of them are personal."

"I would expect them to be."

"Did you jack off while this was going on?" I asked, hardly believing I was asking such a thing. I hated being a man at that moment, hated the ridiculous things a man thinks and feels. The inappropriate, self-absorbed, hysterical kinds of possessive and territorial feelings that seem to be part of the male chromosome.

"No," Nicky said, flatly, without anger or alarm. There was a long pause and then he said, "but I had an erection and I came really close to orgasm."

We let that sink in. "I don't understand exactly how or why," he said. Nicky wore boxer shorts and a T-shirt and sat cross-legged on the bed, facing me. I was naked beneath the comforter, and had propped myself up with pillows against the headboard. He leaned forward. "I'm not going to lie to you about anything," he said. "Ever."

"Good," I said, wondering if I meant it.

"Obviously some part of me responded to what was going on. I'm not making any judgment about it or even any observations about it, other than on some level I must have enjoyed the encounter," he said, looking down at the coffee mug he held. "Some part of me must have liked it."

"What part do you think it was?" I asked.

Nicky thought for a moment, then answered. "Probably the same part that likes it when we're making out and all of a sudden you flip me around, pull down my pants, and bury your face in my ass, or the part of me that likes it when I'm lying naked on my stomach and you're kissing my back and you suddenly grab my hips and jerk me up to my knees and then shove your dick inside me." Nicky shrugged his shoulders, as if he were admitting something he hadn't even articulated to himself, and said, "It's the part of me that likes to be taken."

Sometimes it scared me how much this guy understood himself. I wasn't sure I wanted him understanding me that well. At least not right away.

"Why do you think he did it?" I asked.

"I don't know. I had absolutely no warning. It came straight out of nowhere. One minute I was tending his wounds, the next he was forcing himself into my mouth. I don't think it was the nipple thing," Nicky said, reaching over and placing his mug on the nightstand. "What I mean is, I don't think that little swipe with the peroxide on his nipple could have elicited that kind of response. I think it was something else."

"I really have a difficult time understanding this. If you didn't say anything provocative or give him any encouragement, why would he think it would be all right to do that to you?" I realized I was sounding more like a jealous husband or an attorney for the defense, but it was baffling.

"You forget something," Nicky said with a trace of tears in his eyes.

"What's that?" I asked.

Nicky held his arm up between us, palm toward his face.

"What? I don't get it," I said.

"My skin," Nicky said. "The color of my skin. You forget, because to you it doesn't matter, but other people see me differently. Think about what he said to me when he…when he…just think about what he said to me, what he called me."

"That's right," I said. "He called you nigger. That's sick." I literally had a nasty taste in my mouth.

"It's a lot more common than you realize," Nicky said, smiling a little, sadly. "You don't see the looks people give us when we're out together. Older white man with younger Pacific Island man: that's all they need to know."

"I never notice that," I said, incredulous as much at my own naïveté as the pure fact of the matter. "I just don't. I'm sorry."

"It's no big thing. I'm used to it," he said.

"You're absolutely sure about all this?" I said.

"Nigel, think about it for a minute. When we're out together, who always gets the check placed in front of him at a restaurant? Who does the store clerk hold out his hand toward when it's time to pay? You're a white, middle-aged, middle-class homosexual; you're privileged, a bit naïve, and totally unaware of the world that exists outside yours." There was no malice in his tone. Nicky wasn't trying to be mean; he was being honest. He was holding up a mirror for me to look into and I was seeing something I had never seen before. "Someday you'll meet my family and you'll be shocked at how tribal and parochial they are. I mean it. You'll be shocked. You've only seen me with Nonna in Italy, surrounded by the opulence on my mother's relatively remote side of the family. You have a big surprise in store for you, believe me. There's a lot you don't know about me."

I couldn't shake the image of Nicky being held by his hair and forcibly raped. Neither could I get the word "nigger" out of my mind. "God, I hate that word. I can't even say it without feeling sick to my stomach. Why would he call you that? Why...*that*? You're not African-American."

"Let me tell you a story," Nicky said. "I interned one summer for the Children's Aid Society in New York, taking care of emotionally disturbed kids. Most of them were smart, but emotionally screwed up. The job was part of my training in the seminary. Everyone had to do some form of social work. I lived in a house with 12 boys who ranged in age from 7 to 11. There were two boys who used to fight a lot. They vacillated between being best friends and archenemies. One was Lee Reading, this little nerd with thick glasses, who could do mathematical

formulas that no one in his school could do. He was 9. The other was
Donald Smeed, a black kid who came to the agency at the age of 6. He
was extremely bright too. He could read anything, pronounce any word
you put in front of him, even if he didn't know what it meant. But usually he did. He read voraciously.

The summer I was there, Donald turned 11. One day he came running into the house from the yard where the kids were playing. He was
crying his eyes out, really sobbing. He could hardly breathe, he was crying so hard. It took me almost ten minutes to calm him down.

"Finally I said, 'Donald, what's the matter? What happened?' He said,
'Lee Reading called me a nigger.' I almost laughed, because around there
everyone called everyone that. When I first got there I was shocked, but
then I realized it had nothing to do with anyone's skin color. White kids
called other white kids nigger; black kids called white kids nigger. They
called the staff nigger. It was what they called each other when they were
angry. Today it would probably be 'bitch' or 'faggot' since the word nigger is such a universal taboo.

"Anyway, I said to Donald, 'Donald, you and Lee Reading call each
other nigger all the time. I've heard you.' And Donald looked up at me
with those beautiful big brown eyes of his filled with tears and said, very
softly, 'Yeah, but this time, he meant it.'" Nicky paused a moment, then
added. "You don't know how much hatred is out there for people like
me. You really have no idea."

"I'm sorry," I said. It seemed so trite and pathetic, but it was true. I
was feeling overwhelmingly sad that Donald Smeed or Nicky Borja or
anyone in the world should be treated so badly simply for the color of
his skin. It was so far from my own experience. I felt sad and ashamed.

"People reach for the closest epithet when they're angry," Nicky said,
crawling over and curling up under my arm. I set my coffee mug on the
nightstand next to his and wrapped my arms around him. "Vaughn was
pretty drunk too, remember. And God knows what the fight in the garden was about."

"Yeah, what was that about?" I said. "When did he refer to us being
on a witch-hunt?"

"When we were leaving the bathroom," Nicky said. "He was putting on his pants and smirking, pleased with himself about what had just happened. He looked at me and said, 'Now that you know who's really the boss around here, you and Annarita can end your little witch hunt.' I started wondering then if that might be what he and Travis were arguing about."

"Why would they argue about that?" I asked.

"Maybe Vaughn told him we were going to Scottsdale or something and Travis blew up because people are going to be snooping around his ranch. I don't know. It's just a theory," Nicky said. "But I'll bet I'm right. I can't figure out anyone in that family. I thought my family was fucked up."

"Do you still want to go over there today?" I asked.

"I want to know who's getting the money. Besides, Annarita could use the moral support. Vaughn and Virge are both being nasty to her." Nicky smiled up at me, but it was a weak attempt at bravery.

"I hate him now, you know," I said. "There's a part of me you haven't seen that isn't pretty. I'm Italian, remember, on my mother's side, and it can show itself in ugly ways."

"Please don't make a scene over me," Nicky pleaded. "It will just complicate things. For one thing it will draw his attention back to me and then he might do something even worse."

"His attention is already drawn to you, isn't it?" I said, stating the obvious.

"No, honey. You don't understand how these things work with people of color."

"He virtually raped you," I said. "What makes you think he's not going to try it again?"

"In his mind he accomplished what he set out to do," Nicky said, with a trace of sarcasm mixed with sadness. "He put the nigger bitch in her place by showing he's the master. He thinks I'm going to crawl back to the cellar and curl up on my bed of straw and pray he forgets I'm there. I know how this goes, believe me. He thinks it's over."

"Well, he's wrong about that," I said. Dead wrong."

FORTY-EIGHT

NICKY didn't go with me to Annarita's. He didn't feel like facing Vaughn and I thought being there on my own might draw less attention. We called Annarita and checked it out with her. She was fine with that and said I should come directly around to the puppies' room, where she would be until the attorneys arrived for the reading of the will.

The day was clear and crisp, one of those days that make tourists move to San Francisco on impulse. As I emerged from the Caldecott Tunnel and descended toward Concord, I found the polluted air that never accumulates in the city. The winds that blow through the Golden Gate push all the smog across the bay. In spite of that, the green hills and eucalyptus trees made Contra Costa County a wonderful place to live. I passed estates, small ranches, and open pastures before slowly the buildings grew closer together, then taller.

I used the time in the car to think about what had happened to Nicky. I had so many conflicting feelings about it that I knew I had to be careful about what I said and how I proceeded. Part of me was screaming that he should have stopped and gotten out of there. Part of me wanted to hunt down Vaughn and kill him. Another part of me was just sad and hurt, feeling betrayed and rejected. These were all feelings that I was going to have to remain aware of or I'd find myself acting them out inappropriately.

I didn't know why I felt betrayed, but I did, and the feeling was almost overwhelming. Nicky had been with someone else and he hadn't done what needed to be done to get out of the situation. I would always wonder about that. If I let myself wonder about it, that is. I had no reason to believe Nicky did anything at all to provoke the incident and I knew without a doubt that I loved him. I would try to focus on that.

Nicky said that Vaughn hadn't revealed anything about the incident in the rose garden. I wondered why they would be fighting. It made no sense except that everyone's nerves were on edge. Vaughn and Travis both struck me as being unstable and anything might push either one over the edge. I had to find out more before we went to the desert.

Before I'd left the house Nicky had rebooked our flight for the next day. I was still unsure about what we were looking for, let alone what we'd find in Arizona, but I didn't protest. It would be good for the two of us to get away from all this for a few days and roam around in the sun. I began counting the hours.

I found Annarita in the puppies' room where she'd said she would be. The puppies were twice as big as the last time I saw them. "Boy, they grow fast, don't they?" I remarked, closing the door and blocking one of the puppies' attempted escape with my foot.

"Yes," Annarita said, picking one up, "they're fully grown in about a year, so they have a lot to do in these first few months. Aren't they precious?"

"I have to admit, I'm a sucker for puppies. I had dogs as a kid, but it's been a while since I lived with one."

"The only love money can buy," Annarita said, smiling and handing me the puppy. He began licking my face a mile a minute.

"That one's yours," Annarita said. "I mean that's Beau, the one Nicky asked me to hold. I think he's a hands-down champion if you decide to show him. I mean, if you decide to take him and then to show him." She smiled a knowing smile that said she knew this puppy would eventually be going home with us.

We gathered the pups into their pen then walked down a long, dark hallway. "I hope this is going to be all right," I said. "Are you sure the others aren't going to object?"

"No, not at all," Annarita said, slipping her arm through mine and pressing close. "Since I'm in the middle of a divorce I told them I wanted someone to be with me to help me understand all of this. They're such male chauvinists—Virge included—that they thought nothing of it. It's going to be emotional for all of us, I'm sure. I told them I asked Nicky, too, but only you were available. No one balked. They're all too busy counting the money they're about to inherit. I don't want to feel alone in there."

'In there' turned out to be Evelyn's library, a large, wood-paneled room with leather sofas and chairs and a huge wooden desk with a red leather armchair. By the time we arrived, everyone else was there. The only places left to sit were two leather armchairs sitting at angles toward each other so the corners of their red leather seats practically touched. A small end table was squeezed in between them. They faced the desk, but between them and the desk sat two leather sofas facing each other so that all the furniture formed a square, what Evelyn might have called a "conversation area."

Virginia and her husband sat on one sofa, Vaughn and some man I had never seen, much older than Vaughn, sat on the facing sofa. Vaughn looked at me only once, and there was no indication that he was thinking about the same thing I was thinking about. He looked away without acknowledging me. Travis paced back and forth in front of some bookshelves behind Vaughn. The three attorneys had placed extra chairs behind the desk and were going through some papers. Finally one of them said we could begin. Travis turned and leaned against the built-in bookshelves. He had a matchstick in his mouth and wore new jeans, cowboy boots, and a tight-fitting light blue cowboy shirt with pearl snap buttons. I could see the outline of his nipples through the fabric. He winked at me and smiled. I nodded and turned my attention back to the lawyers, who had begun reading.

They went through lots of incidental things and the bequeathal to the battered women's shelter. One of the attorneys explained how a successor to head the Foundation would be chosen if Vaughn should leave. Finally they got to the part about the children. I didn't understand most of it because it was all about stocks and bonds and things like "the savings account at the Concord Savings and Loan," or "the certificate of deposits at Bank of America, Branch Number such and such." The amounts weren't given, but everyone in the room except me seemed to know how much everything was worth. I watched people's faces, trying to get some idea if things were going as expected. It all seemed OK until they got to the end.

The attorney at the desk read slowly so everyone could follow. "The remainder of my estate is to be divided as follows: the house in Concord, and all its contents, are to go to my daughter Annarita O'Brien Holland, if she survives me for 30 days, along with the sum of 20 million dollars in money market funds held in Fidelity Trust, Dallas, Texas; 10 million dollars each to my children, Virginia O'Brien Leavitt, if she survives me for 30 days, and Vaughn O'Brien VanDeventer, if he survives me for 30 days; the sum of 1 million dollars to Anita Hudson, my friend and personal secretary for over 15 years if she survives me for 30 days; the remainder of my estate, including all stocks, bonds, cash, bank, and market accounts not mentioned herein, the ranch in Scottsdale, Arizona, and all its contents I will and bequeath to my husband, Travis Iversen, if he survives me for 30 days. Should any of my heirs or beneficiaries, whether individuals or corporations not survive me for 30 days, their portion of this estate is to be equally divided among my aforementioned surviving children."

This was the part that brought the coughs, the sighs, the stares—and a smile to Travis Iversen's lips. As soon as the attorney set the will down on the desk and took off his glasses, Travis sauntered out of the room, the heels of his boots clicking loudly on the hardwood floors.

Annarita whispered for me to follow her and led me to the kitchen, where the cook poured us some lemonade. We sat at a small table near a window and Annarita explained what had happened. She was stunned.

"I understand the part about Travis getting the remainder of the estate," I said, "but I didn't understand all the other stuff. I mean, I have no idea how much money the stocks are worth or the bonds or the mutual funds, so I couldn't tell if anyone was being shortchanged. No one seemed too upset."

"You don't know my family," Annarita said. "We don't show anger in public, not even to one another until it boils over. You can be sure that right now Vaughn and Virge are either having strokes or planning murder."

"Why?" I asked. "Translate for me."

"We sat around a couple nights ago when Travis was out somewhere—probably with those drinking cowboy friends of his—and laid out what we thought Mother's will said. We thought we knew, actually, but it sounds like Mother either lied or made some drastic changes just before she died. The way we had heard it from Mother was that we each got the equivalent of about 100 million dollars. The house was to go to all three of us; the ranch and 10 million dollars was supposed to go to Travis. Everything else was set up in trust funds to support the battered women's shelter."

"What about the Foundation?" I asked.

"Oh, she endowed that separately a long time ago. That's all taken care of and runs by itself," Annarita said. "Well, not by itself, I guess. Vaughn runs it. His salary is about $200,000 a year, I think."

"So there were drastic changes?" I asked. "Like how drastic? How much does Travis end up with?"

"Well, if our calculations were accurate," Annarita said, "and we actually thought they were conservative, then the total estate is worth about 420 million. So, figure 20 for me, 10 each for Vaughn and Virge, one for Hudson, the house and ranch are worth about five. The stocks Vaughn and Virginia got add up to about another ten, I think. What does that leave?"

I gasped. "$360 million."

"See what I mean?" she said. "You can be sure both Virge and Vaughn have their panty hose in a twist right now. Sorry if that sounded homophobic. I didn't mean it that way. I meant it to be sibling-phobic." Annarita gave a little giggle.

"Can I ask you something personal?" I asked.

"Sure, why not?" she said, taking a drink of her lemonade.

"Does this bother you?"

"The money part, you mean?"

I nodded.

"Oh c'mon," Annarita said softly. "As if this house and 20 million dollars isn't enough. I couldn't spend that much money even if I tried. No, I don't care very much about money. I have an education and I can get a job any time I want. I have the dogs, which are pretty much my whole life these days. I'm very happy."

"What does bother you?" I asked.

"That this stranger came into my mother's life and saw a good thing and knew how to get it. It wouldn't bother me so much if I knew for sure that he didn't kill her, but I don't know that. I know she was happy at first, then she became unhappy toward the end. They argued a lot, which she never did with Cyril. Travis went out on the town without her, which Cyril wouldn't have even thought of doing. Travis invited rowdy friends over at all hours of the night. He stood her up for dinner engagements, then arrived looking like he just climbed off his horse. I need to know what happened, Nigel," she said, reaching across the table and placing her hand on top of mine. "I need to know that my mother wasn't murdered so this man could party for the rest of his life. I need to know that everything that Cyril VanDeventer—who, by the way, treated me my entire life like I was his own daughter—that everything he worked for all his life didn't just fall into the lap of the man who murdered the only woman Cyril ever loved, the woman he built the empire for in the first place. I just want justice, or to know that justice needn't be concerned."

I clasped Annarita's hand in mine. "We'll do our best, Annarita. I promise."

"That's all I ask," she said.

"We're leaving for Utah and Arizona tomorrow. We'll tell you everything we find."

"Just bring back some answers, Nigel. "Some answers that will let me sleep at night."

FORTY-NINE

I TOLD Annarita I would find my way out, then simply walked around the house rather than going back through it. I was unlocking the door to the car when I heard a woman call my name. I turned to see Virginia striding down the front walk toward me. She didn't look happy.

"Hello," I said as neutrally as possible.

Suddenly she smiled. "Hello, Nigel. I didn't get a chance to speak to you in there and then all of a sudden you were gone. I've been meaning to thank you for looking out for my little sister through all of this, but I never seem to find the appropriate moment."

"It's quite all right, really," I said, trying to figure out what in hell she really was up to. She'd never talked to me except to ask what I wanted to drink. "Nicky is quite fond of Annarita. They go back a ways, I take it."

"Yes, college days," she said, smiling again. She leaned against the side of my car, fingering the strand of pearls around her neck. "There for a time, I think she was stuck on him. Romantically, I mean. I'm glad they've remained friends. I'm glad you're around, too. Annarita tells me you're looking into things for us."

Us? Something has shifted, I thought. "Well, we're just trying to help her come to grips with your mother's death. I can understand how upsetting it would be to have all these uncertainties hanging over the death of a parent. We're hoping to clear some of them up. We'd like to help put her mind to rest about some of the details."

Virginia looped her arm through mine and coaxed me to walk with her. "Let's stroll down the lane a way," she said, smiling and squeezing my bicep a little. "I'd like to chat with you about that."

We walked along beneath the walnut trees. There were hardly any cars on the street, as opposed to the day we walked here with Annarita, the day of the funeral. Two children kicked a soccer ball back and forth in the middle of the narrow street beneath the broad branches of the trees, which practically shut out the sky. They had been pruned over the years so that they made a kind of canopy over us.

"Are your parents living, Nigel?" Virginia asked.

"My father is alive. My mother died when I was young," I said, not wanting to give this woman any more information than necessary.

"How young?"

"I had just graduated from college. I was 22," I said.

"So you know the pain we're all going through," she said. "Can I ask you something quite directly, Nigel?"

"You may ask. I may not answer," I warned.

"Fair enough," she said. "I don't know exactly how far along you are in your investigations…"

"I'd hardly call what we're doing an investigation," I said.

"All right, your research," she corrected herself. "Have you formed any opinion yet on the nature of my mother's death?"

She was fishing in a big, bold way. "Opinion as to what, exactly?" I said, not willing to assume I knew to what she was referring.

"Do you, for instance, think she died accidentally, or do you think there was foul play involved?" She wasn't smiling any longer, but she still held firm to my arm.

"It's too soon to tell, I'm afraid," I answered. "I think we'll have a better idea about that in a few days."

"So you will continue to look into things?" she asked, smiling again, this time squinting her eyes so that there was a pleading quality to her question.

"We're not private investigators in the strict sense," I said. "If you want a real investigation over and above what the police have provided, you really ought to hire someone professional." I wanted to both clarify my position and test her to see just how "official" she wanted this to get.

She gave a sardonic little laugh. "Oh, goodness no. We don't want a lot of strangers rummaging through our private affairs. I'm sure you're quite capable. I only meant to encourage you, offer support. For my sister's sake."

"I understand," I said. "We promised your sister we'd stay with it until we get some sort of answer for her."

"Good," she said, squeezing my arm and pulling me closer. "I want you to know that we're all...well, at least I am very grateful to you. I will confess, but only to you, of course, I have my doubts now."

"Now?"

"I didn't at first," she said, looking up into the branches of the trees as though she was looking back over the past few days. "I mean, I'm no fool. I never thought Travis loved my mother, but I didn't think he would do anything like this. I didn't think he would actually harm her to get her money."

"When did you change your mind?" I asked.

"This is confidential, I assume. What I say won't go any further?"

"Absolutely confidential. How could we get any reliable information if we didn't keep people's trust?" I responded, smiling back at her now for the first time. I was supposed to believe this woman would trust me with something she considered confidential?

"Good," she said. "Ever since the drowning, Travis has been getting telephone calls that he won't take in front of people. At first I thought it was ranch business since I answered the phone a couple times and it was a man on the other end and it seemed to be long distance. I could hear static on the line. Although come to think of it, I guess it could have been a portable phone. At any rate, the calls kept coming at all hours of the day and night. Then, night before last, we both picked up the phone at the same time. I was in the upstairs hallway and he was in the living room. It was late and everyone was in bed. He had just come home and I had only just turned out the lights and gone upstairs. I've been staying here for the past few days, trying to keep on top of business matters.

"I had paused at the telephone table in the upstairs hall to look at a stack of mail someone had placed there, rather than on the desk in the study where it's supposed to be placed."

I resisted the urge to smile at Virginia's obsessive-compulsive personality.

"I heard him stumble in, obviously drunk," she continued. "He went into the living room and I was about to continue into the bedroom when the phone rang. I thought it might be my son, who's studying

abroad and calls me when he can. Sometimes it's late here when it's early
where he is. I picked up, trying to keep it from ringing again and waking anyone up, but before I could say hello, Travis answered. I started to
put the phone down, but, well, frankly, I thought it was an opportunity I should take advantage of. I mean we're all so tense and he's being so
sullen and distant to the family. So I listened in."

"And?" I pressed.

"It was a woman," Virginia said.

"Did you recognize the voice?" I asked.

"No, but he did. She barely said his name, when he snapped at her, 'I
told you never to call here again and I meant it.' After that, I couldn't
put the phone down, now could I?" She smiled up at me and wrinkled
her nose, trying to strike a naughty pose. It wasn't very successful, but I
went along.

"I wouldn't have hung up," I said. "What else was said?"

"She said, 'I'm telling, Trav'-she called him that, 'Trav'—'I'm telling
and nothing's gonna stop me, because you lied to me. You lied and you
ain't never comin' back.' Those were her exact words. She talked like
that—you know, uneducated." Virginia looked at me like I might interpret the caller's words for her.

"What did he say?"

"He just told her not to call here again, that she was going to ruin
everything and she had to be patient. Then he said, in a really mean
tone, 'Unless you want to end up like her, you'll do what I tell you.'
Then he hung up."

"That could simply be an empty threat," I suggested.

"I suppose," Virginia admitted reluctantly.

"Why haven't you gone to the police with this?" I asked.

"It's not enough to nail him. We both know that," she said. "The
police would confront him and then he would just be more careful and
we'd never find out what really happened. That's why I'm telling you. I
want to help you with your invest...your research."

"I appreciate it, Virginia," I said. "Do you have any idea what it all
means?"

"I can take a pretty good guess," she said. "And so can you."

"I don't want to assume anything, but you're right. It does sound like he's conspiring with someone."

"I want to help in any way I can," she said, turning around and heading us back toward my car. "If you need any money for this, please don't hesitate to let me know. I want to get to the bottom of this as soon as possible." Her voice had deepened and she was now sounding like some chief executive officer speaking to her staff.

I decided to bait her. "It's not fair, is it, that he should undo what Cyril and your mother worked so hard to build?"

"No it isn't," she said fiercely. "He's such a philistine. He's unrefined, crude. I can't stand the thought that he could kill my mother and then walk away with everything."

"With your rightful inheritance, you mean?"

"That, too," she said. "I make no bones about that part of it. Look, Nigel, I've seen the bottom of the barrel. I know what it's like to be poor and I have no intention of ever being poor again or having my children poor. My first husband walked out on me, leaving me with two kids, just like my father did to my mother. I decided right then that the next time I married, it would be an investment as well as a marriage. Nothing personal, but I don't trust men."

I was still thinking about something she said a moment earlier. "Your first husband walked out on you, the same as your father did to your mother?" I said.

"Yes," she laughed with bitterness. "At least I didn't have to find a house for me and two kids, like my mother did."

"Three kids, you mean," I corrected.

"No, I only have two children, both boys. You met the younger one at the house after the funeral," she said.

"I meant your mother," I said. "She had three kids when your father walked out."

"No she didn't. It was just me and Annarita then."

"Where was Vaughn?" I asked.

"He hadn't been adopted yet," Virginia said. "That wasn't until almost two years later."

"Wait a minute," I said, grabbing her by the arm and halting our walk. "Vaughn was adopted?"

She looked at me intensely for a moment before answering, as though she was trying to decide if I was pretending I didn't know this. "Yes, he's adopted," she said. "I thought you knew that."

"No, I had no idea," I said.

"Annarita didn't tell you? She never mentioned it to Nicky?" she asked.

"Not unless he's had a severe case of dementia that I don't know about. Are you certain of this?"

She looked at me like I had insulted her.

"I'm sorry. Of course you're certain. I can't believe no one mentioned this before now," I said, running my hand through my hair and trying to think about how this affected things.

"We don't mention it, because he's sensitive about it," Virginia said, taking my arm and resuming our stroll. "Growing up it was a real stigma. He's had a huge chip on his shoulder ever since he found out. That's why he never got along with my mother, and the fact that he treated my mother badly is why Cyril was always fighting with him. Of course, any time he got into trouble it was always because he was adopted. It became a broken record. Does it make a difference that he's adopted?" she asked.

"I don't know," I said. "I don't see why it would. It's just that, well, it's something no one has mentioned."

"Well, don't mention it in front of him unless you want a fight," she said as we reached my car. "And remember, if there's anything you need to help you with this, including money, just call me. Annarita can give you my number. But then I guess that's kind of laughable, isn't it?"

"I don't follow," I said.

"If you needed money, Annarita has a lot more now than I have." There it was at last, that little dig I was waiting for that betrayed something brewing beneath the surface. "Nevertheless," she said, "if you should need money, you call me."

She patted my arm and trotted back up the walk to the front door.

FIFTY

WHEN I got to Nicky's, he was in the garden out back. I stood in the doorway watching him work on a bonsai tree. The tree sat on the round green metal table along with his gardening toolbox, which was actually a fishing tackle box. Also on the table was a boom box playing an esoteric lecture on female archetypes—very Jungian. He wore a skullcap, a brown khaki work shirt, and glasses, and was looking at the tiny pine tree the way a painter might look at a canvas. He would snip something, step back, cock his head one way, then another, squinting his eyes. Then he would turn the tree, cover a branch with one hand, cock his head, and observe it from this new perspective. My mother's wedding ring caught the sunlight once when he moved his hand, and my heart fluttered.

I stood in the doorway for several minutes watching him. Seeing him like this, content, away from the world, absorbed in two things he loved—bonsai gardening and psychology—I felt this sudden surge of love for him. It was one of those moments of complete bliss that overcomes a person every once in a while, usually without warning, and always without words to express it.

Nicky turned to look at one of the trees that sat on the step-backed shelves below the deck and noticed me. He smiled broadly, switched off the tape player, and called out, "Hi, honey. How long have you been standing there?"

"Long enough to fall in love with you all over again," I said, coming down the steps and joining him in the yard.

He kissed me and asked, "How did it go?" He went back to his tree, but was listening to me, I could tell.

"Very interesting, actually, in more ways than one. But first, tell me how you're feeling," I said, placing a hand on his shoulder.

He turned and looked at me with a melancholy look in his eyes. "Dirty, like a whore," he said. "Like I've done something really wrong and horrible. Sad that I may have hurt you. Afraid you're going to go away from me now."

I took him in my arms and held him close. "I don't think you're dirty, or a whore. You haven't done anything wrong or horrible and I'm never going to leave you. Even if I did think you did something horrible, I wouldn't leave you. I'd tell you I thought you did something horrible and then we'd talk about it. That's the work of a relationship, isn't it? Doing all that nasty, difficult, emotionally draining work and then coming out of it feeling closer than ever?"

"I don't know, is it?"

"Isn't that what you did with Rosario?" I asked.

"No, not really," he answered. "Our way of handling difficulties was usually just to go away from each other and wait for the feelings to pass. It worked for us."

"Well it won't work for you and me," I said. "We will always talk about things. You're the one who started that in the first place. Have you completely forgotten Italy and how you saved my life?" I held him at arm's length and he looked at me bashfully.

"I remember Italy," he said softly, "but I hardly saved your life. Besides, it's easier to tell someone else what they're doing wrong than it is to see it in yourself."

"And evidently a lot easier to forgive someone else than to forgive yourself," I added.

He put his arms around me and hugged me again. "I love you, Nigel," he said rocking from side to side a little, almost like we were dancing. "Sometimes I think Rosario and Lyle conspired on the other side of life to bring us together. I think that quite a lot, actually."

"You might be right," I said. "Some force was at work. Whatever it was, I'm grateful." I kissed him, then said, "Show me what you're doing here."

He showed me the tree and told how he was pruning it so it would stay small, and how he had removed some wire from one limb because it was now fully formed and growing in the configuration he wanted. He showed me how it was a masculine form as opposed to the feminine, fluid form of another tree he pointed out. He spoke about the trees as if they were sacred living beings, which they are, I suppose. I realized, as I listened to him talk about the trees, how loving he was toward them and how, partly as a result of his work with the bonsai garden, this would spill over to me.

"I've learned most of what I know about life from working with these trees," he said. "You tend them with love and they grow and mature and prosper. Sometimes you need to restrain or direct or redirect them. Other times they need to be left alone. They need to be fed and nurtured and touched. The soil they are rooted in needs to be replenished from time to time." He looked at me and smiled, "Just like people." Nicky cocked his head and narrowed his eyes. "Nigel, You aren't crying, are you?"

I couldn't help it. It was all so fucking poignant. "I guess so," I said, and he put his arms around me again.

"What is it, honey?" he asked, holding me tight.

I tried to express it. "I never thought I would fall in love again. After Lyle died, I thought I was next and so I was just waiting to get sick and die. I thought I was lucky to have had one good relationship, and that to hope or look for another would be greedy. Then you came into my life and picked up right where Lyle left off. You have a spiritual life, an intellectual life, everything. You aren't afraid to love and you don't shy away from the hard work that's required of two people in a relationship. I'm so blessed, so lucky. I think I love you more than I have ever loved anyone in my life. I can't believe this is happening to me, that's all. Sometimes I just can't fucking believe it."

"We'll have to remind each other once in a while, because I can't believe it, either," Nicky said, looking at me and placing his open palm against my face. "I feel just the way you do and even more. Every day we have together is a treasure, which is why I feel so bad about what happened."

I started to reassure him, but he placed his fingers on my lips to shush me.

"I know, I know," he said, nodding his head and smiling. "It will just take me a little while to get my bearings back. Thank you for loving me so well."

I laughed. "The pleasure is all mine, I'm sure."

"And tomorrow, we get to go on a little trip together," he said.

"A honeymoon in the desert," I said.

"A honeymoon in the desert," he repeated.

FIFTY-ONE

I FILLED Nicky in on what had transpired at the reading of the will and on my conversation with Virge. We agreed there was something strange about the fact no one had mentioned Vaughn's adoption, but we couldn't figure out what. We decided to create a virtual whelping box, like the one that contained Annarita's puppies. We'd put things there that we didn't want to get away from us and we'd take care of them later.

Nicky called Annarita with our itinerary and where we'd be staying in case she needed to contact us. The next day we flew into Phoenix, rented a Toyota 4Runner and checked into the hotel in Scottsdale, where a message was waiting for us from Annarita, asking us to call her immediately upon arrival.

I unpacked while Nicky placed the phone call. I couldn't make out anything from his end of the conversation, but he took notes. He hung up and whistled loudly. "Things are really popping now," he said.

"What happened?" I asked, plopping on the bed in a half-lotus position.

"Looks like your new friend Virge has the sleuthing bug," Nicky joked.

"Huh?"

"Annarita said she came home from running one of the puppies to the vet today to find Virge waiting for her with a telephone number and the name of the person who supposedly made those calls to Travis last week," Nicky said. Then he added, with a mischievous smile, "You and Virge make quite a team, Mr. Bond. Sounds to me like she's got some *Octopussy* ideas about you."

"Stop being ridiculous and explain what's going on," I said, annoyed by even the suggestion that I was on friendly terms with Virge.

"She called in some favor or other with the Contra Costa police and got the name of a Sandy Jo Thomas and this phone number," Nicky said, holding up the hotel notepad on which he had written the number. "Shall you call, or shall I?"

I placed the call. The person who answered was hesitant to let me speak with Ms. Sandy Jo Thomas, wanting to know first if I was a lawyer and next if I was a reporter. When I convinced her I was neither, but needed to speak to Sandy regarding an urgent matter, she put a man on the phone. "This is Neil McBaer, Ms. Thomas's attorney. Who am I speaking with, please?"

"Mr. McBaer, my name wouldn't mean anything to you, but I am authorized by the family of Evelyn VanDeventer Iversen to conduct an investigation into her death." I heard myself and thought I had been watching too many detective series on television. "Several telephone calls were placed to my client's home from this telephone number and I would like to speak with Ms. Thomas about it."

There were some muffled sounds, then McBaer said, "Ms. Thomas isn't speaking with anyone right now. She's under a great deal of strain. Did you get this telephone number from the police or the county clerk's office?"

"No, sir," I said, trying to sound respectful and ingratiate myself as much as possible. "As I said, a simple trace on the call revealed this number. We aren't implying any wrongdoing on Ms. Thomas's part, Mr. McBaer. We simply want to know whom she called and what her business was with that person."

"And you say you're working for Iversen?" McBaer asked.

"No, sir, not Mr. Iversen," I clarified. "My partner and I have been retained by the VanDeventer family, the family of the deceased."

"Just a moment, please," McBaer said. Again there was a muffling of the receiver, voices in the background, then McBaer came back on the line. "What did you say your name was again?"

"Nigel Love," I said.

Nicky listened intently. We had exchanged places so I could make the call and now he was sitting on the bed cross-legged, bouncing up and down in anticipation.

"And who are you with, Mr. Love?"

I fumbled a bit on this one. "Uh, I'm a partner in an investigating agency?" I said, hearing it come out more as a question than an answer.

I shrugged toward Nicky, who was nodding his approval vigorously. He reached for the pen and notepad and began writing something down.

"And is this agency connected with the police or some government bureau?" McBaer pressed on.

"No, sir, it's a private firm," I said. Nicky handed me the pad and I read what he'd written, then said to McBaer. "N. and N. Pinscher, private investigators," I said, giving Nicky an inquisitive look, as if to say, "Where the hell did you come up with this and what does it mean?"

"Well, Mr. Love, if you want to come over here you can speak with me, but I don't think Ms. Thomas will be able to talk with you," he said.

"Why is that, Mr. McBaer? Does she have something to hide?"

There was a loud guffaw on the other end of the line, then, "Excuse me, Mr. Love, but you have no idea how funny that is from this end. Why don't you just come on over and see for yourself."

Nicky and I drove to the address. It was out in East Mesa almost to Apache Junction, about 45 minutes east of Phoenix. We drove through miles of citrus groves, almost overcome by the essence of the orange blossoms. The craggy Superstition Mountains loomed closer and closer as we traveled east.

"Don't you think it's kind of weird that her attorney was there?" Nicky asked, cupping his hand out the passenger window and letting the force of the rushing air swoop it back.

"Very strange," I said. "It's almost as though they were expecting us to call."

"Except they had no idea who we were."

"Well, they were expecting someone to call or that attorney wouldn't have been there," I concluded.

The house was a plain stucco two-bedroom tract home. There was nothing distinctive about it, and I couldn't help but think that the occupant wouldn't normally need an attorney unless she had been arrested.

There was no doorbell, so I knocked on the peeling wood door. An obese man in a suit answered. "Mr. Love?" he asked.

"Yes. You're McBaer, I take it?"

"Right," he said. He looked past me to Nicky and then back at me with an inquisitive look.

And there it was, right in front of me, for the first time since Nicky had explained to me what people see when they looked at us together. We were facing one of those people. Clearly, McBaer was confused by the presence of a man of color.

"My boss, Nicky Borja," I said, making the introduction.

McBaer's jaw dropped a little, then he recovered. "Come in," he said, stepping back into a dark room.

The living room was small and dingy and had only a naugahyde sofa and a plaid recliner sitting at angles to each other. In the corner, opposite the furniture, was a console television that was turned on, but with the volume turned all the way down. Jerry Springer shook his head judgmentally at a pierced and tattooed woman in black leather knee boots and halter top. She was being restrained by a muscular bald man as she tried to pummel what I assumed was her unfaithful boyfriend who had probably been sleeping with either her mother, her sister, her father, or all three.

"Please have a seat, Mr. Love, uh," McBaer said in a kind of Southern drawl, forgetting Nicky's name.

Nicky and I both ignored it and sat on the sofa. McBaer indelicately plopped into the recliner. He wore a gray suit that looked like he had slept in it, a white permanent-press shirt and a skinny gray tie. He was the kind of lawyer you see advertising on late-night television.

"How can I help you?" he asked, straightening the tie, which had flown over his shoulder when he fell into the chair.

"We just want to know if Ms. Thomas knows anyone in the VanDeventer household. We're trying to track down a number of telephone calls and right now the calls we're focusing on are the ones placed from this number."

"Is this a joke, Mr. Love?" McBaer asked, cocking his head slightly and looking back and forth between me and Nicky, squinting his eyes as though we "guys" might be able to share a moment together.

"I don't follow, Mr. McBaer," I said. "Why would you think this might be a joke?"

"Did Iversen send you guys here to intimidate Sandy Jo?"

Nicky and I exchanged puzzled looks. "Mr. McBaer, I told you why we're here. May we please speak with Ms. Thomas?"

"No, I don't think so," McBaer said. "That won't be possible, I'm afraid. You see, Sandy Jo…"

Just then a young, bedraggled woman appeared in the doorway behind McBaer. She must have come out of a bedroom somewhere else in the house. At first I thought she was sick, because all I could see was her head and shoulders and she leaned against the door jamb, holding her forehead with one hand. Nicky and I stood to acknowledge her presence and then I saw why she was leaning and remembered McBaer's laugh on the phone when I asked if she had something to hide. The woman was about 12 months pregnant. I had never seen a woman so pregnant. I don't know how she could even stand up.

"You fellas go back and tell that son of a bitch he had his chance to do right by me," the woman shouted. "He lied and he lied and he lied," she shrieked, beginning to cry. "He fucked me and now he's trying to fuck me over and it ain't gonna happen. Trav's gonna pay, by God. I swear he is. That no-good…" Then she began bawling and couldn't talk any more.

McBaer, who had been struggling his way out of the recliner during Sandy Jo's tirade, finally got to his feet and waddled over to the woman. "Sandy Jo, honey, you gotta rest now," he patronized. "Remember what the doctor said. Come on, now, sugar, back to bed," he said, taking her by the arm and helping her back into the bedroom.

"I mean it, you two," she shouted as she disappeared into the room. "You tell him he had his chance to do right and he blew it!"

Nicky and I stared at one another. Nicky was trying hard not to laugh and I was giving him menacing looks, trying to discourage any incorrigible behavior. McBaer came back into the room shaking his head.

"She's real upset," he said, putting his hands in his pockets a bit nervously. "So you guys really had no idea about the lawsuit?"

"What lawsuit?" Nicky asked.

"The paternity suit. It just got filed this morning, which is why I was flustered on the phone. I couldn't figure out how you found out so fast."

"I take it Ms. Thomas has filed a paternity suit against Mr. Iversen," I said.

"That's right," McBaer said, grinning as he thought about his legal fees. "Ten million dollars, including mental anguish, pain and suffering, and loss of Ms. Thomas's good name."

I caught Nicky turning to look at me at the mention of Ms. Thomas's "good name," which is why I kept looking at McBaer. "I see," I said slowly. "I assume you have some way of proving that Mr. Iversen is the father of this baby?"

"Babies," McBaer corrected. "There are two little angels in there. And yes, we do have proof."

"Just out of curiosity, Mr. McBaer, what would that proof consist of?"

"The damned fool consented to a blood test three months ago," McBaer beamed. "Came down here to take it. Don't know what that boy was thinking."

"Guess he thought Sandy Jo was a loose woman," Nicky posited, managing to keep a straight face.

"And the results of the test?" I inquired, before McBaer figured out he should take offense at Nicky's comment.

"A 99.9% match to Sandy Jo's amniotic fluid. DNA doesn't lie. He's the daddy all right."

FIFTY-TWO

WE DROVE back to the hotel slowly, taking in the lush greenery the intoxicating fragrance of the citrus groves and the wide expanse of desert sky. It was beginning to get hot, so we rolled up the windows of the 4Runner and turned on the air conditioning.

"Now what?" Nicky asked.

"I think we need to pay a visit to the site of the drowning," I said. "I want to see the layout. As long as we're here."

"Aren't we going to go to the ranch?" Nicky asked. "I want to see cowboys."

"Behave yourself and we might go to the ranch," I said, pointing my finger at him across the console. "But stay out of the bunkhouse."

Nicky leaned toward me and wrapped his lips around my pointing finger and began to suck. "That's more like it," I said. "Make sure that's the only thing you put in your mouth today."

He stopped abruptly and leaned back, looking out the side window.

"I'm sorry," I said, reaching over and taking his hand. "I didn't mean it like that. I wasn't thinking. Please, Nicky, don't get upset."

"I can't help it," he said. "I told you, I feel dirty. Let's not talk about it."

We rode back to the hotel in silence. I vowed to think before I spoke from then on, at least about sex.

We got directions to Lake Barnett from the concierge. She gave us a Maricopa County map and circled the lake in red magic marker. How to actually get there was more than she could cope with. "It's really remote," she said.

"We know," Nicky said, wrapping his arm around me and winking at the woman behind the desk. Then he smiled at me and I felt a small rush of relief, thinking perhaps he was back on track emotionally.

The drive to Lake Barnett was stunning. We made our way north, through Scottsdale and Carefree, toward the string of man-made lakes. Houses thinned out, then became five- and ten-acre ranches, then buildings disappeared altogether. The desert stretched on the horizon as far as we could see. Giant saguaro cacti, like supplicants, dotted the landscape, their fat, upstretched arms reaching toward the heavens.

"Are those saguaros?" Nicky asked.

"Yes," I answered. "Supposedly the main stalk represents a hundred years' growth and each arm is 50 years in the making. See those tall spikes over there with the red flowers on the end?" I said, pointing. "Those are Ocotillo."

"Gorgeous!" Nicky exclaimed. "I love the desert." He reached over, took my hand from the steering wheel and kissed it. "Thank you for bringing me here."

I said nothing, but smiled.

"Thank you for letting me work through this and for having patience with me."

"That's what it's all about," I said.

"Can we talk for a minute? Seriously?" he asked, turning sideways to face me, one knee pulled up on the seat.

"Sure, anything your heart desires, my little prairie dog."

"Do you believe in having a monogamous relationship?"

I couldn't tell if this was a trick question or if it had something to do with what had transpired between him and Vaughn, so I had to think for a moment.

"It's not a difficult question," he pressed, only half joking.

"It is and it isn't. Let me answer it this way," I began. "Yes, I prefer monogamy. For me it is the way a relationship works best. But it isn't the only way I've been in a relationship. Lyle insisted on an open relationship. He dragged me kicking and screaming into it, but after a while I got used to it."

"Is that what you want with me?" he asked.

"No," I said flatly, feeling my stomach sink. I remembered the trouble Lyle and I had with my insecurity over him having sex with other men. "You said you weren't going to lie to me, ever. I'm not going to lie to you either. I want a monogamous relationship with you. If I can't have that, I'll take what you have to offer. At least I'll try to." There, I thought that was honest enough.

"Tell me why you prefer monogamy," Nicky said. I still couldn't tell if he was baiting me or seeing if I felt the same way he did.

"I've seen lots of open relationships," I said, "and what happens to each and every one of them is this: Eventually, when things get tough, rather than bringing the energy of those uncomfortable feelings to each other and trying to work it through, one partner takes it outside the relationship, to someone else. And sooner or later, someone else looks a lot better than the current partner, naturally, since there is tension in the relationship at the time. So before you know it, they've broken up instead of dealing with their problems and working on the relationship they're already in. They attach to a new partner and start all over again because that's a lot easier than doing the difficult work of being a couple, especially the inner work that's required of each person individually. You know, the work of finding out who and what you really are, independent of your partner. I don't think relationships break up from the outside. I think they fall apart from within."

"Do you think sex can save a relationship?" he asked.

"What do you mean?"

"Well, if you think it's not OK to take sex outside the relationship, especially when a couple is having difficulties, it implies that they might be able to work out their problems by having sex, doesn't it?" he said.

"What I think is that sex is nothing to build a relationship on, that sex can be a vehicle of celebration, of destruction, or of healing. Sometimes, when words fail, feelings—even sexual feelings—can bring two people closer together. I don't see how a person can have enough energy to give to more than one person at a time," I said, rather finally.

"You don't think people have enough sexual energy to be sleeping with multiple partners?" Nicky asked.

"Oh, that's plenty possible. We've all done that routine at one time or another. But I don't think sex is always about sex," I said. "I think it's a front for intimacy, but men, not wanting to expose their feelings for fear of becoming vulnerable, hide behind sex. Believe me, sooner or later, in the right mood, with the right music playing or the right projection going on inside, that casual sex partner becomes the answer to all a guy's problems. Sooner or later, sex with the trick turns into true intimacy or a reasonable facsimile thereof. If that happens to someone while he's already in a relationship that's requiring a lot of effort, then he and his partner find themselves dividing up the CDs and looking for new places to live."

Nicky sat silent, contemplative.

"So, I take it you want an open relationship," I said, trying not to sound disappointed.

Nicky gave a kind of derisive laugh. "Hell, no," he said. "If you slept with someone else, I'd leave you in a minute."

I looked at him incredulous. "Really?"

"Why do you think I feel so horrible about what happened? It defiled our marriage," he said with anger in his voice.

"Marriage?" I repeated softly.

"Well, I think of us as married," he said. "Don't you?"

I couldn't help but laugh. "Of course, but I didn't think —"

"Oh, please!" he shouted. "I've been running around acting like Mary Haines in *The Women,* living in a fool's paradise. I keep wondering if it's too soon to talk about moving in together."

I must have looked dumbfounded. I had no idea he felt that strongly about me.

"Pick your jaw up off the floor, Mr. Love," Nicky said, his eyes twinkling. "You know damned well I'm over the moon for you. I said I'd marry you didn't I?" He held up the hand with the ring on it. "Well, didn't I?"

"You also said time would tell," I reminded him.

"Well, look at the clock on the wall," he said with a bit of giddiness in his voice. "It's five minutes to wedding. You were more correct than you knew when you referred to this as our honeymoon. This is it. I just wish I wasn't in such a funk."

"Maybe I can remedy that," I offered. "If you'll open yourself up to the possibilities."

"I'm sure you meant something by that, but I have no idea what,"

Nicky said, quoting *All About Eve* yet again.

"I'll interpret for you later," I said.

Then Nicky unfastened his seat belt and leaned over and kissed me on the mouth, complete with tongue.

"Careful, Dorothy," I said. "We're not in California anymore. They shoot boys for doing that out here."

"Let 'em. I'm on my honeymoon. I'll die happy."

FIFTY-THREE

LAKE BARNETT was the most godforsaken place I had ever seen, outside of Area 51 in Nevada. We followed the highway to a state road, then took that to a dirt road, then followed that about four miles to an abandoned parking lot. A sheriff's van parked near a sun-bleached emergency phone said CRIME SCENE LAB on the side. An empty squad car sat next to it. As we pulled up, a uniformed officer stepped out of the van and waited for us to park. He was about 30, had a paunch, and wore those glasses that get dark automatically in the sun. With the gut and the bad glasses, he wouldn't have made it through the first round of auditions for The Village People.

He nodded but said nothing. I was reminded of the posturing that goes on in leather bars. I restrained my grin.

"Afternoon, sir," the deputy said. "Can I be of assistance?"

"My name is Nigel Love and this," I said, indicating Nicky, "is my partner, Nicky Borja."

Nicky nodded at the cop, took in the name on his name tag and said, "Yo! Deputy Holland."

I couldn't believe he said that. I brought my hand up to my eyebrows as though I needed to shield my eyes from the sun and scrunched up my face, like the light was hurting my eyes. It was the only way to camouflage the laugh I couldn't contain. I wanted to kick him. "We've been retained by the VanDeventer family to look into the drowning of Evelyn VanDeventer Iversen," I said. I noticed the frown on the officer's face, so I quickly added, "We won't be in your way. This is mostly related to some personal matters involving the daughters." I smiled, but the cop didn't.

"What are you doing here, then?" he asked. "If it's a personal matter, I mean."

"Frankly, we were in Scottsdale, meeting with one of the parties involved, and, well, curiosity got the better of us. Mr. Borja here is a close friend of the youngest daughter, and we thought since we were this close, we'd come out here and take a look around."

Deputy Holland looked at each of us, but kept his opinion to himself.

"So, could you point us in the right direction?" I asked amiably.

"Depends on what you want to see," he said curtly.

"We were hoping to see where the couple was camped and where the boat was docked," I said, looking out over the lake in the distance.

"Ain't nothin' to see," he said. "Only thing still down there is the boat and that's off-limits to civilians."

"Well, we're here now, so we'll just take a look," I said, a little more firmly.

The deputy and I had a short-lived stare-down, then with exaggerated exasperation, he pointed and said, "About a mile down that dirt road is where the old boat dock is. The campsite is about a hundred yards past that, right on the lake. Can't miss it."

"Thank you officer," I said. "We won't be long."

Nicky and I got back in the 4Runner as the deputy stood watching, his hands on his hips. I could tell he didn't like us being there. As we turned the 4Runner and eased away he yelled, "Don't go disturbing things out there. Don't touch that boat."

"Like there's a lot to disturb," Nicky groaned. "What does he mean, don't touch the boat? Do we really look like we're going skiing? I'm not even wearing Lycra."

"Don't do that again," I said to Nicky, only half joking.

"Do what, honey?" Nicky replied, playing dumb.

"Don't make Daddy slap you in public," I teased.

"No, Daddy, I won't," Nicky promised. "Only in private."

The road was dirt, but it wasn't rough, at least not in the sport utility vehicle. I wouldn't want to drive it in a sedan. We came to the boat dock, but drove past it to the campsite. There was nothing there to see. We got out and walked around and all we found was the remnants of a campfire, but even that could have been a year old.

I walked the hundred or so yards to where there was a dilapidated single pier. The jet boat was tied to it and haphazardly wrapped in yellow police tape. The boat looked brand-new. The only sign of wear was a streak of orange on the outer hull near the bow. Other than that it looked like it had just come off the showroom floor.

About 15 feet from the pier was a piling sticking about four feet out of the water with faded neon orange numbers on it, indicating, I assumed, the depth of the water. The top half of a five was visible and, above that, the numbers went in one foot increments to eight.

I looked at the narrow, sandy path that went from the pier to what I assumed used to be a staging area for boaters to park their cars, although there was no indication of any formal parking places. The path was nothing but a thin strip of sand, mostly overgrown with creosote bushes and brittlebrush. I was thinking about how narrow it was from disuse and wondering how long it had been since this area was a popular boating spot when I heard Nicky call my name.

I turned around, but he wasn't there. I looked toward the campsite and saw him near the water, close to where Evelyn and Travis had pitched their tent, paying me no attention. But I would have sworn I heard my name called. I went to the pier and walked out to the end. Across the lake, I could see another small pier just like the one I was standing on. There at the end of that pier was a young woman wearing a long dark skirt and a white blouse. I waved and she waved back. How odd, I thought.

I called to Nicky, who looked up from where he was crouched, looking at something at the water's edge. I pointed to the dock directly across the lake and he looked in that direction, but when I looked up she was gone. It was the oddest thing. There was no place for her to hide. The terrain was flat and barren; no cars or trucks were visible, not even a boat. Nicky turned back toward me, shrugging his shoulders as if to say "What?"

I just waved my hands in a gesture indicating *never mind,* but I couldn't let go of it. It was too bizarre. We looked around a few more minutes, decided there was nothing there, and drove back to the parking lot.

I stopped the 4Runner and knocked on the door of the van. It opened, and the deputy stuck his head out.

"Yeah?"

"Excuse me, officer, I was wondering if you could tell me what that dock is across the lake?"

"The one directly across from where you were?" he asked.

"Yes, that one," I said.

"Nothing. Used to be a boat dock like the one you were nosing around, but neither one of 'em's been used for five or six years, maybe longer."

"Is that all that's over there?" I asked.

"That and another campsite like the one you were at," he said, avoiding using the term 'nosing around' again, though I could tell he wanted to.

"I suppose that's the place where the men were camped the night the Iversens were here, is that right?"

"As a matter of fact, it is," he said. "At least, that's what Iversen claims. Why?"

"Nothing," I said. "Just wanted to be clear about it. Thank you, deputy. You've been very helpful," I said and got back in the 4Runner with Nicky. I waved as we pulled away.

"What was that about?" Nicky asked.

"Just asking about that other dock over there," I said, still ruminating about the woman I saw.

"What about it?" Nicky asked.

"Nothing, really. I thought I saw someone over there, that's all. I was wondering if that's where the other party was that night," I said.

"The other party?"

"You know, the guys playing the radio that Travis said he had to go ask to turn down the music so he and Evelyn could sleep."

"Oh, right," Nicky said. "Why'd you want to know about that?"

"I don't know. Something's bothering me about it, but I don't know what."

"Did those men ever come forward?" Nicky asked.

"No, and that's one of the strange things," I said. "With all the publicity this has received, they're bound to have heard about it. Wouldn't you think they'd come forward to give a statement?"

"Maybe they're from out of state," Nicky offered.

"This has been on network news and in every newspaper in the country," I said. "Surely they've seen the story."

"Most people don't want to get involved in murder investigations."

"Except there's no murder investigation. He's never been charged with anything. All their coming forward would do is corroborate Travis's story that they were there. They might have heard the boat when she went out in the lake. They could possibly clear all this up."

"Looks like that's not going to happen," Nicky said, slouching down and putting his stocking feet on the dashboard. "Where to now?"

"I think it's time to pay a visit to the ranch," I said.

"It's almost dinnertime," Nicky whined.

"Then we're sure to find someone home to answer our questions," I pointed out.

"Well, I hope they're friendly," Nicky moaned. "I'm hungry. Maybe they'll have a pot of jackrabbit stew!"

FIFTY-FOUR

THE RANCH wasn't in Scottsdale, like everybody always said; it was actually in Carefree, a carefully planned, extremely prohibitive, unincorporated town north of Scottsdale. It sat on the most beautiful part of the desert, with rocky bluffs and rises and countless groves of ocotillo, jumping cholla, and other cacti and bushes whose names escaped me.

When we drove up the drive and parked in front, it was clearly evident that no one was home, at least in the main house. All the shades and curtains were drawn tight. There were outbuildings scattered about: two barns, a bunkhouse, and what I assumed was the foreman's house, along with stables and corrals.

We walked around the outside of the house a bit, trying to look through the windows, but there was nothing we could see. It was a ranch-style house, huge and sprawling, probably about 5,000 square feet. The front had a desert lawn, where someone planted, or left standing, two giant saguaros and an ocotillo, and had spread some red rocks around. The only obvious "improvement" was a cement walkway that led from the front door to the end of the lawn area, a distance of about 50 feet. Cars were left to park randomly in a dirt clearing.

We walked toward the bunkhouse, hoping to find someone to talk with. I had pulled back the screen door and was about to knock when Nicky reached past me and opened the door. Our unexpected entrance startled two ranch hands, who were coming out of what appeared to be a communal shower. Neither one was wet, neither had a towel, and both sported erections. One man, whose dick was pointing straight out, turned and disappeared back into the shower room. The other, younger, brash, and about three-quarters hard, stood there staring at us.

"Welcome fellas," he said, "looking for work?"

I started to answer, but Nicky beat me to it. "Maybe," he said.

"Is Travis around?"

"Nah," the young cowboy said, moving to a round oak table near the window and reaching for a pack of cigarettes. He made no attempt to cover himself. "Travis is still in California. Never know when he's coming back. You a friend of his?" he asked, looking Nicky up and down.

"Friend of the family, you might say, more than a friend of his," Nicky said.

The other cowboy, barefoot and in jeans now, walked back into the room, buttoning his shirt and smiling nervously.

"Friends of Travis," Cowboy Number One said, nodding at us.

"Hi, name's Hank," the fellow buttoning his shirt said, stepping forward and extending his hand. We introduced ourselves. Cowboy Number One identified himself as Terry and shook our hands too, his dick not quite limp yet, bobbing up and down in the process. I felt like I had entered a nudist colony and we were the ones out of sync.

"Austin ain't here right now either," Terry said, "if you're serious about looking for work." He looked us up and down again. "Where'd you say you knew Travis from?'

"Family ties," Nicky said.

"Didn't think you met on the circuit," Terry said. "Don't look like you rope or ride."

"That's right," I said. "Who's Austin?"

"He's the foreman," Hank offered, standing with his hands in his pockets. His sandy hair was disheveled and he looked like a schoolboy. I don't think he could have been more than 25, if that, and Terry looked barely 20. "He does all the hiring. He'll be back tomorrow."

"We're not going to be around that long," I said, "but thanks for the tip. Maybe on our way back."

"Where you headed?" Terry asked, setting his cigarette in a red metal ash tray on the table and reaching at last for a pair of Levi's flung over the back of one of the table's wooden chairs.

"Utah," Nicky said.

The two cowboys looked at one another as though we had said something wrong. "Utah?" Hank said. "Why Utah?"

"Just like being in the desert," I said. "We're seeing the desert in

Arizona and Utah and thought we'd stop in and see if Travis was around."

"You heard about his wife I s'pose?" Hank asked.

"Yes, we did," Nicky said. "That's one of the reasons we stopped by."

"Shit," Terry muttered.

"Terry!" Hank said, almost gritting his teeth.

"I don't give a fuck," Terry said, sneering at Hank. "Everybody knows they weren't gettin' along. And you two ain't nothin' but reporters or lawyers. You can stop bullshittin' us. You think just 'cause we're ranch hands we don't know shit."

"Sorry," I said, rather lamely. "We're neither lawyers nor reporters."

"Right," Terry sneered. "You're not on your way to Utah to see Ruth McGraw either, I suppose."

"Ruth McGraw?" we both said at the same time.

"Travis's second wife," Hank said.

"They know damned well who she is," Terry snarled. "Don't play their cat-and-mouse game. They probably know a lot more'n we do." Terry sat on the Navajo-blanketed sofa now, pulling on his boots. He looked up at us with contempt but also with daring. "Why can't you guys just come in here and ask us what you want to know, 'stead a sneakin' 'round like a bunch of perverts, trying to catch somebody doin' something you can put in the papers? I'm sick to death of you high-toned city boys blowin' in here with muscles you get from gyms instead of honest work and Day-Glo suitcases with designer labels. You boys just better watch your backs is all I can say."

"Don't mind him," Hank said, stepping forward now, trying to get between Terry and us. "He's just cranky. One of them ornery ranch hands. We don't know nothin' about Ruth or anything about that other woman either, the one who's gonna have his baby," Hank said with a breaking voice.

"That's right," Terry said, heading for the door behind us. He bumped his chest against Nicky's and gave him a lascivious look as he passed. "We just poor dumb cowboys what don't know nothin 'bout what the boss man does." He turned before letting the screen door slam and added, "With his time or his dick." Then he laughed loudly and strode down the steps of the bunkhouse.

"Look," Hank began, "I'm really sorry about him. He's pretty pissed off. He was supposed to get a raise month before last, then last month, then this month, and Austin keeps putting him off. He's ready to quit, I think. We don't know nothin', honest. We ain't been here long enough to know nothin'."

"How long have you worked here?" I asked.

Hank shifted from one bare foot to the other. "I been here near six months. Terry's been here since Travis and Ms. VanDeventer bought the place, about a year or so ago. Travis hired him 'cause he knew him from the circuit in Utah. Said he was a good trainer, and he is. But him and Austin don't get along."

"The foreman?" Nicky asked.

"Right. They're at each other's throats night and day. I'm surprised Terry's hung on this long. He'd probably of quit a long time ago 'cept for being so close to Travis. Austin done fired Terry once, but Travis hired him back. They're pretty good friends, I think. Least they was."

"Well," I said, extending my hand to Hank, "thanks for talking with us. Sorry we barged in on you like that."

Hank blushed a bright red and stammered. "That's OK. We wasn't doin' nothin' really. Just gettin' outta the shower."

We left Hank standing in the bunkhouse and closed the door behind us.

"Are you thinking what I'm thinking?" Nicky asked.

"Yeah. Terry's our fountain of information and he's ready to talk," I said. "But which one of us should approach him?"

"Considering the look he gave me when we came nipple to nipple, I'd say I'm the likely candidate," Nicky said.

"Are you OK with that?" I asked.

"Sure," Nicky smiled. "Angry cowboys are my specialty."

While Nicky went looking for Terry, I went back up to the house and nosed around some more, trying to look into windows in the back of the house, but I still couldn't see anything. Living room, dining room, kitchen, and one bedroom. The rest of the windows had the blinds drawn. I decided to wait for Nicky in the 4Runner.

So Travis had a second wife. No one had mentioned that, but obviously it had come out somehow, since we were beaten to the ranch by reporters or lawyers—or both. This could be the marriage Matthew had found in the Mount Carmel Junction records. But what could a second wife tell us that the first one couldn't? And why had she never been mentioned by anyone? Could it be that Travis planned to go back to her? Could it be that they were never divorced? What could the secret of Wife Number Two possibly be? Only Nicky would be able to get us the information we needed. I only hoped it wasn't going to be a repeat of his adventure with Vaughn. All I could do was sit in the Arizona sun and wait.

FIFTY-FIVE

NICKY wasn't gone long, so I didn't have long to fret. Terry seemed like a loose cannon and I didn't want to mess with him. Nevertheless, it turned out that once he was alone with Nicky he was not only forthcoming, but friendly. I didn't know how Nicky had managed it, but I was glad it hadn't turned ugly or sexual. Nicky wasn't the only one still smarting from his encounter with Vaughn.

Terry knew Travis from their days on the rodeo circuit in Utah and Texas, just like Hank said. Travis performed with his Brahman bull and Terry was a roper and horse trainer. Travis had hired Terry to help him train horses and work with his Brahmans at the Carefree ranch and also to help from time to time at a spread he owned near Abilene, Texas.

"What a queer bird he is," Nicky said, as we pulled away from the ranch. He was struggling to fasten his seat belt. "You know they were having sex when we walked in."

"No kidding. It was definitely a strange encounter. I couldn't believe Terry stood there naked for practically the entire conversation."

"I confronted him about it, too," Nicky said smugly.

"You did?"

"Of course. It gave me the upper hand."

"What did you say?"

"When I caught up with him in the corral, I said, 'Sorry about interrupting you guys; we didn't mean to embarrass you.' He just smirked and said, 'No biggie. I'll get me some later.' Just like that, casual as a cat."

"Jeez," I exclaimed, turning onto the main road back to Scottsdale, "I thought that stuff just happened in porn flicks. I had no idea *Bunkhouse Buddies* was a documentary. So what did he tell you? Anything useful?"

"Very," Nicky said, pulling a matchbook from his shirt pocket. "Her name is Ruth McGraw." Nicky was waiting for my reaction.

"Does that mean something?" I asked.

"That name doesn't ring a bell?"

"Other than them mentioning her in the bunkhouse? No, why?"

"It's the name Matthew came up with, the one who married a Thomas T. Iversen in Mount Carmel Junction, Utah," Nicky said, smirking.

"Are you sure?"

"Of course," he said. "I wrote down the name before we left home because I figured we might have to go looking for the woman by her maiden name."

"And Terry knows her?"

"Yeah, they used to hang together. I think they were drinking buddies," Nicky said, putting down the window and hanging his elbow out in the warm evening air. "Evidently she's a real pistol."

"Pistol? Did you say she's a real pistol?"

"Well, that's what Terry called her. Said she had the biggest tits he'd ever seen except for Dolly Parton."

"Nicky!" I protested.

"What?" he shouted. "It's not my choice of words. I'm quoting him. He said she had big...breasts and that she was a pistol. Jeez!"

"Pistol?" I repeated.

"We're in the desert. We have to start talking like these people or they're going to think we're city slickers and not give us what we're after," Nicky said with mock seriousness. "Now I'm mighty hungry after all that dick work—pun intended—so let's go rustle us up some grub."

The sun was just reaching the horizon, and splashing an orange wash across the landscape. The sky went from orange in front of us to blue above us to deep purple in the rearview mirror. We stopped at a steak house and ordered T-bones, figuring we should start acting more cowboy-like, and when we got back to the hotel I showed Nicky how good I was at riding a bucking bronco.

FIFTY-SIX

THE NEXT MORNING we headed north to Utah. We drove through Flagstaff and made our way around the Grand Canyon. Nicky kept saying he wanted to see it, but I promised him grander things to see farther on, free of the busloads of tourists and traffic jams.

It took us most of the day to get to Zion National Park, where we had a reservation at the park lodge. After a shower, we went hiking, past the long lines of German and French tourists and past the parking areas where cars stood with their motors idling, waiting for other cars to pull out so they could pull in. We hiked to where the main, paved path dead-ended into the stream, then we charged into the cold water and made our way slowly through the gorge, where not many people trek. Most tourists don't like to get their high-top Nikes wet.

The cliffs rose above us a thousand feet on both sides, and after a mile and a half we climbed out of the water onto land again, where the gorge widened out once more. We climbed a bit farther, sat on a huge slab of sandstone, and took in the silence. The cottonwood trees along the river swayed in a slight breeze and birds flitted back and forth among the branches. The light made its way through the bluffs into the trees illuminating them in a way that made it look like the leaves were lights themselves—tiny, flat, chartreuse lights waving at us from the arms of the cottonwoods.

We sat in silence for a long time. In places like this there isn't any need for words; nature says it all for you. At last Nicky spoke. "This is the desert?" he asked incredulously. "I thought the desert was sand and camels."

"Not the American desert," I said and laughed. "But this is only the edge of the desert. Tomorrow, we're going to see the real desert, at least the real Utah desert. Then you'll understand why I love it so much."

"I think I already do," he said, taking my hand and kissing it one, two, three distinct times, as if it were a ritual.

We made our way back to the lodge before dark fell. We read, made love, and went to sleep early so we could head out before the masses were up and swarming around the park.

Terry, it turned out, was absolutely accurate in his description of Ruth McGraw. She truly was a pistol. And, yes, she had the biggest tits either Nicky or I had ever seen in person. And they really did have to be called tits, for nothing else could adequately describe them. She had what we used to refer to in high school as "bullet boobs." Her breasts pointed straight out and it looked like she had them packed into huge metal funnels. And she knew how to dress to her—or rather, "their"—advantage. We could tell that she didn't take shit from anybody. She had a look that said "Don't mess with me unless you're looking for trouble," but she also had a smile that would melt the heart of Genghis Khan.

We caught up with her where she worked: the Mount Carmel Gravel Company. She was a truck driver, of all things, driving a dump truck back and forth from the gravel pits to a highway construction site about ten miles away. She was funny and outspoken and very forthcoming, not at all what we'd expected. She told us to meet her at the restaurant at the Best Western motel in Mount Carmel Junction and she'd take her coffee break early. We followed her in the 4Runner, gravel bouncing out of her dump truck and ricocheting off our bumper.

She wore tight jeans and a red, white, and green plaid shirt with a sheer green scarf tied around her neck. "I was half expecting you," she said. We sat in a booth near the window, Nicky and I on one side, Ruth on the other. She had strawberry blond hair, long, but piled on top of her head and fastened somehow. I suspected that at night, after work, when she found her way to the honky-tonks of St. George, she let that hair down.

"Yeah, I figured it was just a matter of time before somebody caught up with me, or him, or us," she said, stirring a mug of coffee into which she had heaped three teaspoons of sugar and some cream.

"Do you want to say more about that?" I said, trying to get her to say what she knew without revealing that we didn't know anything other than the fact that she existed.

"Since Travis and I talk a lot on the phone, I mean. Now with this drowning thing, I figured the police would be tracking me down." She sipped her coffee, then smiled. "Or a couple of handsome reporters like you two."

"Actually, we're not reporters," Nicky offered.

"You mean I'm not gonna get my picture in the papers?" she teased, making a mock frown. "What are you two, then, Heckle and Jeckle?"

"Actually, I'm a friend of Annarita, Evelyn's youngest daughter," Nicky explained. "We went to school together."

"What's that got to do with all this hoopla?" she asked.

"Nothing, really," Nicky said. "It's just that she's been distraught since her mother's drowning and things keep popping up about Travis that make her and the rest of the family wonder how well they actually know the man."

She let out a hearty laugh and threw her head back. "Ain't that the truth. Said the same thing myself the first time he beat me." She flagged down a passing waitress, who refilled our mugs. "What you looking so shocked about? Don't you have wife beaters out in California? I know for a fact you got some." She sipped her coffee and studied our response. "At least one," she added mischievously, with a twinkle in her eye.

"You take all this rather lightly," I said.

"My beatings or that woman's drowning?" she asked, looking me straight in the eye.

"I was referring to the spousal abuse," I said.

"Yeah, you're from California all right," she said, shaking her head. "You folks got a fancy name for everything. Here we just call it beatin' the crap out of your wife." She sighed and there was a moment of silence among us. An angel passing through the room, my mother would have said.

"Blood under the bridge, honey," she said with a wry laugh. "I probably asked for it. Oh, not the beatings, but the trouble I got for running off with him. I met him at a bar across the state line. That's where we go around here for something stronger than three-two beer. That's Mormon beer, in case you don't know, 3.2% alcohol. They want to make sure you drink a lot before you get drunk, that way they make more money than if you was drinking regular beer." She laughed again, good-naturedly. There was no way not to like this woman.

"When was that?" I asked.

"About a hundred years ago. He was still married to Juleen or whatever the hell her name was. The minute I seen him walk through the door I said, 'That's the cowboy I'm gonna marry.' And I did. His body was a lean, mean sex machine. I doubt it's the same now, but he was a roll in the hay in those days, I'm tellin' you. He came up and asked me to dance and I fell in love right then and there, right on that dance floor."

"You said he was married at the time?" Nicky asked. He stirred his coffee absent-mindedly, clinking the mug in a most annoying way.

"Yeah, but I didn't know anything about that then. All's I knew was he was H-O-T hot and I wanted it," she said, and let out a little whoop that caused the two elderly couples in the next booth to turn and crane their necks at us. This didn't faze Ruth McGraw one bit. "We saw each other every night after that until Christmas. Come Christmas, he up and disappeared without a trace." Ruth got a bit more reflective here, staring at her hands, which were wrapped around the thick, diner-style coffee mug.

"That must have hurt," Nicky said. I reached over and placed my hand on top of his to get him to stop stirring his coffee. "Sorry," he said to me.

"Where did he disappear to?" I asked.

"I didn't know at first, but finally I got one of his rodeo pals to spill the beans that he was married. I couldn't believe he'd keep that kind of secret from me, but I come to see it's how he operates," she said. She looked at us and gave a pained grin. "I didn't know he married that California woman until I read about her drowning. Ain't that something? And we been talking to one another on the phone almost once or twice a month for the past two years."

Nicky and I both gave her sympathetic but surprised looks.

"Well, I gave the son of a bitch an ultimatum once I got the news he had a wife up in Wyoming or wherever she hightailed it to. For all I know, she could have lived right down the street. He's such a lyin' little shit. Never know whether to believe him or run over him in my truck."

"So what happened?" Nicky asked.

"We started living together and he filed for divorce from that wife of his. That Juleen," she said with disdain.

"Actually, her name is Tammi," Nicky said.

"With an 'i', I bet."

"Yes," Nicky laughed, "with an 'i.' T-a-m-m-i."

"See? Juleen, Tammi with an 'i.' Same thing," Ruth said, curling her lip. "Anyway, we finally got married. It was my idea, not his, so I can't blame anybody but myself for the heartache he caused me," she said, leaning back now, bullet boobs still reaching the yellow Formica table. "We both got jobs driving trucks, hauling coal for a local mine. It's all dried up now. Feds made 'em close it down so they could add to Capitol Reef. We had a good time while it lasted, though. Built us a ranch up there near Escalante. Did the whole thing ourselves. Borrowed my daddy's backhoe and some of the other heavy equipment he uses on his construction jobs. We even put in the plumbing and wiring. We'd work from sunup to sundown and then fuck like rabbits." She looked up to see if we were offended.

"It's OK," I assured her. "We talk like that too."

"I had a feelin' you boys weren't no saltpetered missionaries," she said, winking at us. "Then things just went sour. He started drinking and then he'd lose his temper at the least thing. He'd hit me, knock me across the room. Once he tied me up and beat me, then just left me on the kitchen floor and walked out. A neighbor found me after he came by to see if he could borrow a harness out of our tack room."

"Did you ever call the police?" I asked.

"Hell, yes," she responded. "You got any idea how much good that does in a place like this? You might as well call and say your pig stepped on your foot or your husband whipped the dog. Shit!" She was bitter beneath the bravado; that much was clear.

"What did you do? Leave him?" Nicky asked.

"No, not at first," she said. "My daddy didn't raise me to be no quitter. We went to a marriage counselor. Once. But then Travis wouldn't go no more. He said if I was a real woman I wouldn't have to go see those quacks. It's taken me five years to get my confidence back, to understand this didn't happen because I wasn't a good enough wife to him. All the son of a bitch wanted to do was be with those goddamned bulls of his and hang around and drink with his rodeo buddies, then come home and ride me till he fell off and passed out, which got to be less and less— the riding that is, not the passing out. That gets old fast, know what I mean, fellas?"

We assured her we did. "But you remained friends," Nicky observed. "Why's that?"

Ruth laughed, tossed her head back, and looked out the window where a tour bus was spitting out a stream of excited-looking but befuddled German tourists. "He's a hard one to resist, kid. Real hard. Kind of a charmer, if you know what I mean." She looked at Nicky now and smiled, like he might understand what she was saying better than I.

"Was he really all that charming, given that he beat you?" I asked, trying not to sound rhetorical.

"Ask that woman at the bottom of the lake. I'm sure she'll tell you," Ruth said, draining the last of her coffee.

FIFTY-SEVEN

WE DROVE slowly from Mount Carmel Junction up through the Escalante Steps, stopping every couple of miles to get out and walk around in the desert. We climbed huge Navajo sandstone formations with juniper trees growing out of crevices in the rock. The views over the Escalante were breathtaking. Far off in the distance we could see the Monti-LaSal National Forest that blanketed the mountains and foothills, and the quaking aspen belt that made it famous. The trees stretched from east to west to the horizon in both directions. In fall they created a yellow swath that extended for 200 miles.

"The largest concentration of aspens in the world," I said. Their white trunks rose from the dark hills like bleached matchsticks. We drove down the escarpment into Boulder, Utah, deviating only twice. Once to investigate a road to a place called Hole-in-the-Rock, but since there had been an unseasonal rain the night before and the red clay road was pretty slippery, we decided to go only about 15 miles, stopping at an area designated The Devil's Garden. We hiked around the unusual rock formations and followed the dry riverbed, ascending and descending through geologic time.

The second time we went exploring off the main road was when we came to a screeching halt after seeing a sign pointing to a dirt road that read DEVIL'S BACKBONE. We looked at one another. "Let's do it," I said.

"These Mormons sure have a thing for the devil," he said, shaking his head.

We turned the 4Runner around and took a winding dirt road for what seemed like 50 miles, switching back and forth through the forest, but climbing the entire time. I was just about to say "Let's turn around" when we came to a small wooden bridge. I eased the 4Runner up to it, but stopped when I saw what lay on either side.

"No way, honey, am I going to take this 4,000-pound vehicle over that Indiana Jones bridge," I said as I backed up and pulled over to the side.

We climbed out and walked to the bridge. Below, stretching away as far as we could see, was what truly looked like a backbone of white rock, descending from where we stood at 8,000 feet to the desert floor below.

We got out the camera and took some photos, mostly of Nicky standing next to remarkably shaped junipers growing out of sheer rock formations. He pointed out several different kinds of trees and talked about their shapes and how and why they grew that way. He told me about the "literary" school of bonsai, begun by Chinese masters, who went into the mountains to pray and meditate and who came back down and developed the art of making tiny trees that looked like the giant trees they had seen at the higher elevations.

I listened to him and watched as he tenderly examined a branch or touched a limb with his fingertips. Then I did what any self-respecting man on his honeymoon would do. I dragged him onto one of the larger, flatter outcroppings, tore his pants off, and made frenzied love to him. Every once in a while he would break his concentration from the sex to look up at me and say, "What if someone sees us?"

"We'll charge them for it," I panted, trying not to lose my rhythm.

The lodge where we had reserved a room in Boulder was like an oasis. A compound of oak and cedar structures that included one long building with normal motel-style rooms, a larger two-story building with four apartments, and a modern octagonal building that was mostly glass and housed a chic restaurant.

Our waitress told us the owner had been living near Zion Park but the town got too crowded for him so he moved to Boulder and built the lodge. Then he went to Boston and hired a graduate from the Culinary Institute of America to come work for him. We couldn't help but laugh at the irony of us coming from San Francisco, restaurant capital of the country, to the wilds of the Utah desert, and finding a gourmet restaurant, let alone the synchronicity of our deciding to spend the night here rather than in one of the other motels that would have been closer to a town.

The next morning we rose early, fixed a pot of coffee, and headed for Moab, our last stop before flying back to California. These last two days of the trip were intended only for us and had no business attached to them, which pleased us both immensely. We checked into our motel in Moab, then headed for Canyonlands, where we hiked some trails and sat on cliff edges. We ended the afternoon at Gooseneck Overlook, a remarkable promontory that afforded a view of the entire western end of Canyonlands National Park.

We inched our way to the flat overlook by negotiating a foot-wide ledge of rock extending from the "mainland" along the edge of the sandstone cliff for about ten or 12 feet. The drop was straight down about 600 feet. The national park service had built an iron railing into the rock so the boldest tourists could get to the lookout without plummeting to their deaths.

We walked to the very edge of the overlook. Actually, we crawled from about six feet away. The height was over 1,000 feet on that side, and I thought we shouldn't take any chances of vertigo. I didn't want to lose my husband—or have him lose me—on our honeymoon.

We sat there in the afternoon light, looking out over thousands of square miles of exquisite desert, much more grand than the Grand Canyon, and all the more impressive since we didn't have to share it with anyone. I don't know how long we sat there in utter silence; I'm sure it was close to an hour. There was simply no sound, save a gust of wind through the branches of a nearby juniper or the whoosh of flapping wings when a hawk flew close by overhead. So we simply sat together in silence at this center of the world.

It was a profound moment for both of us. It seemed as though every road I ever took led to this man, this spot, and this moment. I had never felt so completely alive, never felt such a deep sense of being grounded and centered and focused on what truly mattered. I thought of something Lyle had once said to me when we were in Joshua Tree National Monument, a similarly deserted spot in the California desert. We were hiking through Hidden Valley when he stopped and turned around on the path and said to me, "It would be a privilege to participate in the universe, even without consciousness." That was exactly how I felt at the edge of the world with Nicky.

Finally Nicky turned and smiled.

"What are you thinking about?" I asked. Extreme introvert that he is, I knew his mind was going about a million miles a minute, especially since he had smoked part of a joint before we got out of the car. "Medical marijuana," he'd said, as he always did when he lit a joint to ward off the nausea of HIV. "It's *the law*." He was referring to a ballot measure passed in California making it legal to grow marijuana for medicinal use.

"I'm thinking that this is a perfect manifestation of what is meant by referring to God as the ground of being. It is so immense, so over-whelmingly beautiful, so intimidating, and yet so completely reassuring at the same time. It's a truly spiritual experience," he said softly, looking out over the canyons and valleys and hills of red and brown and white earth that stretched for hundreds of miles. "Maybe the most spiritually complete experience I've ever had. It puts the ego in its proper place."

We sat for another several minutes before he asked me the same question in return. "I don't think I'm thinking anything," I answered. "I'm having a whole bunch of feelings, though."

"What are they?" he asked, smiling in a way that told me he knew what I was about to say, because he was having the same kind of experience, except in his own, intellectual way.

"Mostly I feel humbled by the vastness of this," I said. "When I'm in the desert, I realize why every great spiritual master in history has at one time or another gone into the desert to find God, or to find himself."

We both laughed at that. "Same thing, I guess. Self with a capital 'S.' I'm also feeling terribly mortal right now."

"Say more," Nicky said. "Sitting here with you right now, I want to live with you forever," I said. "I want our lives to go on for a long, long time. I wish Lyle and Rosario could be here. I wish they could have lived for this long, until these new drugs were available, but at the same time I'm..." I couldn't bring myself to say it.

"You're what?" Nicky asked.

"I'm afraid to say it. I'm afraid you might misunderstand."

"Try me. I'm stoned."

"I was going to say that while I'm sorry they died, at the same time I'm glad of it, because if they hadn't we never would have met and never would have experienced the joy of this relationship. I believe this is the relationship my whole life was preparing me for, the relationship that will allow me to know who I really am. So I'm feeling mortal and scared of being mortal, because that means it's going to come to an end at some point and I don't want it to. I want to be with you forever. I believe that in some very real sense both Lyle and Rosario are here with us right now, but I miss them all the same, even Rosario, whom I didn't even know, but feel like I knew because of how you talk about him. I also believe that even after we die it won't be over, that somehow we'll still be together in some way I don't understand. In the midst of all the happiness and sorrow I feel an overwhelming joy, which I suppose is poignancy. Yes, that's it. I feel the poignancy of being here with you."

I looked at Nicky, who was staring at me glassy-eyed. "Jeez," he exclaimed. "And you tell me *I* think too much."

As we were about to leave, Nicky took off an amulet he wore around his neck, one I had asked once about and he told me was the Buddhist Knot of Infinity. It consists of eight overlapping squares formed by a continuous line. He put it around my neck and fastened it.

"I want you to wear this," he said.

"But this is your medallion. You always wear it; you never take it off," I protested. I was humbled and flattered.

"I want you to wear it from now on," he said, smiling broadly and looking at it hanging around my neck.

I touched it and choked back tears. "I love you so much," I said.

"Ditto," he said, and kissed me on the lips in the middle of Mormon country, just as a huge RV filled with a family of five pulled up next to the 4Runner. They were all gawking at us, the kids in the back actually allowing their mouths to hang open. One little girl was giggling.

"My God," we heard the woman on the passenger side say to her husband, "you can't get away from them."

"That's right," Nicky yelled, "'cause people like you keep cranking us out. You probably have one on board right now and don't even know it."

"Keep going George," the woman shouted, pointing toward the road.

"Think of the children."

As they pulled away, Nicky, unable to resist, shouted after them, "We are your children, lady."

He turned to me, looking both proud of himself and sheepish. "Sorry," he said.

"No you're not," I said back to him.

"You're right. Still love me?" he asked, wrapping his arms around my waist.

"Still?" I said. "It's probably *why* I love you."

FIFTY-EIGHT

THAT NIGHT we had crazy, wild, demented sex, fell asleep, then woke up at 4:30 and made love very tenderly. Then we fell back to sleep and the next time I woke Nicky was shaking me and saying, "Nigel, listen to this." The television was turned to CNN. A woman anchor was droning on in her best Columbia School of Broadcasting voice.

"In the most recent developments in the mysterious VanDeventer drowning in Arizona, a paternity suit was filed yesterday by Sandy Jo Thomas of East Mesa, Arizona. The suit names the widower of the late Evelyn VanDeventer, 40-year-old Travis Iversen, as the father. As her attorney filed the $10 million-lawsuit at the Maricopa County courthouse in Phoenix today, Ms. Thomas was giving birth to twin boys at Maricopa County's Good Samaritan Hospital. You will recall that Evelyn VanDeventer, multimillion–dollar heiress of publishing tycoon Cyril VanDeventer, married Travis Iversen, a man nearly half her age, just six months before she drowned on a camping trip with her husband at a remote lake 30 miles north of Phoenix. The VanDeventer family had no comment regarding the lawsuit."

Needless to say, that woke me up quickly. I sat up in bed and said, "Well, I guess we don't have to call Annarita and tell her about Sandy Thomas thanks to CNN."

"I need coffee and glazed doughnuts," Nicky said, hopping out of bed and rummaging for his briefs. "Where's Thao when you need him?"

"You sure are sexy," I said. "Why don't you come back to bed for awhile."

He froze where he was, bending over, looking under the bed, and said, "You need to see a doctor. It's not normal how much sex you need."

"I think it's abnormal how *little* you need," I said, folding my arms across my chest and resigning myself to the fact that breakfast was obviously going to be coffee and doughnuts, not Guamanian buns.

We had arranged to drop the car in Salt Lake City and fly back to San Francisco from there. We hadn't learned much, at least not much that Annarita hadn't found out before we could tell her, but on the other hand I had the gnawing intuition that this trip was going to be more helpful than we currently realized.

If nothing else, we now knew that Iversen had a history of spousal abuse, something neither the family nor the police was aware of at the time of Evelyn's drowning. There was also something odd about the Carefree ranch. Those ranch hands running around naked that way, the brazenness of Terry, the way the house was locked up tight. And where was the foreman? Without Travis there, why was the foreman out of town? And something about the scene at Lake Barnett kept tugging at me as well. I kept seeing that boat moored there, the dock, the piling with the numbers on it and the woman waving at me. These things nagged at me. I felt as though I had seen something crucial but hadn't recognized it. I held the woman across the lake responsible for that. That event had distracted me and broken my concentration.

It took us six hours to get to Salt Lake and we nearly missed our flight. Nicky slept most of the way while I read Martha Grimes's latest mystery. I followed Martha's career, as we were old friends, having taught together at a college outside Washington, D.C. for several years before she hit the big time. We hadn't spoken in a long time, but I held a special place for her in my heart and was always on the lookout for her work. Her success made me happy. Unfortunately, I had just gotten into the latest book when the captain announced that we were making our approach into the Bay Area.

I never tire of flying into San Francisco and am always glad to be home. I never come back from a trip and not think about how many people return home to a place that isn't as nice as where they were vacationing. When you return home to San Francisco, you're usually coming back to a place far better than wherever it was you have been. In this case there was even more waiting for us than I realized.

As we made our way to the baggage area, Nicky grabbed a newspaper to see what details were available on the paternity suit. When he caught

up with me at the baggage carousel, he held the paper up for me to see
the latest banner headline: IVERSEN A WIFE BEATER IN SECRET SECOND
MARRIAGE.

"Man, those reporters must have been nipping at our heels," I said to
Nicky as he folded the paper to read the story to me.

"We should start charging them to follow us around," he said. "Oh
brother, listen to this."

Nicky read from the paper's front page. "Evelyn VanDeventer, a tire-
less crusader for the rights of abused women, never knew her husband
had a history of domestic violence allegations from his second marriage,
her daughters and minister said today." Nicky looked at me and screwed
up his face. "Her minister? What the hell is he doing in the picture? That
Reverend Smarmey worries me."

"Reverend Simmley," I corrected, knowing full well he knew the
man's name.

"Whatever," he said, and went back to reading me the story. "In fact,
VanDeventer didn't know there had been a second marriage. It is only
now, after her mysterious drowning on a camping trip with her husband
of six months, that this detail is revealed. It is a crucial detail, according
to her longtime friend and former business associate, Marilyn Morton,
owner of the fashionable Il Gatto Bianco Boutique in Concord. 'Evelyn
was in the shop just a month or so before she drowned and she was acting strange. I know that Iversen's marital history was important to
Evelyn,' Dunn said when interviewed at her place of business yesterday.
'For one thing, she was interested in finding someone who fit a particular description, someone who would be able to treat her right. She told
me once that part of the appeal he held for her was that he had remained
single for 12 years after his first marriage. She thought that meant he'd
been waiting for the "right" woman to come along. He was with her at
the time she said this to me and he didn't say anything about being married a second time.'

"VanDeventer knew of Iversen's first marriage, which lasted five
years. It was the second marriage that surprised the family today, when
it was revealed that Iversen and Ruth McGraw of Mount Carmel
Junction, Utah, were, until just five years ago, husband and wife.

During their marriage police were called to the Iversen home on three separate occasions on domestic violence complaints. They arrested Iversen once on suspicion of spousal abuse after his wife claimed he had shown up in a jealous rage, choked her, tied her up and punched her, then left her in the kitchen. A neighbor found her tied up when he happened by hours later.

"Other attacks left her with bruises, cuts, and black eyes, McGraw's medical records show. Authorities did not prosecute for reasons unknown." I retrieved one of Nicky's suitcases and dropped it with a thud at his feet. He sat down on it without taking his eyes off the newspaper.

"Oh, now they're on a roll," he squealed. "Listen to this. 'One of VanDeventer's main passions in her philanthropic life was the cause of battered women. The Cyril and Evelyn VanDeventer Foundation built and underwrites the VanDeventer Battered Women's Shelter in Martinez to help women such as Iversen's former wife.'

"Nevertheless, VanDeventer's family continues to support Iversen. Her son Vaughn made a statement to the press today, saying, 'My sisters continue to believe, as I do, that there is no evidence of foul play in the death of my mother. If you look at the investigation report, the autopsy report, and the corroborating evidence from the sheriff's department, you'll reach the same conclusion we have. I know these latest developments don't look very good, but you have to remember, one of the reasons my mother was so attracted to this man is that he is very much a man. Men do those kinds of things.'"

"What a weird thing to say," I commented as I lifted a second of Nicky's bags off the carousel.

"It is a kind of male chauvinist thing to say, isn't it?" Nicky said. "Especially coming from such a big queen."

"Well, some of the worst male chauvinists I know are big queens, honey," I remarked, moving him aside to grab his third suitcase. Nicky doesn't travel light. "Any comment from Iversen?"

"Yeah, and it looks like he's back in Arizona," Nicky said, then read more from the story. 'Remember the source' Iversen said at his Carefree home. 'When you're talking about an ex-wife, you should know if you're talking about a mad ex-wife or not. This one's plenty mad at me.'"

"Doesn't sound like the kind of couple that would be talking on the phone once a month, does it?" I said, more comment than question.

"He's covering his ass," Nicky said. "Who would you be more inclined to believe?" he asked, hailing a skycap. "Buffalo Bill Iversen or Ruth McGraw?"

FIFTY-NINE

WE SLEPT at Nicky's that night, me stopping at my place to get some fresh clothes. Nicky said he would call Annarita in the morning. The next morning, Matthew woke us with coffee, bagels, and the morning paper.

"I thought you might like to see this," he said slyly, then stood by, waiting for our response. Matthew sported pajamas I hadn't yet seen. Elmer Fudd, shotgun aimed, racing round and round Matthew's chest, arms, and legs in a never-ending pursuit of Daffy Duck.

Nicky read the whole story; I didn't have to read any further than the headline: VANDEVENTERS DEMAND POLYGRAPH OF IVERSEN.

"I'm calling Annarita," Nicky said after reading the story to us, which basically said that Virginia had held a press conference announcing that in light of all this new information, the family was requesting that Travis take a lie detector test. "Not that we don't believe him, but just so we can put all this wild speculation and innuendo to rest."

"Can I stay and eavesdrop?" Matthew asked.

"Of course," Nicky said.

"You're Paul Drake in this one," I said to Matthew, who was now standing at the corner window looking out over the city.

"But which one of you is Perry Mason and who's Della Street?" he quipped. Then quickly he turned and said, "You realize, of course, there's no need to answer that. It's obvious just from the wardrobe."

I opened my mouth to make a clever wardrobe remark, but quickly realized I didn't know Matthew all that well. I held my tongue.

"Annarita?" Nicky said into the phone, holding up his hand like a traffic cop for us to shush. "We just read the morning paper. What on earth is going on? Things seem to be happening awfully fast over on that side of the bay."

Nicky talked for about five minutes, then hung up and gave us the poop. "Seems like Vaughn and Virginia had a knock-down-drag-out last night, complete with martinis. Virginia is claiming they really don't know squat about Iversen and the information that's coming out in the press is doing both the family and the Foundation lots of harm."

"And Vaughn's retort?" I asked.

"He says the Foundation is his business, not Virginia's, and that she should keep her nose out of it. Also, he said that if anything was going to bring bad publicity and more attention to the family it would be their publicly challenging Travis's motives for marrying their mother. He said he doesn't understand why Virginia is so hell-bent on destroying the man when he made their mother so happy."

"Sounds like Vaughn and Virginia really hate one another," Matthew said. "You'd think they were actually brother and sister. They sure fight like siblings."

"Annarita said that every other sentence out of Virginia's mouth was about Vaughn being adopted and not having the right to meddle like this, technically speaking," Nicky said.

"No wonder it got out of hand," I exclaimed.

"Right," Nicky said, folding the paper, finally. He reached at last for his coffee and one of the doughnuts he liked so much: honey-dipped maple bars. Just looking at it sent me into insulin shock. "Annarita said Vaughn finally just flipped her off and walked out."

"What now?" Matthew asked. "This is better than my soap opera."

Nicky looked at me, then back at Matthew.

"I don't care if he knows," Matthew said, laughing.

"Matthew likes to watch *All My Children*," Nicky said with a grin, like he was telling a big secret that only family knew.

"He's being coy," Matthew said. "The truth is I haven't missed a single episode in the 27 years it's been on television." He fidgeted with his pajama shirt pocket, which I could tell contained a pack of cigarettes. Daffy with a Camel in his bill. There's poetic justice.

"Not only that," Nicky said through a mouthful of maple bar, gesturing with great flourish, obviously impressed with the additional information he was about to reveal, "he remembers absolutely everything. I swear he has a photographic memory."

"You should try to swallow before you speak, my little gourmand."

"What are you up to today, Matthew?" I asked.

"More genealogical work over in Oakland," he said, walking slowly to the door and taking a cigarette out of his shirt pocket.

"Why Oakland?" I inquired.

"The Mormon Temple Library in the Oakland hills," he said, as though I should know the implication. I didn't. "The Mormons have the best census and genealogical records in the world," he explained. "I'm working on something for a client right now. The library ordered a microfilm from Salt Lake for me about a month ago. I have to look at it today. It goes back to Utah tomorrow."

I pictured Matthew boarding the BART train at 24th and Mission Streets, briefcase in hand, cigarette dangling from his lips, dressed smartly in Porky Pig PJs and Bullwinkle slippers.

"How ironic," I commented. "I mean that the information you use comes from the place we just returned from. Do you ever imagine going to Salt Lake yourself?"

"Not really," he said, almost out the door, the nicotine craving spurring him downstairs. "I can get everything I need here. If I don't find it at the Sutro Library or in Oakland, the Mormons order it for me. They're strange, but they sure do know their genealogy."

"Never trust a religion that isn't strange," Nicky said, again with his mouth full. "Sorry," he mumbled, looking at me and grimacing.

"Like the Catholic Church?" I said.

"Uh-huh," Nicky answered. He swallowed, thought a moment, then added, "Maybe you can't trust them even if they are strange."

"The weird thing is," Matthew said before he left completely, "in the Mormon Church, you can only go into the basement of the temple unless you're a bishop or something."

"What?" Nicky yelled.

"That's right," Matthew shouted as he descended the stairs. "The more important you are, the higher up you get to go in the Tomorrowland exhibit."

"Gee," Nicky said. "I think I like that religion. So what's on the detectives' agenda for today?"

"I want to talk with that woman who owns the boutique," I said. "I'd like to speak to someone outside the family who talked to Evelyn recently and who's known her for a long time. She said something in the paper that intrigued me, something about Evelyn's fascination with cowboys. I want to know more about this cowboy thing. Cowboys in Concord. Who would've thought?"

"Oh Boy." Nicky exclaimed. "I'll wear something boutique-ish."

SIXTY

NICKY and I set out to see what we could learn about Evelyn from Marilyn Morton. I was hoping she could shed some light on why Evelyn would marry someone like Iversen. On the way to Concord I told Nicky to get the pad and pen out of the glove box so we could make a list of the things we had relegated to our virtual whelping box.

First there was the whole idea of Evelyn marrying a cowboy. Not that that was so terribly unusual, considering she was from Texas, but what struck me as really odd was that she should actually find a cowboy who *would* marry her, let alone that he would be the Arnold Schwarzenegger of the rodeo circuit and 25 years younger.

Then there was this business of Vaughn being adopted, but it never coming up anywhere except in arguments between him and Virginia. Why had no one but Virginia mentioned it? Why hadn't the press pounced on it? There was also that really weird scene in the bunkhouse in Carefree. Both Nicky and I believed we could get information out of either one of the two ranch hands if we pressed hard enough.

There were other things, as well: the abused wife who still talked to her attacker regularly on the phone; Vaughn being so defensive of Travis; the fact that no one had challenged the will being changed so drastically to benefit Travis, although Nicky suggested that the last item was now happening in the form of Virginia insisting on the polygraph. I conceded that point. And, finally, related or not, there was that woman I kept seeing. I realized, the more I thought about it that there was a connection between the woman I saw in the abandoned house on Helen's farm, the woman in the window upstairs at Annarita's the day of the funeral, and the woman standing on the pier at Lake Barnett. I hadn't the foggiest notion what that connection might be, but I felt strongly that there was something there I needed to think about.

I learned long ago that there are forces and energies in the world we know little or nothing about. Since Lyle's death, I had come to firmly believe that those who go ahead can and do communicate with those left behind. Perhaps it was a spirit trying to tell me something. I would not normally say that out loud to anyone, and I only asked Nicky to put it on the list because of his acceptance of Nonna's clairvoyance and his belief in reincarnation. He jotted it down without so much as an odd look in my direction.

We tried to rank the list, but I couldn't pick one item I thought was more important than another. Nicky, on the other hand, could. "Vaughn's split from the family," Nicky said. "It's puzzling."

"Don't you think it's just a sibling feud with Virginia?" I offered. "He's really not at odds with Annarita."

"But he is," Nicky argued. "Insofar as he's defending Travis and telling both of his sisters to lay off, he is at odds with her. He's at odds with everyone."

"But it's really about the Foundation, isn't it?" I said. "He's afraid the publicity is going to hamper the Foundation's work, and that's his livelihood."

"Doesn't compute," Nicky countered. "The publicity couldn't get any worse than it already is. For him to separate himself from the family will be seen as distancing himself from the name that's at the very heart of the Foundation he's supposedly trying to protect. And it isn't his livelihood. He just inherited a shitload of money. Something isn't right there." He stewed over it all the way into downtown Concord.

Marilyn Morton's shop was small but elegant, with a brown awning that covered the sidewalk in front. The name of the boutique was printed in white letters on each side of the awning, and the stylistic white outline of a cat appeared on both sides of the words IL GATTO BIANCO.

"Try not to embarrass me in here," I teased, holding the door open for him.

"Like how?"

"Like trying on clothes and making disparaging remarks about them."

"Don't be silly, they only sell women's clothes in here," he said, giving me a puzzled look.

"Like I said..."

The shop was relatively small, located on the main drag rather than in a shopping mall. It was too early in the day for the elite of Walnut Creek to be out shopping for Donna Karan, so we had the place to ourselves.

The owner, Marilyn Morton, was a fashionable and extremely good-looking woman, not the kind of woman I would have expected to find running a shop. She was more the kind I would have expected to see shopping there. She wore her hair cropped short, and had on small gold earrings. Dwarfing her wedding band was a diamond engagement ring the size of a beach ball. She was wearing a white silk blouse, a gold choker, and a brown crepe skirt that clung to shapely hips. She was the kind of woman that straight men turn around to look at.

"Can I help you gentlemen find something?" she asked, approaching casually and smiling.

"Actually, we're looking for information," I said. "We're trying to help a friend of ours solve a family puzzle."

"Oh, you're not reporters, are you?" she said with apparent dismay.

"No. We're friends of Annarita O'Brien," Nicky said.

This meant nothing to Ms. Morton. She gave us a puzzled look.

"Evelyn VanDeventer's daughter," I explained.

"Oh, I see," the woman said slowly, mulling it over. "Are you with the police?"

"No, ma'am," Nicky said, sounding like Sergeant Friday.

"Well, you don't look like reporters," she fished.

"No. Like I said, we're just friends," I explained.

She stood there for a moment, sizing us up, then smiled and said, "I've had enough of these reporters. Sharks, absolute sharks. Coffee?"

We sat in the cluttered back room of the boutique drinking Mocha Java while Marilyn, which she insisted we call her, gave us her part of Evelyn's history. A small antique desk spilled over with paperwork. The top of a telephone was visible in the sea of green, yellow, and pink invoices, bank statements and other related red tape that went with running the place. Marilyn sat near a half-opened Dutch door so she could watch for customers.

"I felt terrible when I read about it in the paper," she said, pouring coffee into white cups that were almost mug-size. "It's so sad. She was such a nice woman. Good to everyone she met. Do you think it was the cowboy?" she asked directly.

"We're just trying to gather information. We're not making any judgments," I said. "What can you tell us about Evelyn?"

"When she came to work here, she was a wreck," Marilyn said in a New York accent, which got thicker as she became more relaxed. "I felt kind of sorry for her, actually. She had been dumped by her husband and had her kids to raise. She'd never held a job and had no skills to speak of, but she was the sweetest woman."

"What prompted you to hire her if she had no experience?" I asked.

"She had a terrific personality," Marilyn said, adding more coffee to her cup. "She was a natural at putting people at ease. She used to come in right after I opened the place. Oh, she never bought anything of course, but she liked to browse. One day, while she was looking at a rack of dresses, another woman knocked over an entire stack of blouses. Evelyn went rushing up to her before I could even react. She asked the woman if she was all right and picked up the blouses, all the while reassuring the woman that the same thing happened to her all the time and not to think another thing of it. Then she stood there and made small talk with the woman and re-folded the blouses. She held one up to the woman and said the color was perfect for her. The woman bought the blouse."

"Where were you while this was going on?" I asked.

"Well, frankly, I stopped and watched. I was curious that Evelyn's first inclination was to make everything comfortable for the woman. I mean, it wasn't her store or anything," Marilyn said.

"Go on," I urged.

"Well she just kept talking and encouraging the woman to look at other things. She even pointed out something she had been looking at herself for the past couple days that she thought was cute. The woman ended up buying that, too," Marilyn said, raising her eyebrows in admiration, "and I offered Evelyn a job."

"That was nice of you," Nicky chimed in, toasting Marilyn with his coffee mug before taking a sip.

"And lucky for her," I added.

"Well, that's just it," Marilyn said, poking at my knee with a red fingernail. "Later on, I figured out that she'd been planning that all along."

"I'm not following," I said.

"She'd been in the neighborhood for days looking for a job and decided the only way to land one without experience was to get on the good side of a shop owner. She also decided this was where she wanted to work because she liked the merchandise. So she started coming in here every day, waiting for her opportunity. Clever, eh? And I fell for it. An old New Yorker like me."

"How did you find this out?" Nicky asked.

"I pieced it together over the next few months from bits of conversation she had with me and advice she gave a couple of the other part-time salesgirls who worked here but wanted to move to larger stores. I eventually confronted her. Not in a hostile way. More girlfriend-to-girlfriend. She was terribly embarrassed, but admitted it. I think that's one of the reasons we became such close friends. I admired her spunk—and her honesty. Evelyn's no dummy, fellas. She knows which end's up. I mean, she did. Especially when it came to men."

"Say more," Nicky urged.

Marilyn kept turning to look at the front door, as though a customer might walk in without her hearing the chime. "I watched her set her sites on Ben Tedeschi. She landed him pretty good." Marilyn winked at Nicky, as though he might understand that kind of "manhandling." I thought it was cute; he noticed my reaction and gave me a look as though he had just found something floating in his coffee.

"Ben had come in to buy his secretary a Christmas gift, and Evelyn recognized him, partly I think because of that silver-handled cane he uses. He was wounded in combat and it left his right leg weakened. That silver walking stick became his trademark as a politician. Lots of votes for a disabled veteran and Ben Tedeschi knew it. Anyway, Evelyn laid it on so thick it was funny, but Ben responded. He came back the next day and asked her out on a date. It was between sessions of the legislature and he was working in his regional office during the break. It was very romantic," Marilyn said, cocking her head wistfully and smiling at Nicky again.

"I'm sure," Nicky said.

"They started dating right after that?" I said before Marilyn had time to interpret Nicky's tone of voice.

"That same week," Marilyn said. "It was touching. Evelyn was so lonely up to that point. She just wasn't cut out to be on her own. All she ever talked about was finding the right man. Oh, don't get me wrong," Marilyn said, "she was plenty glad to be rid of Bill O'Brien. He was a drunk and a wife beater. Beat the kids, too. She was just wandering through life waiting for Prince Charming when she met Ben. Thank God for those kids she found him."

"Yeah," Nicky said. "Thank God."

"But they never married," I added. "Why?"

"I could never figure that out. But by that time she was gone. She'd gone to work over at the chamber of commerce. Ben got her that job," Marilyn said.

"So she moved up in the world," Nicky said. "Improved herself after you gave her a first break."

"I would have been glad to keep her too. I was sorry to see her leave."

"But the chamber of commerce was a much better job," I said. "You can understand why she'd leave."

"Oh, she didn't go there right away. She didn't take that job for almost a year after she left."

"Wait a minute. I'm not following this," I said. "I thought she met Ben, started dating him, and then he got her a better job at the chamber of commerce so she left here to go to work there."

"Yes, but not in the rapid succession you're suggesting."

"There was something else in between?" I asked, perplexed.

Marilyn looked back and forth between me and Nicky, then smoothed her skirt. "I probably shouldn't tell you this. It's only conjecture on my part. I loved Evelyn and I respected her. That's why I never asked her about it directly."

"Please, Marilyn," Nicky pleaded, "girlfriend to girlfriend." The little manipulator. "We're only trying to help the family. Annarita's coming out of an unfortunate marriage and now she has this to deal with. She and I were best friends in college and she's asked us to help her find the missing pieces to this puzzle. We read your comments in the newspaper yesterday and we knew you would be the one to shed real light on this case." Nicky leaned over and placed his hand on Marilyn's, a girl-stuff gesture. I wanted to kick him.

"Well, I make no judgments about any of this," Marilyn said, looking at both of us to make sure we weren't judging her either. "I wouldn't be telling you this under any other circumstances. I'm only saying it now because of the dreadful thing that has happened. I've never breathed this suspicion to a living soul. Not even my husband."

"We understand," I assured her.

"Well…Evelyn left here and kind of went away for awhile before she started that other job."

"You mean she took some time off?" I asked, not following. She obviously didn't want to come right out and say something, but I couldn't intuit what she was getting at.

"I think she went back to Texas. I got a card from Galveston Beach shortly after she quit, saying she had decided to take time off and see the country. But I think it may have been a different kind of trip."

"Ohhhhh," Nicky said slowly, catching on. "And how long was she on this little trip to Aunt Sophie's?"

"Six months," Marilyn whispered.

"You're kidding!" Nicky said.

Marilyn nodded.

"This was when Vaughn was adopted?" Nicky added.

Marilyn nodded and blushed just a trace.

"How old was Vaughn when she brought him home?" Nicky asked.

"One month," Marilyn said, nodding and arching her eyebrows.

"I see," Nicky said, half singing.

"See what?" I begged.

"How many were there when she came to work here?" Nicky asked.

"How many what?" I asked.

"Only the two," Marilyn said softly.

"Ohhhhh," Nicky said. "So when she left, could you tell? Was it obvious?"

"I can always tell. I suspected for a couple months," Marilyn boasted.

"What?" I shouted.

"Calm down, beetle lips," Nicky said, patronizing me and enjoying every second of it. "Marilyn is saying that when Evelyn left here, she was pregnant." He leaned forward, put his hand on Marilyn's knee, and said in a low voice, "Aren't men thick?"

SIXTY-ONE

BEFORE we left the boutique, Nicky gave Marilyn his phone number, made a luncheon date with her, and practically convinced her to add a men's section to the store. She had mentioned that she and her husband were looking for a place in the city because they were tired of commuting to the opera and the ball games—they wanted a pied-à-terre—and Nicky promised to keep his eyes open for her. She said she'd call if she thought of anything else that might be helpful.

We had just pulled away from the front of the shop, Nicky waving good-bye like it was Nonna, when he turned to me and screamed, "Pregnant!" I almost swerved into an oncoming car.

"Jesus!" I shouted back. "Control yourself."

"She was pregnant. Little Miss Good Ship Lollipop was getting ready to lose eight pounds in an hour," Nicky exclaimed.

"OK, so what does it mean?" I questioned.

"You know damned well what it means," Nicky said.

"I'm pretending like I don't," I said. "Say it."

"It means, of course, that she was carrying somebody's baby!" Nicky said. "Either she was still giving it up for her husband, a la battered women's syndrome, or she'd been putting out for someone else."

"But according to Marilyn," I said, "Evelyn was dating…"

"No wonder he's taken such an interest," Nicky said, as it dawned on him who the father was.

"I wonder if Nonna knows," I said, looking at Nicky to see if this would upset him.

"There's nothing Nonna doesn't know. And this would hardly count him out in her book. That old gal's been around the block a time or two," Nicky said. "Vaughn is Ben's son. I'm sure of it."

"We can't prove that," I reminded him. "It's just Marilyn's conjecture."

"I'd trust that woman's conjecture over scientific evidence," Nicky said. "She's got East Coast savvy. A real woman's woman. You wouldn't understand."

"Like my mother always said, takes one to —"

"I'd expect something crass like that from you," Nicky said, reaching into his pocket and pulling out a pack of cigarettes. I watched, incredulous as he lit up.

"Exactly when did you start carrying cigarettes full-time?" I asked.

"When this got pregnant with possibilities," he said.

"I don't get this smoking thing," I said. "Explain it one more time."

"It makes life more like a movie," he said, crossing his legs and folding his arms. He punched the radio button and said, "*Liebestraum!*"

"What?" I said, turning onto the freeway on-ramp.

"*All About Eve,*" he sighed. "*Liebestraum.* Don't you feel just like Karen when they were stranded on that road in Connecticut in the snow?"

"I have no idea what you're talking about," I said, shaking my head.

"And in the last analysis," he said, quoting the movie, "unless you can look up at the breakfast table or turn over in bed in the morning and there he is, you're not a woman."

I looked at him like he was crazy.

"Evelyn, nitwit," he explained. "She's just like that. Not like Margo Channing, but the kind of woman Margo was talking about. She just had no self-esteem without a man in her life. Poor baby. After Cyril croaked she was a sitting duck, all right." Nicky thought for a moment. "Sitting bull might be more like it. But he couldn't train her, so he drowned her."

"Don't you think you're jumping the gun a bit?" I asked.

"No. You need to get up to speed."

"I beg your pardon?"

"Sixty-five, honey. You're doing 40 and the speed limit on the interstate is 65. We're going to get creamed unless you get up to speed. Here, let me help," and with that, he disappeared into my lap. This time, I made him open his mouth and show me his tongue before we reached the toll plaza.

SIXTY-TWO

I DROPPED Nicky at his place and went home to pay some bills and water the garden. I told Nicky I would phone him later. About 9:30, he phoned me. "Listen," he instructed, "and don't ask questions. Just do as you're told. Meet me across the street from 2500 Steiner. Be on the steps to Alta Plaza Park at exactly 10 P.M. and wear dark clothes."

I was about to laugh when I heard the click of the receiver. I tried calling back, but in his flair for the dramatic he had taken the phone off the hook.

Reluctantly, I followed his instructions, parking my car on Clay and walking up the hill to the other end of the park. Nicky was already waiting, sitting on the steps, drinking a beer out of a paper bag. He was wearing baggy green work pants, a sweatshirt, and a brown fedora.

"What the hell is going on?" I asked as I sat down next to him. "Why are we out here in the middle of the night and what are you doing drinking beer out of a paper bag like some homeless alcoholic?"

"Good," Nicky said. "That's just the effect I'm after. See that building over there?" Nicky asked, nodding at a white, 16-story deco apartment building across the street. It was famous in the city because each floor had only two units, each with a 360-degree view.

"Yes," I said, like the straight-man sidekick he was making me out to be. "I see the building."

"Know who lives in that building?" he asked, swigging from his beer.

"No, but I'm sure you do," I said.

"Vaughn VanDeventer lives there," Nicky said with exaggerated precision. "Apartment 1002."

"OK, Vaughn lives there," I said.

"Vaughn *VanDeventer*," Nicky repeated.

"I don't get it, Sherlock."

"Vaughn was adopted," Nicky said. "By VanDeventer. Matthew found the records at the county clerk's office." Instantly, the image of Matthew in Flintstones pajamas and red Roy Rogers bathrobe flicking through file drawers in the Mormon Temple Library popped into my head.

"So Virginia is telling the truth?" I asked, confused as to what Nicky was getting at. "Marilyn was wrong about Evelyn being pregnant?"

"No, I don't think so," Nicky said. "I think Marilyn was right. I think Virginia is lying."

"Oh," I said, not following.

"She's also telling the truth."

"I'm leaving," I said and started to get up.

"Nigel," Nicky said, grabbing my arm. "You're ruining my fun."

I plopped back down on the cement step, a bit too hard. "Ow!" I hollered.

"Shh!" Nicky said, looking around. "You're going to give us away."

"I wish you'd just explain this to me instead of trying to do an Ellery Queen," I pleaded.

"My sister, my daughter, my sister, my daughter," Nicky chanted, tossing his head from side to side like he was being slapped over and over.

"Huh?" I grunted.

"Faye Dunaway. *Chinatown*." Nicky said. "Now follow this: VanDeventer adopted Vaughn when he and Evelyn got married, but Vaughn was already with her because he was hers. VanDeventer adopted him to give him a name."

"So," I said. "Now can we go home?"

"No," Nicky said. "I'm going in there."

"You're what?" I croaked, not believing my ears.

"I've got to find out what he's hiding," Nicky said, more in a way that was asking my permission than expressing a desire. "I know there's something in there that will explain things, and I'm going to go in and find it."

"That's breaking and entering," I said. "He'll have you arrested."

"I don't think so," Nicky said. "I don't think he wants any more publicity than he already has, and I know he doesn't want any more adversaries than he already has."

"I won't allow it," I announced.

"Yes you will," Nicky countered.

"And what makes you so sure?"

"Because you love me," he said, kissing me on the cheek, then putting his head on my shoulder.

"That's precisely why I don't want you to do this."

"I know, honey, but you will let me."

"What if he's in there?" I said.

"He's not. I just got off the phone with Annarita. He's with her at the house in Concord and should be there for at least another hour, but I have to hurry. Wait here. I'll be right back." And with that, he leapt up and skipped down the steps. Before I knew it, he was ringing doorbells at the front of the building. Sure enough, someone buzzed him in.

SIXTY-THREE

ALL I COULD do now was wait. This seemed like the craziest thing he'd pulled yet. What if Vaughn came home? What if building security caught him? There would be no valid reason for him to give as to why he had broken into the apartment. What if Vaughn had an electronic security system wired to the police precinct?

A light went on in one of the tenth-floor windows. It was a dim light, but I knew he was in there rummaging around. I couldn't believe I had let him do this. Now there was a light in the adjoining room, the bedroom, probably. It seemed like hours went by and I couldn't see Nicky in any of the lighted windows. Then, all of a sudden, a pair of headlights blinded me as a car turned the corner onto Steiner. When I could see again, the car, a black Lexus coupe, sat waiting in the driveway of the apartment building for the garage door to swing open. It was my worst nightmare come true. In the driver's seat of the Lexus, his arm hanging out the window, hand tapping in rhythm to music, sat Vaughn.

I looked back up to the apartment, as though I might be able to telepathically transmit a message to Nicky to get out. The garage door swung open, the car pulled in, and the door swung shut.

"Get out, get out, get out," I said over and over to the lighted windows on the tenth floor, hoping my message would somehow work its way into his mind.

The lights went out in the windows, one at a time. Thank God, I thought, he's going to get out just in time. I relaxed for a moment, picturing him rushing down the hall, then descending in one elevator as Vaughn ascended in the one next to it. My heart sank as another light went on in two more windows. *Damn!* He was exploring yet another room, this one on the far right of the tenth floor. Just then, a light came on in the window that had lit up when Nicky first entered. Vaughn was inside the apartment. *Shit!* I looked at the two windows on the far right. The light went out. Nicky had heard him come in.

I didn't know what to do. Should I try to get in? Should I go up and try to help? What if Vaughn attacked him? What if he…I couldn't even think of the next thing. I put it out of my mind immediately and stood up. The light in the far room went on again, this time brighter. Vaughn appeared in the window, taking off his jacket and throwing it down. Then Nicky appeared in the window next to that one, which had its blind drawn. It was a Roman shade, so I could see Nicky's silhouette. He was standing there flailing his arms around. Then they both disappeared from view. I ran across the street and frantically pressed doorbells.

It took what seemed like hours, but finally someone buzzed me in. I couldn't believe how careless people in this building were about security. I ran to the elevators and pressed all the buttons. It was one of the old-fashioned elevators that has an analog dial that moves like a clock, showing you what floor the elevator is on. It was now on seven. Six, five, four. It was taking forever. I was panic-stricken. He could be hurt badly by now, even…no, I know nothing bad is going to happen, I told myself. Not now, not when we've finally found one another. Then I prayed, actually whispering out loud. "Please, God, please don't let anything happen to Nicky. I couldn't bear it. Please, please, please."

The elevator doors finally opened and I leapt in, right into Nicky. He was hopping up and down, trying to put on a shoe. His sweatshirt was in his hands; his pants were unzipped and unbuttoned but he was laughing, so I knew he was all right. A flood of relief swept through me and I thought for a minute I might actually faint.

"Come on!" he yelled, grabbing my arm and heading for the door. He was laughing, giggling like a high school girl.

We raced across Steiner Street, up the steps and into the park. We ran along the path that led into the trees and sat on the first bench we found.

"What the hell happened?" I asked, out of breath, clutching his arm tightly.

"Ow, Nigel," he said, still giggling. "You're hurting me, honey."

"Sorry," I said, loosening my grip. "I was frantic. I thought he was going to kill you or something."

"Not likely," he smirked. "He came in just as I found something. This was all I could get before I had to put things back and jump in bed." He held up a single sheet of note paper. It was too dark to read anything.

"Jump into bed?" I said.

"I didn't know what to do, so I took my clothes off and got into his bed," Nicky said, laughing and throwing his head back. "God, I don't believe myself sometimes," he said. "I'm amazing."

"Keep going," I said. "I'll be the judge of how amazing you are."

"Well what else could I do?" Nicky said, turning sideways on the bench, getting into the storytelling now. "I was just beginning to go through things in his desk—which is in his bedroom, by the way, not in the study, although there's one in the study, too. I heard him come in, so I closed the drawer and just stood there, thinking the jig was up. All I could think of was the scene in the bathroom, with him calling me names. I didn't know how to get out or how to explain what I was doing there. So I did the only thing I could think of that would repulse him. I got in bed and pretended I had broken into his apartment to be with him."

"What?"

"I know. Isn't it too divine? Vaughn with a one-man-of-color fan club? I knew he'd freak." Nicky was way, way too happy with himself. "He came in and flipped on the light and there I was, lying in his bed stark naked. Well, not stark naked. I kept my underwear on."

"What did he say?"

"He said what I thought he'd say. Nicky affected a deeper voice. 'How the hell did you get in here and what are you doing?' So I said, 'I let myself in to wait for you. After the other night I couldn't stop thinking about you.' Good, huh?"

"Oh, brother." I moaned. "I don't believe this."

"Isn't it fab? Then he yelled, 'Get the fuck out of here.' I said, 'I thought you liked me.' He started shouting that I'd be the last person in the world he would want and that if I wasn't out of there in one minute, he'd phone the police and have me arrested."

"And?"

"I got out, of course. I jumped up and grabbed my clothes and scampered out like a scared little bunny," Nicky said, in a childlike voice. "That's what he wanted to see, so that's what I did. It saved my ass, I'll tell you."

"I was worried."

"You're sweet. I love you so much," Nicky said. He took my hand and kissed it three times—the ritual again. "But you should know by now that I can take care of myself."

"Yeah, and give me a coronary in the process," I said, starting to feel my irritation rising up to rival my sense of relief. I cut it off before it got too serious. "What's that?" I asked, pointing at the paper.

"I don't know," Nicky said, holding it up as though we might be able to read it. There wasn't a street lamp or a moon, so it was useless. "It's some kind of master plan regarding his mother. I only got to glance at it. Let's go home and read it," he said, standing now and pulling me up by my arm like a kid wanting to go on the Ferris wheel.

"How about let's go home and give you a spanking?" I said, stumbling along after him, my arm being tugged half out of its socket.

"That too," he said.

SIXTY-FOUR

MATTHEW was at the kitchen table reading and drinking tea when we came up the stairs at Nicky's. Tonight it was Bugs Bunny. He poured us each some herbal tea and Nicky read the single sheet of paper he had purloined from Vaughn's desk.

"Image Maker Plan: Year One, Black. Mother mourns for Cyril. Year Two, Mother pays tribute to memory of Cyril; establishes charitable foundation, engages in philanthropic activities, promotes herself in the media. Year Three, Mother gets her new husband."

"It sounds like he was going to help her get back on her feet," I said, dunking my tea bag.

"Sounds like he was going to run her life," Matthew said, lighting a cigarette.

"But why would he be the one to do this?" Nicky asked, tapping his finger on the paper.

"Why not?" I asked in return. "After all, he is the only son. Isn't that the kind of thing sons do for their mothers when their fathers die? Especially gay sons?"

"Actually, no," Matthew said. "It's more the kind of thing daughters do. At least where I come from. The men do other things, like fix the lawn mower."

We laughed, but took Matthew's point. "Also," Nicky said, "wouldn't you think this would be something Virginia would be more likely to undertake, since she's the one who's always so worried about her mother giving away all the money?"

"Or even Annarita," Matthew chimed in, "since she seems to be the only one who really cares about her mother's well-being."

"Ordinarily I would agree, except for one thing," I said.

"What's that?" Matthew asked.

"That last item."

Nicky read it again out loud. "Year Three, Mother gets her new husband."

"What strikes you as odd about that?" I asked, taking my tea bag out of the mug and laying it on a saucer Matthew had placed in the center of the table which already held his used tea bag.

"Let's see," Nicky mused, then asked more than stated, "It's odd that he would want his mother to get married again, given his relationship with Cyril?"

"That's odd, I grant you," I said. "But something else."

"What? Tell us," Matthew said.

"Vaughn has written 'Mother *gets* her new husband,' not 'Mother looks for a new husband,' or something more indefinite," I pointed out.

"Right," Matthew said. "It almost sounds as though he were going to see to it that she got married."

"Oh, I think you two are just nitpicking," Nicky said. "You're so obsessed with language. I just think it means he was going to see to it that she started looking for a husband or something like that. I think you're making too much of it. Besides, we don't even know for sure that this is Vaughn's."

"One way to find out," I said.

"In the meantime," Matthew announced. "I have some interesting news."

"What?" Nicky asked excitedly.

"Today while I was over in the East Bay I decided to do some digging of my own." Matthew picked up the papers that were lying in front of him and read to us. "Travis County, Republic of Texas. September 30, 1968. Eight pounds, four ounces, male, Vaughn Alexander. Mother: Evelyn O'Brien. Father: Arthur German. Mother's place of birth: Fredricksburg, Texas. Father's place of birth: Gwynda, California."

"Holy cannoli," Nicky exclaimed. "Nigel was right. He isn't adopted...and he is adopted."

"That's exactly correct," he confirmed. Matthew consulted his papers and said to me what he had said to Nicky before we met in the park. "Cyril VanDeventer adopted Vaughn O'Brien German and legally changed his name to Vaughn O'Brien VanDeventer on January 31, 1971."

"But who is Arthur German?" I asked.

"Yes, precisely," Matthew chimed in. "Who is Arthur German? There are no such people listed anywhere in the entire state of Texas or California in the year 1968. Frankly, I was surprised. I thought it would be a common name, but I was wrong. Lots of Germanes, lots of Germains, and some Germans, but none of them with the first name Arthur."

"So who is he?" Nicky asked.

Matthew folded his hands on his stack of papers. "He's fictitious. That's who he is."

The next morning I awoke to Nicky sitting up in bed talking on the phone to Annarita. They were laughing and having a fairly good time. When he hung up he confirmed that the paper he had found in Vaughn's apartment was indeed Vaughn's. "The Image Maker Plan," he said, as I scooted over and laid my head on his bare chest, "was Vaughn's idea, but everybody thought it was a joke. But guess what? She had never heard about Year Three. There was never any talk about their mother getting married again. None whatsoever."

"That's interesting," I said in my gravelly morning voice. "He added that later."

"Yes, and in our excitement over Vaughn's little Image Maker plan last night, I forgot to tell you and Matt about the other thing I found on Vaughn's desk—a plane ticket to Phoenix for today. He's leaving at noon. Annarita just confirmed it. Supposedly he has to go to the ranch to do an inventory of the house."

"Too bad you didn't wait until today for your little breaking and entering foray," I said, reaching down and pinching his inner thigh. "You might have spared me my heart attack."

"Ouch!" he yelled. "My *chachaga*!"

"Your what?"

"That's what you call the thigh in Chamorro," he said. "Now, since you mentioned it, I have one more tiny topic to discuss."

"Mmm," I groaned.

"This should help wake you up," Nicky said.

I wrapped my arm around his bare chest and squeezed. "Your naked *chachaga* could wake me up, honey, especially if it was wrapped around my naked face."

"No, I mean my next topic, which is sort of related to Vaughn going to Arizona," he said.

"Hunh?" I grunted, not comprehending.

"I have to go back in that apartment. I have to look in the other desk, the one in the study."

"What?" I sat straight up in bed, just as Nicky scooted out and ran into the bathroom and locked the door.

He shouted from the other side, "I can't hear you, honey. I've got the water running."

SIXTY-FIVE

I COULD not believe that he had roped me into this a second time. Here I was, sitting in the car across the street from 2500 Steiner again, waiting while Nicky, dressed as a plumber and carrying a ridiculous— not to mention completely empty—tool kit, rummaged through Vaughn's apartment. If I hadn't been absolutely certain Vaughn was in Arizona, I never would have allowed this. At least that's what I told myself as I sat strumming my hands nervously on the steering wheel of the Celica.

It was a little after 4 o'clock, Nicky having taken the better part of the morning and early afternoon to find just the right plumber's coveralls and tool kit. Then, of course, he had to go to a mall and have a blue baseball cap stitched with the name "Plumb Loco." He was like a deranged Hollywood producer.

So I was greatly relieved, when at precisely 4:37 P.M., Nicky strolled out of the main entrance of the apartment building and sauntered, unlike, I might add, any plumber I have ever seen, even in San Francisco, over to the car and got in.

"Bingo!" he said, jumping up and down in the seat. "I struck pay dirt."

"And it's a fucking good thing you struck it when you did, Emma Peel. Look," I said, pointing toward the apartment building. There, at the main entrance, emerging from a blue DeSoto Cab, was Vaughn. He carried a single green and black leather tote bag with a silver diamond insignia on the side. Vaughn slammed the cab door and rushed inside, looking none too happy.

"Oh, shit," Nicky said. "Let's get out of here."

Back at Nicky's, I fixed us a BLT on toast. It wasn't much of a dinner, but neither of us was hungry and I was getting tired of Chinese takeout, which had become standard fare of late.

What Nicky found in Vaughn's apartment was, I had to admit, impressive and incriminating. The first item was a boarding pass from Southwest Airlines.

"You actually took that?" I said, nearly apoplectic.

"Yeah, of course," he said. "It's evidence."

"It's stolen property, you mean. Nicky, don't ever do that again. We can't be stealing things we may need later as evidence," I pointed out.

"Well we can't be leaving evidence around in people's apartments for them to destroy once we accuse them of …"

"Precisely," I said, making my point by jabbing a cooking fork in his direction. "We're not accusing him of anything. What could we accuse him of, flying to…where's the boarding pass to?"

"Phoenix," Nicky said.

"What could we accuse him of, flying to Phoenix?"

"Yeah, flying to Phoenix *the day his mother drowned in Lake Barnett*," Nicky said, waving the boarding pass in the air like it was a winning Lotto ticket.

Nicky did have a point. "I admit that is a bit odd, but it doesn't prove anything. He has every right to go to the ranch in Carefree, assuming that's where he was going," I said. I laid the bacon strips on paper towels to soak up the grease while I thought about Vaughn's trip to the ranch. "Speaking of Carefree," I said, "he sure did come back from the ranch today in a hurry, didn't he?"

I turned to say something else to Nicky and caught him stuffing something into his coveralls. "And what is that, please?" I asked, coming to the table and standing over him like a schoolmarm.

"What?" Nicky said, knowing full well I had seen him sneak something into hiding.

"Right here, young man," I said, holding out my hand. "Put it right here or I'll be forced to call your mother."

He reached into his coveralls and produced a three-by-five–inch photograph of Vaughn.

"And the reason for this, pray tell?"

"Intuition," he said sullenly.

"Explain," I said, losing my patience.

"Don't worry, it was in a photo album. He won't miss it. He probably never looks at it since he has his clothes on in the picture." Nicky looked at the photo again, then held it up for me to look at. "See? He'll never notice. He's not wearing anything Armani," Nicky said snidely, an obvious attempt to distract me from my irritation.

"Anything else I should know about before I take you upstairs and paddle you?" I asked, hand on hip.

"Well, now that you mention it, there was one other thing." Nicky grinned like a cat full of canary.

"I hope you left it there, for God's sake," I groaned as I returned to finishing the sandwiches.

"Yes, I left it there," Nicky mocked. "He would have noticed if I had taken it."

"And what was it?" I asked, my curiosity piqued.

" A silver and turquoise bolero tie," Nicky answered smugly.

"Huh?"

"You heard me, a silver and turquoise bolero tie. A western tie. A string tie." he elaborated with a tone of exasperation.

"So?" I said, placing the plates with our sandwiches on the table.

"Duh!" Nicky said.

"What? He can't have a silver tie? You said he was a big jewelry queen."

"I didn't say that; Annarita did," Nicky corrected, taking a huge bite out of his sandwich and chewing it with his mouth open to annoy me.

"OK," I said. "Annarita said it. Why does it matter?"

"You are so dense," Nicky said.

"What do *you* read into it, then?"

"That Travis has been in Vaughn's apartment, of course," Nicky said.

"So? He *is* married to Vaughn's mother. Or was. They probably went there for dinner or something."

"When was the last time *you* went to dinner and left your tie?"

SIXTY-SIX

I SAT straight up in bed. "Nicky," I whispered loudly, as though there were someone else in the room I might wake up. "Wake up."

Nicky stirred, rubbed his eyes. "What? What time is it?"

"I don't know, late. Early. That's not the point."

"Are you all right?" he asked, waking up more fully, thinking I might be ill.

"Yes, but wake up. We have to go to Arizona. I'm going to my place to pack. You make the reservations." I got out of bed and pulled on my pants.

"What is it, Nigel?"

"I'm still piecing it together, but we have to talk with that ranch hand again," I said, pulling on my socks.

"Which ranch hand?"

"What's-his-butt. The one who used the word 'tits'."

"Oh, you mean Terry," Nicky said.

"Right, Terry. Make plane reservations for as early as possible, then call me and I'll call us a cab."

Nicky leaned up on his elbows. "You're serious."

"Yes, I'm serious," I said, leaning over the bed and kissing him. "Now hurry, Della, we have a plane to catch."

"Can't we just call him?"

"No," I yelled as I went down the stairs. "We have to show him the photo."

We arrived at the ranch in Carefree around two in the afternoon only to find that Terry had been fired just before Austin and Travis left for a livestock auction in New Mexico. Terry had packed up and cleared out the day before. Hank was a bit coy, but couldn't resist telling us that Terry got what he deserved since he was always complaining, not to mention snooping around the main house.

"What was that about, do you think?" I asked.

"Hell if I know," Hank said, pulling on his crotch. "He started getting all fruity about two weeks ago, right after the first bunch of newspeople showed up."

"Is that why he got fired?"

"Sort of," Hank said, pushing his cowboy hat back a little. Sweat ran down the sides of his face from where the hat brim pressed against his head.

"Sort of?" Nicky said, screwing up his face. "What do you mean 'sort of'?"

"Well, he got fired for snooping around the main house the day after Austin moved in there."

Nicky and I exchanged puzzled glances. "You'll have to be more specific. Why would that get him fired?" I asked.

"Cause it ain't none of his business what the foreman does," Hank says. "Quickest way I know to get fired is to question the boss."

"Why did Austin move into the house in the first place?" Nicky asked. "What's wrong with the foreman's cabin?"

Hank gave Nicky a real wiseass sneer, like he knew what Nicky was trying to do. "Guess you'll have to ask Austin about that," Hank said.

Hank did volunteer to tell us some of the places where Terry hung out and where he thought he might be staying until he got resettled. We drove to the address Hank gave us, but he wasn't there. Another cowboy-type stuck his head out of a window and told us we'd find Terry at Black-Eyed Peas, a restaurant about half a mile up the road. "Said he was gonna get him some lunch," the guy said, giving us the once over and then closing the window.

"Sounds appetizing," I said.

"Hey, don't knock it," Nicky replied. "I went to school in Texas and there's a chain of restaurants called Black-Eyed Peas and they're really good. Fried chicken with pan gravy, mashed potatoes and black-eyed peas. Mmm-mmm."

We found Terry sitting in a red vinyl booth, hunkered over a plate of food that in California would get a restaurant closed down, but anywhere else would be referred to as comfort food.

We slid into the booth on the opposite side from Terry, in an exceptionally good mood for someone who'd been fired the day before. He wore Levi's and a blue denim shirt.

"Hey," Terry said. "What're you two doin' here?"

"We need to ask you a couple of questions," Nicky said. "If you don't mind."

"I don't mind," Terry said. "Want some lunch?" He held up a fork mounded with mashed potatoes, dripping gravy.

"No, thanks," I said, watching Nicky drool over the mega-cholesterol meal on Terry's plate. "We ate on the plane."

"When did you guys get in?" Terry asked.

"Just this morning," Nicky said flirtatiously, warming up his victim.

"We were wondering if you could identify the man in this photo," I said, pulling out the photo of Vaughn that Nicky had taken from the apartment.

Terry wiped his hands on his jeans and took the picture. He replied immediately, almost before he had taken it from me. "I'm not sure. All you San Francisco boys look alike to me," Terry said and grinned. "No offense."

"Why do you think he's a San Francisco boy?" Nicky asked.

"Well, he looks a little like someone who was here once to visit Travis, but I couldn't be positive," Terry said, looking at the photo again.

"Someone who came to visit Travis and Evelyn when they were spending some time here?" I asked.

"No. Mrs. Iversen had gone back to California. I remember that for sure, because I drove her to the airport. When I got back I was getting out of the Land Rover and some dude came screeching up in one of them fancy Mustang convertibles. He got out and walked right into the house like he owned the place. Never seen him before and he only stayed till the next mornin'. He was all pretty and had one of them gym bodies, too. Looks like him, I think."

"Did he have a suitcase with him?" I asked.

"Not a suitcase, more like a duffel bag. Pretty, too," Terry said. "I looked for one like it, but couldn't find one."

"Aren't all duffel bags pretty much the same?" I baited.

"Not this one. It was green and had this really pretty shiny diamond on it. Like it was made of real silver or something," Terry said.

"Is that what you were referring to the other day when you said something about people coming in here with their Day-Glo suitcases? Was it that silver diamond you were thinking of?" I asked.

"Yeah," Terry said, impressed. "How'd you know?"

"Just a hunch," I said, turning to look at Nicky, who was right with me on this. "one last thing, Terry. I hope you won't think I'm being too nosy. If so, just tell me. I was wondering why you were fired?"

Terry became sullen.

I pressed on. "Hank said it had to do with snooping around the main house after the foreman moved in. Is that the reason?"

Terry stared at his plate and mumbled something unintelligible.

"I'm sorry," I said. "I didn't hear you."

"I said, 'Fuck Hank.'"

"Well, at least you might clear up one mystery for us: Why did Austin move into the main house to begin with? What was the reason for that?"

Terry looked up, his mouth tight, jaws clenched

Nicky took up the persuasion. "Terry, this could be a matter of life and death."

"Are you a cop?" Terry asked, looking straight at me.

"No, I told you before, I'm not with the police."

"You?" he said to Nicky.

"No, Terry."

"Can I get in trouble?" Terry asked.

"Not unless you broke the law," I said.

"You guys are tryin' to find out if Travis killed Mrs. Iversen, huh?" he asked.

"Something like that," I said.

"I don't know nothin' about it. I swear."

"OK. Fair enough. Sorry we made you uncomfortable, Terry," I said discouraged. "You've been a big help. C'mon, Nicky. We'd better go." I started to slide out of the booth when Terry said, "He's what Hank and me call a pendalam."

"What?" I said, turning back to look at him.

"Travis. Me and Hank call him Pendalam."

"You mean pendulum?" Nicky asked.

"Yeah, a pendalam. That thing on a grandfather clock," Terry said, stifling a little grin.

"I don't get it," Nicky said.

"He swings both ways. Travis likes both kinds. That's how I met him. That's why he hired me," Terry said, pushing his plate away and taking a drink from a quart Mason jar filled with iced tea that came with his meal.

I slid back into the booth.

Terry continued. "Then Austin come along and busted us up. He's a son of a bitch. Don't care how many women Travis fucks, but Austin wants to be the only guy. Jealous little pissant's all he is. Probably cries when he gets it."

Nicky and I sat silent for a moment, as though we might be able to comprehend this new information and apply it. We couldn't. Terry stared out the window, a blank expression on his face.

"Terry," I said softly, genuinely, "that took a lot of courage. You're a good man to tell us this. Thank you."

Nicky and I slowly slid out of the booth and stood up. "You take care, Terry," Nicky said.

"Say," Terry called after us. "If you ever see one of those duffel bags, would you pick it up for me? I'll pay you."

"Sure thing," I said. "Count on it."

Nicky and I got in the car and headed north.

"Where are we going now?" Nicky asked. "The airport's in the other direction."

"One last hunch," I said, patting Nicky on the thigh. "Bear with me."

Hank was out near the barn when we arrived back at the Carefree ranch. "What you guys doin' back so soon?" he asked, hoisting a saddle onto the corral fence as we approached.

"I forgot to ask you something," I said. I took the picture of Vaughn out of my pocket and handed it to Hank. "You ever see this man?"

"Sure. He was here yesterday," Hank said, handing me back the photo.

"This man was here yesterday?" I asked.

"Yep, didn't stay but a New York minute," Hank said. "He drove up in a fancy red car, pranced into the house real cocky. Tripped on the top step. All show, no blow. Then, about five minutes later, he stormed out like he'd seen a ghost. Tore out the driveway like his pants was on fire. Fuckin' city slickers. Present company excepted," he said apologetically.

"No offense taken," I assured him.

"Hank, if we should need to get in touch with you later, is there a phone number or an address?" I asked.

"Yeah, I'll give you the phone number of the bunkhouse if you want," he offered.

"We'd appreciate it," I said, handing him a pen and turning the photo over for him to write on. "And your full name, too, please, just in case we have to ask for you."

"OK, but that's never any problem," Hank said, writing down the number and his last name. "There's never more than one Hank anyplace I ever been." He smiled and handed the photo to Nicky. "Call if you need to. Or even if you just want to. I got lots of free time. Nights especially."

Nicky winked at him. I reached out and took the photo they both had a corner of in their hands. "We'll remember that, Hank. Won't we, *honey?*" I said to Nicky.

SIXTY-SEVEN

WE SAT at the Phoenix airport trying to sort things out. All around us drifted hundreds, if not thousands of senior citizens dressed in every pastel color imaginable. I think clothes made from petrochemical bi-products can take only so much pigment. Polyester pantsuits always look like they were dyed then set in the sun too long to dry. The preponderant favorite color in Phoenix was sky blue. Fitting, I thought, since the airport was dubbed Sky Harbor.

"So what does all this mean?" I asked out loud, but more to myself than to Nicky.

"I'm not sure," Nicky said. "Do you think Vaughn's trying to frame Travis?"

"That doesn't make sense. How can he frame a guilty man? And how would he do it?"

"I mean frame in the sense of making sure he's charged with murder," Nicky said.

"But why? I can't think of a reason unless it has to do with the inheritance. But I think there's more to it than that."

"Like what?"

"I don't know, but something more," I said. "Why would Vaughn come here and then leave immediately? That doesn't make sense. If he was here to do business or…"

"That's right," Nicky interrupted. "Annarita said that he had come here to do some sort of inventory. He hardly could have done that in two minutes, or however long it was he was inside the main house."

We sat mulling it over for a long while as we watched travelers milling around, dragging suitcases, wiping spilled ice cream off their bosoms, checking their watches. Then, for no apparent reason, it struck me what was really going on. Nicky thought of it at just about the same time. I turned to him slowly as the revelation dawned. Nicky was already staring at me, the concept forming slowly and painfully in his mind, causing him to have a rather comical facial expression, like he was constipated.

"Could Vaughn have…?" he said.

"Not by himself," I answered.

We sat in shocked silence for a moment. Then Nicky said he'd be right back. He went over to the Southwest ticket counter, returned about five minutes later, and began gathering our things. "Come on," he instructed, "our flight is boarding."

It was at least an hour and a half before our flight was scheduled to take off. "Your watch is wrong. We've got plenty of time."

"Come on," Nicky snapped, grabbing his leather backpack and my jacket.

"Did you get us on an earlier flight?" I asked, running to keep up with him.

"Sort of," he answered.

"Sort of? What does that mean?"

"I'm playing a hunch," he said. "I'll explain on the airplane." Nicky was way ahead of me in the sleuthing department.

We touched down in Sacramento at 7:05 P.M.. Nicky had called ahead and had a car and driver waiting for us. I'd thought he was calling Hertz, not a limo service.

"A rental car would have done just fine," I said, climbing into the back seat of the black Cadillac.

"I'm too tired to watch you drive, camel lips," he said, sinking into the plush seat. "Besides, the driver already knows where we want to go."

"And where is that again?"

"The Double R Ranch in Grass Valley," Nicky said, smiling and closing his eyes. "Let's nap until we get there, honey. I'm pooped. All this thinking wears me out."

He leaned on my shoulder and was asleep in seconds.

The owner of the Double R Ranch was a woman who could have passed for Evelyn VanDeventer's sister or Ruth McGraw's mother. This woman was well-preserved, shapely, and way too sophisticated to have grown up on a dude ranch. I figured she had been widowed by some New York tycoon and then retired to this life. She was in the barn with a vet tending to a lame mare when we caught up with her.

"Ms. Kaiser?" Nicky inquired as we approached.

She stood outside a stall, looking intently at whatever was going on inside, and turned toward us when Nicky called her name. She was a classic: perfect makeup, coiffed auburn hair, high cheekbones and sparkling green eyes. She wore jeans and what I can only describe as a cowgirl shirt, red satin with white pearl snap buttons.

She looked like a movie star from the 40s and 50s. Rita Hayworth with straw in her hair. I guessed she was close to 60, but only because Nicky had taught me to guess high with women who took care of themselves. If I had met her before I met Nicky, I would have guessed 48 tops.

"Gentlemen, can I help you?" she asked, the way you would say that to a couple of trespassers.

"Ma'am, I hope this isn't a bad time, but we need to ask you a couple questions," Nicky said.

"It will only take a moment or two," I assured. I could see inside the stall now, where the vet and a stable hand examined the hoof of the mare. The horse was slate black, shiny, and had a mane like spun silk. Definitely show material.

"Frankly, gentlemen, this isn't the best time," Ms. Kaiser said. "My girl Maggie here's got a lame foot. Doc Sutter's trying to determine the cause. Could it wait until tomorrow?"

"No, ma'am, I'm afraid not," Nicky said. "But I promise this won't take more than a few minutes."

She looked at Nicky, then at me, then at the mare, then back at us. "Can we do it here?" she asked, smiling slightly, knowing how to get her way with men.

"Absolutely," I said. "It will only take a minute."

"All right," she said. "What can I do for you?"

"Do you remember the fund-raiser that the Cyril and Evelyn VanDeventer Foundation held here a year or so ago?" I asked.

"I certainly do," she said. "It was one of the most successful events we've ever hosted."

"Really?" Nicky said.

"Yes," she replied, "and I'm damned hopping mad about it."

"Excuse me?" Nicky said.

"That Foundation representative promised me that if that rodeo went, and they reached their financial goal, he'd give us the event every year. All I asked was that he give me at least six months notice. It's been 13 months since then and I've never heard a single word." She scowled at us like we might be from the Foundation. "Not one word."

"Really?" I said. "Ma'am, do you remember the Brahman Bull act you booked for that event?"

She rolled her eyes and placed a hand to her forehead. "Do I!"

"I take it that's a yes," I said.

"That ridiculous act was the hit of the weekend, and I fought like a bobcat with the man who insisted on booking it. Guess I don't know everything after all." She paused a minute, then added, "Of course, I feel a little guilty now, considering what happened afterward. With Ms. VanDeventer and all. Are you men from the police?"

"No, Ms. Kaiser. We're private investigators," Nicky said.

"You say someone insisted on booking the act?" I continued.

"That's right, the representative from the Foundation. Not the one who came originally, another fellow. About a week before the fund-raiser. Surly kind of guy, actually. Didn't like him much, but, hey, they were paying the tab and he gave me a bonus for having to book the act at the last minute."

"Ms. Kaiser, would you recognize that man if you saw him again?" Nicky asked.

"I suppose so," she said. "We talked right out there near the corral and it was around noon. I got a pretty good look at him."

"Is this him?" I asked, pulling the photo from my jacket and handing it to her. She reached into her shirt pocket and pulled out a pair of half-glasses. "Yes, that's him. He looks different in this picture, though. He had longer hair and wore black-rimmed glasses then. Also, he spoke with a funny accent. Does this man have an accent?"

"What kind of accent?" I asked.

She laughed. "Funny you would ask that. It's the same thing I kept trying to figure out. I've traveled quite a bit and I couldn't place it. It was like some made-up thing I'd never heard before. You know, like that comedian used when he played Latka on *Taxi*. He was very abrupt. A nasty man. Don't know how he could ever raise any money for them with that attitude."

"You're sure this is him?" Nicky asked again.

"Young man," she said, looking at Nicky over the top of her glasses, "I'm not *that* old."

"No ma'am," Nicky said. "I didn't mean anything by it.

SIXTY-EIGHT

NICKY paid the limo driver to take us back to San Francisco over my strenuous but insincere objections. We were both exhausted. I got out of the car and went inside before there was any chance of hearing how much it cost him.

"Do you always spend money like that?" I asked, as he reached up and flicked off the lamp on his side of the bed.

"Like what?" he asked, clearly tickled at the question and knowing exactly what I meant.

"You know," I said, poking him with my elbow. "Hiring limousines in Sacramento to drive you to San Francisco."

"What's money for, if not to spend?" Nicky said, wrapping his arm around me. "Turn over so we can spoon."

I turned and pressed my back up against him. He tightened his grip around me.

"Besides, I don't think of it as spending money," he said, already starting to fade into sleep. "I think of it as creating experiences, or making life easier." He kissed the back of my neck. "Or worshiping you by making your life easier."

I lay awake for a few minutes after that, feeling his breath growing increasingly heavy on the back of my neck. Soon he was purring, his fingers dancing against my skin as the nerves in his extremities settled into sleep. The last thing I remember before falling into a dreamless sleep was whispering, "Thank you, Lyle. Thank you, Rosario."

Once again I awoke to Nicky on the phone with Annarita. I could smell coffee and doughnuts, but didn't feel like opening my eyes yet. I lay there listening to Nicky say, "But that can't be right, Annarita. We *saw* him come back day before yesterday, the same day you said he left. In fact, we happen to know he didn't stay at the ranch for more than 15 minutes."

I opened my eyes to find Thao sitting at the foot of the bed staring at me. "Good morning," he whispered, then held out a half-eaten, chocolate old-fashioned doughnut. "Want a bite?"

I laughed. "No thank you," I whispered in return. "Does he have you assigned to bring doughnuts on certain days?"

Thao nodded enthusiastically and took another bite of the doughnut he had offered me.

"What time is it?" I asked.

"Three o'clock," Thao whispered.

"You're kidding," I said.

Thao made a cross over his heart. I knew we were tired when we arrived home, but I don't think I've ever slept quite that long before. At least not since Saturday mornings when I was in high school.

"Are you absolutely sure about this, Annarita? It's very important that you're sure about this," Nicky said. Then, "OK, OK, I'll call you back. Don't go anywhere."

He hung up the phone and Thao asked, "What's going on?"

"He's back in Carefree," Nicky said.

"Who is?" Thao asked.

"Vaughn," Nicky said solemnly, looking at me to see if anything was registering.

I sat up and leaned against the headboard as though that might help me think better. Nicky added some sweetener and cream to a mug of coffee and handed it to me. "OK, let's think this through," I said. "What the hell is all this commuting back and forth to the ranch about?"

"Will someone please fill me in?" Thao said, reaching into a square pink bakery box nestled in the goose down comforter in the middle of the bed. Thao's hand withdrew clutching another chocolate doughnut.

Nicky began the story. "Two days ago—at least I think it was two days ago; I'm beginning to feel like the Secretary of State with all the jetting around we've been doing—Vaughn went to the ranch in Arizona for some reason we haven't yet quite figured out. When he got there, he went into the house and about five minutes later came storming back out and drove away in a hurry."

I picked up the story from there. "Nicky and I flew down there to find out what was going on and found that Vaughn had also been there one other time, shortly after Travis and Evelyn had bought the place. Evelyn was in California, but Travis was there. Vaughn stayed one night that time. We're not sure if it means anything. He flew down two days ago, supposedly to take some sort of inventory for the estate. Now Annarita says he's gone back to Phoenix."

"Carefree, darling," Nicky corrected.

"Phoenix, Scottsdale, Carefree," I litanized. "They're all the same to me. We also discovered that it was Vaughn who arranged for Iversen to perform at the rodeo shindig where Evelyn first met him. Which makes us wonder why he did that and how he even knew about Travis and his rodeo act."

"But this business of him rushing back to the ranch is really weird," Nicky said.

"Why would he do that when he was just there yesterday and didn't stay?" I mused.

Nicky and Thao gave one another a knowing look and then said slowly, in unison, "Or wouldn't stay."

"Huh?" I grunted.

"OK," Thao said. "What does this sound like? I pack up a weekend bag and trot off to Carefree, Arizona. I love that name, by the way. I arrive all sweetness and light—"

"As though that *diable* could ever be sweetness and light," Nicky spat.

"Whatever," Thao said. "So I arrive all sweetness and light, ready to have a fun time. I waltz into the house, looking for someone. Then something happens—or I see something unexpected—and I become enraged. I storm out and fly back to where I came from."

Then, together, Thao and Nicky sang in the best twangy voices they could muster, which, for Thao, was not terribly twangy, "Your cheatin' heart will tell on you."

"Come on, guys," I whined. "Let me in on the secret." I was growing more and more exasperated with this conundrum by the minute.

"Don't be thick, Nigel," Nicky said. "Vaughn was acting like a jealous lover. Living in a fool's paradise."

"Poor Mary Haines," Thao said.

I looked at Nicky like everyone was speaking in some foreign language. Then, slowly, like a ten-ton metal crusher, it came down on my weary mind. "Of course. That would explain so much."

"Right," Nicky said. "What if Vaughn's collusion with Travis was more than financial? What if they were secretly lovers? Then Vaughn goes down to the ranch—"

"Unannounced, I dare say," Thao added.

"Right," Nicky repeated. "Unannounced. He was going to surprise Travis. Or sneak up on him. Vaughn's not exactly an innocent."

"But he ends up being the one who's surprised," I continued, "because Travis was cheating on him with Austin."

"Who," Nicky said, "was always jealous of Terry because Travis was hot for him, too."

"Jesus," Thao exclaimed. "This Travis guy must take Viagra."

"Oh, shit!" Nicky shouted. "Nigel, what if Vaughn is going back there to do something ugly."

"How ugly can he get?" I asked, reaching for a doughnut.

"Pretty ugly, honey. Maybe he's the one who took Evelyn's gun."

I stopped mid-bite. "Fuck! I forgot about the gun. Do you think...?"

We threw off the bedclothes, jumped up and began scurrying about, causing Thao to run downstairs, shouting, "You two are nuts! I'm calling the police!"

SIXTY-NINE

WHAT Thao meant, of course, was that he was calling the Maricopa County Sheriff's Department to warn them that Travis's life might be in danger. We got to the airport as fast as one of Nicky's limos could get us there. I swear, I don't know how he gets those limo drivers to "hop-to" like that, but he does. The car was waiting out front by the time I was done shaving.

We got to the airport and found that all flights were delayed because of fog, which, of course, there was no sign of. The only fog we could imagine was in the control tower. Nevertheless, we waited until after 8 o'clock to take off.

Then the plane had mechanical trouble and we had to make an unscheduled landing in Las Vegas, where the plane was promptly declared unfit to continue and all 116 passengers went scurrying to find other flights. Naturally, there were no more flights to Phoenix that night, so the indomitable Nicky rented a car and we drove to Arizona. And what did he rent?

"I've always wanted to drive one of these," he said, turning over the engine of the Lincoln Town Car. "They're so debauched. A really sensible car, don't you think?"

We took turns driving through the night, watching the nearly full moon rise and set across the star-filled desert sky. We arrived at the ranch in Carefree a little after 5 A.M., just before sunrise to find three sheriff's deputies in two squad cars posted at the gate.

"We got here about 5 P.M.," one said, struggling to lift himself out of his white and blue squad car, then leaning his bulk against the door. He was grossly overweight. If he ever had to chase a culprit it would be fatal—and not for the culprit.

The deputies had posted themselves at the gate when they arrived at the ranch, then walked up to the house.

"Wasn't nobody home," the deputy said as he unwrapped a Butterfinger and popped half of it into his mouth. The wrapper got tossed into the air. Nicky watched it float across the hood and disappear on the other side of the car. The cop added that he and his partner had been there the entire night and no one had come or gone since they arrived. "We're short a couple men this week so we pulled double duty," he informed us.

I turned to look at his two partners in the other car. The driver was catching 40 winks, but at least he looked like he could chase somebody more than a block if he had to. I rapped on the window and gave him a start. He put the window down and I introduced the two of us, then asked if anybody minded if we just went up and had a look around the property. They said to go ahead, since the place was empty.

Nicky and I started with the bunkhouse, which they said they hadn't bothered to check. I opened the screen door and Nicky tried the handle of the wooden door. It opened. We stepped inside and I felt around for a light switch. I flicked it on and sitting at the window, swigging a fifth of Jim Beam, feet propped up on the windowsill, was Hank.

"Have you been here all the time?" Nicky asked. I wouldn't have been so diplomatic. I was tempted to walk over and kick his chair out from under him.

"Yep," he answered, his voice sloppy with liquor.

"Why didn't you talk to the sheriff?" I demanded, a little more forcefully than I had actually intended.

Hank turned his head and gave me a sneer. "They didn't knock on my door," he said.

"Jesus!" I muttered.

Nicky squatted down next to Hank and put his hand on Hank's thigh. Hank gave him an unsteady gaze, then smiled. "Hank, do you know where Travis is?"

"Uh-huh," he said, and swigged on the bottle again.

"Where is he?" Nicky asked.

"Lake Barnett," Hank said.

Nicky and I exchanged glances. "Why did he go to the lake,

Hank?" I asked.

Hank glowered and said nothing.

"Hank, why did Travis go to Lake Barnett?" Nicky repeated. It was clear that I was persona non grata as far as Hank was concerned.

"That guy wanted to go see where his mother drowned," Hank said. "Whatchamacallit. Van."

"Vaughn?" Nicky said.

"Yeah, whoever. That guy you showed me the picture of." Hank gave a wicked laugh. "This place is really fucked up, you know that?" he said, looking Nicky in the eye and trying his best to focus.

"It is?" Nicky said.

"Yeah. Austin fired me last night. Gave me till mornin' to clear out. Now I ask you," Hank said, slurring his words badly, "how the hell they gonna keep this fuckin' ranch goin' if the foreman keeps firin' everybody? Huh? Answer me that, if you can."

"I don't know," Nicky said. "Maybe we'll just have to fire the foreman. Do you know where he is?"

"Tore out of here after he fired me. Came flying out of the house after a ten-minute screaming match with Travis and that city slicker. He busted in here, said, 'You're fired. Get out by tomorrow.' Then he picked up his hat and drove off in the pickup. Dumb fuck. I hate this place. If he gave me my job back, I'd quit."

"Nicky," I said softly. He turned and I motioned for him to step outside with me.

"Don't you think we should go look for them?" I asked.

"Yes, I was just trying to decide if Hank had any more information, but it looks like he's told us what we need to know."

We walked back to the gate and told the fat deputy there was a ranch hand in the bunkhouse, but that he was harmless. Then Nicky and I got in the other police car with the two deputies who were not on the "Butterfingers diet" and drove out to Lake Barnett. They radioed for backup to meet us there.

The sun was easing up over low-lying hills to the east as we pulled into the same parking lot where Nicky and I had encountered the sheriff's deputy the first time we were there. Travis's jeep was parked at the far end of the lot near the rest rooms and an emergency phone. I wondered if it was the same emergency phone Travis had used just a few weeks ago to call 911 and report Evelyn missing. Only this time it was Vaughn talking on the phone when we pulled up. We all jumped out as he hung up the receiver.

"I just called 911," he said to the deputies, avoiding us altogether. "It's Travis Iversen. He shot himself."

"Where is he?" one of the deputies asked.

"Back at the campsite," Vaughn said, pointing. One of the deputies took off running in that direction. "I was asleep when this awful bang woke me up. It scared me to death. I'm not used to being around guns. I hate them, actually. I sat up in my sleeping bag and called for Travis to ask him what that noise was. There was no answer, and so I got up and went over to where he was sleeping. That's when I saw the blood."

"Is he dead?" the deputy asked.

Now Vaughn looked at us, first Nicky, then me, as he said slowly and very distinctly, "Yes, officer. He's quite dead."

SEVENTY

EVERYTHING happened quickly after that. The body was taken to the county morgue, where an autopsy was performed. By the time we left Arizona, it had been concluded that Travis put the revolver—Evelyn's missing revolver, of course—under his chin and fired up through his mouth into the cerebral cortex. Death was instantaneous.

Vaughn flew back to California the next day, as did we, although on separate flights. We didn't want to be in the same plane with him any more than he wanted to be with us. We called Annarita to tell her about the shooting. We didn't implicate Vaughn. She sounded more relieved than anything and said she would meet us at our house when we got home. She said she had a surprise for us.

We arrived home a little after noon. Matt and Thao met us at the door, welcomed us with a hug, and then we all went upstairs. There was coffee brewing and two of those ubiquitous pink pastry boxes sat on the kitchen table. Matthew set out mugs and napkins.

"You look good," Nicky said to Thao. "New suit?"

"I got another raise," he said. "Armani. Black label. Good value."

That was Thao's way of saying Nicky was not to ask how much it cost. Thao stacked four chocolate old-fashioned doughnuts in front of him on a saucer, like the leaning tower of Pisa, then started eating his way toward the bottom. He sat in his black Armani with chocolate on his upper lip. His eyes darted back and forth from person to person, waiting for someone to start talking. At last he broke the silence. "So what did you uncover in Arizona?" he asked.

"It was pretty straightforward, actually," Nicky said. "We went to the ranch and found that Travis wasn't there and neither was Vaughn. One of the ranch hands told us they'd gone to the lake camping."

"Remember, now," I added, "this is after the flight from hell which included an unscheduled stop in Las Vegas. We drove from there to the ranch, which took all night. We arrived just before sunrise."

"Oh, those friendly skies," Matthew quipped, leaning back in his chair, coffee mug in hand. Popeye peeked out from beneath the lapel of his Roy Rogers bathrobe.

"So we drove to the lake with a couple of sheriff's deputies who were waiting for us at the ranch," Nicky continued. "When we got to the lake, Vaughn was phoning the police to report that Travis had shot himself."

"Who pulled the trigger?" Thao asked, between bites.

"The coroner ruled it a suicide," I said.

"Of course he did, but who pulled the trigger?" Thao asked again.

"I doubt we'll ever know for certain any more than we'll ever know what happened the night Evelyn drowned."

"I know what happened," Matthew said.

We all looked at Matthew.

"Yeah?" Nicky asked.

"Simple. Vaughn went down there, lured Travis out to the lake, then bang. Just like he and Travis did to Mommie Dearest. What comes around goes around," Matthew said.

"Why would Vaughn do all that?" Thao asked. "Where is the motive?"

"Actually, we have Nicky to thank for figuring out the last piece of the puzzle," I said, putting my arm around him.

"Only the *last* piece?" he said with mock indignation.

"All right," I conceded, "and a couple of pieces in the middle. Somehow Vaughn met Travis, probably in a bar, but we'll never know for certain. He had this planned a long time ago. Probably since Cyril's death. Since he was adopted, he believed his mother would leave most of her money to his sisters. It only reinforced his belief when he and Cyril got into it and Evelyn didn't stick up for Vaughn. But don't forget: This was a woman who was without her own identity. She felt helpless unless she had a husband on her arm. She wasn't about to jeopardize her marriage—not for a gay son, anyway. So after Cyril died, Vaughn plotted to have her meet Travis, who was only too willing to go along for the ride, since it was going to make him rich."

"And since Travis swung both ways, it was no big deal," Nicky chimed in.

"Swung both ways?" Thao said, cocking his head.

"That bolero tie with the turquoise and silver I found in Vaughn's closet," Nicky said by way of explanation.

"What about it?" Thao asked, reaching for another doughnut.

"Vaughn wouldn't be caught dead in anything like that," Nicky said. "Travis must have left it there one night when they had sex."

"Ick!" Thao said. "Don't say that. I'm eating."

"Vaughn made sure Travis was booked for the rodeo fund-raising event in Grass Valley because he knew his mother would be smitten with a cowboy like him," I said. "Remember, she was looking for a cowboy to replace old man VanDeventer. Travis worked his charm on her and within six months they were married."

"*L'amour, l'amour,*" Nicky said wistfully, "how it does let one down."

"But, my, how it does pick one up again, doesn't it, ducky?" Matthew finished the quote.

"The poor Countess DeLave," Thao said, identifying the movie, "on the train to Reno—again."

Nicky nodded his assent and raised his mug to Matthew, who toasted back.

"It was nothing, then, to get her to change her will. He probably didn't even have to do anything. She probably did it herself," I said.

"With the right amount of coaxing from hubby in the bedroom, I'm sure," Matthew added.

"Then came the big payoff," Nicky said. "And figuring this out is where Nigel really showed his stuff. Tell them about the boat, honey," Nicky said, rummaging through the doughnut box and giving Thao dirty looks because all the good ones were gone.

"The first time we were out at the lake, I noticed several things that I didn't link together until later. First, I noticed the pylon that had orange neon numbers painted on it sticking out of the water a few yards away from the boat dock. Then I saw the second pier across the lake just like the one we were standing on. Then I saw that there was a scraping of orange paint on the side of the jet boat that Evelyn had been out in the night she drowned."

"Meaning what?" Matthew asked.

"Well, at the time it meant nothing, but when I put those things together with two other things, the narrow path and the boarding pass Nicky found in Vaughn's desk, everything came together."

"OK," Thao said, "Make it come together for us, too."

"Vaughn flew to Phoenix the day of Evelyn's and Travis's camping trip," I continued. "He rented a car and boat and drove to the lake after dusk so there was no chance of his mother seeing him. He camped near the second boat dock, the more remote one, directly across the lake from his mother and Travis. That night, Travis plied Evelyn with champagne, as if he needed to weaken her, being the hulk that he is, and led her to the boat."

"But I thought there was only one set of footprints to the dock," Thao said.

"That's right," I said. "But that assumes that two people would walk single file down that narrow, overgrown path. If the boat wasn't tied up at the pier, but was tied to the marker pole with the numbers on it so that Travis had to walk off the path through the brush to get it and bring it around to the pier so Evelyn could get in, there would be only one set of footprints on the path."

"Oh, I get it," Matthew said. "He made an excuse to not walk on the path."

"Right," said Nicky. "If he even needed to. She probably wouldn't notice whether he was walking behind her on the sandy path or next to her on the hard clay. If he said the boat had drifted off a ways and he would wade out and get it and meet her at the pier, then he could walk off the path and there would be no trace of him."

"Then how would he get back without leaving footprints?" Matthew asked.

"He didn't," I said.

"This is where Vaughn comes in, I take it?" Thao asked, reaching for doughnut number three.

"Very astute, counselor," I said to Thao. "Vaughn had a boat as well.

Whether they both held her under or whether it was only Travis is a moot point. The important thing is that they conspired to kill her. Once the deed was done, Travis climbed into Vaughn's boat and left the jet boat to drift. He helped Vaughn load his boat into a trailer, went back to the camp, waited a while, and then phoned the police to report his wife missing. By that time, Vaughn was long gone."

"And the story about the other campers he asked to turn down their radios was pure fabrication," Nicky added, "just in case someone decided to check out the other boat dock and found evidence of someone having been there recently. The sheriff would think it was the campers Travis had mentioned."

"Vaughn flew back to San Francisco and was home by the time Annarita called to tell him the news, since they didn't recover Evelyn's body until the next afternoon."

"My God," Matthew said. "I just realized they pulled off the perfect crime."

"Well, Vaughn has pulled off the perfect crime, but Travis didn't get away with it," I said. "At least he ended up paying for his ways."

"So what went wrong between Travis and Vaughn?" Thao asked.

"Vaughn didn't plan on Travis being such a slut," Nicky said.

I gave him a disapproving look and he shrugged and slunk down in his chair. "Well, that's one way of putting it," he said.

"Vaughn hadn't thought about the fact that someone as unethical as Travis, who would do such a thing for money in the first place, would also cheat on him," I said.

"You think they were actually an item?" Matthew asked.

"I don't know. I doubt it, but finding out that Travis was fucking his foreman must have made Vaughn realize Travis was uncontrollable and could jeopardize everything.

"Actually," Nicky added, "there was probably a perverse sexual thing between them, because that's what sparked the end of it. Vaughn went down to the ranch in Carefree to do God-knows-what, probably make sure Travis wasn't getting some second bimbo pregnant, when he caught on to the fact that Travis was not only sleeping with other women—he was fooling around with Austin."

"Right," I said. "Remember, by this time Travis was under heavy fire. Sandy Jo Thomas had filed her paternity suit and the media had latched on to Ruth McGraw and the wife-beating charges in Utah."

"Which, by the way, no one here knew about," Nicky said. "One of the things that Evelyn was so drawn by, according to her friend Marilyn, was the fact that after he and his first wife divorced, he waited 12 years to marry again. What no one knew, of course, was that he actually got married to Ruth McGraw the same day his divorce was finalized with his first wife. Not to mention that he had been living with Ruth McGraw for a year before that."

"So," I picked up the story, "Vaughn goes to Carefree to do damage control and what does he find?"

"He finds," Nicky interrupted dramatically, wanting to tell the juiciest parts himself, "that the foreman, Austin, has moved into the main house and things are more out of control than ever."

"So?" Thao asked, eyeing the last doughnut on the plate in front of him. "Is that unusual on a ranch? I don't know these things; we don't do cowboys and Indians in Vietnam."

"Yes, it's very unusual," Nicky said. I decided to let him tell the good part. "When Vaughn went into the house and found the foreman had not only moved into the main house, but he had moved into the main bedroom…"

"Now wait a minute," I said. "He didn't move into the main bedroom. He was living in the bedroom on the first floor."

"You know what I mean," Nicky whined. He turned back to Thao and Matthew. "Travis's bedroom was filled with toys. Dildos and whips and funny ridged things tied to a leather cord. All kinds of kinky stuff. Evidently they didn't put all of it away, so when Vaughn walked in looking for Travis, he came upon the scene of their passion," Nicky said with melodramatic flair.

"Then, when he found out that Travis and Austin had gone to New Mexico together, he realized he was about to be double-crossed," I said. "So he had to act."

"What I don't quite understand," Matthew said, "is why he acted so hastily. Why didn't he bide his time and wait until things cooled down before he put Travis out of the way?"

"Because he's very clever, that's why," Thao said, seeing the legal implications immediately.

"Explain, please, counselor," Nicky said, giving the floor to Thao.

"You see," Thao began, wiping his mouth and sitting up straight now, as though he was lecturing in a graduate seminar. "It is standard practice in writing wills to include the clause, 'if this person should survive me for 30 days,' whenever you bequeath something to a person. Otherwise, it's possible that all your money would go to your heir on Sunday—the day you die—and then that person might happen to die on the following Friday and that person's heirs, whom you don't even know, inherit your money. The 30-days clause prevents that from happening. So Vaughn had to act within 30 days to activate the contingency clause. I assume that any part of the estate that wasn't legally inherited within 30 days went to the children. Am I right?"

"Right," I said.

"So," Thao continued, "if Travis died before he could legally inherit the estate, it was to be divided among the surviving children. Of course, it is illegal to profit from a felony, so Vaughn also had to make sure he wasn't charged with murdering Travis or he wouldn't get the money he was after in the first place. Simple, really." Thao sat back in his chair and rewarded himself with the last chocolate doughnut.

We sat silently for a moment, sipping our coffee and taking in the complexity of it all.

"But," Thao said loudly now, having thought about it for a moment, "I still don't understand why Vaughn did all this in the first place."

"That," I said, "is the supreme, if not tragic, irony. Vaughn honestly believed, and probably still believes, that he was adopted by Evelyn and Cyril. Only Virge knew the truth and she would never tell Vaughn, at first probably because her mother swore her to secrecy, and later because she hated him and could use it to torture him. The fact is, Evelyn gave birth to Vaughn about a year after she left her first husband."

"Then who is Vaughn's real father?" Thao asked.

Just then the doorbell rang.

"That must be Annarita," Matthew said, getting up to answer the door. "She called just before you guys arrived to say she was on her way over."

"Yay!" shouted Nicky. "She has our surprise, and I think I know what it is." He leapt from the table and followed Matthew downstairs. Thao and I shrugged and followed.

When Matthew swung open the door, there stood Annarita holding a three-month-old Doberman puppy with his ears bandaged. They stood straight up like two white goal posts. He had on a tiny blue nylon collar and wagged a little stump that would have been a tail if they hadn't docked it at birth.

"Harry!" Nicky shouted, grabbing the puppy out of Annarita's arms. "I can change his name, can't I?" he asked Annarita.

"Naturally," she said.

"Harry, you're so beautiful!" Nicky turned to me. "Now our agency will be N., N., and H. Pinscher, Private Investigators," he said.

Annarita stepped inside. We hugged. "You look good," I observed as we hugged. "But how are you feeling?"

"Actually, I feel better than I have in a long time," she said, smiling a bit. "I even slept for eight and a half hours last night." Then after a moment, "Harry?"

"Don't ask me," I lamented. "I just married him, I don't claim to understand him."

"That's his name," Nicky said, holding him up and spinning round and round him. "Harry Krishna."

SEVENTY-ONE

IT DIDN'T TAKE long for all of it to come to trial. Maybe crime isn't as rampant in Arizona as it is in California, so justice is meted out in a timely fashion—if this was justice. Nicky and I attended the trial. It lasted less than a week.

One by one, Vaughn's attorneys, led by the old man who was sitting next to him at the reading of Evelyn's will, discredited the witnesses, what witnesses there were. Neither Terry nor Hank would—or could, for that matter—swear under oath that they'd had a sexual encounter with Vaughn or seen him in any sexual context with Travis. Neither would they testify that they had witnessed sexual contacts between Austin and Travis, thereby diminishing the theory for the motive that Travis was about to dump Vaughn for Austin, which spurred Vaughn to murder him. Both Terry and Hank had minor criminal records, but in Arizona with a jury of retirees, anything more serious than a parking ticket is looked upon with a jaundiced eye.

It was no surprise to anyone that the clothes Vaughn wore the night of Travis's death had been dry-cleaned and given to Goodwill, along with a bag of other clothes, of course, Vaughn being such a philanthropist and all. It was days before anyone could get an order for a gunpowder residue test and then his lawyers successfully convinced the court that it was far too late for that to be effective, even if it weren't opposed, which it was. By the time they finally conducted the test Vaughn didn't even have dirt under his fingernails, let alone gunpowder residue.

The other witnesses, brought in to attack Vaughn's and Travis's character, people like Austin and Sandy Jo Thomas, were of no help. Everything they had to offer was hearsay. The closest the prosecution could come was the supposed screaming match among Austin, Travis ,and Vaughn, and for some reason, probably with six figures, Austin testified that it was over whether or not he could use Travis's Lexus. "No big deal", he said, shrugging and turning to look at the jury, which was made up of ten men and two women in their mid to late 60s who thought Vaughn looked like their grandson.

The most credible witness, and the most lively, was Elizabeth Kaiser, the owner of the Double R Ranch in Grass Valley. She said she didn't care if the guy wore a Clarabell costume and spoke Greek backwards, "That was the guy," and she pointed a jungle-red fingernail in Vaughn's direction. It was only when she couldn't read the clock at the back of the courtroom without her glasses that the defense came even close to shaking her credibility. "I was wearing my glasses, sir. They're too expensive to leave lying around," she said. The defense argued that even if for some bizarre reason it was their client, which they insisted it wasn't, it would not be a crime to arrange for the rodeo act to appear at the benefit. There was no direct link.

So by the end of four days, Vaughn's defense attorneys had created what they summed up as "reasonable doubt beyond dispute." But their real winning ploy was to paint Travis as the horrible perpetrator of the first murder, bound and determined to inherit a vast fortune so he could run off with Sandy Jo Thomas, who had testified that he promised to marry her after Evelyn was out of the way.

They pointed to the will as proof that Vaughn had relatively little to gain by his mother's death. And they painted Travis in the worst possible light at every opportunity. It was all too sordid and pansexual for the jury to follow by the time it was over. They just kept looking at Little Lord Vaughn, who wore a black suit from Sears—the same one every day of the trial—a white shirt—probably a vintage Arrow with snap collar—and a thin black tie like he was still in mourning for his mother, whom he referred to over and over as Mom. The jury liked Vaughn.

It was exasperating, and Nicky was more shocked and disappointed by the outcome than I was. Not guilty. I think his chagrin at the verdict had as much to do with his encounter with Vaughn in the bathroom in Concord as with the murder.

The only moment of levity we got out of the entire trial was Nicky going up to the evidence matron one day after adjournment and asking if she would give him the brand name of the green knapsack with the diamond logo on it. Then he went to Goldwater's and bought one and had it delivered to Terry with a cute little thank-you note. I thought that was sweet and quite typical of him, to bring the only element of caring into the picture.

The only time Vaughn showed any emotion at all came and went in a flash, when the prosecution brought forth Vaughn's Texas birth certificate, proving he wasn't adopted, but was Evelyn's biological son. Vaughn noticeably winced, then bowed his head, but raised it immediately when his attorney nudged him with his elbow. The birth certificate would have been on the prosecution's evidence list, so Vaughn's attorneys had forewarned him. I would like to have been in the room when he first heard that bit of news.

Annarita stayed away from the trial. Virginia had a front-row seat, along with us. She latched onto us like we were old friends, probably only to make Vaughn nervous. It made *us* more nervous than it did Vaughn, I suspect. I don't think anything makes him nervous. I'm not sure he even has nerves. The day he stood to hear the foreman say "The jury finds the defendant not guilty," he was expressionless. Like he was never worried about the outcome in the first place. He shook hands with each of his attorneys, then turned and blew Virginia a kiss. He glared at Nicky and me for the briefest moment, and then was whisked out and away in a black limousine.

"Going to the bank, no doubt," I said to Nicky as we watched the car screech away from the curb.

"More likely to a sex club, I would imagine. Now that this fantasy is over, he has to find another one," Nicky said without emotion. He reached into his coat and retrieved his silver cigarette case. We stood for a few minutes on the courthouse steps in the warm Arizona sun as Nicky finished his cigarette. I watched the reporters and attorneys huddled in clusters, asking and answering questions. They dispersed before long. There really wasn't much to say. The judge had said it all in the end. "Mr. VanDeventer, you're free to go."

SEVENTY-TWO

MILAN was cold and wet when we landed and the train to Florence pushed through rain the entire way. Nonna had sent a driver to meet us at the *stazione,* and within half an hour we were sitting in front of a fireplace the size of Rhode Island, warming ourselves, sipping Grand Marnier, and bathing in the warmth of being together at Christmas.

Nicky and I had broken all the rules, which he pointed out wouldn't even be possible if the concept of breaking them wasn't inherent in the act of making rules on the first place: We moved in together on the Fourth of July. We decided I should move into his place since he owned his house and I rented. It made more sense than the other way around, what with Matthew and the new puppy and Nicky's bonsai garden. So we trucked everything up the hill and spent the evening of July 4 sitting on his rooftop deck looking toward the marina, where we knew, somewhere in the fog bank creeping up the bay, pyrotechnics were celebrating our moving in together as well as my birthday and, incidentally, Independence Day.

Harry grew by leaps and bounds, making me wonder if his father, whom we had never seen, might not have been a Great Dane. By the time we left for Nonna's for the holidays, Harry weighed 80 pounds. I trembled to think of how big he would be when we returned in January. I had images in my mind of coming home to find Matthew in his Roy Rogers bathrobe and a black cowboy hat riding Harry around the neighborhood, handing out cigarettes to the children, a modern good humor man.

Annarita assured us that if we wanted to show Harry, she would do all the handling. She said he would easily be a champion, but she wouldn't pressure us. But we neutered him when he turned eight months old. We decided to spend our weekends at the beach with

Harry rather than at dog shows.

Annarita remained in the house in Concord. She turned what had been the west wing of the house—where the puppies had been whelped—into a kennel. She began breeding Dobies seriously and confessed to Nicky one day over a latte that she had found herself looking at women in a peculiar way. She wanted to know if that made her a lesbian. Nicky said looking didn't make her anything, and the two of them embarked on the journey of finding out what Annarita really wanted out of life.

Meanwhile, Nicky kept in touch with Marilyn Morton, calling regularly, lunching with her, and finally, driving her and her husband to look at the house next door to his when it came on the market. They bought it, but only as an investment, turning the top floor into a unit they used as a pied-à-terre. The rest they rented out. Marilyn and Nicky became shopping pals and one afternoon, after returning from an especially heavy bout of consumerism, I threatened both of them with commitment to a mandatory 12-step program. Naturally they just laughed and went on showing me their purchases.

In Florence Nonna gave us our old room at Nicky's urging. He insisted we return to the scene of my attempted seduction so I could finish what I started that morning long ago.

"You mean so I can finish what *you* started," I corrected.

"Same thing," he said, unpacking his suitcase, carefully laying his knit shirts in a drawer.

"It is not," I protested.

He smiled at me as he came back toward the bed to take more shirts from his suitcase. "It will be soon," he said. "Already I can't remember if you're the one who prefers the aisle seat in the plane or if that's me."

On Christmas Eve we went to midnight mass at Santa Croce. I was told that usually Nonna had a priest come to the family chapel and say mass for family and staff, but this year she wanted to "show off my new family", as she put it. "*Guarda, Firenze! Mia famiglia bella,*" she said as we entered the basilica; "My beautiful family."

After mass we went back to the house, had a light meal of prosciutto, mortadella, bel paese, provolone, champagne, and pannetone, the traditional Italian Christmas bread. Then Nonna allowed each of us to open one present before we trundled off to bed. Mine stunned me. Nonna presented me with her ancient deck of alchemical tarot cards. I said I couldn't accept them, but she waved away my protestations, saying it was not possible for a person to procure his own tarot and she was convinced it was time I had my own deck. "These are for you," she said. "They were meant to be passed to you, and now I do so."

Nicky escorted his grandmother up the grand staircase to the third floor. I lagged behind with Ben, taking the stairs one at a time, Ben's silver walking stick tap-tapping on the marble risers.

I paused on the landing to look at a Fra Angelico hanging on the wall. Ben waited for me. As I turned I asked, "Ben, do you have a middle name?"

"Yes," he said, "as a matter of fact, I was named after my grandfather, Arthur."

"A noble name," I said, as we continued our climb. The house staff was extinguishing candles and electric lights on the lower floors, the darkness ascending with us at our heels.

"Correct me if I'm wrong," I said, "but doesn't Tedeschi, in Italian mean 'German'?"

"That's right," he said. "Why do you ask?"

"Oh, nothing," I replied. "I just think it's an interesting name. There was a Tedeschi family in the little town where I grew up in California. They were friends of my parents. I haven't come across the name since."

"Yes, it's rather uncommon," he said. "I suppose we could be related."

We arrived at the sleeping floor. Nicky had already said good night to Nonna and deposited her in her suite. He passed us on his way to our room.

"Good night, Ben," he said as he passed, lightly touching Ben's elbow. "And Merry Christmas."

"Good night, Nicholas," Ben said softly.

"Good night, Ben," I said, shaking his hand.

"Good night." He turned and made his way down the hall. Ben seemed to have aged considerably since we last met. I wondered how closely he had followed the trial and if the outcome might account for the slowness of his gait, the weariness in his eyes.

"Oh, Ben," I called after him.

He turned, a pained expression on his face.

"Are you all right with how things turned out? In California, I mean."

He smiled, but the look of anguish didn't disappear from his face. He thought for a moment, then said, "You boys did the best you could. Now we're all family together and I will think of each of you as the son I never had."

"The son you never had?" I repeated.

"The son I was never allowed to have," he said, nodding his head slightly, and we understood each other.

It was only in that moment, there in the dimming light, beneath the Fra Angelicos, Botticellis, and Raphaels, that I really realized what a passive-aggressive, manipulating woman Evelyn O'Brien VanDeventer Iversen had been. Here was a man who would have gladly and proudly married her, even before it seemed necessary. But she held out for something "more," something complete with title, land, and money. After all, when she met him, Ben Tedeschi was only a state legislator, not a member of the United States Senate.

Had she accepted Ben's proposal, would Vaughn have turned out to be a different person? Would Evelyn have come to such a karmic end, floating in her bra and panties in a remote lake of central Arizona, put there by a cowboy also pursuing "something more?" And was Vaughn, free now to run the Foundation as he wished and to enjoy his third of the nearly half-billion-dollar estate, also in pursuit of "more"? I couldn't help but wonder where he would surface again in our lives. I had a strong feeling we hadn't seen the last of him.

"Well, good night, then," Ben said, and disappeared into the darkness of the hall.

I opened the door to our room to find Nicky already asleep. He lay on his stomach, naked, of course, blankets down to just where the crack of his butt began. He had probably intended this as a Christmas present, but couldn't stay awake until I got to our room. That's all right, I thought as I undressed. We have the rest of our lives.

I climbed into bed, pulled up the comforter, and reached to turn out

the lamp, when my eye caught the gift that Nonna had given Nicky for
his Christmas Eve present. It was a triptych of three framed photo-
graphs. One from her youth, one from middle age, and one taken shortly after her wedding, the last time we were here. It was folded closed on
the nightstand, but I wanted to look at it before I went to sleep, as I had-
n't gotten to look at it downstairs.

I opened it and felt my heart miss a beat when I looked at the first
photo. It was, without any mistake, the young woman I'd seen that day
in the empty house above Helen's farm. It was also the woman I'd seen
looking down at me from Vaughn's old bedroom in the house in
Concord. Now I found myself wondering if it was the same woman
who'd waved to me from the dock on Lake Barnett.

I stared at the eyes in the photograph, yellowed a bit with age, but
unmistakably it was her. I remembered Nonna's response to me in the
chapel the day of the wedding, when she referred to her dream, saying
later to Nicky that I was the man she saw in her dream on a hillside in
the rain. I had been chilled by the thought of appearing in another person's dream, but now I was even more taken aback to think the dreamer had appeared to me, however fleetingly, in my waking moments.

At Annarita's house that day in Concord, what was Nonna trying to
tell me as she peered through the curtains of Vaughn's old room? Had
she been trying to tell me the former occupant of that room was the one
we should be seeking out? At Lake Barnett, she must have been telling
me to cross the lake and look at the other dock, the other campsite, that
it was the place where the answer to the mystery of the single trail of
footprints lay.

I wondered, as I replaced the triptych on the table, turned out the
light and settled into the down pillows, if this would teach me to pay
more attention in the future to my intuition, to things that appear but
may not make sense. Nicky stirred, moved onto his side, and put his arm
over me. I turned and kissed him lightly on the lips. He moaned softly.

"Merry Christmas, Nicky," I whispered.

"Mmm, Merry Christmas, Nigel," he said and sighed. " I love you."

In spite of the hour, I lay awake for a long time, my mind whirring.
I kept thinking of the juxtaposition of love and death. Death had swirled

all around me for so long, I hadn't recognized love when I encountered it, even when I felt the zest of it. It was Nicky and Nonna who slapped me into full consciousness. It was love that called my name when I had sealed myself in Lazarus' tomb, convinced that my life was over.

What a strange contrast I was to someone like Evelyn VanDeventer, who, when her husband died, went on an all-out search for love. Unfortunately, what she ended up with was death. I, on the other hand, having accepted my own death, was brought back to life by love. There was a lot to learn from Nicky and Nonna about one's attitude toward life and death and love.

As I drifted gently into sleep, the sun began to break across the Arno and a tender, golden light filtered through the slatted shutters covering the huge windows. The soft light, dusty, warm, and liquid, spilled gently across the marble floor. A new day, I thought, as I held my lover close to me, felt the warmth of his body, heard the steady rhythm of his breathing, a rhythm I would hear night after night for the rest of my life.

A new life, I thought. Like a gift from the gods, a gift I will cherish every day, just the way I cherish the days themselves, days I never thought I would live to see.

Christmas, I thought, smiling and remembering the 20-foot tree downstairs covered with ribbons and ornaments and lights of every imaginable color.

The rest of my life, I thought. With Nicky it was bound to be an adventure. I was learning to like adventure. Nicky was teaching me how.

ON THE LOGGIA

I FELL asleep eventually, the light washing across the floor, over the bed, into my dreams. The sleep was peaceful and the dream was gentle. In it, I was hanging upside down, suspended from what I could not tell, since I was laughing too hard to bend my body upward to see what grasped me by the ankles. Below me on a vast expanse of lawn, their heads just level with mine, stood Nicky and Nonna and Helen. They too were laughing. We were taking great glee that everything in my pockets was falling to the ground. Coins, a silver cigarette lighter, keys, a ruby ring. And these things kept falling out over and over. Then other things fell out, larger things. Nonna's car, a painting, Harry, who began running in circles and barking at my curious situation. The bigger the objects that tumbled from my pockets, the harder we laughed.

That's how I woke up this morning. Laughing. Nicky was lying next to me smelling of soap and that intoxicating scent that is his alone. We made love, bathed, then lunched with Nonna, Ben, and our friend Helen, whose Christmas gift was twofold: a key to her farmhouse and a confession. She admitted she had told us both to go to the farm in May with the intention of throwing us together. She said Nicky was the only person she knew who would be too much fun for me to resist, and I was the only person she knew who was smart enough to hold Nicky's interest. This admission of guilt put to rest something we had wondered about for months.

Now it is Christmas day and I am once again on the loggia of Nonna's palazzo in Florence. This time I am waiting to be called to a more intimate supper. I am bundled in a wool blanket that is heavy as a rug and, I am told, was brought from the Orient by Marco Polo on his last expedition to the East. I have no reason to doubt it.

A gaggle of faceless Christians, no more from this vantage point than scarves and hats and fine leather shoes, scurry about on the street below. They are, no doubt, working their way through the crisp afternoon toward warm dinners with family and friends. Their arms are laden with colorfully wrapped boxes and tins. They are rushing to celebrate the birth of someone they never knew, never even met, but into whose hands they place all their hopes and fears, all their dreams and disappointments. As I spy on them from my eagle's perch here on the via di Genori, it occurs to me that this story I have told you is a tale more of dreams than of death. Of dreams lost, dreams destroyed, dreams pursued, and dreams envied. And not my dreams only.

It is dark now and I must go indoors, back to the warm golden light of the dream that is my life now. The dream my story ends with. It has turned cold out here on the loggia, too cold even for Marco Polo's blanket to keep me warm. I have been called to Christmas supper. Ben, who came to fetch me, has left the door open, and I can smell the warm meats and pungent vegetables steaming on the sideboard, waiting for the gloved butlers, like uniformed nutcrackers, to lift them onto silver trays and parade them around the table for our pleasure.

The stars twinkle brightly on this night of Christ's birth, pouring their light down on the city, the duomo, the Arno, and me. My life is filled with light these days. Sometimes it is almost too much, almost blinding, the way Lazarus must have been blinded when that huge stone rolled away from his tomb. I wonder if he wanted to come out from that place. Or did he want to stay where he was? Perhaps he had grown comfortable in the dark, accustomed to the damp and the cold. Or was he simply afraid? Perhaps that's why he had to be called more than once. Like me.

I want to take Lazarus' cold hand on this Christmas night, this night of births and new beginnings, and urge him on. I want to say, "Don't be afraid. This dark resting place will be here when you truly need it. Go. Love is waiting for you. I promise. There is love after death, if only you will sit still and let it find you. And it will, Lazarus, it will. Love has the power to heal us, to save us, to free us from the softest and the harshest fetters. It will be your eyes in the dark. But it finds only those brave few who have the courage to seek it. For it is not love that is elusive. It is the courage to step out of the comforting darkness and open yourself to love's infinite, disturbing possibilities that is difficult. How much easier to die than to be saved. Ask Him who called you forth if you don't believe me."

This is what I would say to Lazarus. But alas, he is not here. So I repeat it to myself. Frequently.

I go inside now to the warmth of the house, the comforting aromas, the blazing hearth, and the laughter of my new family. And to the sad and happy ghosts that haunt every brave home. And we are brave, Nicky and I. Brave enough to give love one last chance.